SELLING *Scarlett*

Sandra U rock!! :)

Ella J

ELLA JAMES

Selling Scarlett

Cover design by © Regina Wamba of Mae I Design
Book formatting by JT Formatting

ISBN-10:0989508404
ISBN-13:978-0-9895084-0-7

Printed in the United States of America

This is a work of fiction. Names, characters, places, brands, media, and incidents are either the product of the author's imagination or are used fictitiously. The author acknowledges the trademarked status and trademark owners of various products referenced in this work of fiction, which have been used without permission. The publication/use of these trademarks is not authorized, associated with, or sponsored by the trademark owners.

Find out more about the author and upcoming books online at **www.ellajamesbooks.com** or friend her on Facebook at **www.facebook.com/ellajamesbooks**

SEE WHAT OTHERS ARE SAYING ABOUT

SELLING Scarlett

BY ELLA JAMES

"I was flat out blown away by this book."
- *Bend in the Binding*

"Definitely a 5 out of 5 star book!"
- *Weet Weets Bookshelf*

"Selling Scarlett was amazing and engaging. It made me cry, it made me laugh, and at times I was sitting on the edge of my seat wondering what was going to happen next."
- *What Stina Thinks*

"I (recommend) this book to anyone looking for a hot steamy roller coaster, I promise you won't be disappointed!"
- *Book Wormie*

"I was up all night finishing this book, but I couldn't help it. I had to know what happened next."
- *Delphina Reads Too Much*

"I'm reading this one right now and I'm loving it!"
- *The Book Hookers*

"The concept was different, and there was mystery, drama, and hot sex!"
- *Bookbabe*

PROLOGUE

Hunter

SEPTEMBER – LAS VEGAS

IT'S SATURDAY NIGHT, and I'm coming off a two-day tournament. I'm tired and hungry, chugging back a DeVille bottled water as I steer my Aston Martin through the clot of traffic on The Strip, toward the private airport behind the golf club.

I won again, with a full house over queens in the last hand, but it was close. I was tired—*am* tired. Not enough sleep. I collected my chips just after midnight and we wrapped the show at one-thirty. There was a room at the Bellagio for me, but I'm sick of the Bellagio. The last two times I stayed, I found company in my suite. I didn't ask for any company.

I'm flying to the vineyard: my house, my big bed, absolute quiet. I won't get to sleep for another couple hours—I can't sleep on my Gulfstream—but it's worth it. I'm tired of Vegas.

I'm still dressed in my poker black, and the jeans and button-up feel like sandpaper on my skin. I take another gulp. My head is throbbing like I just snorted a gram, but I didn't. Four months sober. Four months celibate, too. No real reason why. I just got bored.

I'm starting to get that empty, ill feeling in my stomach that comes from lack of sleep when Marchant starts blowing up my phone. I let it ring as I navigate South Maryland Parkway. I pull off my Stetson and run my left hand through my hair. Kinda makes me want to go to sleep. Maybe I *can* sleep on the plane.

Marchant just won't quit it with the phone. On the fifth call, I pick up, sounding more pissed than I mean too. "What do you want?"

"I've got a favor, man."

I groan, because I can hear it in his voice that Marchant is all hyped the hell up. "You got a favor you want to do for me?" I drawl. "Cause I could use a favor."

"Nah, man." He hesitates, the way he always does before he drops a bomb. "I need you to come out here. I've got something going on. I need you to run backup."

Run backup? I'm not sure what that means, but I can already tell it's going to be a pain in my ass. "You must be out your mind. It's two forty-thirty." I move the phone away from my face, scowling. "Are you rolling?"

"What? No. Look, just—hold on just a second." I hear shuffling, followed by Marchant's hiss as I roll into the parking lot of the tiny private airport where I keep my plane.

"Dude," he says, after a moment of muffled static. "I got Priscilla Heat out here."

He pauses, I guess expecting me to be impressed. When I'm not, he says, "She wants me and some of the girls for one of her videos."

I shake my head. "I'm at the airport, March. I'm going to the vineyard for a little R&R."

"You're a bourbon heir, Hunter. You shouldn't even have a fucking vineyard."

I hit a button on my steering wheel, the garage door lifts, and I slide into the fourth slot in the garage. It's dark in here, making me ache for sleep. "The word is 'no.' Have Rachelle watch the ranch for you."

"C'mon, man, this is *Priscilla Heat*."

Marchant is the kind of guy that has a favorite porn star, and Priscilla Heat, the lasered, lipo'd two-time World Boner Award winner, has been Marchant's ultimate fantasy since college.

"I get it, dude, but use Rachelle." Rachelle is Marchant's right-hand woman. She can watch the cameras at Love Inc. just as well as he can, and besides, he's got Richard on the ground. Richard and a team of big-ass bouncers.

"Rachelle is out," he says sourly.

"What do you mean, she's out?" I know for a fact she lives at Love Inc., Marchant's fluffy bunny brothel.

"I mean her sister died. Breast cancer. Rach won't be back till October first."

I rub my eyes. "Then tell Priscilla Heat to wait a week."

"She won't." Marchant's voice is low, almost a growl.

"Why not?" I throw my car door open, wincing as the garage's interior lights blink on.

I hear another puff, a pause where Marchant hesitates. Then he lowers his voice another octave. "She wants you here, man. She wants to spend the night with you and shoot the video here all week. It's more than a video. It's like a doc-u-fuck-ery or something."

I lean my hip against my ride, looking out the garage window at my waiting jet as I start to understand.

"You need the money."

"I didn't say that."

"Damnit, Marchant." I squeeze the bridge of my nose and swallow a sigh. "When this is over, I'm chaining you to one of your beds. No more going to Tao on Rach's nights, either."

I'm backing out of the garage a minute later, wheeling around and heading out toward I-215.

MARCH AND I met at Tulane, at the frat house. I had a shitty attitude because I joined under pressure from my father, and March was a party boy, moving through sorority girls like an assembly line. I thought he was full of shit, and he thought I was an uptight prick. But somehow the next semester we got stuck in adjoining rooms, and we've been good since.

March's parents died our junior year—plane crashed into the peaks of the Ecuadorian Andes—and around then my dad won his U.S. Senator gig and left for D.C., so we said fucks to the frat house and moved into West Manor. Marchant rented the entire downstairs, parading women in and out like cattle. The weird thing was, they always stayed friends after, so he had a lot of chick buddies. Sometime in our senior year, I bedazzled some of his inheritance, and he decided to use the money to open a Vegas brothel. A very Marchant thing to do. And Marchant being Marchant, he doesn't go for something reasonable like Radcliffe Ranch; he names it Love Incorporated.

It's a two-thousand acre, dusty, barren strip of Nevada desert, but the three sprawling, English manor houses and the forty or fifty acres around them—Marchant's got them looking like the Garden of Eden. He sold that image to a lot of people, too. Mostly people with dicks.

I'm not charmed when I give my Aston Martin to the valet and follow Krista, one of my least-favorite escorts, into the vast Love Den. She's got her strawberry-blonde hair thrown back over her shoulders, and it's kind of curly. Her blue eyes twinkle with a genuine smile, something I just don't understand.

Tonight she doesn't stop me in the den, with its many cozy alcoves, to ask me how I'm doing and bat her pretty blue eyes. In fact, I'm staring at the back of her head as she leads me down the nearest of four wide, candle-lit hallways. I watch her black silk dress sashay around her upper thighs, listen to her designer heels tap on the oriental runner. Against the soft brown wallpaper, her pale skin looks ghastly white.

For some reason, her silence makes me feel compelled to speak. "You doing alright tonight, Krista?"

"Just fine, Mr. West. Thank you for asking." She says it without missing a beat. "How are you?"

I rub my forehead, trying not to watch the crease between her thigh and ass. "I could be worse."

It dawns on me that most people would probably be happy with my weekend. I just won five million dollars. But one of the strange things about being rich as shit is five million's just not that exciting.

What most people don't know is that I haven't gotten my pocket of gold coins from great-granddaddy West. Not yet. Not until I'm thirty-five. When I turned eighteen my father gave me one of his stock portfolios to manage. He's fond of trial by fire, and I think he wanted to see if I would sink or swim. Before I graduated college I was able to triple what he gave me. Since then, I haven't stopped.

March's suite is behind a large mahogany door at the end of the hall, but I can't see it because there's a film crew camped outside. A few of them must recognize me because they tip their hats or nod as we squeeze through. I nod back, and Krista knocks briskly when we reach the door.

The camera mounted on the wall makes its creepy-ass mouse squeak, and I hear Marchant's voice over the intercom. "Good to see ya, West. Krista, thanks."

I press a Benjamin into her palm, because that's what any other guest would do, and the door swings open as she walks away.

Marchant is grinning. I can see relief and jubilation shining on his face as he pulls me into a bro hug. As always, I try not to wince.

"Thanks for coming, West."

I roll my eyes after taking in his black silk robe and spiky, dark blond hair. "Thanks for inviting me to the slumber party."

From behind March's wide shoulders, I hear a feminine laugh that makes my skin crawl.

"Hunter West!" I see a slim, tanned arm reach around Marchant's robe, and then she steps out from behind him. Priscilla Heat. Tonight she's decked out in a zebra striped teddy with red lace garters, black thigh highs, and six-inch heels. Her breasts are perkier than melons, and my eyes go there on their own before I jerk them back up. Priscilla's eyes are pale blue. Her smile is lasered, her teeth veneered. As she clasps my hand, I smell a whiff of sex.

"Hunter West." She smiles coyly. "I'm so glad to finally meet you. I'm a big, big fan."

I try to smile. I swear to God, I really do, but my mouth muscles aren't working. I'm pretty sure I wince instead. This is confirmed by the small notch between her thin, dark, drawn-on brows.

"I've seen some of your films," I said. "You run a tight ship."

She bursts out laughing, then grabs my arm and jerks me to the giant, claw-footed dining room table. Tonight, it's piled with hors d'oeuvres and liquor. I'm eying a meatball, thinking how hungry I am, when she grabs my ass and squeezes. "Christ, you're tight."

"Hands off," I growl.

She grabs my jaw, and as she lowers her mouth to my ear, I know that she'll be trouble. "I do what I want."

She grabs my cock—or tries to. "I don't know much about your business," I say as I catch her wrist, "but in my line of work we shake hands."

"Funny!" Her red smile curves, stretching her face. Applause erupts from all directions, and it's nothing like the polite applause from an audience watching a round of Texas Hold 'Em.

"How would you like to be in an adult film," she croons, "opposite me?"

"I'm busy tonight." I strut over to Marchant, ignoring my giant hard-on, and grab his shoulder. "Sarabelle, my room, now."

I keep my head down as I stride into the hall, shouldering past a smug-looking guy with sunken cheekbones and slick black hair; a short, bespectacled girl holding an enormous camera; and a couple of others I don't see because my eyes are on the carpet. In seconds, I'm at the suite that Marchant built for me, back when we were young and I was snorting blow and fucking like a demon.

I figured Sarabelle would be free, because she keeps Tuesdays open for her favorite clients. But even if she was working, she would have cleared her schedule. I strip, stashing my clothes in the chifferobe, and slide into a cool, silk robe. By the time Sarabelle arrives, wearing nothing but a blue teddy and wicked grin, I'm sprawled out on the bed, stroking my dick.

"Mr. West, how can I help you?"

I eat her out, then fuck her. When we're both satisfied I buy her for the rest of the night, as per our old arrangement. I'm ready to split when Donnie, one of the male escorts, knocks on the door. He's got a bottle of West Bourbon and two glasses already poured over ice.

Under the bottle is a note, scrawled on a receipt: *For being such a good sport. ~P*

I toss back one of the glasses, then shove the note into the pocket of my robe.

I tip Donnie with the bottle and the other glass, and by the time he closes the door, the room is spinning.

I hear a woman's voice as I sink to my knees, but I'm not sure which woman. Sarabelle is asleep. At least I thought she was. The voice is high-pitched, kind of like my stepmother's when she's angry at me. I blink at the swirling ceiling. Maybe it's my mother's—but I can't remember that far back. I can't remember...anything.

The next morning, I can't even remember if Sarabelle spent

the night in my room. All I know for sure is that she's gone.

CHAPTER ONE

Elizabeth

NOVEMBER – NAPA, CALIFORNIA

THIS IS WHAT happens when you don't leave your house for weeks on end, trying to prep for grad school finals. For the first time in my life, I'm looking at a man, imagining him naked.

Not just any man—my host for the evening, Hunter West. With tweed pants hugging muscular legs and jacket carelessly unbuttoned so I can see his undershirt and black vest, he screams sex. The kind of sex that's all slick skin and pheromones, bulging biceps and a six pack that ripples as he leans closer to plant kisses all over my face.

The little fantasy makes me blush, but I don't look away from Hunter. We're in the same room for the first time in at least six months, and I'm entranced. I pretend to tuck my wavy brown hair behind my ear as I steal another glance his way. He's standing by a massive stone fireplace, surrounded by some of California's most eligible bachelorettes. I recognize a few of them from Hargrove Day School: Honey Neighton, a former cheerleader who missed senior year due to some kind of Ambien addiction; Brina Lulle, a pretty, petite figure skater who once qualified for the Olympic team but broke her ankle and didn't go; Mary

Baldwin Greese, the über shy daughter of one of L.A.'s best talent agents. There are more of them, decked out in designer gowns every color of the fall and winter fabric palette.

Hunter is more than a head taller than most of them. His wide shoulders almost triple the width of teeny, tiny Brina. He's nodding at something she's saying, the look on his face politely solicitous, but I tell myself that underneath, he's brain-killingly bored. Honey Neighton fans herself with her hand, drawing attention to her breasts, and I smirk down at my gown. It's like a bad regency romance: Everyone gathers at the nobleman's estate for a hunt and the unmarried ladies fawn all over the awkward and ornery—but charming!—duke.

Hunter West isn't a brooding romance novel hero, though. He has too much breeding to be awkward and he's too straightforward to play at anything—although he *is* hard to get.

I watch him produce a convincing and completely gorgeous grin for Brina before he turns to Mary Baldwin, ruffling her chin-length hair and laughing with his blond head thrown back. This earns him a small smile, which, coming from Brina, is like a lap dance.

Suddenly, Hunter turns and looks over his shoulder, and I can see his eyebrows arch. Marchant Radcliffe, one of Hunter's hell-raising friends, tosses a glass bottle over the heads of a cluster of guests, and Hunter catches it with one hand, saying something that makes his admirers smile before turning to the wet bar behind him and opening a cabinet.

He pours, and his ladies wait. Even filling shot glasses, he seems completely in command of himself and what's around him. I've moved in or near his circle for a while, despite our seven year age difference, and I've never seen him *not* look like that. Like a man at the helm of the universe.

It's kind of surprising, considering he spends most of his time in Vegas, playing poker, man-whoring, and tossing back his family's infamous Louisiana bourbon. That was his great-grandfather, Willard West's legacy. Hunter's father, Conrad West, after a long life in politics, is Secretary of State.

He disapproves of Hunter's lifestyle, or so I've heard. I've only actually seen Conrad West in person twice, and both times from a distance, so I don't know much about him, but I wish I did. I collect Hunter details like my best friend Suri collects Hermès jewelry.

Watching Hunter turn around with a platter of tall shots balanced on his big hand and a sly smile on his face, I can't help imaging him lying on the Egyptian cotton sheets I know hug all the mattresses here at his Napa estate.

It wouldn't start there, though. As he tosses back his shot, I envision him backed against a wall, his shoulders bare and round and wide, that plump lower lip just begging to be bitten. Something about him makes me want to bite. If I was anybody else, maybe I would try to arrange that.

As it is, I'm Elizabeth DeVille, super spy and resident poor girl, and watching him out of the corner of my eye will have to do.

I nod at something my best friend Suri is saying to me, then feel bad because I'm not really listening.

"I'm surprised she's wearing Oscar because I heard she's not modeling for them anymore," she says.

"Oh really," I reply, hoping that's the right response.

"Maybe someone on the design team is a friend of hers, because otherwise I don't know how she would get her hands on it."

Hunter leans against the fireplace, fingering a flask that sticks out of his pants pocket. I catch him wipe a hand back through his slightly wavy hair as his groupies shift their attention to a curvy black-haired girl who's gesturing wildly about something. For half a second, Hunter's gaze lifts. I think it rests on me, but then a blonde bombshell in a wispy red gown steps around me, and I'm sure his attention is meant for her.

I'm watching him more brazenly than ever now, curious to see how he reacts to the sexpot stalking his way. I'm surprised when his jaw tightens. He almost seems to wince. Then she is close enough to reach for him. He drapes an arm around her shoulder, a gentleman greeting a fond acquaintance, and I realize who she is: Priscilla Heat, infamous porn star and my good friend Cross's arch nemesis. I don't know what went wrong between the two of them—he hasn't even told me how he knows her—but Cross seriously hates the woman.

I wonder if he's seen her yet. I wonder how she knows Hunter.

A soft giggle pulls me back to earth, to Suri, who's standing beside me in front of a wall of glass doors that lead onto a balcony overlooking Hunter's vineyards. I turn to Suri, but I can still sense Hunter at the other end of the room, exuding a low-level hum that makes my electrons feel unstable.

"I knew you still wanted to do him," Suri giggles, wiggling her eyebrows like she's trying to attract attention.

"I do not," I hiss.

Squinting my left eye, I look around us, mindful of who is close enough to eavesdrop. I can't see faces clearly because my left contact fell out in Suri's limousine, but I think I spot Carolitta Hamshon in a circle of gowns just beyond the couch in front of me.

I angle my body more toward Suri. "I do not," I whisper, even lower. There's no way I want Carolitta's coven of bitches to hear this. It's embarrassing enough that Suri spotted me ogling.

"Yes you do, girlie. You've wanted him since sweet sixteen."

Suri knows all about the time Mom's Porsche broke down on the winding road that runs past West Vineyard. Hunter came to my rescue at just past midnight, leaving a beautiful brunette in a silky gown watching from his front door as he pushed Mom's

Porsche down his long driveway and into his garage. He'd pushed it up a ramp and stripped down to his jeans, then pulled out a rolling body-board, eased his broad torso onto it, and scooted his fine self beneath the belly of the car. He emerged twenty minutes later covered in oil smudges, with grease in his golden hair and a self-satisfied smile on his tiger face, inexplicably smelling slightly of bourbon. He'd insisted I stay the night in his spacious guesthouse. Suri also knows how, the next morning, I'd heard moans coming from the direction of the pool. And how, from that point on, my insides have quivered every time I see him on Moneyline or read about his poker tournaments. It's even worse when the gossip blogs feature him toting a trophy date to this event or that. Every time I read about him with a woman, I feel like scratching her eyeballs out.

I don't like it, but it's something I've resigned myself to living with.

"I'm not lying," I mumble, but Suri's no longer paying attention to me. She's shifted slightly in her silver Manolos, tossing a not-at-all-discreet glance Hunter's way.

"Suri, stop," I hiss.

"His eyes are almost yellow," she murmurs, this time having the tact to lean her head near mine. "You told me they were green, but when he passed by earlier, I swear they looked like cat eyes."

I nod. I think of him as part tiger. He's languid to the point of appearing almost lazy, and yellow or green, those eyes are framed by ridiculous lashes, set in a strong face with prominent cheekbones, full lips, and a sensuous smile.

I hear his chuckle, low and warmer than a gulp of bourbon, and I swear my knees shake under my slip like a debutant on her first night out.

"Elizabeth DeVille, I think you have your first boy crush."

She says 'boy crush' because Suri has a long standing joke-suspicion that I'm gay.

"He's not my crush," I whisper, tight-jawed. I can feel sweat prickling underneath my arms, and the truth is, I'm starting to get a little upset as I worry Hunter will somehow *know*.

"Suuure he's not. Save it for the funnies, girlie-o." Suri winks, and her boyfriend Adam Hamilton is there, smiling at us both and holding two wine flutes. He hands one to me and presses the other into Suri's dainty hand. He glances from my face to hers and frowns, his eyebrows crinkling.

"What is it?" Suri giggles. Suri is always giggling. If she were a party drink, she'd be champagne for sure.

"There's something here," he says, pointing accusingly from Suri to me. "You're doing one of those girl things where you talk about someone and they don't even know it." He shakes his head. "It's not fair."

"Well it wasn't about you," Suri says, propping one hand on the hip of her burgundy, silk sheath Valentino gown. She slides her eyes to me, and Adam grins his dimpled grin. "Oh, I see. Miss Elizabeth."

"No, not Miss Elizabeth." I scowl, because I resent the simpering nickname.

"She has a hot crush," Suri murmurs, barely containing another giggle behind her wine flute.

"I do *not*." My face is flaming. I seriously consider smacking Suri, except I know that would draw even more attention, and I am not a fan of attention.

"Bet my crush is even hotter," Adam says, taking Suri's hand. He brushes her brown curls out of her face and nods to the doors behind us, most of which have been propped open, letting in the nippy November air. "Want to dance?"

I roll my eyes at their cheesiness, but truthfully I'm glad Adam got the heat off me.

"Why of course, my love." Suri curtsies, and I have the wherewithal to flush on her behalf. Someone from Suri's family should act a lot more reserved in public. Suri's like an oblivious nine-year-old.

I, on the other hand, am absolutely conscious of the eyes pulled to my orbit as Suri and Adam pass through the doors behind me, leaving me alone with my half-empty wine flute. I hate moments like these, where I know what everyone is thinking: *Look at Elizabeth DeVille, left alone by the only friend she has. With a mother like hers and hardly any money left, it's a wonder she has even one.*

Mentally shoving off their judgment, I lift the tail of my green dress in my right hand and gently pick my way through the crowded room, toward a slender hallway just beyond a staircase. I can't resist a glance over my shoulder as I go; I'm looking for Hunter, but he's nowhere in sight.

To my left, beyond a wine-gurgling fountain and across a vast oriental rug, I spot my friend Cross Carlson with his arms around the red-haired Cole twins: identical, including their D-cup racks. He winks, and I give him a genuine smile, hoping the black-haired, blue-eyed devil in the bespoke tux is actually Cross. I really can't see. I curse the loss of my contact, and my own vanity. I have a pair of glasses in my clutch, but I'm too vain to wear them with my emerald satin, mermaid-cut Vera Wang.

Not that it would change my aesthetics much. With or without glasses, I'm still a fat girl. Not a lot fat. Just regular, eats-too-much-good-food fat. The kind of fat that curls the waist of my blue jeans down and creates an unattractive line of back fat between my pants and my top, just over the butt, when I sit cross-legged, hunched over one of my textbooks.

Since finishing undergrad—since my mom threw my dad out before having her third nervous breakdown in as many years, and dad went running to another family, complete with two new daughters—I've gained probably fifteen or twenty pounds, and the thing about the new me is, I don't care. I like Phish Food ice cream. I like beer, wine, and whiskey. I like Dove dark chocolate even better than the fancy imported stuff, and my mystery novel fetish is such that the time I don't spend studying for a PhD in Ethics is devoted to figuring out whodunnit.

With the exception of Hunter West, who's been my own personal porn since that fateful night Mom's Porsche broke down, I don't find that many men attractive. Maybe I am a lesbian, but I don't think so. I've never had the hots for another woman. I think most guys are just boring.

I clutch the tail of my dress a little more tightly as I glide down the hallway just off the great room. The wall on my right has turned from stone to glass, and I realize I'm approaching the atrium: a glass-walled garden in the middle of the octagonal house. Through the glass wall on my right, I see a swatch of starry sky, and I remember three nights ago, at Mom's house. Cross and I went to the front lawn to watch a meteor shower, and I think he wanted to kiss me.

He's always been like that when he drinks. Needy. Turned on. Most girls love it, but Cross is one of my oldest friends. I know how closed off he is to everyone, how shallow he keeps things, especially with girls he "dates," and I can't risk that happening with me. I need our long, deep talks, just about as much as I need his unwavering friendship. Besides, if we hooked up and it went wrong, Cross wouldn't have anywhere to live.

I let my mind linger on Cross's troubles only for a moment before I hurry past the atrium, knowing everyone standing in the glass-framed garden is probably making out or gossiping in cliques. I don't need their eyes on me.

My destination, a replica of an old-fashioned powder room, should be just past a serving closet up here on my left. I look at the rug as I walk; it's red, ornate, and old, and it covers most of the hardwood in this hall. My lack of sight in my left eye makes my right eye jump around, taking in the Sanskrit wall-hangings and the glittering, crystal light fixtures on the ceiling—and all the space in-between. I want to be sure I don't run into any company.

Cross texted the directions to the powder room earlier today when I asked for an escape place if I found myself alone. *Mom built room on request, 4 his women,* Cross told me, adding a winking smilie at the end. Cross's mom, Derinda, is a well-known California architect, and this octagonal mansion in the spot where the original estate burned is one of her most recent creations.

The *'something brass'* Cross told me would mark the powder room is a brass door-knocker in the shape of a tiger's face, and I smile when I see it. My hand is on the doorknob when I hear a moan: a woman's moan, followed by a man's moan.

I should move. I know I should, but I just can't. My BCBGs are pasted to the rug as my whole body heats to a boil.

Hunter is in there. I know that moan.

He moans again, and I hear a strangled "no" from low down in his throat. My body slumps against the door as my pulse dances. Sweat blooms on every inch of me. I can't swallow or breathe as the woman whispers something in an enticing alto voice, and Hunter's baritone voice purrs, "Such a bitch."

"You're the bitch," she laughs, and I hear the smack of a hand on skin. She moans like she's turned on, and I imagine Hunter's golden hair around his tiger face, the sexy curve of his lips as another slap rings through the room and the woman laughs again, high-pitched and off-key like the whinny of a horse.

Holy crap.

His release is rough, too. I can easily imagine his hips swinging, his ass tightening as he pumps into her from behind. His moan is guttural, almost a grunt. It sounds like pain but I know it must be pleasure.

"Jesus," the woman pants. "You're worth the trouble. Really, Hunter...what a fucking stud."

I listen with my heart in my throat, but Hunter is silent as the woman makes a little mewling sound. I can hear the shuffling sound of fabric over bodies, but there are no words—just the woman's panting.

A second later there's heavy footfall, followed by the low squeal of a closing door.

"Jesus," the raspy, female voice whispers.

Looking down at my hand on the doorknob, I realize there's a key hole and I peek through it, getting a fleeting glimpse of Priscilla Heat in her red taffeta gown. Hunter has left her there with swollen lips and wild hair, examining her manicure as she leans on one of the ivy-covered columns framing a sunken tub.

Hunter—well-mannered, charming Hunter—slapped her ass, bruised her lips, and then he left her there. For some reason, that does crazy things to me: the image of Hunter, pulling down his expensive trousers and taking out his cock. Quick, rough sex, and then he's gone.

I glance behind me and, seeing no one, stumble farther down the hallway. I'm weaving like a drunk, and I am drunk: drunk on pent-up lust and yes, a silly, juvenile crush. I stumble past a row of dark wood doors, stopping for a breath when I reach a bend in the hall.

I lean against the burgundy wallpaper, shocked by the intensity of my arousal. Every breath only steepens my desire. I think about how long it's been since I took care of myself. I've been busy studying for finals, so I guess it's been about a week. As I stand there, throbbing, I look down the remainder of the hall and notice there are no doors beyond the one I just passed. The hall turns to the right and leads around to the massive foyer, if I'm correct about where I am.

I glance left and right again. No one is around. I can't even hear the string band playing in the great hall. I take a deep, shaky breath. Then I grab the handle of the door behind me. It's taller and wider than the others, and to my surprise, it gives when I turn the knob.

Blinded by a haze of lust, I sail into the room, flaps of emerald silk flying around me, my hand already reaching between my legs.

Through my mental fog, I notice the vastness of the bedroom. My eyes slide over the flames blooming in a marble fireplace and I spot a tasseled pillow tossed haphazardly, inches from the fire. My attention settles on the bed; it's huge, with four mahogany posts and a deep green bedspread that matches my gown almost perfectly. I dimly note a surprising lack of pillows, just before I trip on one. I glance down at my feet, surprised to find I am standing in a sea of pillows. I glance around, still panting, and notice a broken mirror hanging beside a small armoire.

I'm confused and for a second, worried, but another glance around the room reveals nothing else out of the ordinary. I assume someone has used the room for a party quickie. That turns me on even more, and I rush back to the door, locking it behind me before striding to the bed.

It's ridiculous. I'm still blazing hot. I feel full and restless. Desperate. I know what I need. I've never done this outside my bedroom, but Hunter West does something strange to me, so I'm not entirely surprised—nor am I inclined to stifle my desire. I'm a grown woman, and God knows I'm the only one with a say-so in my sex life. Why not do what I want? Ten minutes, and I'll be back out in the hall, feeling a lot more level-headed. It's win-win.

I grin as I scoot up onto the mattress, inhaling the sweet scent of leather and cologne as I lean back on the only remaining pillow. Sweaty and trembling, I part my legs and reach under my gown. My fingers have just found their mark when a shadow rises from the floor space on the other side of the bed.

CHAPTER TWO

Elizabeth

HUNTER IS SHIRTLESS and sweat-slicked, with dark eyes and a twisted mouth. He wipes his forehead, squinting, and speaks in a voice that sounds strangely far away. "Is that you, Libby?"

I can't speak. I can't even move for the longest moment. When I find my voice, I sound like I'm choking. "Libby? N-no."

Oh dear God, he's beautiful. I am in awe of his shoulders. His pecs. My heart is racing, and under my gown, I quiver in response to—well, it must be pheromones. I have the urge to grab his arms and pull him down beside me on the bed. Instead, I squeeze my eyes shut.

Oh God. I'm done. I was an outcast before, but my old crowd will really slay me now.

Slowly I lift my eyelids, finding Hunter closer; he's leaning over the mattress, the weight of his gorgeous upper body propped on his thick arms. His face softens when his eyes meet mine, and he nods slightly. "Yes it is."

I have no idea what he's talking about anymore, because my brain has turned to soup. I'm all glowing, glittering sensation as his green gaze sweeps me from toes to crown. His brows are slightly gathered, his mouth still tight. Firelight illuminates his face, so I can see the exact moment he realizes what I've been doing. His torso stiffens as his hands, pressed against the mattress, curl into big fists. He makes a low, approving sound and speaks in a voice that sounds like molten lava.

"That's so sexy."

I look down at my hand, still tangled in my gown. "It is?" I search his face.

"Oh, yeah. Hell yeah." He's on the bed with me that next second, his gym-ripped body licked by the glow of flames. I gasp when he grabs my hips and turns me toward him. His eyes are flaring, and I expect him to let go of my fleshy hips. I'm already recoiling, hating myself for humiliating myself in front of this man. Instead he pulls me closer, locking both hands around my big ass and squeezing.

"Let me get you off," he purrs. I feel a throb between my legs, followed by a rush of needy warmth.

Oh God.

Somehow I manage to nod, and his hand is fishing in my gown. I can barely stand to watch him. I'm already panting, and my eyes want to squeeze shut. I won't let them. Fate has given me this gift, and I intend to experience it. I inhale deeply, trying to hold off my release.

Hunter's eyes glow as he strokes my calves and traces up my thigh, across my hip. He looks dazed as he lifts my panties with his finger, stroking oh so gently over me.

I whimper and he moves to straddle me, the fingers of his free hand tangling with mine, guiding my fingers, stroking me lightly, making me want to burst as he positions my finger, wraps his palm around my hand, and gently urges me inside myself.

His fingers are working my clit, and I'm wet...*so* wet. I am gasping, clenching and unclenching. My legs are locked, my feet dancing. All my blood has rushed under our joined fingers.

"You like it," he rasps, and then my finger is joined by his.

This is the most I've ever had, and I moan with the fullness of it. As I reach for him, clutching at his golden hair, he tugs away, ducking under my gown. I feel the soft heat of his tongue and shriek. My thighs clamp down around his head and it's like the universe is ripped apart. I groan and push his head down, nearly coming off the bed as he works me into what must be nirvana.

Holy shit.

I've never had an orgasm like this.

I'm bereft and shaking, gasping; humiliated and sated. I close my eyes and wrap my arms around myself, feeling like the child I clearly am. But as I peek shyly up at him, he grins, surprising me by stretching his gorgeous body over mine, hovering for a moment just above me before he dips down, kissing me lightly, even sweetly, on the lips. I can taste the salt of him. His breath smells like bourbon and when he tickles his damp mouth down my neck, I shudder so hard I think that I might burst.

And then I do—again. He cups me over my gown and strokes and— *Oh my God.*

From somewhere far away, I see him moving off the bed, standing wide-eyed at the foot of it. He's tugging at his golden hair, rubbing his eyes. Something is wrong, I think. He looks upset. I have the drowsy urge to hold him close and soothe the stress etched on that handsome face. But he is gone before I fall back down to Earth.

DID THAT REALLY just happen? Oh my God, I've stumbled into a fantasy. My legs are still shaking when I stand forever later. I grip the green duvet and set my gaze on the open door through which Hunter West disappeared; apparently this room has an attached bathroom.

I rub my temples, wondering if he's in there, or if the bathroom attaches to another room as well. Where did he go? Did that really just happen? I feel slightly sick about this. I feel gleeful. Hunter West! I picture him in the black button-up and Stetson he wears for poker tournaments. I picture his lazy smile as he waves at paparazzi from the red carpet at the premier of a movie his production company financed, his strong arm locked around a starlet's waist.

I shut my eyes and conjure the image of him above me. His eyes on my face are gentle as he leans to kiss my lips.

Still clinging to the duvet, I make my way around the bed and toward the open bathroom door, pausing to examine something on the floor, where Hunter was sitting when I came into the room. It looks like an old-fashioned cravat. On a whim, I scoop it up and bring it to my nose. It smells like Hunter. I tuck it in my clutch and turn back around to see the bedroom one more time. With a clearer head, it looks more damaged than it did before. The broken mirror and strewn pillows remind me of the carnage left after one of Mom's breakdowns.

I do a quick sweep of the furniture and walls, looking for any tell-tale trinkets, but other than Hunter's scent, there is no evidence that this room is his. I notice something blue glowing in the fireplace and step back toward it. It's a broken wine glass, cracked and glowing with the heat.

It gives me an uneasy feeling, which intensifies when I remember what Hunter was doing just a few minutes ago—or rather, *who* he was doing. It's not Priscilla's profession that gets to me. I don't think there's anything shameful about a woman who has sex in front of a camera. It's the memory of Hunter's footsteps on the bathroom floor that bothers me. The way he left her there, even if sex was the only thing between them. Also bothering me is the proximity of that encounter to the one he had with me. I want to be okay with it, to just not care, but Hunter is still my crush, and care I do.

Why did he leave the room without saying anything? Is he some kind of sex fiend? A bedroom Batman?

I can't decide if I'm amazed that this just happened, or if

I'm angry that he treated me like Priscilla Heat. He just *left*.

I gather my gown in one hand and step through the door to the bathroom, holding my breath because I expect to see Hunter. But I don't. I glance around the empty room. The walls are decked with heavy, gold mirrors; the floors, the massive tub, and the even more massive shower are brown and gold marble; there's a glass-encased painting on the wall between the tub and the shower; it looks like Dali and I wonder if it's real.

I'm looking in the mirror, giving my body a rare critique and trying to put things with Hunter in perspective, when someone enters from the other end of the bathroom.

My stomach dips like I'm riding a roller coaster.

Not Hunter. Another woman.

I notice she's wearing a prim black dress and a crisp white apron. *Not another lover*. She gives me a shy smile and as she steps forward, I can see that her dark brown hair is tucked into a tidy bun.

"Miss DeVille?" she says softly.

"That's me," I say, hands on my hips.

She nods at the tub. "Would you like a bathe?"

Her accent is French, I think. "A bath?" I correct her automatically, then feel guilty; it's the soon-to-be professor in me.

"Yes." She nods vigorously. "Would you like to get into the bath?"

I narrow my eyes at the massive, square tub. "Um, that's not necessary." I stare at her and fold my arms. I'm not sure what to say.

I decide to be blunt. "Where is Hunter?"

"Mister West is tending to some business."

Oh, I just bet he is.

"Did he send you to offer me a bath?" I ask.

The girl hesitates, then nods.

"Thanks for the offer, but I'll take a few minutes in here by myself and I'll be gone."

The girl starts to go, and I put a hand over my breasts. I feel like someone's shoved a spike into my chest, and I tell myself that's what I get.

Who do you think he is, Lizzy? He's a freakin' man whore, and he found me in one of his bedrooms, funking the fuzzy franny. What the hell do I expect? That he'll rush back in and get down on one knee?

I step closer to the mirror, frantically smoothing my hair, and the housekeeper turns. "There is one more thing," she says.

I wait, brows arched.

"He does not make this a habit. He says he found you, he had been drinking, you were beautiful. If there is any forgiveness to be asked, you will speak with him?"

I frowned, confused until I realize this must be Hunter West's damage control. Ouch. I swallow. Nod. "Yeah, whatever. Sure." She turns again, to go, and I say, "Wait." Her dark eyes meet mine, and I spit it out: "Tell him that's fine. I wasn't looking to get married, either."

After that, I lock the doors, pull my gown up, and work carefully to restore myself to my pre-Hunter state. I also give myself a mental shake.

He didn't use and abuse you, silly girl. You were both in the right place at the right time, and you had the best orgasm ever. If anything, he gave you stud service. It so happened to occur right after he was with another woman, but he didn't design it that way.

I try to believe my own propaganda as I smooth my hair, reapply my lipstick, and stuff the Hunter-scented cravat deeper into my clutch. I look perfectly respectable—and I am. I had a pleasant experience, and now I'm going back to the party. Maybe Suri will feel I've served my time, and I can go home and finish my reading for class on Monday; the subject is fitting: the morality (or amorality) of sex.

After a few more minutes of deep breaths, I start toward the door the maid went through, but as soon as I do, I can see royal blue and gold curtains. I don't want to come out in another bedroom, and I damn sure don't want to bump into Hunter again, so I turn around and open the door leading back into the emerald room.

What I find on the other side stuns me. Priscilla Heat is naked, lying on her back beside the fireplace, and Hunter is leaning over her. I'm so distracted by his amazing, taut backside, it takes me a second to notice what he's doing with his left hand.

It's pushed against Priscilla's throat. She moans. I gasp and Hunter's head whips my way. The look on his face is horror. I imagine mine is much the same. I fly through the blue bedroom as fast as I can move.

I'M DASHING THROUGH the hall, toward the vacant part that leads to the foyer, and I guess I must be freaking out because I don't even notice Cross until he and I collide.

"Whoa." His hands close on my shoulders as he holds me at arms' length, his blue eyes narrowing and then widening as he realizes I'm me. "Where have you been?" His voice is low, and I can smell the vodka on his warm breath.

"Is something wrong?" He moves his hand up to my face and cups my cheek. "You look upset."

Without waiting for my answer, he pulls me close. With my body pressed against his, I realize that I'm shaking and I pray he doesn't notice. "I'm okay," I lie. And even though I'm not nurturing romantic feelings for Cross, being so close to him makes me feel warm. I imagine him sitting at his desk with a sketchpad and a pencil, dictating the design of a new Cross Hybrids motorcycle, rough around the edges and pretty damn sexy.

"What's got you all worked up?" he asks. "I know Hunter West and his parties, and he's—" Cross inhales deeply, his nose in my hair, and then pushes me away, his eyes flying to mine. "Elizabeth, you *didn't*."

"Didn't what?"

He looks me over, up and down, and when his gaze falls on my left arm, all the color drains out of his face. "Fucking hell," he whispers.

"What?"

He snatches my clutch, which has come unclasped and is hanging open, pulling out Hunter's cravat and waving it around. "Jesus, Lizzy. Really? *Hunter West?*"

I nod, because I'm not sure what else to do. "What's wrong with—"

I'm going to ask what's so wrong with Hunter West—a rhetorical question whose answer is among the hundreds of scandalous rumors I've collected about Hunter over the years. But before I can finish my question, Cross turns around and slams his fist into the wall, striking it hard enough to cause a loud boom.

I grab his arm, stunned and appalled. "Cross! What the hell is wrong with you?!"

For half a second, I can feel the pent up rage seethe in him. Then it's gone.

He gently removes my hand from him and turns to look at me, his expression carefully subdued. "Do you need a ride home, Lizzy? Do you want to talk?"

"I'm fine," I say, and his mouth twists. He tugs me down the hall, back toward the green bedroom, where I hear slapping and Hunter's moan. My stomach lurches.

"Don't think that you're the only one," Cross says. His eyes bore into mine, looking for something I can't name. "Did he force you, Liz?"

"No way! Of course he didn't." I grab Cross's hand and drag him back the other way, toward the empty foyer. "Call off the state of emergency. I've still got my V-card. *Unstamped*."

"For how long?" he asks darkly, and I've had enough.

"I don't care how much you've been drinking—" I begin, but he cuts me off.

"Do you really want to be just another fuck?"

I recoil, feeling like I've just been slapped. It takes me a full half-second to gather my thoughts, and when I do, I'm irate. "I could never be 'just another fuck,' so don't you say that shit to me. I'll make my own choices and I don't do a bad job, unlike some people who drink themselves stupid and sleep with any warm body that will have them."

He works his jaw, and I know it was a low blow. He's told me practically all his secrets since we were kids, and I know he uses sex to get affection.

"I'm just trying to be your friend, Lizzy."

I feel steam coming out my ears. "Why were *you* back here?"

The look on his face tells me exactly what I had suspected: he was looking for space for his two redheads. *Not* for me.

"I'm not like him," he starts.

"Right."

I can see the hurt in his eyes. Instantly, I'm gutted.

"Cross, I'm sorry—"

But he's out the front doors in a gust of frigid air, and I can't take back what I've said. I stand there, trembling with anger and remorse.

For a few long seconds, my stomach clenches as I ask myself *why Hunter?* I know that he's a man whore. I know he doesn't 'like' me. He doesn't even know me. And yet...I've never even had a crush on anyone but him. I realize now how messed up I must really be, and it makes me want to cry.

My shoulders heave as I stare through the wavy glass panes on the ornate doors. I can hear Cross's bike crank from somewhere in the direction of the front of the house, and despite how terrible I feel, I can't leave without linking up with Suri, my ride.

I press my back against the wall and take big, deep breaths.

I refuse to cry. For the next five minutes, every time my eyes start to sting, I refuse to give in. When I finally make my way back around to the great hall, the first thing I do is scan for Hunter. He's easy to spy, surrounded by a flock of women, missing his jacket and his tie—or rather, cravat—the sleeves of his shirt rolled up to his elbows.

My body throbs, and Hunter's gaze flickers over mine—there, then gone without conveying anything.

Then Suri is in front of me, cheeks flushed, eyes bright from wine. "Woman, where were you? Cross almost ruined his cover!"

Cross lives at my family home, in my childhood bedroom. It's a secret. His family disowned him, and Cross doesn't want them to know where he is. His father, Drake Carlson, the governor of California, actually said he didn't care if Cross turned up dead. I wouldn't have believed it, but Cross let me hear the voice mail.

My family has fallen off the social grid, and Mom's in rehab and I live with Suri, so we think he's well hidden. Just in case, Cross and I try to stay away from each other in public.

"Yeah, I just ran into him." My eyes widen warily.

"What happened?"

"He freaked out," I say. It's the only thing I can manage. "I guess I should go find him." He'll be at Mom's, alone. At least I think he will be. Cross isn't the type to hit the bars when he's upset, much as he'd like everyone to think the opposite.

Suri agrees to ride home with Adam and loans me Arnold for the night. A butler fetches Mom's worn, white mink and escorts me down the wide, brick walk, to the line of limousines where, years ago, our own driver, Wilson, would have been waiting. The door is opened, and I climb in, feeling weighted.

I lean forward and give Arnold instructions he doesn't really need.

"We'll be there in forty minutes or less, ma'am," he says.

"Thank you, Arnold."

The divider wall locks into place, and I'm alone under the starry sky, staring out the sunroof, looking for constellations I can't find because we're moving too quickly down the little vineyard road.

A computerized refrigerator offers me a bottle of water and I take it, smirking at the green and blue label: DeVille. This is how my great-grandfather made his fortune. It's good water. Almost as good as West Bourbon, which I find in the liquor console. I take a deep swing, remembering the taste of Hunter West's mouth. I wrap the cravat around my wrist. Wrong or right, I'm keeping it.

I'm ashamed to say my mind is still on Hunter when the limousine slows. Arnold lowers the shield, his face taut as he says, "Miss DeVille, please remain inside the vehicle." The wall goes up, and I feel a weird energy. A kind of darkness.

I'm not sure what compels me to open my door, but as I step into the road, I think some part of me already knows, because my arms and legs weigh two tons each.

My good eye blinks and there is Cross, lying on his side in the damp grass just beside the road. At first glance, it looks like he is simply relaxing. His arms are raised over his head in the position he adopts sometimes while sleeping. His legs are scissored, his pretty mouth parted just a little.

I see blood oozing from his lips. The dark smear on the asphalt—that's Cross's blood. His bike, a renovated '73 Norton Commando Mark III Roadster he loves like a person, is smoking in the road beside him.

CHAPTER THREE

Hunter

A FEW WEEKS LATER – LAS VEGAS

I CAN'T GO back to Love Inc. I know I should, to try to jar my memory of that night, but I can't. So we're at Batshit Ranch, a fifteen-thousand-square-foot California red roof on my little patch of sand, just outside the Summerlin community. I own ten-thousand acres out here, and besides grazing some cattle, I don't do much with them. Some things should be for enjoyment only, and I enjoy staying at my country place. It's my Vegas home when I need to get away from the bustle of the Wynn.

March and I are in my study, and I'm behind my desk, cradling March's iPad as I scrutinize the chart that my friend and his private eye, Dave, put together. I turn the tablet sideways, frowning.

'To Catch a Criminal'. I flick a withering glance his way. "Enjoying the drama, Radcliffe?"

"Not enjoying," he says, his voice faintly defensive as he kicks his feet out and crosses his long legs at the ankles. "Just making do. I figured we should have a project name."

"Right." I look it over, curious to see the revised list of suspects. I note the absence of two names I'd expected to see: Bill Percy and James Meyers, both deviant little fucks who've bruised some of the girls at Love Inc. before.

"Percy wasn't there," Marchant says, reading my mind. Bill Percy was a prick in college who is now a prick lobbyist for the gambling industry. He got rough with one of Love Inc.'s employees; he claimed he was drunk, and she decided not to press charges. "His wife caught him boinking the housekeeper that night," March tells me. "He checked into Bellagio around three. Meyers was at an electronic cigarette convention in Virginia, so they're both in the clear."

Marchant takes a sip of his whiskey, then rolls up the sleeves of his rumpled button-up. "All in all there are twenty-six suspects, including you and me. Eleven stand out."

I scan the eleven bolded names. "My guy's been on Rutherford and Kriss for going on sixteen days. He says they're both clean as a whistle."

Marchant passes his almost-empty glass from one hand to the other, looking moody and restless. "I say we drop Rutherford. He likes it weird, but I think that's only when he fucks Brad. Everyone seems to like it weird with Brad. Devotion to the pacifier does not a kidnapper make," Marchant mutters.

I lift my head, brows arched. "A *pacifier*?"

March shrugs. "That's what Brad says."

"That goes on the list of kinks I'll never understand."

"So now it's a list of one?"

"Funny. We've got a more important list to worry about." I bring each name up as a slide, and flip through one at a time. Name. Picture. Possible motive. "Let's keep the tail on Kriss. There's just something about him."

Marchant nods, punching something into his iPhone.

Since the evening Sarabelle vanished from my room, almost two months ago, we've paid a couple of Vegas private investigators to track people of interest. So far all we've learned is Vegas has a total of three decent PIs, and there's no limit to the number of affairs a determined man of means can have. That, and one of

Priscilla Heat's screenwriters looks at kiddie porn. Dave, a Vegas local and ex-FBI dude, is our lead guy, and he's the one who provided us with this list.

I flip through a few more slides. "Are we still on the ex-boyfriend and the stepbrother?"

"Sarabelle's ex-boyfriend doesn't do anything but a waitress," Marchant says blandly. "Her stepbrother doesn't do anything but Oxy."

"Tell Dave to keep tracking them. I'll add Michael Lockwood to my list, you add Caleb Zeuss to yours."

Michael Lockwood was one of Priscilla's film crew; he quit his job just a few days after that night at the ranch. He's come up clean so far, but something about him smells off. Caleb Zeuss is one of the cooks Marchant employs. He was on the clock that night, but no one seems to have seen him.

The cameras are useless, because while March was fucking Priscilla for *Pimps and Princesses*, someone turned them off. The woman watching the monitors assumed the system glitched. Naturally, when she tried to convey this to Marchant, he did not want to be interrupted.

I hand Marchant his iPad and pull out my smart phone, blinking at a new text.

"Cumming to your place tonight. Bringing a surprise. ~P"

I squeeze my eyes shut, opening them some seconds later to find Marchant out of his leather chair and standing in front of my desk. He leans over, pressing his palm against the sleek oak. "You alright, dude? You look amped."

I glower. "Thanks." I'm not doing coke, which March should know, but I'm sure as shit not justifying anything to him.

"You sleeping okay?"

I snicker. Marchant drains his glass and rolls his brown eyes. He slinks back to his arm chair, reminding me momentarily of the Pink Panther. "You gotten any more calls from Smith?" he asks me. Josh Smith is the LVPD's lead detective on this case, and he's been on me like white on rice since the morning we called to report Sarabelle's disappearance.

I toss back the remainder of liquor in my glass and stand, stretching my sore legs. "I think he's finally gotten the hang of calling Lehland," my attorney.

"What about your old man?" Marchant asks.

"His people have stopped calling, too. I guess they've got all their fires put out." No one but Josh Smith and a few others from Love Inc. and Priscilla's company, Heat Enterprises, knows Sarabelle disappeared from my particular room. Given the political sensitivities, it needs to stay that way.

Marchant, on the other hand, has been all over the news. His business hasn't suffered at all. In fact, he says it's picked up. Bunch of sick fucks out there.

His phone buzzes, and I feel a jab of guilt. He should be at work. He's busy, week night or not. I should have met him there instead of being such an avoidant fuck.

Now I have to get him out of here before Priscilla shows up. He has no idea what's going on between the two of us, and I'd like to keep it that way for a while longer.

TWENTY MINUTES LATER, I'm on the balcony attached to my bedroom, pretending to read *The Financial Times* on my tablet and wishing Priscilla would hurry the hell up.

My life has been fucked up this way ever since that night with Sarabelle. I woke up the next morning stark naked, sprawled out on my back, with a splitting headache, a killer case of dry-mouth, and a lipstick heart drawn around my left nipple. When I sat up, the room tilting around me, I spotted a yellow note stuck to the nightstand by the king-sized bed. Large, loopy hand-writing I recognized from the note that came with my bourbon night before.

"Last night, the Hunter was hunted. Do you remember how hard I made you cum? xo, P"

I didn't remember, but I'd been roofied before, and I knew what the hangover felt like. Not sure what I'd done with Priscilla Heat and hoping to hell and back that the answer was *nothing*, I slung my clothes on and left without giving Sarabelle a second thought.

I got the call from Marchant on my phone about an hour later. "Did you take Sarabelle with you?"

Now, sitting outside on this cold Nevada night, I take a sip of my brandy, remembering how suffocated I'd felt sitting beside Marchant in the private waiting room inside the LVPD. And how ill I'd felt when I learned that another escort had gone missing a few weeks before. Ginnifer Lucky, a 22-year-old from Arkansas. Vanished just after her last shift at another brothel. I had an alibi for that night in August, but Marchant didn't. It had been his night off, and he'd spent it at his private home in Summerlin.

Neither of us answered any of their questions. The LVPD didn't need to know anything except that Sarabelle fell asleep in my room and I awoke the next morning to find her gone. I was back at the Wynn two hours later, wearing the floor thin as I paced my suite with Marchant, trying to find some clue as to where Sarabelle had gone.

Donnie, the escort who'd brought me the drugged drinks, confirmed they came from Priscilla herself. According to the sticky note I'd found in my room the day after, I fucked her that night, but I didn't remember doing so for obvious reasons. I could have performed in my juiced-up state, but it seemed unlikely. Had she really come into my room after filming all night with Marchant for a sunrise fuck with a man she roofied? What would be the point of that, anyway?

For that matter, why roofie me? My only theory was that she'd been angry at how I'd rejected her. But it was still really fucking weird considering Sarabelle disappeared that night.

The person who'd tried to send Marchant an S.O.S. about the camera malfunction was an escort named Geneese Loveless. Richard, March's head of security, had been out with the flu, and with Rach away at her sister's funeral and March chasing his dick, Loveless had volunteered. I know Loveless well—I used to be one of her regulars—and I can vouch for her trustworthiness. She wouldn't hurt Sarabelle, and she wouldn't have let anyone else, either.

It's always possible that Sarabelle got up and walked away on her own, but she never returned to her room, and she left her purse in mine. She didn't have her phone or her car keys.

Clearly, someone took her.

It took me two weeks after Sarabelle's disappearance to track down Priscilla. When she finally surfaced, the shit really hit the fan.

I check my watch and stroll into my bedroom, remembering the night Priscilla surprised me here. I had stepped out of the bathroom, near naked from my shower and planning to hit the hay. I sensed company before I saw her, and I stepped toward the cabinet beside my bed, where I keep a loaded .45. I don't think she knew that, but she must have guessed based on the way I moved.

"Calm down. It's just me, Hunter."

I turned to find her in a form-fitting trench coat and high-heels. "What the hell are you doing in my room?"

I can still see the determination on her Botox'd face as she smiled. "How many people know about your mother?"

My gut clenched, but I held my poker face. "Rita?"

"Your biological mother: Roxanne. The escort who worked for Lotti Bleaufont at the Hartland Casino in the early '80s. She died in child birth. Some big-headed boy." Priscilla grinned wickedly and held out a folder. I snatched it from her hand and flipped it open. Mine. From my safe. My birth certificate, which lists the name of my biological mother, and the certificate of adoption, from when my father's high school sweetheart and second wife, Rita, adopted me. Both certificates had been kept under lock and key my whole life; no one could know my up-standing paps had once been head over heels for a Vegas escort.

"This would be such a lovely story for Page Six, don't you think? Your father would be known for something besides piss-ing off Syria."

"What do you want, Priscilla?"

She'd smiled. "I just want to get into your bed. I think you'd enjoy it." She shrugged. "If you disagree, I think you will agree that your story is just *too* salacious, given what's happened lately. Mother was a prostitute. A prostitute disappears after you fuck her. Sounds kind of creepy-kinky, doesn't it?"

"Sounds like you know a lot of things that aren't your fuck-ing business."

Her eyes widened, and she smiled widely. "Of course it sounds that way to you, silly man…"

I INHALE DEEPLY, returning to the here and now. I hear the sound of fabric swishing on the other side of my bedroom door, and seconds later, Priscilla strolls in.

"Hunter."

I hate the way she says my name. Like she's talking to a puppy. Like she owns me, and for a secret I don't give a shit about, not directly. It's other things I need kept quiet—things more likely to come to light if a bunch of reporters start snooping around my family's past—but I know Priscilla doesn't know those things. Almost no one does.

So am I fucking her to decrease the already very low odds

that my dirty secret will come to light via increased West family scrutiny, or because it's prudent, because she might be tied to Sarabelle's disappearance?

This is a question I ask myself daily, but in the absence of an answer, I'm just fucking her.

Maybe she's the one who kidnapped Sarabelle—out of jealousy that I chose Sarabelle over her that night they were filming. Until I know for sure she's not, I'm going to keep this hellish charade rolling.

Priscilla reaches behind her back and the long, suede robe she's wearing tonight falls dramatically to the floor, revealing ...only skin. She's on me, has me stripped and on my mattress in a matter of minutes. Her hand slides around my cock, and I can't help but respond. I grit my molars as I harden and throb, forced along by nimble fingers and a warm, damp palm.

"Cum for me, Hunter. Cum for Mommy."

I slit my eyes open, and the glare of the bathroom light on her face causes them to shut again. I'm having trouble finishing. I squeeze my eyes shut more tightly and think of another face. I'm done in no time.

"What a good man. If you want to keep your mommy happy, we'll do chains tonight. It's your night to wear them. I get to hit."

I shut my eyes again. Truth be told, I like that best.

"I brought your surprise."

It's E, and I roll my eyes at the little pill. "I've never been a fan."

"I think you'll like it this time."

I pretend to take it, we fuck, and when Priscilla leaves, I follow her, thirteen miles to a small brick home with a familiar address. It's the home of Michael Lockwood, the film assistant who recently quit working for Priscilla. The one who used to work security for Governor Carlson. Drake Carlson—the political heavyweight Priscilla used to fuck.

I park down the street and dial our guy, Dave. “I’ve got a change of plans. You remember Lockwood? Lives on Anderson? I want him followed, night and day. Priscilla Heat, too.”

CHAPTER FOUR

Elizabeth

NAPA, CALIFORNIA

"I ALREADY TOLD you, I'm his sister." I look the evil nurse right in the eye and lock my jaw, like I mean business, because I do.

"Mr. Carlson doesn't have a sister," she says after glancing at her clipboard.

I reach into my worn Coach bag and grab a fifty, shamelessly sliding it across the high-gloss counter. If I had more, I'd offer it all. But the only rehab I could get Mom into this time is seriously pricey, eating up our meager allowance from the DeVille Trust, and my fellowship money only goes so far. If Suri didn't let me live at Crestwood Place with her for free, I'd never make ends meet.

The nurse raises her right eyebrow and looks from my money to me. I cross my arms in front of my chest. "How many visitors?" I ask.

"Excuse me?"

I meet her pale brown eyes and hold her gaze. "How many visitors has he had since I came Monday?"

Her lipsticked mouth twists, and her eyes flicker down the

hardwood hall, toward Cross's spacious, private room. "Thirty minutes," she says, shoving the fifty back at me. "That's all you're getting. And I know you're not his sister."

I slide the fifty into the pocket of my pea coat, where my iPod Mini is hiding, and hold my contraband-filled purse close to my side. I walk quickly to Cross's room, the way I always do, because I truly am eager to see him, coma or not.

For the first four weeks, it was medically induced, but when he began healing from his neck and hip surgeries, they decreased the sedatives so he could wake up. But he hasn't. I think I might know why, and I can't stand how much that knowledge hurts. But Cross's secrets are safe with me.

I push through the door, the lemony scent of Lysol fills my nose, and I feel angry that I'm the only person who visits him. Suri came the first two weeks, but she had to stop. All she can do when she sits in Cross's room is sob, and the nurses think he can hear us. Cross's parents—I could skin them both alive. They got him his swanky room at Napa Valley Involved Rehab, but neither Cross's mom nor his dad has visited since the first twenty-four hours after the accident.

It makes me queasy remembering that first day. How I couldn't sleep at all and how I itched to be here by him. I even bought a fake ID with the surname 'Carlson' so I could slip into the ICU with him.

The next few weeks weren't much better. He looked a lot different, then, all bruised and swollen. One of the saddest things about right now is that he looks like Cross again.

Today the top half of his bed is raised. His head is propped between two pillows. As always, he looks peaceful. Beautiful. His almost-black hair is short—they shaved it for his surgery—and his long, dark lashes make his face seem pale as porcelain. The awful tube that once went down his throat has been removed, because he's breathing on his own. A tube that feeds extra oxygen into his nose is taped to his cheeks, and I know that under his gown, snaking into his abdomen, is a feeding tube. Sometimes I peek because I want to understand what's going on with him. I wish I was his next of kin, so I could truly get all the information, but there's a nurse who likes me—Nanette—and she's told me they think his brain is fine. He sometimes squeezes my hand, and once when I kissed his forehead, he moaned. He just won't wake up. Not yet.

As soon as I make it across the fluffy, olive-colored rug and over to his bed, I grab his wrists and squeeze his hands. They smell like Betadine and are striped with tape that holds IV lines in place.

I lay one of his hands back on his blankets, but keep the other one sealed in mine. I force myself to look at his still face and smile as if he's really here.

"Hi, C. How's it going?"

I imagine him answering, because otherwise having a conversation with myself is just too weird. I kiss him on the cheek and sit in the biege wing-backed chair I've come to think of as mine.

"When I called the other day, Nanette told me you opened your eyes for a few minutes. I can't believe I missed that! I had a test that day. You'll be glad to know I passed." The machines around him hum their response, and for a second, I get tripped up. It's been two months now, but sometimes it's still too strange to see Cross like this. "So...what else is there? Suri and Adam might be having problems, but she keeps it quiet. I think she likes to pretend they're okay. Probably because she wants them to be. You know she loves her decorating stuff in San Fran and I think Adam is pushing her to move to New York with him again. It is the place for literary people I guess, but it's just not Suri. I think she's coming here tomorrow. If she gives you the scoop, I want to know."

I babble some about classes. In the time since Cross's accident, the new year has come and gone, and I've started the last semester of my second year of grad school. I search my mind for other updates, skipping over Mom (still in rehab), pop culture (Cross wouldn't care), and my non-existent dating life. I look down at my jeans. "I've been on the caveman diet, just for kicks. I've lost some weight. I feel good, so I might keep going."

I tell him more, sharing everything with him except for Hunter. Not that there's anything to share. I haven't seen him since that night at his vineyard, and my thoughts about him pull me in two directions. The main one, though, is interest. I still want him, more than ever, and more and more I'm coming to understand that there is something seriously wrong with me. I'm not sure I want a real relationship, and for me, Hunter is just a fantasy. I think about his soft kiss on my mouth and I want to tell Cross, *"He wouldn't treat me like he treats the other women. I'm different."*

Except, of course, that's stupid.

Putting Hunter out of my mind, I let Cross hear some Neil Young and Grateful Dead on the iPod and then I use a straw to dip a little Sunkist into his mouth. He loves Sunkist, and I firmly believe that he can taste it. I put some strawberry lip balm on his lips and tuck the covers around his broad shoulders. The sheets and blankets are all mine. I wanted him to have things that smelled familiar.

When I get up to leave, fifteen minutes after the arbitrary deadline assigned by Nurse Bitchface, I kiss him on the cheek. It's selfish to play on the feelings he might have had for me, but I need him to wake up.

"I've got to go and read some Victor Hugo, but I'll try to come back tomorrow. I want to hear about your next N-therapy session." N-therapy is where they use some big, swanky machine this clinic patented to stimulate Cross's brain. They talk to him while they wave a wand around his head, and supposedly that helps. It must, because people with brain injures come from all over the place to get treated here. In my mind, this is the very least his awful parents can do.

I stuff my hands into the pockets of my coat, feeling sad again. "I don't want to pressure you, Cross, but I really do need you back. I miss you." Tears fill my eyes, and on impulse, I lean down and kiss his cheek again.

When his eyes flutter, I think I'm seeing things. As soon as I realize those are really his blue eyes, I feel my throat constrict, like I'm going to get sick or cry.

"Cross?" My wide eyes cling to his.

I almost faint as Cross blinks. His eyes tear, and he makes a face like he's tasting something really sour. I feel something tickle my abs, and I realize he's grabbing my shirt. I back up, gaping at him. Laughing. "Oh my God, Cross. Hi."

His mouth lolls, and I can see he's trying to speak. I look down at myself and start to cry as I watch him white-knuckling my shirt. My heart is beating so fast as I clasp his hand.

"Are you okay?" I would do anything on Earth to take that lost look off of his face. "Do you want me to call someone?"

His eyes squeeze shut, and his chest makes a rumbling noise. "No."

"You don't?" I whisper through my tears.

He shakes his head just a little and mumbles something. His lids drift lower, and I grab his cheek, frantic he is falling back asleep. Instead, his eyes peek up at me again, and he mumbles, "...bitch of a headache. And..."

He swallows, and I squeeze his hand. "What was that?"

His eyes shut, and I bite my lip—but again, they flutter open. "I'm sorry," he rasps.

"For what?" My voice cracks. "You don't have anything to be sorry for."

His eyes roll back slightly, but his arm is tugging me closer. Still sweating and hardly able to breathe from shock, I lean down and wrap my arms around his shoulders.

"It's okay," I whisper against his cheek. I'm rubbing his

back, wanting to be sure that he knows someone loves him. Someone misses him. “I’m sorry, too. We’re friends again. You’re my best friend. Stay here with me, please.”

I hear him swallow. Then his eyes are fluttering again, his eyelashes like butterflies against my face. They’re closing as he says, “Stay…”

The soft word is the last thing that I hear before a nurse bursts into the room, and Cross is gone again.

THE REST OF the week passes slowly. I’m spending a lot of my time in mandatory group study sessions, which I definitely don’t need in order to understand and apply our class material. If I wanted to spend all my time with other people, I’d have joined a think tank, not signed on to become an Ethics professor.

I’m grouchy and tired when I come home from campus Friday afternoon, toting a little brass scale for a presentation my Plato & Aristotle group is making to a high school honors class next Wednesday.

The driveway at Crestwood Place is almost half a mile long, taking me through a beautiful apple orchard and then around several fields where horses graze. The horses belong to Suri’s parents, who are so seriously amazing, at times I pretend they are my own. Trent Dalton is the most modest big-wig computer software dude you could ever meet, and Gretchen is an elementary school counselor, working every day of the work week entirely pro bono. Suri has two younger sisters, Rachel and Edith, and I spot Edith’s white horse, Samson, as I pull into the circle drive directly in front of the house.

I toss my leather pack over my left arm and scoop the scale up in my right. The columned brick home has a wide, stone staircase, and it takes me forever to drag my tired self up it. I press my thumb against the keyless entry and the door pops open immediately—so quickly, in fact, I worry that it wasn't locked. Which is strange since Suri always uses the kitchen door.

I wiggle my cell phone out of the pocket of my baggy Lucky jeans and quickly pull up the emergency services phone number, conveniently stored as No. 2, in honor of the bullshit usually going down with Mom when I have to use it. I'm not sure what scares me most as I slowly step inside: the idea of Crestwood being burglarized like the Dalton's city home has been a time or two, or the images that resurrect themselves inside my mind: visions of my mom lying in a broken heap at the bottom of the stairs or passed out in a pile of Oxy.

Thinking of Oxy—or any drug, for that matter—makes me think of Cross, which makes my heart ache.

After the miracle of Wednesday, I skipped my classes Thursday to be at the hospital with him, convinced he would finally wake up. He squeezed my hand when I asked if he was glad to see me, but that was all. This morning when I called, Nanette sounded weird.

I'm wondering if I can slip in during her shift tonight when the scent of cinnamon rolls hits my nose.

I race through the foyer, past the spiral staircase, through the formal dining room, and into the massive kitchen like a kid hot off the school bus.

I come to a stop on the rug that spans most of the kitchen with a satisfied smile. Suri, in a pink and green paisley apron, has her back to me. Her curly brown hair is locked away in pigtails, and she looks like she just stepped out of *Martha Stewart Living*.

My smile disappears when she turns.

I hold up my hands, trying to ignore the sinking feeling in my stomach. "Remember what we said last time with Mom. Just spit it out, Sur. No sugar coating, 'cause that makes it worse."

I bite down on my lip when Suri's eyes tear and she steps over, closer to me, fiddling with the oven mitt and meeting my eyes with a deep frown. "You're going to be so upset, Lizzy. I am, too."

"Suri, spit it out!"

She wrings her hands and starts speaking on fast-forward. "My mother told me today. She heard from their new housekeeper—she cleans the Carlson's home, too." My stomach takes a nose-dive. "They've dropped him off their insurance. They're not going to pay for his healthcare anymore. They've moved him, Lizzy. This morning, to a state-run place down in L.A."

"What?"

Suri's eyes are wet. "Sunshine Acres Assisted Living. It's part of the Los Angeles County Public Hospital System."

My heart drops. I know that name. "Isn't that the one mom went to when she was sentenced for violating her parole? The one with no visiting hours and those shitty double rooms and that bad pee smell?"

Suri bites her lip. "I looked up the visiting hours. Noon to three p.m. Except on the weekend." I feel like I've been punched. Suri sniffs. "It's closed to visitors on the weekend."

CHAPTER FIVE

Elizabeth

SURI'S ARMS COME around my shoulders as I sob, and I smell the cinnamon rolls burning. "I can't believe they're doing this to him." She pats my back and I hide my face in her chest, feeling like a child—I never cry—but unwilling to pull away because I know how hideous I look when I do, and I don't want to subject Suri to that even though she's seen it before.

When I finally compose myself, there's a definite smoky smell in the kitchen. Suri squeezes my arm once more before dashing to the oven and yanking the cinnamon rolls out. They look like they've survived a volcanic eruption at close range.

"I'm sorry!" She looks anguished as she stares down at the cinnamon rolls.

"Suri." I can't help laughing, because this is classic Suri, dealing with a crisis via yummy foods, concert tickets, fruity daiquiris, and spa trips. It's actually pretty great, and I've enjoyed it since we were kids.

"I don't care about the cinnamon rolls," I say, unable to swallow a laugh at their horrible appearance. "It's the thought that counts." I smile, although my tears have started up again. "Do you want to go out or something? Maybe we can break Cross free from that shithole and move him here."

"That's the thing," she says, her voice going all high-pitched like it does when she's really distressed. "Adam is making me fly to New York tonight. Some special occasion he won't tell me anything about."

My brain shifts gears immediately. "Do you think that he's proposing?"

"I don't know, but he better not. He knows how I feel about New York, and he can be a literary agent on the West Coast much more easily than I can run Northern California Interiors from New York! His clients are all virtual. Mine have homes."

She bares her teeth and mimes a cat scratch, and I know things must have gotten really rough with Adam. I think it's safe to say he's not proposing.

"So the two of you are still at an impasse about where to live?"

She nods miserably but quickly finds a smile. "Maybe he's finally going to give in. I would so accept a Cali-shaped cupcake or...I dunno, Alcatraz earrings."

"Alcatraz earrings." I smile a little, and Suri giggles.

"I can hope," she says.

She pulls a napkin from the pocket of her apron and dabs at her eyes, and I put my arm around her. She wraps hers around me, and together we walk over to one of the windows. I'm not sure who steered us here: her or me. It's like a game of Ouija Board; maybe we both needed a look outside.

It's quiet inside the house, so the low whoosh of the heat through the vents down by our feet seems loud. When Suri speaks, her voice is high and shaky. "Remember when we were in seventh grade and Cross invited you to Fall Ball?"

I nod, smiling at the memory. He came to my house to ask, wearing a black leather jacket and jeans with holes. I frown next, because I remember how his parents never drove him anywhere. It was always Renault, the Carlsons' butler.

Suri inhales softly, and I watch her face as she sucks her lips in and makes a classic Suri Thinking face. Then she drops a bomb. "Ever since then I kind of had a secret crush on him."

I shriek. "Suri, you have got to be kidding me!"

She shakes her head, blushing three shades of pink. I slap her arm. "How could you harbor such a huge secret?"

"I don't know." She smiles, and shakes her head, and I know the answer before she says it.

"I guess I just met Adam and...that was that." Her eyes tear again. "I still love my Cross."

"Me, too."

"I want to do something for him," Suri says.

I do, too. In fact, I have to.

MAYBE IT'S BECAUSE of Mom that I freak out. I don't have that many childhood memories of her being whisked away to rehab, and I think that's mostly because she never went. Not until I was a teenager. But she was locked away from me in other ways. Always in and out of altered states, sleeping just like Cross is now.

I have too many memories of watching from the foot of her bed as one of many private nurses dabbed her forehead with a damp cloth or hooked up saline to the IV stand she stashed in her make-up room. Sometimes, when I was really little, I would cry and my dad would tell me she was sleeping.

"She loves you, honey, but she's sleeping today."

After Suri leaves, I feel gripped by that old sensation, panic at my lack of access to someone that I love. But I'm not a child anymore. I grab my car keys and race to my old, powder blue Camry. I'm out of breath by the time I crank it, but that doesn't stop me from speeding to Mom's house, a massive, white Southern antebellum-style home with a huge wrap-around porch, situated in the rolling hills fifteen miles northwest of downtown Napa.

The gate password is still the same. It's been a month since I've been here—several weeks after Cross's accident—but I don't see any spider webs stretched between oak trees as I fly down the arrow-straight driveway. I remind myself that a maid service is still coming; I hired them myself after Cross got hurt, mainly to check on the house so I don't have to drop by regularly.

The front is lit up to deter gate-hopping criminals, and as I see it for the first time in weeks, my heart squeezes, because no matter how much time passes and how much changes, this awful place will always feel like home. I throw the car in park and fly up the square staircase, unlocking the door and stepping inside quickly, so I can disable the alarm.

The code is my birthday backwards. I picture Cross pressing the keys, probably standing in this very spot wearing old jeans and one of his bomber jackets, and tears sting my eyes.

I'm here for one thing and one thing only, and that's Dad's new phone number. I don't keep it in my cell, because it's too enticing. I don't allow myself to call him on a whim. When Dad wants to talk to me, he calls, and as soon as we're finished talking, I delete the number from my call log. It's a Salt Lake City number, so it's not one I could accidentally memorize.

When I call from the rotary phone in our vast, dark kitchen, I'm grateful that it's new wife Linzie who answers and not one of her daughters, Fern, thirteen, or Hollow, nine. Her hello is flat and Midwestern; I can almost see her on the other end of the line, clutching a cordless phone and standing in a slightly dated kitchen. The picture of normal: that's Dad's new family.

"Um, hi Linzie, it's Elizabeth."

She pauses for a second, then responds in a crisp, telemarketer-sounding voice. "Elizabeth. Can I help you?" Whoa, her tone is brisk. I swallow back my irritation.

"Yeah. I want to talk to my dad." Biotch. I want to stick my tongue out and tell her he was my dad first, but instead I calmly say, "Is he around?"

"He is." I think she's gone to get him when I hear a breathing sound and Linzie says my name again. "Elizabeth?"

"I'm here."

"I know you are. Uh—" there's a fuzzy sound, like she's covering up the phone's mouthpiece. When she speaks again, her voice is tight. "Elizabeth, is this about your mother?"

Now it's my turn to be surprised. And peeved. "Why do you ask?"

Linzie sighs. "I know that she's in rehab again, Elizabeth."

"Yeah. That's not news." I squeeze my eyes shut, wanting to bang my head against the kitchen wall. What the hell does Linzie care what my mom's up to?

"I know it's how things are there, but it's not normal here for us." She pauses, like she's rallying herself, and I try to put my armor on, because I can tell this is going to get me right between the ribs. "Your father is damaged from what he went through with that woman. You know how she treated him. But when things happen with her, he still feels responsible."

For some reason, this makes me want to punch Linzie in the nose. "Um, I'm not trying to be rude, but of course he does. He was married to her for more than twenty years." I inhale deeply, fighting to control my off-the-handle temper. "Anyway, I'm not calling about my mom, so can I talk to my dad now please?"

I hear silence, and for a long moment, I think she's hung up. Then my dad is on the phone.

"Elizabeth."

"Hi Dad." In the background, I can hear a girl's voice, and I know it's one of them. Fern or Hollow. 'One of my new girls'. I lean my head against the wall. "Look Dad, I just had a quick question for you."

"Okay. What's your question?"

I wrap the curly cord of the olive green phone around my finger, biting my lip, because I hate to ask this—but I have no choice. "I was wondering if I could get a loan. From the DeVille Trust, or from you."

My words are followed by a long pause, during which I honestly have no idea what he will say. Then I hear a sort-of snort.

"Elizabeth, are you serious? We've talked about this. You can't spend money like your mother used to. I know it's hard for you, growing up the way you did, but this is life now and you're twenty-three—"

"Dad, I'm not. I'm not spending any money." I clench my jaw, breathing deeply as my pulse races. "I never buy anything. It's not for me."

Pause. "So you are calling for your mother?"

"No." I grit my teeth as rage builds in me, pooling underneath my breastbone and radiating out over my shoulders like venom from a snake bite. I huff my breath out, so angry now I'm seeing stars. "Dad, did you tell Linzie to screen my phone calls?"

"Screen your calls? Of course not, Elizabeth. Linzie would never do something like that. She cares a lot about our relationship."

I can feel my lower lip tremble. "Why don't I believe you?"

He sighs, and it's the sigh he used to save for Mom. I get the eerie feeling Linzie is standing right beside him, encouraging him, with her deep brown eyes, to stick it to me.

"Elizabeth. You have issues with trust."

"What?"

"There's money available for counseling—"

His comment takes me off guard and makes me furious. "Oh yeah?" I demand, cutting him off. "You think so? Maybe Linzie could see me. Do herbalists take insurance? I know they're great advice givers, so maybe I could fly out—"

I'm still going—verbal vomit, that's what Cross would call it—when the dial tone dings.

My mouth stays open and my eyes fill up with tears. "I need

counseling?" I slam the phone down with all my might, feeling the impact in my fingertips as I whirl around to face the empty kitchen.

At least, it's supposed to be empty. I'm supposed to curl into a ball and sob, because when I get this mad, it's the only thing I can do to discharge my anger. Instead, I find myself staring at Hunter West.

CHAPTER SIX

Hunter

HER FACE IS blotchy, like she's been stung by a bunch of bees. I can tell she's close to crying because her sea blue eyes are glowing, and she's got them wide open, the way girls do when they don't want tears to spill and smear up their mascara.

Her wavy, red-brown hair is messy, hanging just above her shoulders, and I want to run my fingers through it.

Shit.

I shouldn't even be here.

I saw the gate open and I threw on my superhero cape. Then I saw the unfamiliar car and found the door unlocked. I know nobody's living here. I keep an eye on the place, because I want to buy it soon; its acreage backs up against my bird-hunting lodge, which is where I was heading when I made this detour.

Batman or not, I've screwed up. I shouldn't be in Libby DeVille's childhood home, standing in this massive, outdated kitchen with her, just like I shouldn't have crept close enough to hear her conversation with her father.

I tell myself to turn and go—after all, Priscilla's waiting for me—but my feet aren't listening. I take a small step closer, my eyes never leaving hers, even as she looks me over, Lakers cap to boots.

"Asshole father?" In the tomb-like silence of the house, I'm surprised at how deep my voice is.

I can see her shoulders rise and fall; she's trying to control herself. Judging by the bit I heard, it makes sense that she would be worked up. If his reputation is anything to go on, Benjamin DeVille didn't do much for his wife or daughter when he was with them, and does even less now that he's left town.

Libby quickly smooths the pained look from her face and crosses her arms. "How much did you hear?" she asks me with a wary wince.

"Enough to know you're probably not the one in need of therapy."

She squeezes her eyes shut, running a hand through that silky hair. "Wow, well that's embarrassing."

If only she could be a fly on the wall at the family home in NOLA back when I lived there with Dad, Rita, and my half-sister, Amber. This wouldn't even register on our drama-meter. I want to tell her that, but I've got no clue how. Besides, the best way to keep a secret—that Rita is not my real mother, for instance—is to avoid mentioning anything to anyone that even comes close to the truth.

Libby chews her succulent lower lip, and it's my turn to stare her down. I've only seen her once, from a distance, since the night of the party, and I'm surprised by how much weight she's lost. I wonder if it's intentional, or if she's stressed, and I'm surprised by how much this question concerns me.

She plays with the ends of her hair, and I let my gaze linger, from her low-cut royal blue sweater down her loose jeans to her suede shoes—some kind of moccasins. She looks cute. Casual. I feel a pleasant tingle just from being near her.

Finally her eyes flick up to mine, like she's waiting for me to say something. So I do. "What do you need money for?"

Her mouth draws up like she's sucking on a lemon. I like this face on her. The you-should-be-ashamed-of-yourself face; it's kind of sexy mistress. To top it off, she arches her eyebrows primly. "That's not really your business, Hunter West."

Maybe not, but I have a pretty fair idea. "Is it the governor's son?"

Her eyes flash, dark blue now. "The son the governor cut off and sent to a shitty state hospital because he's a dickhead who deserves to be ridden out of California on a rail?" Her cheeks flush. "You probably shouldn't ask me about that right now." I watch her delicate eyebrows meet as her sea blue eyes narrow to slits. "What are you even doing here?"

Her eyes wander the expanse of my chest and I know she's taking in the size of me. I saw the Mace on her key chain in the parlor, and I wonder if she's thinking about running in there for it.

I nod toward the back of the house, relaxing my shoulders so maybe I look a little friendlier. "I saw the gate open and wanted to check in on things. I own the property behind you."

Her furrowed brows crease more deeply. "The old retreat?"

"I bought it off the Anglican church a few years back. Turned it into a quail hunt." She still looks wary, so I give her a little more. "Just being neighborly."

Her face is blank, and I can't tell what she's thinking. I wonder the odds of her having heard about my connection to Sarabelle's disappearance, and decide they're nil.

Next I think about that night on my bed: her head pressed into my pillow, her hair spread out around her face. The memory of it makes me hard, but then I remember how it ended, with Libby seeing me with Priscilla. Impotent anger washes over me, but I'm still hard as a damn diamond. I shift my weight; that makes it worse.

Libby's eyes are on mine, thankfully. "Well I'm okay," she tells me, tucking some hair behind her ear. A tiny pearl gleams from her earlobe, and I have the odd thought that I could buy her something so much bigger.

"I appreciate you stopping in to check on things, and I'm

sorry you got an earful of my business." She waves at the kitchen doorway. "You're free to go."

I don't want to go.

"Really, I'm good here." She's got her hands on her hips, and I notice she's closer to the parlor door than she was before I looked away. For a fraction of a second, I allow myself to play out a fantasy. Libby runs and I bolt after her, capturing her upper arms and whirling her to face me. I plant my mouth over hers and press her gorgeous body against mine.

I can't contain a hungry smile, and Libby side-steps, now even closer to the parlor.

I arch a brow. "I make you nervous?"

She smiles smugly, and the nervousness I thought I saw looks more like impatience. "I have my black belt in Judo. Do you?"

A grin blossoms on my face, but my lips aren't sure what to do with it. It falls right off, and I press my mouth into a more familiar solemn line. I adjust the bill of my cap, feeling the weight of the last few months. "You'd be right to be nervous. That's a good thing. You never know whose room you could be wandering into."

"So that *was* your room that night."

More statement than question, but I say, "Who's asking?"

She looks at me strangely, and I realize I've become too paranoid.

"Sorry." I rub my brow, feeling frustrated and tired. "It's been a long...long week."

I'm shuffling my feet, headed for the parlor, when her mouth does something soft. I want to kiss it. My cock twitches as she nods, like she's looking in a crystal ball and seeing every sleepless night and fucked up, dead end day that's led me here, to her kitchen. I'm trying to play superhero and it's just so stupid. I feel revulsion rise in my chest. Then she says, "I believe it." Her words are soft silk, and when they leave her ruby-colored lips, her radiant eyes are on me, gentle and perceptive.

My throat tightens. I remember her that night at the party—the warmth of her, the weight of her. I need to leave, but I'm rooted to the kitchen floor.

Libby's eyes flicker to my clenched fists, and I imagine what I must look like: two-hundred-twenty pounds of head-fucked male, product of an escort and a professional asshole. But instead of bolting for the Mace, she tilts her head, regarding me like she would a puzzle. "Do you stay at the vineyard often?" she asks quietly.

"Sometimes." I'm not sure why she cares.

The corner of her mouth lifts, a lovely little half-smile that makes me wonder if she has any idea what effect she is having on me. "I'm sure you don't remember this, but you helped me fix my car once, years ago."

I nod, but I don't return her smile. Even then, when she was just a kid, she captured my attention.

She turns and walks into the parlor, and I follow her into the spacious room, decorated in dark browns and reds. She looks over her shoulder as she grabs her keys from a Victorian secretary.

I can tell she's thinking about something. She hesitates before casting a troubled look into my eyes. "Did you do that to your room?"

"Do what?" I frown, annoyed at how I can't seem to make myself leave.

"At the party," she says. "Your room was a wreck."

I flinch at the memory, debating only briefly whether to be honest. "I was very angry that night." My voice is ultra-deep; husky. As I drink in Libby, I go back there.

I remember the sensation of choking—a sensation Priscilla sometimes likes to experience with a collar, or—so much worse—my hands around her neck.

I'm holding Libby's stare, hoping she'll see these things inside me and tell me to get going. I notice I'm holding my breath, waiting for her wary dismissal. Instead, her mouth softens again. I wait for her expression to morph into pity or sadness, but she looks serene. "I think there are two sides to you," she says quietly.

She must think one of my sides is a psychopath. At least she won't be disappointed if I ever become an official suspect in the escort disappearances.

Thinking of that, while looking at her delicate face, makes my heart pound uncomfortably, and I realize how afraid I am that it might come to that. I'm completely innocent, I remind myself, but I know better. There's a common perception, partially true, that rich people are above the law. It's true for a lot of us, but I have a feeling my notoriety could work against me. I'm the kind of guy prosecutors like to stick a case to.

Libby can read my mind. I think she can. Her eyes are latched to mine, and I see my heaviness reflected on her face. She slides her hands into her pockets, stepping closer as she speaks. "What I mean is, most people only see what you want them to see. Like the night my mom's Porsche broke down."

I remember that night. It was back when I was fucking an escort from Los Angeles. The sex was explosive, but I always felt like shit after, and I'd been relieved when my security manager interrupted over the intercom. A few minutes later, after pulling on some pants, I'd gotten my first glimpse of Elizabeth DeVille. She'd had her hair in a pony-tail that stuck up off the side of her head, and she'd been wearing short red shorts and a light blue tank top with a whale on it.

"You like whales?" I'd asked her when I finished with the car.

Her face had gone all soft and pretty, making me feel more like one-hundred-and-three than the twenty-three I was, and she'd shrugged. "Yeah, but not a lot more than any other animal. I just like saving things."

The car was a piece of junk that likely wasn't going to make it a hundred more miles, so I convinced her to spend the night in my guest house. After Marietta went to sleep I found myself sitting out by the swimming pool, hoping Elizabeth might wake up and come outside. It was ridiculous. Embarrassing, even.

She's inches from me now, and reaching toward my face.

For a second, I feel a thrill of fear I haven't felt since I was a boy. It settles deep inside my stomach. Then her hand touches my shoulder, and I start to sweat from every pore.

Her free hand grabs one of mine, and she closes the distance between our bodies with a gentle tug. I lean closer to her, moving in slow motion. I'm getting seriously dizzy, as her thumb touches me between my brows.

"I see a frown mark, though," she whispers, "right here." I blink, surprised to find the soft sensation makes my eyelids heavy.

"I thought you were upset that night," she murmurs as she strokes. "After..." She colors, and I blink my heavy lids.

"I could see you at the foot of the bed, and I was kind of worried for you. I don't know why, but something about you..." That frown is back, visible through my lashes, and someone is scooping out my insides. I feel gutless and emptied, like I might dissolve into a puddle at this woman's feet.

"Something about you just seems sad. I don't know what about poker-playing would make a man sad, but I'm watching these," she says, gently thumbing my frown lines one more time. "Try not to let them get any deeper."

I nod at her, feeling like I'm in a dream. As I'm walking out the door, I turn again, fighting a vision I have of kissing her mouth.

I take her porch stairs two at a time, and my knees ache from my misadventures with Priscilla. I swing into my F-250 and before I can get a handle on myself, my phone buzzes. Priscilla. Seeing her name on the screen is like jumping into icy water.

I hit the button to answer, but I can't bring myself to say 'hello'.

I can hear the static on the other end, static and the clinking sound of hooker heels. "Hunter?" she says; it sounds like the lash of a whip. "Where are you? I'm waiting."

"Keep waiting," I spit out.

"Believe me, I will. But you'll pay for this."

I grip the steering wheel and wonder if Sarabelle is dead already. I'm playing this fucked up game in part for her. And in part because I can't bear what would happen if people found out that Rita wasn't my real mother. If people found out what I did to her.

I can still hear her low voice, a whisper in my memory where it should be a scream, and for the briefest moment I can feel the sticky sweat I used to get when she was mad. I can hear her say, "You're trash, just like your mother."

And I can see her crumpled in my arms, as her pretty face turns white.

I lower the phone and I am punching the 'end call' button when I hear Priscilla on the other end of the line. Her voice is low and sultry, but it's wicked all the same, giving me flashbacks of another evil bitch.

"I know where you are," she says. "And I don't like it."

CHAPTER SEVEN

Elizabeth

I LEAVE MY mom's house feeling like a changed woman. It's dangerous for me, because it involves Hunter. I can't imagine what gave me the courage to be as forward with him as I was. It's true I'm not exactly shy, but this is Hunter, golden god, my oldest, only crush.

In one fleeting interaction he went from Hunter West Fantasy to Hunter West Real Person, and the bad thing is, I like him even more now. He was sympathetic when he asked about my dad. He cared that I was upset; at least that's the feeling I had in my gut. I could be wrong.

But not about the end, when we were in the parlor and he told me he'd been angry that night at the vineyard. I know I'm not wrong about that, and while I admit maybe I'm being self-indulgent, I feel like I can say almost for sure that what I saw between Priscilla and him wasn't really…accurate somehow. Hunter seemed disgusted with himself when he looked at me that night. And tonight... He seemed kind. Not at all the kind of guy who gets off strangling porn stars.

I can hear Cross's voice in my head, telling me I don't know anything about Hunter, and I admit maybe I'm star struck. But I just don't think so.

If he's only a playboy, would he have been as nice as he

was to me tonight?

Yes, idiot. That's what puts the 'play' in playboy.

I sigh, because I can't heed my own warning, and all I can think about as I park in front of Crestwood Place is when I'll see Hunter again.

SATURDAY MORNING, I wake up early and make the six-plus-hour drive to Los Angeles. I could have asked Arnold to take me, but seeing Cross for the first time at this new place is something I want to do alone. I've still got Hunter on the brain, so as I fly toward the city, my mind is a tangle of feelings. For Cross, I feel anxious. I'm afraid I won't be able to help him out of this. I'm longing for his friendship. I'm hoping that maybe when I get there—*if* I can get them to let me in today—he'll be magically awake again.

I'm curious about Hunter. Wildly curious. I'm practically craving him, although all fond feelings vanish as I drive through a dreary patch of East L.A. I pass a familiar-looking exit, then the one that's mine, and I know—I know for sure—that this is going to be that same hell-hole where Mom served a court-mandated week two years ago.

I pull onto a run-down service road, then hang a right onto a dead-end street, and there it is: Sunshine Acres—the building right next door to Sunshine Rehab, where mom was sent by court order. Both buildings are tall and Soviet-esque—completely void of frill. The parking deck is dark and dank, even by parking deck standards. I tell myself my imagination is exaggerating, but I swear there's a thick layer of grime on everything.

The lobby, accessible from the third floor of the deck, is a vast space under a low-lying ceiling, filled with plastic chairs and smelling of stale carpet. There's a cut-out in the wall where two women and a man sit behind a counter.

I stop in front of a stick-thin woman with short black hair and ask for the charge nurse. I'm not nervous, because I know that if she says "No," I'll come back in a few hours, and I'll find a way to sneak inside. I'll wait for Cross's nurse to take a bathroom break. I'll decide for myself how well he's doing, and damn their lousy visiting hours.

The person I think is in charge has a name tag that says OLIVE. She's wearing bright green, sweat-stained scrubs that hug her spare tire and compliment her creamy chocolate skin. She looks me over, from my Ugg Moccasins to my jeans and discount designer sweater and she folds her arms across her chest. "It's Saturday," she says. "What do you want with me?"

I can tell she's a straight-shooter, so I match my tone to hers and cut right to the chase. "My friend Cross Carlson just got here, and I'd really like to see him. I know it's a Saturday, but I'm desperate. So I'm asking for a favor—just this once."

She blinks at me. It's an exaggerated blink, almost comical, and after that she bugs her eyes out, like she's just heard something sensational. "Do you know who's running this place today?" she asks me in a deadpan tone.

I shake my head, and she says, "Frankie, and Frankie's not here right now. I can let you in this once, but you've got fifteen minutes before Frankie gets back from lunch. If Frankie catches you, you're shrimp."

I frown as she turns her back to me, then hustle to follow her down the wide, gray-carpeted hall. "Um, just out of curiosity, what's shrimp mean?"

She shoots me a menacing look over her shoulder. "It means you'll get your head bit off."

I follow her around two corners, and at this point, my heart is pounding. The hall has started smelling more like a nursing home—that smell of soiled linens, cleaning chemicals, and sweat. We pass a row of tiny metal doors, Chiclets punched into the drab, white wall, and I want to turn and run away. Cross can't be here. It was bad enough when Mom was in the psych ward next door, but Mom had earned that.

Olive stops before a small metal door and says, "Better hurry."

I nod and thank her. I push through the door without taking time to calm myself, and the sight of a stained blue curtain dividing the room shocks me. There's barely enough space for a hospital bed between the curtain and the wall, and as my eyes move over the bed's metal rails, I know it can't be Cross because this patient is lying flat on his back with his—or her—head wrapped in gauze, and he or she is intubated. The breathing machine looming beside the bed makes a noise that brings back memories of a childhood full of ICUs.

I'm headed for the curtain, hoping against hope that Cross will be sitting up in his bed, when the curtain parts and a freckle-faced nurse appears. She's frowning like she's confused, and her shirt is tugged halfway over her head, exposing a lacy, black bra.

My heart leaps in elation. *Cross...you wicked thing.*

Then I smell the vomit. The nurse is holding a garbage bag, I realize. I quickly notice that the pale pink scrubs shirt she's pulling off is flecked with orange bits. Did Cross puke on her?

I frown as she pushes down the stained shirt.

"What happened?"

"Mr. Russell, next door." She frowns, and I realize she's holding a clean shirt in her left hand. "What are you doing in here? You subbing for Nancy?"

I nod behind her. "I'm here to see my friend, Cross Carlson."

Her face scrunches, unreadable. "Oh."

I try to see past her, but she's blocking my view.

"Hun, this is the professor." She leans her head back. "Dr. Dottswold."

I look from left to right. "So this isn't Cross's room?"

"He's right behind you."

My chest winds tight as I whirl to face the bed. I can't wait to tell Miss Black Bra she's wrong.

The second I really look, I see Cross's face. A cry rises in my throat, and there it dies. It's like a giant is stepping on my sternum as I whirl on Black Bra, finding the curtain in place. I can hear a rustling sound as she changes behind it. I don't care. I snatch it open.

I hear her swift intake of breath, and then she's there in front of me, reddish hair rumpled, eyes wide and alarmed.

"What the hell happened to him? Why is he intubated? Who's in charge here?"

I can tell by the way her eyes widen that she's clueless, even before she presses her mouth into a line and says, "I don't know, ma'am. You know, it's a Saturday and we don't—"

"No." I grit my teeth. "I don't care what day of the week it is, I want to know what happened to him." My voice is raised, almost to a yell. "If you can't tell me what happened find me someone who can."

She's looking at me like I belong in the psych building next door, but I don't care. "What has he been like today? Has he moved or anything?" I glare at the gauze around his head. "Did someone drop him when they moved him here?"

The nurse scowls at me. "I can't share details with you. You're not family. You're not supposed to be—"

I whip out my phony license, the one that says Elizabeth Carlson, and shove it in her face. Her eyes harden, and she practically spits, "He had a bleed."

"He had a *what*?"

She nods, folding her arms. "He had a brain bleed during the transport over. He had a stroke." A small sigh escapes her lips, and she gives me a tired look. "I don't know much about it 'cause I wasn't here. They said he might have been experiencing some pain."

"That caused a stroke? How the hell does that happen?

Like, his blood pressure went up really high or something?"

The nurse is moving closer to the door and I am moving with her, fully prepared to block her way if she tries to leave without giving me the long explanation.

"I don't know ma'am." She shrugs. "I'm not the one in charge. The doctors are."

Her hand is on the door, and I step in front of it. "What's he been doing today? Are you weaning him off the ventilator?"

"No. He needs it."

"Has he moved or anything? Squeezed anyone's hand? Like, a visitor's?"

She blinks. "I don't know. We can't sit in here with them all day."

I know I promised to be in and out, but now that I've seen Cross, I just can't do that. "What nurse is watching him this shift?"

She's defensive now. "I am."

Obviously. I swallow, putting my hand on Cross's bed railing. Suddenly I'm feeling faint. I glance at Cross. He looks so pale and...dead. He looks dead. Helplessness floods me, and I want to scream, but I can barely whisper. "So he's just...pretty much lying here?"

It's a stupid thing to say, but I'm holding back tears.

"That's what they do mostly."

My blood boils. Did this woman go to nursing school? He's not some vegetable! He had a stroke, apparently, but he's going to be okay. She doesn't know jack. No one here does.

"He's been getting N-therapy. He opened his eyes and talked to me the other day." Tears fill my eyes, and I do my best to blink them back as her frown deepens. "He's not in a persistent vegetative state. He's responded to stimuli, just this week. He's doing some kind of therapy here, like N-therapy, right? You have something similar?"

I look at the dark-haired guy in the bed, still wide-shouldered, still handsome, even with his chapped lips and the tube stretching his mouth.

The nurse dips her head again, and when she raises it, I can see pity in her eyes. "I'm sorry," she says. "I shouldn't have said it like that. I don't know about him yet." She shifts the bag, holding her soiled shirt, from one hand to the other, looking contrite. "Why don't you stay here a minute. Talk to him. You can come back Monday, when hours are open again."

"I can't come Sunday?"

She shakes her head. "Tomorrow we're closed for therapy."

"What do you mean?"

"We have a physical therapist come twice a month."

"Only twice a month?"

The nurse shrugs. "I have to go but I'll be watching on a monitor." She points to something over my head, and I struggle with the urge to grab her arm and hold her until she tells me something I want to hear.

Somehow, I force myself to turn around and face Cross's bed. I step over to it, starting to quietly cry as I scan the machines, analyzing the numbers I came to know so well during the first few weeks after the accident.

I check his blood pressure—136/95—and then his pulse—102. The ventilator is taking 24 breaths per minute for him, which means he's hardly breathing on his own at all. I wonder why that is. I tell myself they gave him sedatives, so his body can rest and recover.

I stretch out my arm to touch his face, vowing to do something to make this situation better. As I do, the door behind me opens and I turn.

Standing in the doorway is a middle-aged Hispanic woman with her hair pulled into a tight French braid. She's shorter than I am, but everything about her exudes power. "You must be Pushy." She sticks her hand out. "I'm Frankie. And I know this SOB doesn't have a sister."

I balk. “Did you just call him a son of a bitch?”

She shrugs. “Governor’s son, hurt himself riding a motorcycle drunk. I could call him worse things, but I’m sorry all the same. You need to get off my floor. Visiting is closed today.”

I shake my head. “Not until you tell me what happened.”

“I can’t do that. What I can do is promise that if you don’t leave now, I’ll be sure you see the inside of a jail cell.”

I put my hand over my chest, unable to believe that this is happening.

“I’ll leave,” I rasp, “but I have one last question.”

She presses her lips together, like a disapproving teacher.

“Do you have N-therapy?” I sound composed, and Frankie’s expression loosens a little as her mouth turns down.

“N-therapy?” She looks like she’s never heard of it. Of course she hasn’t.

“They call it N-therapy. I don’t remember the full name. It stimulates the brain and makes them want to wake up.”

“Neurostimulation therapy.” She shakes her head, still brisk but not quite as stern. “I know it helps, but we can’t afford to purchase those machines. This is a county treatment facility. Just the basics.”

I can feel her hand close around my elbow. “I’m sorry, but visiting is closed. You need to leave.”

I nod absently as I step into the hall, vowing Cross will leave soon, too.

CHAPTER EIGHT

Elizabeth

IT TAKES ME almost seven hours to drive home to Napa,_and the whole time, I feel like I'm in a trance. It's early evening on a chilly, gray day when I park my car in the cul-de-sac at the end of Brison Way and walk half a block to the massive gray stone home behind the pointy, black iron gates. Surprisingly, the gates are open, so I walk down the long, cement drive and up the pale staircase Cross jumped off so many times when we were kids.

I hold my fist over the door, wanting to knock with all my might, but decide to ring the bell instead. Seconds pass before one of the massive doors swings open and I find myself staring into the eyes of an unfamiliar, gray-haired housekeeper.

I stand up a little straighter and pretend I'm wearing a designer business suit. "I'm here to talk to Derinda Carlson."

The housekeeper frowns at me, then puckers her lips and shakes her head. "Mrs. Carlson is unavailable."

I press my lips tightly together. There's no way in hell I'm leaving here without speaking to Cross's mother. "Look, ma'am, I'm a family friend." I nod behind me. "I recognize her BMW and I know she's here this weekend. Tell her it's one of Cross's friends. I have something of his."

I don't, of course, but I'm hoping curiosity will draw Derinda to the door. I haven't seen much of her since I left for college, but I remember she used to be a vibrant, funny woman —if a little cowed by her powerful husband.

I spend the few minutes I'm kept waiting sending out pleas to the universe. *Please let her come to the door. Please help Cross.*

I'm almost surprised when the door opens again and she's standing there in front of me. When we were in high school, Derinda Carlson was thin, elegant, and well-dressed, with vibrant blue eyes and short, stylish blonde hair. I remember her sorting through papers as she drew up house plans, but she would always make sure the housekeepers kept Cross, Suri, and I well-fed, and the few times she greeted me upon arrival, she was always kind and smiling.

This woman is much different. Still dressed stylishly in an ice blue pant suit, Derinda has definitely aged. I can tell because her face looks ridiculously smooth, and the areas around her mouth and eyebrows don't move much as she looks me up and down. Her pale blonde hair, swept into a casual up-do, bobs a little as her eyes travel from my moccasins to my hair, which is probably a mess.

Her arms are hanging at her sides, but I notice her hands are splayed and stiff, even as she bends her mouth into a sour-lemon smile and nods slightly at me. "Elizabeth, how can I help you?"

Tears flood my eyes as I think about Cross, with a tube down his throat and all that gauze around his head. My voice cracks as I struggle not to sob. "Why is he in that awful place?"

She frowns, and lines appear—well-worn tracks she can't completely hide. "We can't insure him anymore. Drake is paid by taxpayers these days."

My face says I'm not buying it, and Derinda's frown deepens. "I really don't need to justify anything to you, but do you have any idea how much the facility he was in cost?"

"No."

"Two thousand dollars every night he's there. That's after

insurance pays a percentage."

I blink, stunned that these things matter. "He was waking up! He talked to me."

She's shaking her head briskly, like she can't stand to hear my words. "There's been no response for months."

"This was days ago! I told the nurse. It's probably on the cameras! They were doing that therapy on his brain and it was working. I could tell!"

Derinda shakes her head. "We love our son, Elizabeth. We just simply can't afford it."

I want to call her on her bullshit. Governor Carlson was a prominent litigator before he entered politics. And they certainly aren't acting like they love him. I want to tell her she's full of shit, that I know she never visits, but all that will get me is a door slammed in my face.

I change the subject. "What happened in the ambulance?"

She opens her mouth, pauses as she fixes me with an even stare. "They're not sure. He was on so many different medicines ..." The corner of her mouth tucks down, like we're talking about a broken vase.

"He had a stroke," I snap. "You don't know why?"

"There are no whys, Elizabeth. Don't you think I'd be crazy if I sat around asking why any of this happened. Maybe you can tell me. You were there that night."

I clench my jaw. I want so much—so much—to tell her how their estrangement impacted Cross. How after his father banished him, he'd lost weight. How he spent most of the time he wasn't working at my Mom's house all alone.

My eyes simmer with angry tears. "They said he had the stroke because he was in pain. That sounds like someone's fault."

Her mouth draws up like a rotten fruit. "They shouldn't be discussing this with you."

I ignore her. "He was waking up. Why did you move him?

He was doing well."

"He has no idea where he is, and he isn't doing anything, Elizabeth. I know it hurts, but it's time to be realistic. Cross is gone, and he's never coming back."

I flinch. "I'm telling you, he talked to me the other day. Just ask Nanette or anyone who's there. I don't get why you don't seem to know this!"

Derinda's face is hard when she says. "You love him, so you want him to get better. I love him, too, but palliative care is the best we can do for him now. We must also be prepared for his condition to…deteriorate."

I feel my heart go cold as stone. "They said that?"

"It's too soon to tell, but with what happened..."

"With what happened, you're just giving up? Sending him somewhere that's a day's drive? That place in L.A. is *not* the best. Not even close! He won't get well in that hellhole!"

Her eyes go cold, and I can tell I've crossed a line. "You have no idea what's best for him—"

"I think I'm the only one who cares what's best for him!" I whirl around and fly down the driveway before she has a chance to slam the door.

I DRIVE TO a park and spend the next half-hour crying again, reliving every detail of that night. It doesn't help. There's one detail I can't reason away, I can't forget, I can't ignore, and that's this: He was upset—because of me—when he left. It doesn't matter that he had upset me, too. I hurt Cross bad enough to make him climb onto his bike half-drunk, and even if it was his choice, even if he made the wrong one, I was the precipitating event. I was the catalyst. And I'm not sure I'll ever be able to get over it.

CHAPTER NINE

Hunter

PRISCILLA IS HAVING Libby followed. That means when *I* follow Libby, I have to be discreet. The last thing I need is Priscilla knowing that I know what she's doing. It would ruin everything. And I'm beginning to think there's really something here.

According to my guy, Priscilla has visited Michael Lockwood twice in the last week. The rumor was she'd fired him in a fit of rage—no one knew what over. So why visit? In the meantime, my bank girl found a Swiss account in Michael's name with more than $5 million. That's a lot of money for an unemployed video production tech. How does it connect to Sarabelle? I'm not sure, but I have a terrible suspicion.

In the meantime, I'm fucking Priscilla, and when I have a spare moment, watching Libby's new watchers. Of course, I'm also watching Libby. Like now. Bright and early on a Sunday morning, I've followed her to Napa Valley Involved Rehab, where Cross Carlson enjoyed seven weeks of the best care available before his family moved him to a county dead-end. I watch her walk in with a notebook, see her greeted at the door by a nurse in pink and purple scrubs. Half an hour later, I see her fly through the door and sink into the grass, sobbing into her hands. I have to cross my arms to keep from opening my car door and going to check on her.

Priscilla's spy doesn't follow Libby home, but I do. I tell myself it's out of guilt. If I'd never stopped at Libby's parents' home the other day, I wouldn't have put Libby on Priscilla's radar. Of course, if I'd never stopped at Libby's parents' home, I also wouldn't have known Priscilla was having *me* followed. How fucking sketchy is *that*? She's fucking me, sure, and maybe she has some twisted thing for me, because I rejected her, but having me followed? I smell something fishy, and it has Sarabelle's name written all over it.

I watch until Libby is in range of Crestwood's security cameras and the driveway guard. I shut my eyes and imagine that warm, sweet hand closing over my cock, and it's all I can do not to bust a load right there in my pants.

Instead I drive a little over half an hour to the vineyard and jerk off in my bed. When I'm finished, I call Marchant.

I can't tell him about Priscilla's threats, because even March doesn't know about Roxanne, but I can tell him I'm fucking her for information. So I do. I come clean, and then I tell him about how edgy she's seemed lately—I don't mention the whips.

When I finish, he drops a bomb: "She's also fucking Josh Smith. You know, LVPD Detective Smith? I'm looking into it."

"Well fuck." That little bit of info makes my head reel.

"One more thing," March says slowly. "A woman from the FBI came out to the ranch today. She interviewed just about everyone. She said she's looking into 'several' disappearances. And as far as I could tell, she had the most questions about you."

Elizabeth

ARNOLD IS DRIVING me home from a swim at the country club's heated pool, and Crestwood's porch has finally come into view. Someone is waiting there, and I activate the security system app on my phone to find out who. I pick the porch feed, and immediately recognize Suri's favorite lilac Vera Wang day dress and Alice + Olivia flats. She's waving at me. I glance up, smile, then turn back to my phone. I'm reaching to shut the app down when I notice Suri is waving her left hand. I zoom in...

"Holy *moly*."

I'm out of the car before it comes to a complete stop. I fly up the stairs, and she's beaming, laughing, and then we're both screaming. She shoves her hand into my face and a giant rock winks at me; it's surrounded by tiny fire opals: Suri's favorite.

"Holy crap, Sur, HE DID IT!"

"And he's moving back to Napa!"

"Oh my God you're getting married!" I grab onto her and we're swinging in a circle in front of the rocking chairs, both screaming like lunatics, and suddenly my throat is squeezing like I might cry. But Suri's giggling, and the crying feeling turns into hysterical laughter.

When we finally stop spinning, I'm dizzy and giddy. I grab her left hand and pull her inside, where it's warmer. In the full light I can see how pretty her makeup looks, and I can see the fire opals in her ears, surrounded by tiny diamonds.

Suri beams.

"Sur, how did he do it? I want every single detail right now. I can't believe he finally made the move!" Suri tried her best to act cool about it, but I know that girl, and she's been wanting to marry Adam since our freshman year of college.

She grabs my wrist and tugs me toward the kitchen. "Come in here. I made this tea that has a dash of vodka in it. It's called wedding tea. You're going to love it."

We walk into the kitchen, and, ever the hostess, Suri pulls out a chair for me and then sits herself. The tea is already cooling in crystal glasses beside wedding cookies that look homemade, and I laugh when I realize she's been waiting here for me—almost the whole time I've been at the pool if I'm correct about how long it takes her to make wedding cookies.

"Lizzy, it was *perfect*. We went to Banana Beau's"—Suri's favorite piano/ice cream bar—and they started playing 'Rhapsody in Blue', and then they brought out this huge cake, and it was a red velvet cake, and I realized that the whole place was empty, and Adam tells me he got a new job." She grins. "All I could think about was how it was going to be in like Bangladesh or some craziness, and then he says it's a freelance job with several different options, and he says he's thinking San Francisco or Napa, and he slid onto his knee and he reached into his pocket and pulled out the ring!"

I listen to Suri for the next hour, and then we talk weddings. I'm not surprised to find she wants to get married here at Crestwood, with white bows on everything—even the horse's necks.

I'm caught up in her happiness and slightly drunk when we take the elevator to bed.

"Screw toned thighs," Suri giggles.

"Screw 'em." I grin. "Why worry about being in shape when you've got a freakin' rock?"

Suri flashes it one more time, then leans down to kiss it. "I love my ring."

"I love it, too." Feeling spontaneous, I pull her into a bear hug. "You're the awesomest, Sur."

"No, you are."

She wobbles off on the second floor, and I manage to get off on the third without face-planting. When my buzz wears off,

I get a glass of cold water from my kitchenette and go into my study, where I keep my new friend the elliptical.

I work out for an hour and ten minutes, reviewing the events of the night before I get a shower. I think through the Suri-Adam thing, which from all angles seems to be awesome. Then I make myself revisit the subject of Cross. Within five minutes, I'm feeling so sad I can hardly move, so I deliberately turn my thoughts to Hunter.

I climb into bed, and I want him so badly I can practically feel him here beside me.

MONDAY MORNING, I'M up early. I'm doing an analytical paper on Victor Hugo's portrayal of prostitutes, and in the drama of the past few days, I've gotten behind. Still, I'm having trouble focusing as I sip my French vanilla coffee in one of the massive window seats that line the left side of my room.

I cross my legs and balance my laptop on my thighs, skimming that passage in *Les Misérables* where he compares prostitution to slavery. My fingers hover over my keyboard, poised for insight…but my brain follows my eyes out over the dew-drenched pastures, glowing orange with the sunrise.

Suri's paint horse, People Whisperer, prances near the white fence closest to the house, and I'm thinking about Cross again. We rode horses here just two weeks before the accident, and I remember how he grinned after he'd run on Trojan.

He'd tugged the horse's reins, slowing to a trot, and Suri and Adam had raced past us.

"How'd you know I was going to slow down?" he'd asked me.

I shrugged. I remember thinking on it for a second. "I guess I just saw your face or read your body language," I'd offered.

Cross just nodded. He sucked his lip into his mouth. I remember the dusky, indigo sky reflecting off his high cheekbones. How blue his eyes had looked. "I used to want to do this, remember?"

"Breed horses?"

He nodded.

I looked down the length of him—strong arms, lean, muscled legs—and back into his eyes. "I bet you would've been good."

"It's the speed I like," he'd told me, and after a quiet second: "It sounds trite, but it really does push everything else out of your mind."

And I had known just what he meant, because I'd always felt that way, too. Whether I was swimming, riding, or even reading—maybe especially reading—I liked being in motion, because it let me go away.

"I know just what you mean," I'd told him, and he'd leaned over, just close enough to skim my blue jeans with his fingertips.

"I'm really glad we're friends, Lizzy."

As I think about that now, tears well in my eyes. Why couldn't I just like Cross back? Why is he my old comfy sweatshirt instead of the hot designer outfit I covet from the window? Why have I always felt so at ease with him, my hair never standing on end in that perplexing and wonderful way it does when Hunter is near? Cross is such a good guy. Loyal, funny, complicated. A talented bike designer and a good friend. He's always been there for me when I need him.

I think about my conversation with Dad the other night, and I want nothing more than to talk to Cross. I blink at my computer screen and two tears slide down my hot cheeks.

I look down at my abs—flatter than they've been in years—and think about my kidneys. How much are they worth on the black market?

I sigh. Private care is so expensive, one Grade A kidney probably wouldn't last Cross a week.

I shut my eyes and lean my head against the wall, trying to think of a way to get a loan. I wonder if I could sell the house while Mom's in rehab. No. It's not in my name. It's in Dad's, and I'm sure as hell not calling him again.

I think about my car and want to scream. Three days. Three days is all my car would buy Cross at Napa Valley Involved Rehab. And that's if I got a good price.

I think about Suri again. I think about robbing a bank. I feel so trapped right now, prison doesn't seem much worse, and as soon as I have the thought, I start to cry, because the truth is I'm *not* trapped, and Cross is.

I think about the story of Sleeping Beauty, about how I used to kiss Cross after every visit. I know he cares for me—why can't I get him to wake up?

My thoughts wander to Hunter. For some reason, I think I could get *him* to wake up. I also bet he could pay for Cross's care. I wonder if I have enough money in my savings account to ask Hunter to gamble for me. He's a good gambler. He plays poker professionally.

But I've only got $7,000. So no.

Still, I imagine Hunter sitting at a poker table in a Vegas casino. He's resplendent in black jeans, a black shirt, and a Stetson. His poker face is beautiful; intriguing. I feel my body heat again as I think about kissing his lips. I wonder if the women there fall all over him. I bet the escorts would pay *him* to take a tumble.

My throat goes dry.

That's it.

My eyes fly to the soft, damp spot between my legs, and the room around me tilts.

Holy crap. Holy insanity. Holy vagina.

I know what I can do to help Cross.

CHAPTER TEN

Hunter

I'VE WATCHED LIBBY'S house almost the entire last twenty-four hours, and I don't like what I've seen. Priscilla's got someone following Libby at times that to me seem random, and at least once I've seen Priscilla herself do a drive-by.

I don't get it. For one, Priscilla's California home is in San Francisco—so why the hell is she spending so much time here in Napa? Yeah, she's fucking me, but we haven't seen each other in days, and since then, she hasn't even mentioned anything to me about being in California. Even if she *had* a home in Napa, what's with the Libby fixation? All Priscilla's spy would have told her is that I stopped at Libby's parents' home for fifteen or twenty minutes one day. Unless she's got my brain tapped, she's clueless about the burgeoning fantasies that plague me, so why this level of interest in Libby? Why would she prefer her spy, an older man in a battered Ford Ranger, follow Libby rather than me? If Sarabelle's disappearance is at the heart of this madness with Priscilla and I—and it seems to be, seeing as how Priscilla is fucking Detective Josh Smith—then maybe it makes sense that Priscilla was keeping her eyes on me, but what does Libby have to do with it?

I'm losing my patience with this game we're playing—more so because Dave, our PI in Vegas, told Marchant that the

LVPD doesn't have any leads on Sarabelle's whereabouts. Knowing Priscilla is probably fucking Josh Smith in exchange for some twisted favor really makes my hair stand on end. But I can't seem to find anything to fill in the wide gaps.

There's only one reason I can think of that Priscilla would be in Napa all the time—only one reason excluding the fucked up business that she has with me, and that's Priscilla's ex: the governor. Drake Carlson and his wife live here some of the time. Drake Carlson is also the only link I can find between Priscilla and Michael Lockwood.

Which is why I'm here at the courthouse. According to my PI in Napa, Priscilla arrived in the courthouse parking lot an hour ago—on the morning of a hearing regarding the governor's son, Cross. It doesn't seem like much, but I'm chasing any lead I can find, and with the governor linking Priscilla and Lockwood, I'll take it.

I feel confident she doesn't expect to see me here, and catching her off guard is important to me. I slide my Audi into a narrow space and put it in park, then step into the radiant California sun.

I've got on one of my Vegas getups: cheap suit—still tailored for my shoulders and chest, but not from Seville Row—and my regular joe shoes, a pair of Ralph Lauren loafers. Marchant likes to look like a slick bastard wherever he goes, but I'd rather not stand out.

The Napa County Court House is a smart, Italianate building: two stories of smooth stone arches and brick detail-work with cement stairs that lead into a covered entryway where people like to mingle. I get a fucked up feeling when I come here, probably because the scent of cheap floor shiner reminds me of Rita; she worked, for a time, as a secretary to the probate judge back in Orleans Parish. I try not to think about that.

The judge today, Diana Mendez, is an old friend of mine. She's objectively beautiful—long black hair, fantasy-long legs, doe brown eyes. Her ambition—she's the youngest probate judge in Napa County's history—only adds to her appeal. I try to imagine her naked as I make my way from my spot to the building's front—I have actual memories of her naked body to draw on—but Diana turns into Libby. Just like every other woman I've tried to jerk off to in the last few weeks.

I sigh, only because no one is around, and I want to let the birds know how troubling I find it.

Speaking of trouble, Priscilla is standing by the courthouse doors in black stilettos and a shiny silver dress that, in her fashion, shows too much thigh and too much tit. When I see her, I paste on my surprised expression. The look on her face is confirmation: She's not expecting me. As I start up the steps, I notice a news van pulling up and I wonder if my Libby will be here. I wonder if *he* called her Libby, too, and decide it's unlikely. Lizzy, Liz, or even Beth are more likely. I like to think Libby is all mine.

"Hunter, darling." Priscilla grabs me by the shoulders, like she owns me, and plants a kiss on my mouth. I know from experience that it leaves a slick red mark, just like I know that if I wipe it off, I'll pay with skin later.

"You look surprised to see me. I take it you don't know what's going on today?"

"What?" I lie.

"There's a hearing. The governor is coming."

"A hearing for what?" I ask, sticking my hands in my pockets, a submissive move I'm adopting purely for Priscilla's benefit.

"For poor Cross Carlson." Her voice oozes insincerity. She isn't able to feel empathy.

"He get a speeding ticket?" I ask dryly. The truth us I feel bad for the guy, but Priscilla doesn't need to know that.

"No, the governor and Mrs. Carlson are cutting him off."

"Come again?"

"He'll belong to the state, soon."

I arch a brow. "How do you know the Carlsons?"

I know this answer, of course, but I'm interested in hearing what she'll say.

She rolls her eyes and gives me a you-should-know-this look. "I was almost his step-mother, Hunter. Surely you know that. I care for him. They say he'll never be the person that he was."

She's wearing her liar's face, the one where her big, blue eyes are bigger and her skinny, sharp-looking brows are almost in her bleached hairline.

"I'm surprised you and the governor still keep in touch," I dare.

"We don't," she says, and this is what makes my morning. I happen to know, thanks to the efforts of my new Napa PI, that she was spotted pulling out of the governor's driveway yesterday. "That man has forgotten me entirely," she continues. "Son of a bitch, I'd like to have his balls in a glass jar by my bedside." She says all this in a sing-song voice.

"You and the rest of the state," I say.

Priscilla holds out her arm for me, and I dread the next hour the same way I dread getting my blood drawn and flying in helicopters.

I'd rather be anywhere but here. Then I step into the courthouse, and my day gets ten times worse.

Elizabeth

I CAN TELL he sees me, but he's acting like he doesn't. He's got Priscilla Heat with him, and they're en route from the courthouse entrance to the courtroom. At first I outright stare, but when his gaze jumps over me and then sticks to Priscilla's face, I drop my eyes to my feet and keep on walking. I feel sick to my stomach as I veer the other way, away from the women's bathroom where I'd hoped to close myself into a stall and wrangle up some nerve, and back toward the front door of the courthouse, where Governor and Mrs. Carlson should be arriving any time now.

I realize for the first time how much hope my stupid little nothing with Hunter has been giving me, because seeing him with that—with that…*woman*—sucks it all away, making what I'm about to do feel much more difficult.

Nevertheless, I keep a straight face. I take a spot in the chair nearest to the courthouse's lobby doors and wait with the reporters, who are double-checking microphones and reapplying makeup as they wait for Cross's deadbeat, shithead parents to arrive.

I look down at my aqua pantsuit and tell myself if nothing else, I can be glad about the way I look for the first time since high school. I've really taken to the elliptical and the caveman diet, losing almost fifteen pounds, and I'm kind of surprised to find I don't miss my old friend chocolate much at all.

I could let my Hunter sighting throw me off, but I'm determined not to—not yet, anyway. I need to get through this, to make good on a promise I made Cross when we were in ninth grade: that I'd always have his back.

While I wait, I open a window on my cell phone and revisit the web site I scoured earlier, feeling nervous butterflies just from looking at the discreet pictures. Even now, with the wheels of my plan already spinning, I'm not sure if I can really do this.

The crowd of reporters packed into the lobby stirs, jarring me out of my thoughts, and then the cameras start rolling. A second later Governor and Mrs. Carlson stroll through the front doors, looking like they've had a thorough spit-shining.

I grit my teeth and follow them with my eyes. As soon as they're through the arched entrance to the courtroom, my lawyer Donald Hartley comes to stand in front of me, arm out. I stand and give him a tight-lipped smile, but don't take his offered arm, choosing instead to walk into the courtroom a half-step behind him.

Donald is dressed in his signature pinstriped Armani suit, the one that makes my stomach churn because it reminds me of the many times we've appeared in court for my mother's violations. He pats my shoulder in a fatherly fashion, and we take our seats in the third row. Immediately I feel the stares burn into my back.

I wonder if I can feel Hunter's even hotter than the others, but I can't think of him right now. Seeing Cross's parents take their seats on the other side of the aisle, I feel nauseated. I don't trust them. If they can cut off their own son, who knows what they might try to do to me. At the very least I expect I'll become even more of a social pariah than I already am. That thought only strengthens my resolve, though.

As I wait through the proceedings dealing with other people and their problems, I run Nanette's words through my head. What she told me, when I visited Sunday, about Cross and how 'exceptionally' well he'd been responding to the N-therapy.

I rehearse my lines, putting some effort into not glancing over my shoulder to look for Hunter.

Finally, the Carlsons' lawyer stands and explains the family's position in a crisp monotone.

Diana Mendez, the judge, nods patiently, just the way she

did for my parents' divorce proceedings.

She looks curious when Donald rises. "Permission to speak?" he asks smoothly.

Diana's lips bunch. "Permission granted."

Donald holds a folder in one hand. He clasps his free hand over the one holding it. "My client, Elizabeth DeVille, is a life-long friend of Cross Carlson, and is interested in his care." I hold my breath while quiet sweeps the courtroom, and it is in that moment that I spot Hunter, seated on the fourth row across the aisle. I inhale deeply, trying not to focus on the outline of his form. "Miss DeVille would like to pay for Mr. Carlson to be returned to his previous facility. In fact—" my stomach squeezes — "she'd like to cover all his medical care for the remainder of this calendar year."

I hear a collective gasp go through the room as cameras start to flash. For a split second, my eyes are pulled toward the wooden chairs on the other side of the foot-worn aisle, where Cross's parents are sitting. I want to see their faces, but they both stare straight ahead. Instead, the eyes I meet are Hunter's.

They are wide and ultra-green, and they're trained on my face like they're seeing right through my clothes. Despite my topsy-turvy stomach, I can feel myself warming from the inside out, the flush starting on my breasts and climbing up my throat.

Diana's brows meet over her nose, and my attention is, thankfully, diverted. She looks unhappy. Maybe confused. She gives a slight shake of her head. "You would need to work that out with the medical center. There's paperwork involved. For it to factor into the change of Cross Carlson's medical custody today—"

"It's all here," Donald says smoothly, walking forward to hand the judge the folder full of documents I faxed him an hour ago. "You'll find the appropriate signatures enclosed."

Diana takes the folder, pulling out the paperwork and examining it, her long black hair falling over her gown. I watch the way her face loses its puzzled expression, and I can tell she's surprised. Maybe even shocked. She purses her lips again, and when she looks up, I think maybe there's respect in the x-ray look she pins on me.

Half a second later, the Carlsons' lawyer is on her feet. "This isn't legal," she says sharply. "There's no provision for non-family—"

"Yes, you're correct," Diana interrupts, looking short on patience. "There's no provision either way. And trust me, Ms. Chufunneker, if the bills are being paid, the state has no interest in picking up the tab."

The lawyer looks back down at the governor, and I can tell they're exchanging wordless information. Her gray head raises, and she's looking at the judge again. "Does this grant Miss DeVille the right to make medical decisions on behalf of the younger Mr. Carlson?" Chufunneker sounds mildly outraged.

"Would your clients like that granted?" Diana asks coolly.

"Of course not," Ms. Chufunneker says, having the nerve to look offended on behalf of the horrible Carlsons.

"Well that's good, because they will remain in charge of Cross's medical decisions as long as he's unconscious."

"Including where he's...housed?"

"That included." Judge Mendez tucks her silky hair behind her ear. "If they wish to downgrade to a state facility at taxpayer cost, they certainly may." Her gaze locks on the governor.

The governor colors, and reporters' cameras flash.

Minutes later, the hearing is adjourned. The Carlsons have agreed to move Cross back to Napa Valley Involved Rehab. With all the press here, they have no choice. Which is why I didn't call them at their home after I signed the paperwork early this morning.

I hope if news of how I paid for his care leaks out, the press will use it to crucify the Carlsons.

DRIVING DOWN I-5 South, toward Los Angeles, the flowered hills seem to roll past me too quickly. The sky above is flat, pale blue. Watching the horizon line makes me feel dizzy—like I'm stuck on a carnival ride and can't get off. I try to swallow back the sensation, but it builds within my chest, making my hands tremble on the wheel.

What am I doing?

I can't do this.

I just said I would do this.

Suddenly tears are pouring down my cheeks, and I want to pull my car over by the tall grass with its tiny flowers and sob.

I feel a thousand years old as I speed toward Mom's rehab. I have an appointment with her care worker. To lay the groundwork for my grand deception. I have an appointment at four fifteen, and my mom's expecting me, but I don't go there.

Instead I find myself at Cross's cement high-rise. I'm skirting around the sign-in desk and I'm sprinting down the drab hall toward his room. I think that when I get there, things will be different. The gauze will be gone. Maybe he'll even be sitting up and extubated. All I want in the world is to see my friend again before I go to Vegas. Or maybe, if he's already awake, I won't even have to go…

When I get through the door—which, thankfully, is cracked rather than closed—he's still in bed, and he looks much the same. The gauze is partially unwrapped, so I can see the tube is still in his head. His eyes are taped shut. His lips are super chapped, but I have lip balm in my purse. I'm reaching for it when I realize he *is* extubated! There's no more ventilator, just oxygen tubing in his nose. I want to scream with joy, and at that moment, the door cracks open.

This nurse is petite, with short, spiky pink hair and a diamond nose ring. She smiles at me and says, "I heard about you.

Elizabeth DeVille?"

I nod, and she explains that she has just seen me on TV. That makes my belly clench, but I try not to show her how rattled I am.

"Are you guys an item?" she asks quietly.

"No. We're best friends." I step closer to Cross, taking his hand, which feels warm and surprisingly soft.

"She put some lotion on him right before you came."

I frown, my head snapping around so I can meet her eyes. "Who did?"

"She comes in sometimes in the afternoons. I think her name is Sari."

Well, hot damn. That's news to me.

"She was here when we extubated him." The nurse smiles. "His eyes were open because they were changing out the medicine in them. To keep them from getting dry, you know? It might have been just reflexes, but she thinks he smiled at her."

I stroke my thumb across Cross's cheek and squeeze his hard hand in my small one. "Geez, Cross, you guys are keeping secrets."

The nurse eyes our fingers. "So you really aren't a thing?"

"We really aren't. He's been my friend since first grade."

"Well, I think he's lucky to have a friend like you."

Is he? I'm not so sure, but I smile anyway. "Has there been any talk about moving him yet?"

She nods. "Tomorrow morning."

"That's amazing."

"Your friend thought so, too. She seemed really surprised when I told her what you'd done."

I rub my eyes. "I bet she did."

CHAPTER ELEVEN

Elizabeth

I'M SO EXHAUSTED after seeing Cross, I decide to rain check with my mother. I'll plant the seeds of my lie another day, when I know for sure what's going on and when.

On my drive home, I call Richard Waites, the man I spoke with early this morning. He answers on the second ring. I can hear laughter and talking in the background, and through the phone line I swear I can smell stale smoke and alcohol.

Our connection is fuzzed by static, as if it's trying to discourage our contact. I think of Cross and press on. "Richard? This is Elizabeth DeVille again."

"Elizabeth, yes."

"I've thought about your offer, and I've decided that I want to do it. Can you tell me what the next step is?"

He pauses for a second, and I think he is surprised. "The next step? Well, you come out here. Come to Nevada and let me get this rolling."

"What does that entail?" I'm not going to a brothel without a detailed road map in my hand.

"It entails a lot," he says bluntly.

"Where does it start? I'd like to have some idea."

He pauses again, just long enough to take a drag on a cigar. "We do this from time to time, but never with a girl like you.

Don't get me wrong. Our girls are beautiful, valuable, talented girls, but they don't have their own bottled water," he says with a chuckle. "They're not Elizabeth DeVille." Another pause, and I decide to put it to him straight.

"DeVille doesn't mean much anymore."

"Yes, and I appreciate your candidness, Miss DeVille, but let me share my own. Our bidders aren't buying your money. They're wealthy men, and what they'll pay for is your high-class hymen. You follow me? All I need from you—well not all I need from you—there's a lot to this— But what I really need is you to come here, do a little training—"

"Prostitution?"

"Well you can't do that. Not and have a decent auction. But I'm saying you learn from our women. Learn the ropes. It's not for long. Maybe two weeks, three. Whatever's enough to get you ready for your big night."

I nod. "I follow you."

I'm navigating the congested interstate, headed back up toward Napa. The sky is purple. Dramatic, like it knows what I'm up to. "And you said the prices on this are pretty high?"

"In the hundreds of thousands, yes ma'am. We've done two this year and both were over five hundred thousand. One last year even fetched a million." There's another pause, while I zip around an eighteen-wheeler. "Now all of these girls were models, and we had them on the menu for several months before their auctions giving other types of pleasure, so the men had built up some interest in them. Curiosity."

"Are you saying I have to...have my own clients?" I hold my breath. This wasn't mentioned earlier, but now that I've signed on to pay for Cross's care I don't think I can back out.

After a moment, he says, "Well, no. You're a different sort of girl, or so we're going to say."

"But I don't want to use my real name."

I hear his low intake of breath. "You don't want to use your name? Well Elizabeth, what do you think we're selling?"

"My body," I say. "Isn't that what you sell? Women?"

"I don't sell anyone," he says, and I bite my lip because he sounds a little defensive. "The women—and men—who work here sell themselves. I'm more landlord than pimp. And with all due respect, Elizabeth, the photos I've seen of your body...well, it's not compliant with the standard of this industry."

I bite my lip, trying my very best to swallow back my pride. For Cross. Telling myself it's nothing personal, I plunge ahead.

"I understand what you're saying, Richard. The truth is, I've recently lost some weight, but I can lose some more."

"I'm looking at the photo you sent me, taken in November. Why don't I put your weight at 165. Is that about right?"

I gape. "You really know your stuff." I'm not 165 anymore, but I was in November.

"I'd like you to have it down to 140. I'd still like some curves, so I want you tight and toned."

I look down at my body, already so much leaner than it was. Screw the numbers. I know where I look my best. I'll make that mark.

"You do that," Richard says, "and then come here. We'll take care of the rest, and you can use an industry name. We could do a wig or something, too. We'll put you up on bill boards around Vegas and we'll talk you up. Something like… 'Selling Scarlett.'"

"And I'm Scarlett?"

"Yeah. You like it?"

I'm not sure how I feel about it, but I say, "Yeah. Scarlett sounds good."

I hear his fingers snap. "There, the hardest part's over."

He laughs, and I know my chuckle has to sound weak. "How soon can we hold the auction?" I ask.

"I think three months, if you want to rush it."

I feel a wave of cold sweat wash over me, and I want to

kick myself for not going into detail this morning when we first spoke. "Three months, no. That's not soon enough."

"Miss DeVille, we aim for healthy loss and toning. We care about our women—and men."

"I understand, but I need the money in a month." I told NVIR I would have it to them then.

I can practically hear his shock in the static coming through the phone line. "A month?"

I rub my brow. "Is that doable?"

"Doable." He chuckles. "Isn't that the word? Of course it's doable. Let me get off the line and get you started. We take twenty percent of the final bid, and we reserve the right to manage the bidding. Understand?"

I swallow. "Yes." I don't know what 'manage the bidding' means, but does it really matter? I've already signed on for this. I'm in.

"One month." He laughs again. "Why don't you get up here as soon as you can, and we'll get you started with the girls."

I nod and drive the rest of the way home in a fog of disbelief. The only thing left now is to tell Suri.

"YOU'RE DOING *WHAT*?"

Suri's mouth is filled with cashews, but she doesn't spit them out or even choke. She simply speaks around them and then swallows, and I have the hilarious thought that Suri would probably be a great prostitute.

"I'm selling my V-card," I tell her again, leaning on the iron breakfast table.

Her face is comical. All her features twist, like she might laugh. Then her mouth pulls down, like a sad clown. "Lizzy, why? Why would you do that?!"

I think for a second before replying, because I need to give

Suri a certain impression. One that will prevent her from trying to stop me. I go for casual and shrug.

"I have it, and I definitely don't need it." An image of Hunter and Priscilla flits through my mind; I shove it away. "I figured why not do something useful with it? I'm thinking of making it a project for my PhD. You know, writing about value judgments people place on things. One sexual encounter is just that: it's a twenty minute thing. And virginity? It's just a hymen, an antiquated measure of a woman's value," I say, pleased with myself.

Suri is shaking her head, her horrified face the same color green as her polka-dotted blouse. "Lizzy, you're wrong. It's not like that. Sex is intimate, it should be done with a lover or a boyfriend or at least a really good friend."

Someone like Cross, I think, and really wish I hadn't.

"It's not just physical. It gets into your head. I know we're not the same, Lizzy, but I have trouble believing you'd be happy if you just...sold it to some random man." Her nose wrinkles. "What if they're ugly or old or they want to do disturbing things?"

All I can think about is Hunter as I try to mold my face into something reassuring.

"They can't be criminals," I tell her. Richard told me that much. "I can even decline them if I want and choose another bidder. And if we leave the premises, I'll have the option of taking along a team of guards."

"So they're...what, renting you? For a night? For a few hours?" Suri's face is grave. "Lizzy, if this is about money, if it's about Cross, and after what you did today I *know* it is—"

"But it's not," I interject. I'm waving my arms now, my heart beating fast as it becomes clear to me how much Suri's opinion matters in this. I don't want her to see me any differently. I don't want her pity. I want her support.

I think, not for the first time, how ridiculous it is that someone taking charge of their sexual assets, someone like me who's making money off them, is looked down upon. I can't wait to write about this.

"It's not about money, not all the way. It's about me doing something interesting, doing something that I want. I see it the opposite of how you do. I'm tired of waiting for the right guy. As you've known for years now, he doesn't exist." She opens her mouth, I'm sure to say something like 'You could meet him tomorrow,' so I beat her to the point. "I don't even think I'd *want* to lose it to a boyfriend, to be a virgin when he's not. A twenty-three-year-old virgin." I make a face. "I want to go ahead and experience this, put it behind me. And if I can make half a million dollars in the process, what's wrong with that? In fact..."

I trail off, because Suri's mouth is hanging open. "Did you say half a million dollars?"

"Maybe," I say, like it doesn't matter.

Suspicion stretches her features as she stands up, grabbing for a napkin on the counter and using it to dab her mouth. She lowers the napkin and frowns. "So this *is* about Cross."

"It's about me," I insist.

"You're not planning to use the money to pay for his medical bills which, you know, you told a judge you would pay?"

I open my mouth, then close it, not sure what to say. Suri's eyes narrow to slits. "I saw the news today, Lizzy DeVille. I'm your BFF, not a moron. Remember, I have money. I can help. I'm Cross's friend, too. In fact, I think it would be a travesty if you went out selling...selling *yourself*, when I'm right here and perfectly willing to help Cross."

"You just bought this huge house, Sur. Listen to me." I catch her hand in mine. I press our joined hands on top of the stylish flowered table mats, which coordinate perfectly with the green gingham table cloth beneath them. "Have I ever done anything I regretted? Have I ever made a really big, bad, stupid choice, one I ended up hating myself for?"

"There's a first time for everything," she says. "I have money, and I *want* to use it to help Cross. You need to let me, and you need to forget this craziness."

I shake my head. "This is something I want to do. It'll be an experience. And as for money, this was my idea. If you had extra money to throw around, I have no doubt you would have already thrown it. You can chip in if you want, but I'm doing this, too," I say vehemently. "You might not understand, because you've had sex. You've done it. I'm just...waiting. Like...I don't know...a dairy product outside the refrigerator."

Suri screws her face up, then lets out a little hoot. "Did you just take the extremely anti-feminist stance that you are somehow spoiling?"

"No! All I'm saying is it's bugging me. That I haven't done it. I feel like...the suspense is just getting to me. I'd like to have it *done*."

"What about...opinions?" she asks quietly.

I squeeze her hand and let it go. "I'll be using another name, and my face will be shadowed the night of bidding. When they advertise me, it'll just be my body on billboards or whatever. No one will know."

I've already called Richard back and asked him not to reveal my true identity to anyone, even—*especially*—Marchant Radcliffe, Hunter's friend. Marchant owns Love Inc., where the deed is getting done.

Suri's eyes are swimming with tears, and I feel a spark of annoyance.

"I know you're just showing me you care, and I appreciate it, Sur, I really do. But I'll be back in two weeks or so, just the same as I am now, but a little more experienced. I'm having one sexual encounter with a man who'll likely be very nice to me, and I'll have more protection than the Pope. I'm okay with this. It's my choice."

"You're doing this for Cross," she says again.

"Part of it is for Cross. Doesn't that make it even more meaningful, though?"

Suri nods slowly. "I guess…maybe."

"See, I'm fine." I stand up, spreading my arms, and she hugs me, speaking into my hair. "You're a good friend, Lizzy, a really good friend. Just remember you don't have to do this. I don't think Cross would want you to."

"I want to do this. It's an experiment for me."

In more ways than one. A good twenty percent of this idea's allure is in my eagerness to get rid of my V-card so I can stop saving it for Hunter. I need to be freed of that idea. Freed of my crush. I hope that after spending some time at Love Inc., I never blush in the middle of a sexual encounter ever again. No Hunter West or anybody else will be able to knock me off my feet, and I like that idea.

Suri hugs me one more time and we call Albert. We're going shopping for gowns and robes in every color of the rainbow. As we walk down the stairs to our waiting ride, I feel more peaceful than I have in weeks.

CHAPTER TWELVE

Hunter

I SWEAR TO God, Priscilla is psychic. That woman knows how to find me after a bad day. And the worse the day is, the more likely it is that I'll end up rolling in the covers with her, whipping her and spanking her, pulling her long hair and pressing my hand over her mouth until her eyes are wide and I'm afraid I'm gonna kill her stupid, spray-tanned ass.

Tonight I'm on my jet. There's a bed and a recliner but I'm too worked up to relax. Instead I'm sitting at the table, twirling an unlit cigarette around in my fingers like a showgirl's baton. I want the damn thing, but I quit. I keep a pack of Marlboro Reds in the freezer of every place I have, but I don't smoke them.

I've got my fingers tightened around the cigarette, thinking about snapping it in half, when the intercom crackles and Frank says, "There's something on the runway you need to see, sir."

I dim the lights and look out the oval window, and the cigarette snaps. Of course it's fucking Priscilla. A brisk breeze is tossing up her ass-short, blood-red skirt and I can see her panties. There are sequins around the seams, so they sparkle in the runway lights.

I can tell by the way she steps toward the plane, waving as she moves, that she's in high heels. I can see the red light of her cigarette's cherry.

My head pounds, letting me know it doesn't appreciate the handle of bourbon I gave it last night. I press the call button, sinking a hand into my hair and rubbing hard. "Let her in, Frank."

I sweep the pieces of the cigarette into my hand and dump them in a garbage can inside a cabinet. Then I sit back down and watch her sashay into my cabin.

"Well hello there, big boy."

I grit my teeth. I am so not in the mood for her bullshit.

"I've got a little exhibitionist fetish I'd like to indulge with you," she purrs.

"How do you want to do that?" My gaze roams up and down her body, making her think I appreciate her so she doesn't feel the need to make any points.

She grins, crossing the space between us to straddle me.

"I want to fuck you somewhere public, Hunter. Somewhere like this runway."

She says it like she's doing me a favor. Like I've never been fucked before and she's the most fuckable woman on the planet.

Priscilla lowers her red mouth to mine, and I close my eyes, meeting her for a rough kiss. *Sarabelle, Sarabelle, Sarabelle,* I chant silently.

Today, I was questioned by the woman from the FBI, who came to my home in Napa while I packed my bags for Vegas. I'm not a formal suspect yet, and I intend to keep it that way.

I SWEEP PRISCILLA off to Beau's, the gym I own in downtown Napa.

While she steps into the ladies' room, I tell Harriet at the desk to cut the cameras in one of the private cardio hubs. I also send a text to Marchant, telling him to send people to both of my Vegas residences. I can't think of another reason Priscilla would've dropped by just in time to stop me from departing for Vegas.

I know from our Vegas PI, Dave, that she spent yesterday at Michael Lockwood's place there. My California PI, Todd, told me she spent most of today with the governor she claims to hate. I still don't know how all this adds up, but I know Priscilla is using up a lot of jet fuel. I also know she's lying to me.

When Priscilla strides out of the ladies' room and squeezes my ass, I guide her hand around to my erection. Priscilla overestimates her appeal and expects my lust. She tries to unbutton my jeans as we step into the 3,000-square foot weight room. I push her against a wall and kiss her up and down her neck, cupping her ass and grinding my cock into her hips, and she laughs that sultry laugh. I've always imagined she practices until she sounds as close as she can to Marilyn Monroe. Which isn't close.

"I don't know how you get by out here without me. Why don't you come with me back home to Vegas?"

Wrapping one arm around her waist, I guide her through the weight room, where a handful of men and women are working out. "You already know I'm going to Vegas for a tournament. I thought you were the one who wasn't going to be there."

I wait for her answer, curious to know if she'll go back on the tale she told me the other day—about how she'll be out of town while I'm in Vegas—but she just makes a sour face and acts as if she's just remembered her plans.

"Such a pity."

Priscilla has led me to believe she'll be filming in Vancouver for the next six days. But Dave says her personal chef in Vegas has prepared a menu for the rest of the week.

As we walk through the back doorway of the weight room, Priscilla's fingertips graze my wrist, and I feel a strange ache behind my breastbone. I know why—and I wish I didn't. I want Priscilla to be someone else. Someone I have no business thinking about, especially considering what kind of black cloud I've got over my head at the moment.

I push that out of my mind, vowing to try harder to keep it out in the future.

Our little space, known to the Beau's security system as Cardio Hub 4, is a glass-walled room just behind 2,000 square feet of women's-only weights space. It's got six elliptical machines, three treadmills, and an adjoining sauna and massage suite. The room is almost always used by members with personal trainers, and since it's almost nine p.m., no one is around.

I pull Priscilla inside, and when I reach behind me to flip the lock on my glass prison, she shakes her head.

"I want it unlocked." She smiles, straight blonde hair falling around her face as she cups me through my jeans. "Part of the thrill, Hunter."

Her palm against my dick makes me lose some of my steam, but I imagine she's Libby and I'm stiff as steel. I grab Priscilla by the wrists and lay her over the deck of one of the treadmills, buns up. I jerk her red skirt up and use the cord that goes to the machine's heart monitor to whip her ass, and she starts panting.

I still haven't puzzled out why Priscilla wanted me that night at Love Inc.—or why she hasn't gotten bored with me yet. We hadn't met before that night.

I still don't know what happened after she drugged me, either. She says she fucked my brains out, but I didn't feel like I'd had my brains fucked out. I'm sure if Lisa from FBI knew Priscilla claimed to have roofied me and fucked me, she'd be looking at Priscilla with a magnifying glass, but I didn't tell her that, and I'm not going to. Not yet.

Because the more I think about Priscilla coming out with the news that Rita wasn't my biological mother, the more I worry about what could come out next. I don't think I could get prosecuted for what happened, but the awfulness of the whole world knowing… The horror of being pitied by the number of people who know me from TV… It makes me ill.

So I'm letting fear dictate the vile things I do with Priscilla. Letting fear keep me in this trap until Marchant and I figure out who really kidnapped Sarabelle—or Lisa, from the FBI, does. I wonder how long that will take, being certain, as I am, that Josh Smith from the LVPD is covering Priscilla's ass.

I feel a pang of regret for not being completely straightforward with FBI Lisa about Priscilla and the roofie and the fucking of lead detective Josh Smith. But the FBI hasn't taken over the case yet, and Lisa told me they likely wouldn't unless another girl went missing. So, for right now, Josh Smith is the top dog responsible for finding Sarabelle—and if Priscilla is one of the guilty parties, Sarabelle's only hope is Dave, Marchant, and I. At least, that's what I tell my guilty conscience when it starts howling.

Speaking of howling…

It doesn't take Priscilla long to grow tired of the hair-pulling and whipping. I can't appease her by slapping her pussy, either, and I don't have the right kind of condom to do her in the ass.

"A condom's a condom, Hunter." She twists her red lips into a pout.

"You know damn well that's not true." I'm not a fan of anal, but we both know a thicker, tougher condom is required.

I can see it in her eyes when she decides she's pissed off. She shoves my chest, and when I just stand there, she slaps my face. I haven't been slapped since I was fourteen, and the fierce sting sends me reeling back into the past.

While I'm off balance, Priscilla shoves me again. I wobble into the wall between the workout area and the sauna, and she giggles, then whistles seductively. "I think I've figured out what you like, big guy."

I feel the trembling start in my chest, and I want to throttle her. I don't care if she's a woman. I want to grab her hair and throw her against the wall and tell her to go fuck herself—and extra fucks for trying to dig into my family's past.

"You don't know shit about me," I tell her, struggling to breathe as I lean against the wall.

"I know you're nice and hard and I like to slap you around." She grins and slaps me again, and it takes all the self-control I have not to lose my shit.

My heart is racing. Fucking flashback land. "You're a cunt —you know that, right?"

I feel my cock twitch as I look at her, and I hate myself for it. I'm becoming just as deviant as she is.

She bites my neck, the sting hard enough to draw blood, and I push her head away. I scoop her up in one arm, shove through the glass door to the darkened sauna, toss her onto one of the benches that line the four walls of the room, and start the steam. I turn her over and spank her again, hoping to ward off what I know we'll end up doing, but of course it only makes her shriek and pant.

She glances back at me and I can see it in her eyes that all she really wants is to be hit. A dom who wants to be dominated. It's what she thinks she deserves, and I know all too well the reasons why.

One night at my house she drank too much and spilled the story. How her mom left her with an uncle who sold her to his friends, and when she was old enough to change her fate, she ran off to a brothel where she made her own money and set her own rules. Later, she started making films. Got herself a C-Class ticket to the Hollywood shindigs and fucked some desperate actors, desperate politicians, desperate gamblers. Got herself a red Jaguar and tattooed eyeliner, eyelash implants, breast implants. God knows what else on her is fake.

She leans closer, giving me a nose full of expensive perfume, and whispers something in my ear. Not understanding it, I blink at her. As much as I loathe her—even loathe her beautiful face—I wonder for the first time if perhaps I should try to make the best of this: our fucked up coupling. I don't do sex with regular women, because too many of them expect affection in return. I quit going to the brothels months before the night with Sarabelle; escorts don't excite me anymore. So maybe I should be glad I have Priscilla. Maybe she and I deserve each other.

"What did I say?" she purrs.

"I have no idea," I tell her, squeezing her big, fake tits.

"I said who's your mama now, you son of a bitch."

My heart pounds in my chest, and for a second it doesn't seem real. That I'm here with Priscilla Heat. That Sarabelle is gone, Sarabelle who always did what I wanted and never asked questions. I didn't know her well, but she was always pleasant to be around.

"It's sure as hell's not you," I growl.

"Oh, you better not back talk mama." She squeezes my balls and I let out a moan. I lay her down and thrust three fingers into her, stretching her as she writhes against my hand.

"You know who's a little slut?" she pants. "Elizabeth DeVille. I want to hear you say Elizabeth is a slut."

Shock like a bucket of ice water slides through my veins, and for the first time I'm actually worried for Libby. True, Priscilla's been following her, but I'd begun to assume that was to keep tabs on me. Now I wonder if she knows what happened between Libby and me at my vineyard shindig. Maybe she's jealous?

She sinks her nails into my wrist. "I'd like to fuck that little bitch. Shove a dildo right up that tight ass just like Marchant did."

I tense, and Priscilla grins—more a leer. "Hunter West, jealous," she says. "I never thought I'd see the day."

"You think I'm jealous?" I am. Blindingly so, even though I'm sure she's just lying to bait me. I bite her mouth, and Priscilla moans. "I don't give a damn about Elizabeth DeVille."

"You lie," she hisses. She puts her hand over mine, and she guides it to her throat. She wants me to choke her. I'd like to, because I'm angry, but still I hesitate, a crime for which I receive a slap.

I see Rita's angry face and am too disarmed to do anything but gasp for air.

"What a little bitch," she hisses.

As our night winds to an end, I'm on top of her again with my hands around her neck. I can feel her tendons strain under my fingers as she jacks me off, and it's everything I can do to stay hard. There was a time, a few months back, when all I could do was watch Priscilla, worried I was hurting her, but I've had to stop that. I can't get off if I'm worried, and she demands that I do.

I spend the next two hours getting whipped and slapped and trying not to get too head fucked. I'm not a child anymore. I can fight back, if I choose.

But I don't.

CHAPTER THIRTEEN

Elizabeth

IT'S KIND OF like what I imagine getting sent off to college would be like if you're in a normal family, where at least one person really cares that you're leaving.

Suri fusses over me like a mama bird, making me egg soufflé and sparkling green tea for breakfast, plus a giant bowl full of perfectly gooey orange cinnamon rolls for the road. As we sit and eat our soufflé at the breakfast table, she watches me like a mama bird, too.

In the last two weeks, I've hit the elliptical hard, and I've even worked out at a real gym three times a week, with a trainer, going through photocopied exercises Richard sent. I look better than I have in a long time. I refuse to weigh myself, on principal, but I'm wearing size six pants. I actually teared up a bit when they slipped on.

I smile a little, figuring Suri must be thinking the same thing, but instead of complimenting me she frowns a little and shakes her head. "This is your choice, Lizzy. Remember you don't have to go. I have money."

I snicker. "I do realize I'm not a sex slave."

"Speaking of sex slaves!" She hops up and opens the drawer of the desk where she keeps her fabric swatches. She holds out something small and black, and I'm appalled to find that it's a gun case.

I wobble backwards when she tries to push it into my hands. "Suri, have you lost your mind? I'm not touching that death machine."

"It's a .38. You need it! Some escorts have been kidnapped and sold into sex slavery or murdered or eaten!"

"Really?" I pause, mid-chew. I've heard a lot of things about Las Vegas, but not that.

"Well, the cannibalism is just a pessimistic guess." She rolls her eyes, like the specifics don't matter. "They've gone missing. Two or three, I think. One of them was even from Love Inc. Surely you've heard about—"

"I have," I lie, because really—I don't need any added stress. I probably *would* have heard about it, had I done excessive Googling on Love Inc., but I didn't. Because I really don't care to know more about it than I do. I'll be there for two weeks, and then I'll be back home. Surely I can avoid getting cannibalized or kidnapped in less than fifteen days.

Suri pushes the gun into my hand, and I take it. Not because I'd ever shoot someone, but because I want to ease her mind.

"Remember, if you have a problem, call me," she says, with her lip between her teeth.

"I'll just shoot 'em dead." I smile, waving my gun, and she says, "Don't do that! It may be loaded."

"You just gave me a *loaded* gun?"

"No, but you're always supposed to act like it's loaded!"

With a wide-eyed look at the little black case, I tuck the gun into my bag and turn to Suri, who's holding out the plastic box of cinnamon rolls.

"Don't forget these."

"How could I?" I'm an absolute sucker for orange frosted cinnamon rolls.

Together we walk to my jam-packed car, where I put that awful handgun in the trunk and Suri checks the tire pressure. She once had a flat outside Chula Vista on one of those lonely country roads. She was rescued by a border patrol agent who was dressed like a smuggler; the experience was scarring, so since then she's always checked my tire pressure.

"Looks like you're good," she says, holding out the gauge. Then she throws her arms around me. "Lizzy, you look wonderful. I hope it's perfect and whoever wins the bid is a total prince charming. I'll come visit soon."

I squeeze her close. "The bidding's not for a week and a half, remember?"

"I can't be away from you for that long, crazy woman."

Suri and I hug once more, and when she closes me into my car, I roll down the window, preparing to wave until I reach the end of the driveway. Suri will do the same; it's our thing.

"Lizzy," she calls, as I shift into drive. She trots over to my window, her long sweater trailing behind her. "I'll visit Cross. Every day, if you want."

If I want...

It's hard to hide my smirk, but I manage. "Suri, that would rock."

She smiles a smile that's bigger than it ought to be, and then says, "Tell him 'hi.'"

"Huh?"

"Cross. Aren't you seeing him on your way out?"

"Yeah."

"Tell him I said 'hi.'"

I VISIT CROSS at Napa Valley Involved Rehab and am thrilled to find him doing better. The gauze is off his head, and Nanette says his brain scans look much the same as they did the last time he was scanned at NVIR—meaning the stroke was minor and hasn't affected his long-term prognosis. Amazing. His eyes drift open once or twice, which leaves me feeling buoyant. I'm similarly thrilled when I speak to Mom on the phone and find out it's a 'busy' day at Ultra Mod/Hip Rehab, and she doesn't have time to see me before I leave town.

It takes me an agonizing ten hours to drive to Vegas, but the driving is important. I have a lot to think about, and I need time to process it.

I'm really doing this. I'm really on my way to the Love Inc. ranch to sell my virginity.

I've dressed up. I'm wearing my new brown Armani slacks, the ones that make my butt look tight and perky, and a low-cut, sea blue wrap-around blouse that matches my eyes. I've pulled my dark hair into a playful up-do, and for once, I'm actually wearing lipstick. I feel sexy.

For a few hours, my mind cycles through practical concerns, like whether I have enough lingerie, and what kind of man likes garters. Superficial thoughts, like what kind of lotion I should use on the big night, and whether I need to shower right before the bidding or if I'll have time after.

Richard and I have agreed that I'll get more money if I offer myself to the winner the night of the bidding. What will I feel like, lying on a stage under those glowing lights, with my face shadowed and steam rolling around my mostly naked body?

What if I'm still to pudgy? What if the winner doesn't like having sex with me and wants a refund?

Will the escorts treat me nicely?

The California hills flatten and the grass turns into sand. The air through my vents feels crisp and dry. I loosen up a little and my thoughts dip deeper—to Cross. It's still so strange, the way things are now. He should be talking to me. He should be on a bike.

I have a strange and fleeting memory of the shape of Cross's fingertips, holding a pencil as he sketches. How, as a girl, I used to picture those hands when I thought about being fingered.

My eyes water as I think about his hair. How soft it was when it was long and dark and messy. How brilliant blue his eyes are. How they widened that night in the hall when I ran into him at Hunter's party.

He was just trying to watch out for me, even if he was being a prick about it.

I go another round of wishing I'd acted differently. What the outcome would be. I think of Suri, secretly visiting Cross while he was at the county hospital. For how long? What were the logistics? I try to imagine her sitting in that awful, stinky place, legs crossed, her curly brown hair pulled back, and everything about her radiating Suri; privileged Suri. I wonder if Cross felt safe when she sat there by him. I wonder if he felt loved when she pecked him on the forehead or smoothed his covers—two so very Suri things to do, I know she must have done them.

The sun climbs into the middle of the sky and starts to fall behind me. Cacti dot the barren land. For the longest time, I think of random things, like the Kenneth Cole cologne Cross wore in high school, which I loved so much. I remember Suri telling me one night when I slept over that if she turned thirty and she wasn't married, she would marry Cross. At the time I was surprised. She'd acted nonchalant and shrugged. *"I bet I would never get bored with Cross."*

I remember how Cross's jackets used to smell when he put them around my shoulders: like pepper and mints and that Reaction cologne. Remembering a time when Cross lent me his jackets reminds me of being younger, and of course, I think of Mom. How she never had sex with my dad, and how I really wished I didn't know that.

Thinking of Dad makes me think of Hunter. I remember a younger Hunter West, grinning, on his back, gliding underneath Mom's Porsche. I remember his gorgeous golden hair. How, for years, I thought he was the consummate playboy, fucking wealthy, silk-robed women by the pool before the sun was fully up. I recall the glitter of his eyes as he looked up from Priscilla, on the fireplace, in the same room where he and I had...

I don't know if it's because it's dusk and cool, or if it's that thought that gets me, but I'm shivering. I feel naked, and I hate it.

In a few days I'm going to sell my body. I'll strip naked and let a stranger inside me.

And it's true, I don't place much value on it: my virginity. For eons it was traded in exchange for land, cattle, power, whatever, so I know full well I'm in good company. I'm okay with that. But the idea of the act as a sensory experience—the knowledge that someone I won't choose will invade my body... I guess I kind of hate that.

Okay…I really hate that.

The image of Hunter leaning down to kiss me flits like lightning through my mind. I can almost feel his lips on mine—so warm and soft and gentle. The look in his eyes as he watches me from the foot of the bed, and I can see he's haunted by something and I know I'll never know what it is.

Tears start to fall as I think of Hunter finding me in his bedroom, ravaging me like we're characters in a romantic movie. Is that the closest I'll ever get to a fairy tale?

I wrap my hands around the wheel, and I can't help but think of mother, in her curlers, behind the wheel of a much older, larger car; her foot on the pedal; my foot on the pedal. And for a long second, I want to run the car into the crag of rock off to my right.

I really kind of want to. Crazy is a siren call.

But I'm too practical. Practical Elizabeth. Elizabeth the whore.

I wonder what Cross will think. I wonder what Mom would think. I wonder what my dad would think.

I wonder what Hunter West would think.

I pass the sign marking the Vegas city limits with a lightness deep inside me. Like the part of me that matters is somewhere up above, floating in a helium balloon. This me behind the wheel is hollow. Brave and ready.

This me is older and stronger and smarter.

This me can handle anything. At least that's what I tell myself.

Hunter

I'VE GOT ON my penguin suit when Priscilla calls. The Heat Enterprises Brawl for Innocence Gala begins in an hour, and I'm pacing around my penthouse, chewing on the laundry list of bullshit I just got from Dave the PI.

I feel a hot stab of guilt deep in my gut—that I'm worried about myself when Sarabelle is God knows where—when my phone rings, flashing a red "P." I groan.

When Priscilla heard I volunteered for the 'brawl' tomorrow night, earning myself an invitation to the gala even after all the charity plates had already been purchased, she demanded to be my date, but we're not riding together, so I shouldn't have to see her until I arrive at the Heat Enterprises Mansion in an hour.

"Damnit." I bring the phone up to my ear, working to sound calm and aloof, the way I used to sound before I realized Priscilla was going to Michael Lockwood's house on a regular basis, in addition to fucking Detective Josh Smith.

I take a deep breath. "Priscilla."

"Hunter."

I roll my wrist, which is sore from the last time I saw her.

"What can I do for you?"

"I'm coming up in ten." I can hear her Cheshire grin through the phone, and then her laughing hiss. "Get ready."

I strip out of my tux and swear that this will be the last time. Tonight, I'll figure out Priscilla's game and end it. Josh Smith will be at the gala, as will Michael Lockwood. If I can find out what Priscilla wants with Smith—other than his dick—or the nature of her relationship with Lockwood, maybe I can finally put a stop to this farce.

I wait behind the front door of my penthouse. I'm planning to grab her from behind when she walks through it. Maybe rip her gown off. Bind her wrists with my neck tie and fuck her doggy style.

I shut my eyes, inhaling slowly while I wait in my darkened foyer like the crazy S.O.B. I am. The small amount of enjoyment I've begun to get from these games with Priscilla makes me sick. I'm further disgusted by my cowardice. I pretend I'm keeping her close for Sarabelle's sake, but the truth is I won't turn her in, just like I won't stop fucking her, until I know my skeletons will stay in the closet where they belong.

It's not just my father's political career I care about—although, as a West, I'm forced to consider that, at least minimally. His reputation would be tarnished if people knew he'd knocked up an escort, and tarnished further if they knew the measures he'd taken in order to cover it up.

My father returned from his business trip to Vegas with a newly pregnant Roxanne, but for most of her pregnancy, she stayed secluded in West Manor. Less than a week after she died in labor—at the house—Rita came knocking. Dad was somehow able to hush the whole thing up, and I was presented many months later as Dad and Rita's child.

Things went just the way Rita had hoped, and ten months later, my half-sister Amber was born. She still lives in New Orleans, managing the advertising arm of West Bourbon, and she knows exactly what kind of insanity went on in our house before Rita's death. What she doesn't know is how Rita died—and that's the part that keeps me up at night. That's for me and me alone to know. Well, and the coroner my dad paid off.

It's a secret I plan to take to my grave, and damned if I'll let a meddling, rumor-spreading porn star expose my greatest shame.

I lean my head against the wall and go over what we've got so far. The PIs—Dave and the two other Vegas PIs we just hired, Julie and Roberto—have found a few good leads:

1. Josh Smith is Michael Lockwood's third cousin. This gives him more incentive than Priscilla's willing pussy to cover up any Priscilla or Lockwood involvement in the disappearance.

2. The night Priscilla invaded my plane, a man searched both of my homes in Vegas. Marchant's guy, Dave, captured the whole thing on film, indicating that, for now at least, the bad guys have no idea that we are onto them—or rather, no idea that we've got Dave on their asses.

3. This one is the big kahuna. The one that gives me hope. Apparently about a year and a half ago, just before Priscilla's affair with Governor Carlson began, one of the governor's mistresses went missing. Maybe. Missy King was a working girl — an exclusive, 'private' escort—the governor met at a brothel on The Strip. He saw her regularly, even took her to social engagements—that part, we've confirmed is true—until he didn't anymore. There are no missing person reports, and there has never been a police investigation. But her friends—some of them Love Inc. women—tell Dave they think she was kidnapped, and the LVPD did nothing to find her.

Priscilla's cell phone is bugged as of today, so I'm impatiently anticipating the next time she talks to the governor. Or to Smith. Or Lockwood, for that matter. I'm hoping they'll fill in some of the pieces, because right now I don't know what this is.

I'm inclined to speculate that the governor is in all of this somewhere; he'd serve as a link between Lockwood and Priscilla, and if I'm being generous or hopeful, he could tie both Priscilla and Lockwood to another disappearance. But again, that's hopeful. Right now I've got nothing.

The most important thing I can do to remedy that is go to the gala. In my most ambitious plan, I can get my hands on Lockwood's cell phone. He'll be there because, like me, he's brawling at the Joseph Club tomorrow night in the name of charity.

Marchant wouldn't sign up for the brawl—something about winning making him look like a pimp and losing making him look like a loser—so I paid my five grand and slid into a spot vacated by a Vegas councilman who sprained his ankle.

There was nothing Priscilla could do to keep me out of the party at the Heat Mansion, so she pretended to be pleased. I wonder if she's coming up here now to try to keep me away.

As if on cue, the door to my penthouse swings open with a whoosh of air. I let her get a few paces inside before I slam the door shut, jumping on her from behind. I sweep her up into my arms and tear her mink coat open.

She squeals, and I hear something drop. I spin her in a circle and see a big, leather bag sprawled on my floor.

"What did you bring me?"

She winks. "Why don't you open it and see?"

I strip Priscilla to her open-nipple bra and crotchless panties before I dump her on the bearskin rug in front of the fireplace and open the bag.

What's inside is vile. And it doesn't make my cock soften at all.

CHAPTER FOURTEEN

Elizabeth

WHEN MARCHANT RADCLIFFE started Love Inc., it was a high-end brothel on the Vegas Strip. According to the Wikipedia page, Marchant never wanted to open 'just another brothel'. He wanted a place where the escorts were treated like any other profession—they have excellent health insurance, 401Ks, and the top performers can even buy a stake in the company.

He wanted a different kind of clientele, too. Wealthy. Connected. Men and women who appreciated an upscale ambiance and a whole lot of privacy.

I'm guessing this must be Wiki's way of saying he wanted to keep the riff-raff out. Eliminate tourists, bachelors, and shut-ins.

After only a year or two, he opened another location in a rural area southwest of Vegas, on a plot of land so large it's a bonna fide green spot on my GPS. If I recall, it's something like two hundred acres. For several years, the location on the strip acted as a sort of gatekeeper. If the escorts liked a client or the client was regular enough, they got invited to the ranch. The strip location was swanky enough that it competed easily with more established places, so Love Inc. grew as a name-brand, but all the while, the ranch was building an identity of its own.

According to Forbes, the ranch location made more than

$600 million last year. It has two dozen full-time female escorts and seven full-time male escorts who live on the grounds, setting their own prices and choosing their own clients. Many of them have worked there five years or more. The place has a job-satisfaction rating higher than Google.

Somehow, the Love Inc. Ranch has come to be known as the 'fluffy bunny' ranch. I've heard it's not fluffy—all kinds of prostitution goes on there, even some of the more hard stuff—but it's nicer than most similar places.

I bypass Vegas, veering onto an interstate and following it southeast. It's eight thirty, and I'm starting to get a serious case of belly bats: the more menacing cousins of butterflies.

It takes me almost forty minutes to get past Vegas and into the dry, flat land to the southeast of the city. In that time, I manage to contain my excitement/horror/hysteria by clinging to the 'fluffy' part of this place's nickname. I think about sparkling fixtures; plush, animal skin rugs; gleaming hardwoods; gourmet foods; and beds so soft you might actually want to climb into them with a stranger.

I veer off the highway onto a smaller, freshly paved two-lane road, its dark asphalt gleaming in the glow of an almost-full moon. Suddenly there are lamplights, and although the land on each side of the road is desert dirt, my GPS tells me I'm within eight miles of my final destination.

Holy belly bats!

I can't believe I'm actually doing this.

As I grip the wheel, I wonder who will greet me. Richard? The manager, Rachelle? What if it's Marchant? When I spoke to Richard this morning, he didn't say. Why didn't I ask?

I look down at myself. What if I'm not dressed right? Should I have worn a skirt or something? Maybe something more glam? Black slacks? My trusty old Manolos? I slow my car, pulling over on the side of the road, and reapply my lipstick. It's red, at least. That should be a good thing—I think.

As I flip my mirror shut, headlights, then tail-lights, wink past me. I recognize the shape of the vehicle: a limousine.

I pull back onto the road, excited and frightened to see that, just ahead, a billboard shines over the road.

I squint and slow down.

'Selling Scarlett'. And there I am, stretched out on my stomach, airbrushed and fake-tanned, but still very much the version of myself I was about a week ago when Richard asked me to send these pictures. I'm on a billboard, stamped with the Love Inc. Symbol.

Holy moly. Suri did a nice job posing me against white sheets in the great room. I don't even look like me. I look...like an escort.

My stomach clenches, and I try to feel okay about that.

Another half-mile, and there's another Love Inc. billboard. This one features a stunning black-haired beauty with yellow eyes and a supple, suntanned body clad in jade green lace. She's opening a bedroom door, beckoning with her finger, the tiniest smile on her cat-like lips.

Another half-mile and another one. Except that this one has an arrow, pointing to a road that intersects this one. There's a brick guardhouse, and metal arms blocking both the entrance and exit.

Oh my God. I'm really here.

I roll my window down with a sweaty fingertip, and the beautiful face that appears behind the glass is framed by long, curling red hair.

"Scarlett!" She grins. "You're the VIP tonight." She leans to the left, and a door behind her, inside the guardhouse, opens. Out steps a tall, bulky man with thinning brown hair and a devilish smile.

"Scarlett." He stretches his hand out the window.

I grab it. "Richard." I recognize his voice.

"How do you like the sign?" he rumbles.

I blush. “It looked very...professional.”

The redhead laughs. “Nice save.” Her voice is kind. Warm. “I’m Marie V.” She stretches out her hand, and I smell a pleasant scent that reminds me of sunlight and linen. “It’s my off-night,” she explains, “so I’m on booth duty for a few hours. The clients like being welcomed by a familiar face.”

I nod, because my brain is blown. “Why don’t you drive on through?” Richard says. “The valets will take your car and you’ll be met in the doorway by some very friendly women who will help you get acquainted with the place.”

Marie V. leans forward. “There’s food, too. Make them take you to Alan, our cook-slash-guard. Or,” her eyes gleam, “if he’s already on his way back out here, just go grab a sweet roll. They’re amazing.”

She looks so mischievous, so gleeful, that I can’t help smiling. “Thank you. I feel ten percent less nervous.”

“Make it one-hundred,” she says, and Richard chuckles.

“There’s nothing to be nervous about, Scarlett. We don’t bite—unless you ask.”

I can barely think straight as I drive ahead, following a curl of asphalt that rolls through unnaturally green grass, beneath enormous trees between whose branches I can see the winking stars. Lamp posts line the road, but it’s the greenery that really gets me.

It doesn’t belong anywhere near here. In fact, it reminds me a little of New Orleans. Then I remember that Marchant Radcliffe went to Tulane—where he met Hunter—and I shake my head. Well, duh.

The driveway rolls on forever. After almost ten minutes, the trees thin and the iron lamp posts glow a little brighter. I’m reminded of my Hugo readings as I notice the stone wall rising ten or fifteen feet above the drive, on my right side; a fountain featuring mermaids, lit with spotlights; bird baths; benches; gardens.

Then I crest a small hill and see an expanse of soft, gold light, and my eyes focus on the largest English manor house I've seen in all my travels.

Holy crap, it's bigger than a castle. My gaze clings to the balconies, doors, windows, and ivy crawling the stone mansion, visible behind the flickering light of torches. My mouth drops ever further when I realize there are two smaller manors situated in a horse-shoe around the driveway.

I gape at the brutally trimmed shrubs and the fruit-bearing trees that blot my view of the open sky. I feel like I'm in the South. Of England.

"Gorgeous..."

A plump white rabbit flits in front of my car, and I laugh. So that's the fluffy bunny thing! I roll another hundred yards or so and come to a stop right in front of the manor. A valet in a red and black uniform comes down the stairs, trailed by two bellmen pulling a cart. My luggage is loaded onto the cart while a woman in a beautiful royal blue gown appears on the stairs. She steps out to greet me.

"Scarlett. I'm Juniper Francis. Come inside. Your luggage will follow you." She's British—or a prostitute that specializes in voice fetishes (if that's a thing). She's got coal black hair with stylish bangs; her hair is pulled into some kind of up-do that compliments her flawless, porcelain doll face.

I glance at my brown slacks and soft blue blouse, feeling dowdy. My heart beats hard as I step up the stairs, and the woman—Juniper—holds out both hands to me. I take them, with only a little hesitation, and she squeezes my hands.

"You're the one on the billboard," I realize.

She laughs. "So are you."

We pass through two huge, thick wooden doors held open by women wearing black and red skirt uniforms, and I try not to gape at the vast foyer. It has to be at least thirty feet high, with ornate, white-washed wood walls and three-pronged iron candelabras that flicker as we move. Directly above my head is a sparkling crystal chandelier, and a few steps in front of me, an ornate double staircase that seems to fall out of the sky. I'm blinking up at it when I hear a good-natured chuckle. I look down, into the laughing brown eyes of a striking African-American woman. She's tall and curvy, dressed in a cream gown that's part partywear, part nightgown.

"Hi." Her red lips curve. "I'm Geneese Loveless. You must be Scarlett." Her smile widens. "You're so pretty!"

Geneese holds out her hand, and Juniper clasps my other one, and together we walk around the stairs, through another set of smaller, but just as ornate double-doors, and into a room so huge I can only describe it as cavernous.

I'm struck first by the size of it—it's as big as half a football field, for sure—and next by how *much* there is. There are so many little nooks, each with its own couch, love seat, and recliner; right offhand, I count at least twenty of them. The room is further divided by huge bookshelves, made cozier by coat racks and partial walls and house plants. The three dark wood walls framing the room are punctured by huge, two-story windows. The rug running under everything—a soft, camel-colored fabric—spans the entire room.

"Holy heck—" I say, embarrassed by my language.

"The rug?" Loveless asks. "Yeah, it's really, really big."

"It's a custom job, of course," Juniper says, and all I can think is blow job.

We stop beside a big desk that looks like it belongs in the oval office. The woman sitting behind it, looking at several rows of security monitors, smiles at me and says, "Hello. I'm Rachelle."

"Nice to meet you," I murmur. I'm hardly even looking at her, although she's very pretty with blonde Curly Temple hair and doll-sized blue eyes. There's so much going on behind her shoulder, I feel A.D.D. trying to take it all in. There are several mini bars, two elevator banks, a hallway cutting into each wall, and so many decorative details: moldings, glasswork, antique-looking fixtures, you name it.

"This is the heart of the main house," Rachelle says kindly. "It can be a little overwhelming at first, but it's really very cozy."

As if on cue, a beautiful blonde in a ruby red gown leads a young man in an obviously bespoke suit to one of the elevators. I can hear him telling her about his day as they pass.

"All that's left is the signatures."

She applauds. "Your first merger!"

This is real, I want to say out loud, because it seems like—okay, I guess it is a (former) frat boy's idea of paradise. *This place is really freakin' real. This is where people come to sell their bodies*.

The notion makes me feel frozen, so it's a good thing Geneese tugs on my hand. "Want to work out with us? Our shift just ended, and it's boxing night."

I'M TIRED, AND I don't really want to work out, but if this is what they do at Love Inc., I will do it. I can already tell this place is its own little universe, and the last thing I want is to stick out more than I already do.

Juniper and Geneese have let go of my hands, so I feel a less like a five-year-old.

"There are stairs that we could take," Geneese says, as we pass a brunette in a pale green gown, sitting on one of the couches, reading a magazine, "but it's hard to look elegant going up the stairs. Anyway, you ever boxed?"

"I have before." I spot another couple—both with black hair—sitting together on a love seat, and Juniper explains, "This is where we meet our clients. They have to pass Rachelle and the cameras and then they wait for us in a pre-set spot. It's a security measure. Marchant Radcliffe—that's the guy who built this place—based it on the dormitory system at his uni."

I nod as we pass a beautiful bookcase and a little nook filled with suede bean bag chairs. The rug under my feet is spotless and looks soft enough to lie on. About twenty yards ahead, rising from the floor and up into the ceiling, is the nearest elevator bank. The elevator is old-fashioned and iron—pretty, if an elevator can be pretty.

"It's beautiful here."

"Some of us have rooms here," Juniper says. "The others bunk in the whorehouse."

I must look surprised, because she blinks. "You do know there's an actual whorehouse where we're made to fuck for our dinner, yes?"

I'm totally confused, and totally at a loss for what to say, when Geneese elbows Juniper. "Girl, that's so wrong."

"So I hear, so I hear." Juniper smiles wickedly, and Geneese presses the "4" button on the elevator.

"Your room will be here in the main house, with some of the girls who can't get on with the others, or have a wooden leg, or need to be watched closely," Juniper says as the doors glide open.

I smile weakly, hoping she's joking.

Geneese pulls me inside and then releases my hand. "I'm kind of a touchy feely person," she says smiling. "You have to bat me off."

I smile back at her, and she laughs. "You look nervous. Don't be nervous. This is a good place. You'll like it here."

I nod. "This is a first for me."

"Well of course," Juniper says. "You're a virgin."

The doors ding open, and we file into a hardwood hall with a deep crimson runner. The walls are done in creamy velvet wallpaper, and the ceilings are high, dark wood, punched in little hexagons where the chandeliers are mounted. On this floor, they're spindly and brass.

"It smells delicious," I say, and Geneese smiles. "This place is supposed to be appetizing."

The hall ends in a rounded nook where a portrait of a half-nude woman hangs, spotlighted and framed by gold tassels.

We walk a few more steps and Juniper pulls out a key, sticks it in the antique-looking brass lock on one of the wide, wood doors, and pushes the door open. It creaks, and as soon as it swings open I can smell flowers.

Geneese waves her hand for me to go first, and as I step inside the lights come on automatically. A few steps on lush hardwood topped by a thin oriental rug, and I'm out of the small foyer and into a large living area. I've been in enough million-dollar homes to know the furniture and fixings are all nice, none of that mass-produced hotel crap. The claw-footed Victorian couch is really a Victorian couch, and the dainty chairs on either side, covered in lush lime green fabric, are probably also from England. A glance beyond my immediate surroundings reveals mirrors, original artwork, and framed photos adorning the walls, and a full kitchen to my left. There's a dark hall out in front of me, and at the mouth of it is all my bags.

"That was fast," I say.

"We aim to please. Why don't you come and see your room?"

Geneese waves me down the hall; she and Juniper follow. I almost gasp when I see the bedroom. At the center is the biggest canopy bed I've ever seen in my life, with lush crimson bedding, yellow and cream pillows, and a canopy so thick it actually creates walls around the bed.

At the foot of the bed is an old-fashioned soaking tub, and all along the outermost wall are windows—no, doors. Doors that lead onto a candle-lit balcony.

"This is really nice," I say, feeling almost intimidated.

"We want you to feel like a princess when you are here,"

Juniper says.

"Oh, I do." I turn a slow circle, and Geneese says, "I've always liked this room. You got a good one."

"I believe it."

They go into the living area while I change, and as soon as the bedroom door shuts behind them, I drop into the nearest chair and put my head into my hands. My cheeks feel warm, my heart is racing, and my stomach is about to fly out of my chest. Damned belly bats.

I stand up, dig some work-out clothes out of my bag, and pace as I wriggle into them. It's not just nerves, I realize. Some of what I feel right now is real anxiety. That I don't belong here. That I can't handle the task ahead of me. That I'll fail.

A virgin at a brothel...

I'm in way over my head.

I try to talk myself up as I pull my hair into a ponytail. I think about Cross and Suri and Crestwood Place, with its familiar fields and my familiar bedroom, smelling like my favorite vanilla bean lotion and coffee from the Keurig I keep right beside my bed. I picture myself reading one of my text books, and I remind myself that I can use this experience as school research. That makes me feel a little more level, so I'm gathered as I make my way into the living area.

Juniper grins as I step out of the hallway. "Looking sharp," she says, and Geneese points. "Your legs are so long and tight."

"I bet yours are much better," I say.

"Psshh. I don't think so. You sure you're game for working out? You had a long trip if you drove. I wasn't thinking about that earlier."

"No, I'm okay. I want to see more of the place, and I missed my work-out today, so this is good."

Juniper gives me the story of how Love Inc. came to be as we walk back to the elevators, and it's pretty much what I read on Wiki. Back on the first floor, we exit out a side door and follow a tree-lined stone walkway around a small garden. The path leads us to one of the smaller manor houses, and as we approach it, I can see the curtains hanging in the windows don't match—some are red, some blue, some pink.

"This is where the escorts and the trainers and the tutors live," Loveless tells me. "Behind the main house—" she points between the main house and the manor where the staff lives—"is another wing where Marchant and his buddies have their private suites. The other building across the way," she says, pointing across the courtyard at the third manor house, "is where we do official things, like see a doctor or go to the media lab or study if we want. If someone comes out here, like to fix the roof or a plumber or something, that's where Rach meets them. Can't have strangers in and out of the main house."

"There are privacy issues," Juniper says.

"That makes sense. Is Marchant Radcliffe here often?" I ask. I feel slightly nauseated, but Juniper shakes her head. "He's in and out. He trusts Richard and Rachelle to keep us straight."

The door opens for us from the inside, and we step into a smaller, more relaxed version of the 'main house.' It's decorated in vibrant lavender, deep purple, and silver, with silver fixtures, a ping-pong table, a pool table, and a cheery fireplace.

"This is our building," Geneese says. "You can call me Loveless, by the way. Everybody else does."

I follow them to the second floor, past identical faux wood doors decorated by welcome mats and the occasional potted plant. While we walk, Loveless and Juniper tell me about the gym below the building. As I wait for them to change, sitting in a plush chair outside Juniper's room, I feel awkward again, like the new girl, and I wonder how much they like me, or if they feel obligated to entertain me. I decide eventually that they both seem real enough, and even if they're being phony, there's no point in worrying about it.

A few minutes later, Juniper emerges from her flower-adorned doorway in nothing but a black leotard and hot pink sneakers. She smiles and hands me a bottle of Evian. "I'm glad you're working out with us. I was wondering about you." Before she says exactly what she was wondering, she asks, "Do you have your own bag?"

"Gym bag?"

She shakes her head. "Punching bag."

"Not my own, but I've used them at gyms."

"It's therapeutic," she smiles, but I get the feeling she doesn't have too many demons.

She slants an eyebrow at me and gives me a look that's caught somewhere between a smile and a smirk. "I know what you're thinking," she says coyly. "I'm British, and I don't seem like a whore."

I gape, although that isn't really what I was thinking—I'm too shell-shocked to have gotten that far—and Juniper bursts out laughing. I make a mental note that *she* doesn't think she seems like a whore. I'll enjoy dissecting that later.

"I am an escort," she says, "but I'm also a cliché."

"Huh?"

She grins. "I'm a student. I'm studying at a distance, and later I'll probably also teach that way. But this has been my job for seven years."

My eyes widen, and she nods. "I'm an expert in the field of cock and balls."

Now it's my turn to crack up. We're both smiling when we get to Loveless's room.

She comes out in turquoise tights, an orange sports bra, and high-top trainers, looking like a model for sports clothes. As she turns to lock her door, she looks over her shoulder.

"I can't wait to get to know you. We haven't had any new blood in months."

"Druscilla," Juniper reminds her.

"That girl's as exciting as a roll of toilet paper."

Juniper elbows Loveless. "A soft, sweet roll."

"True," Loveless says. "But Scarlett, she's got secrets."

I laugh, though my heart is in my throat. "Secrets?" I shake my head. "I'm afraid I'm an open book."

But Juniper nods. "Richard hasn't told us anything about you. I mean, flat-out nothing. You're shrouded in mystery."

"Am I?"

"Well, a few of us know you want to keep everything quiet," Loveless says.

I chew my lip. "Wow. I didn't realize Richard had discussed me with anyone else."

"Just Loveless and Rachelle," Juniper tells me. "Rach is the manager here, as I'm sure you know, and Loveless is the Head Girl." I arch a brow, and they both laugh. "We try to keep it light," Loveless says. "And I do give mean head."

I blush, and Juniper says, "You will, too, before it's over. We'll teach you."

When my eyes widen, she says, "Don't worry. We'll use a dildo."

Loveless nods as I try to get my face to return to its regular color. "You've got a whole box of treasures waiting in your room. But we can talk about the sexin' later. For now, we want to hear more about you."

My stomach flips, and I hate myself for it. For being so unsmooth. I'm in my twenties now. I should be more confident. Less afraid of what everyone thinks. After firing off a quick, sarcastic thank you to my Mom, who's got to be the source of my perpetual fear of others' judgments, I sigh. "What do you want to know?"

"Where are you from?" Juniper asks.

Seeing no reason to lie, I say, "I'm from California."

"Wouldn't be the Napa Valley area, would it?" Loveless asks me. She's wiggling her eyebrows.

I gape, truly taken aback, and they eagle-eye me.

I quickly pull it together, feeling a little more confident as we file into a stairwell. "Why do you ask?"

"No reason," Juniper says. "We've got one of those Superman kind of clients. Loveless and a few of the other girls are half in love with him. Quite pathetic, really."

"I am not," Loveless says defensively. "He's just a mystery. Well, he was," she says, looking troubled.

"Who is he?" I ask, trying maybe too hard to be one of the girls. Honestly the thought of any client scares the crap out of me.

Loveless looks over her shoulder, casual as can be. "His name is Hunter."

"Hunter." I barely have enough air in my lungs to get the word out; I'm slayed by the image of Hunter locked around beautiful Loveless.

"We should go by first name only," Juniper interjects. "Privacy," she tells me with her brows arched. "Hunter's been a client here for years, but he mainly just sees Sarabelle, Loveless, and Marie V."

I'm silent as I imagine Marie V. and Loveless with their paws on Hunter.

Hunter visits Love Inc.? The shock of it makes my chest ache, although why am I surprised? His BBF owns the place.

We push through a metal door, into a hallway that quickly leads us into a fabulous gym, and my brain is so rattled I'm barely able to follow them over to a hot pink mat. Hunter visits escorts to have sex. Hunter comes *here*. Holy shit, this is bad news. Holy shit. I can't run into Hunter *here*!

"What happened to make him stop coming?" I manage after a moment. Automatically I expect a joke about my wording, so I'm kind of surprised when they exchange a dark look.

They both look somber. Loveless, especially, has a blank look in her eyes. "It makes me so upset, to think about that," she says quietly. "Something terrible happened."

CHAPTER FIFTEEN

Hunter

I GO THROUGH Priscilla's handbag while she's cleaning herself up in the guest bathroom. Just when I think my efforts are futile, I find a receipt from a couple of days ago, signed by M. Lockwood, from a place called MIGHTY'S down in San Luis, Arizona, of all places.

I fold it and slide it into a desk drawer. I'm surprised to find my fingertips shaking just a little. With what? Anger? Excitement that I'm adding another flag on the trail of clues, even if I still don't know where it's leading me yet?

I realize belatedly, as I sink down on a leather chair to catch my breath, that I'm shaking because my back is ripped to shreds. The next heartbeat, I'm raging, because she *did* come to my place to keep me away from the party tonight, and my stupid ass let her. I let her flay me because when she placed the whip in my hand and bent over in front of me, I heard Rita's voice inside my head, telling me what an evil little shit I am. I started having flashbacks of the day when I proved to both of us that she was right, and I would rather be whipped than have to feel like I'm the perpetrator—even if in this case, I'd just be giving a fucked up woman what she wants.

Now that the fog has cleared, I feel so stupid that I let her whip me. I also feel sticky blood on the back of my boxer-briefs.

I stand up. "Fuck." I even got a little on the chair.

I'm shaking in earnest now, because if there's anything I hate, it's fucking blood. I turn a circle, squeezing my eyes shut as I realize I can't go clean this off of me, because I can't leave Priscilla alone in my house.

I grit my teeth against the throbbing pain and push a chair in front of the bathroom door. Then I rush back to my bedroom, where I keep a first aid kit. I grab a fresh pair of boxer briefs, a black towel, and an Ace bandage, figuring gauze won't be enough to keep the blood off my tux.

My stomach churns as I stride back into the living area. Priscilla is pounding on the bathroom door. "Hunter, you bastard! I have a party to host at my mansion!"

I shove the chair aside and she strides out, looking like an evil creature in her fluffy coat. "Hunter," she says with mock concern as her eyes flick over my face and shoulders. "You're bloody and you're pale as a ghost. You need to go lie down. You look like hell."

When I lock my jaw and hold out the bandage, her blue eyes widen. "Surely you don't expect me to..."

"Yes, I do, Priscilla." I hand her the bandage and the little metal clasps and turn around, trying to ignore her as she gasps and starts piling on the faux sympathy. "Oh you poor doll. This has to be excruciating."

"Yeah, yeah," I mutter. "Just start wrapping."

"But Hunter, what you need to do is shower. If I wrap it like it is, you'll get an infection." I can hear the subtle note of gladness in her tone, the satisfaction as she assumes her plan is falling into place. "Hunter, I know we agreed to go as a pair, but why don't you stay in tonight? Just relax. You've earned it, surely?"

"Wrap my back, Priscilla." I level a look over my shoulder that I hope kicks her ass into gear, and a second later she starts wrapping.

She works quickly, and she's not gentle. The bandage is tight as she steps in circles around me, wrapping me from abs to collar. I clench my jaw and shut my eyes and inhale through my nose. Fucking Priscilla.

I can gauge the width and depth of the wounds by the way they feel under the bandage. The superficial cuts near my shoulders and my hips just sting, but the deeper slashes in the middle of my back throb with every heartbeat.

"Tell me if I hurt you," she says in her sing-song voice.

I wouldn't tell her this shit hurt if my life depended on it. Priscilla is a masochist, but she has a sadistic side, I learned tonight. She brought the whip to keep me out of the party, and she probably knew from the beginning that I'd never use it on her.

"All done," she says after what feels like a thousand years. Pain is a hot vice around my throat, clouding my mind, making my body cold and light enough that I feel like I could float away. I ignore this and dress myself, trying as hard as I can not to wince or even move stiffly.

"You have a high pain tolerance," she remarks as I slip into my coat. My stomach is churning because it hurts so much to lift my arms, but I give her a smug smile and move briskly as I grab my keys and slide my phone into my pocket.

Priscilla wants to take her limo, and I make the calculated decision to indulge her. I'd like to get as far off her radar as I can tonight, and acting easy-going will help with that goal. I tell her as we slide into the limo that I don't plan to be at the party long. I can see her perk up as she pours two glasses of chardonnay.

I arch my brow, roll my window down, and dump my glass out, and Priscilla laughs like it's the funniest thing she's ever seen. I smirk and lean forward a little in my seat. There's something irritating about being around a woman who knows she got the drop on me. Makes me feel weak.

I'm pissed off by the time we roll up to the gaudy monstrosity that is the Heat Enterprises mansion: two stories of sleek gray stone with massive gold lions guarding the blood red doors. In between the street and the mansion, there's a moat and drawbridge. The water in the moat glows sparkly red.

Priscilla grins when she sees the place.

We spend thirty minutes, if not longer, greeting a long line of Priscilla's acquaintances, everyone from city officials to local mafia. I get caught with her when a gossip columnist pulls out her camera. I don't duck out of the picture, but I don't smile either.

The house is tricked out with cameras in every wall; speakers in every ceiling; and a red, orange, and yellow ("heat") color scheme in every room. Every table is stocked with pamphlets explaining domestic violence, the charitable cause to benefit from tomorrow night's fights.

Priscilla flits off with one of her camera people to pose for a photo with the assistant mayor—only in Las Vegas would the assistant mayor attend a porn star's benefit—just about the time I start feeling sick.

It's my back. I can feel every fucking heartbeat in the gashes there. I'm on my way to the bathroom when I get intercepted by Marchant's cousin, Samuel. I talk to him for twenty minutes about some development ordinance he wants the city to pass. He wants me to help, and I have no fucking idea what he's talking about, my back hurts so bad.

I mutter an "excuse me" and shake my head. "Migraine," I croak, and he says, "Ow. I'm sorry, man. Those things hurt."

"They do."

"Take care."

Fat chance.

I spend the next five minutes in a frou frou yellow bathroom, where I text Dave and let him know I haven't seen Smith or Lockwood yet.

'I'm here, outside,' he replies. *'Lwd just arrived.'*

Hell, yes. I'm stepping back into the formal dining room

when I feel something trickle down my back. My stomach heaves—blood—and I whirl around to step back into the john just in time to see some lady close the door. Fuck. I step toward the food-piled table, telling myself to quit being such a pussy, but the punch is blood red and there's steak laid out on a platter right in front of me, swimming in...

Fucking fuck!

I set off down the hall, swallowing repeatedly, ignoring one of Priscilla's cohorts, a pretty porn star named Cinnamon Vern. The nearest door is only steps away, and I'm reaching for the crystal knob when I hear Priscilla's voice.

I lean closer to the door, but her voice gets softer. She's not in this room, but she's somewhere nearby.

I notice another door a few feet down and walk swiftly to it. In the seconds that follow, I hear a male voice, too, rising and falling in turn. I'm only standing there for a moment when I recognize it from a tape I heard in Marchant's office: It's Lockwood. He says something low that I can't hear, and Priscilla laughs.

"I ripped up his back. He's trying to play it off, but he can barely walk."

Lockwood chuckles, and my throat feels tight. My heartbeat races as I stand there, stiff as a statue with my head leaned to the door.

"Go for his left shoulder blade. I think there's some ceramic impacted, broken off from the end of my cat. It was swollen, and I noticed in the car he's not moving that arm much."

I clutch my stomach; it feels hollow.

"I don't want to do that," Lockwood says. I frown, confused. "I don't give a shit about the fight, and it's a bad idea to match me up with him anyway. I don't want anything to do with that sonbitch. I'm keeping my nose clean."

"Honey, there's not a thing about you clean," Priscilla drawls.

He says something angrily, but for some reason it's muffled.

"Don't be silly," Priscilla says, and Lockwood groans, "Just finish the damn job."

Priscilla murmurs something I can't hear, followed by: "He doesn't like to hurt a lady." She snorts, like the notion is ridiculous.

"Which is why you're supposed to *make* him like it," Lockwood snaps. "And get it on tape."

She laughs under her breath. "I never have time for that."

"Yeah, because you're thinking with your pussy."

"He's a good fuck."

"Congratulations, now do you want to do time in prison, or do you want to frame this son of a bitch and go to Mexico with me?"

"Is she still alive?" Priscilla asks softly.

"Yes," he says, after a moment's pause. "Now get down on your knees and—"

I slip into the next room and get sick.

Elizabeth

I SEE LOVELESS'S big, brown eyes, and I see her swallow, like it hurts to even think about. Juniper squeezes her arm and Loveless's mouth flattens.

"Maybe we shouldn't talk about this," Juniper whispers.

Loveless shakes her head. "Scarlett should know."

"If you think."

And I can't hold it in anymore. "Are you talking about the

girl who disappeared?"

They both freeze. I watch as their mouths curve down in unison. Juniper nods. Loveless says, "Yeah. She was my next-door-neighbor. Sarabelle. I trained her when she started. Three years ago, I think." She opens her mouth, like there's so much more she wants to say, but in the end she just shakes her head. "We're praying for her."

"It makes me furious," Juniper says.

"Me, too, but here's the thing, Scarlett. You need to know a girl disappeared from here. I don't know if Richard told you but I'm the Head Girl and I want you to know. If you ever feel uncomfortable around any man, or something happens that doesn't seem right, you need to let me know."

I nod.

"Probably best not to bring it up," Juniper advises me. "We miss her, some of us more than others, but we're family here, so it's a hole in all our hearts."

"I'm sorry to hear about it," I say as we reach the punching bags. "But, uh, what does—was Hunter the name of the guy from California?" They nod. "What does Hunter have to do with this?"

"He was the last one to have her," Juniper says with one eyebrow raised.

THE NEXT MORNING, when I eat breakfast with Juniper, Marie V., and Loveless, all I can think about is Hunter and whatever happened here, with Sarabelle. I'm disappointed when the subject doesn't come up again over breakfast, and I tell myself that's crazy. I should be glad no one's talking about Hunter. Just like I should be glad he doesn't come here to see the escorts anymore. I'm not glad about the reason he's staying away, but I'm glad I won't run into him.

Juniper has today off, at least until four, so she shows me all around the place and I learn a little more about Marchant. Rachelle and he have known each other since college, and everyone used to think it would be just a matter of time before they wound up in bed together.

"But they use restraint," Juniper says. "I'm not sure who they fuck. Marchant seems positively virginal when he's out here, although I know he must get most of his pussy in the city. Rachelle is different. I really think she's sworn it off. I'm not sure how. Orgasms are the best thing in the whole wide world. Don't you think so?"

I blush, but I'm proud that I can manage a response. "They are."

"So tell me how it is that you're a virgin, darling? Just never met the right one?" I think about Hunter and feel my cheeks and throat color again.

"Yeah. Just haven't found the right one."

"Well Mr. Right will pay you rather handsomely I'd bet. In fact," she laughs, "we're all betting. I'm putting my money on a randy bidder for those long legs of yours."

I smile, feeling warmed by her compliment. "I've never heard anyone use the word 'randy' outside regency-era novels."

"I bet you've never had a lesson on deep-throating, either, am I right?"

We're en route to one of 'the rooms,' and I've been wondering exactly what we'll do. Hearing this, I nearly fall flat on my face.

Juniper smirks. "I guess you do have virgin ears, but a virgin throat?" She shakes her head. "No more. No worries, though, you're learning from the best." She gestures to herself. "Men pay thousands for this throat. It's not as unpleasant as you might expect either, if you know what you're doing."

"So you're my sex teacher?"

She winks. "Anything you want."

"Does that mean I'm supposed to...give the winner a blow job?"

"No, not at all. But Richard felt you might appreciate some bonus lessons, for whoever might be Mr. Scarlett one day, or boyfriend of Scarlett." She smiles. "If it weren't for this, you'd be with Brenda all day, and that's not good, I'm afraid."

"Who's Brenda?"

"Your trainer. She'll be responsible for all your beauty matters. And though they're few, she's sure to make them count. She might order you a waxing, or many miles of running, or perhaps a new hairstyle." Juniper yawns, and mutters, "Sleepless night. I've got a boyfriend in London."

"You do?" I gape, and she nods. "He wants me to quit my job, but he's a poor man and he can't support me. A soldier, in fact. Coming here in several weeks. I'll have to take the time off, but truth is I'm rather excited for it."

We slip into easy chatter, but behind it I'm thinking about Hunter. An escort disappeared from his room. What happened? The girls have all been careful not to say, so I know there must be something there.

BY THE END of the day, I still haven't learned anything else about what happened. I have, however, been waxed, tanned, toned, and pampered with an hour-long massage, and given several new outfits selected by Brenda's personal shopper.

"We like our girls and guys to look a certain way. One that speaks to a certain kind of luxury," she explained. "You might have wonderful clothes, but we'd like you to wear ours while you're doing business here."

The outfits are beautiful—rich, soft fabrics and complimenting cuts—and the truth is, I love them. I feel sexy. I call Suri after dinner and get an update on Cross, who squeezed her hand today, and then call Mom, who's spending an evening away from rehab. I wonder who authorized that.

After an hour alone, most of which is spent wondering about Hunter and the missing girl named Sarabelle, and Googling my butt off but finding nothing, I grab my bag and head downstairs, wearing gray leggings, a royal blue sweater, and tall brown leather boots, to meet the escorts who worked day shift. Those of us who have tonight off are going somewhere fun.

As soon as I arrive in the nook nearest to the side door, Juniper pulls me into a hug and begins to brag about my prowess today. It makes me blush, but it also makes me a little happy.

"I want to know how your next guy likes it," Juniper tells me.

Everyone laughs, and Hannah, an escort all the way from India, asks if we want to see Thomas Bourne.

"Who?"

"He's a poker player," Loveless explains. "And one of Marie V.'s, but Hannah wants to recruit him."

"He's a beautiful man," Hannah says.

"Too skinny," says a girl named Cat.

"That's not why he's beautiful. It's more than just his body. It's his...everything." Hannah holds up her hands, miming a swoon, and Loveless bumps into her. "You sure it's not that dick you want?"

"Is it big?" Hannah asks innocently.

Five minutes later, Hannah has been outvoted. We won't be going to watch anyone play poker, which leaves me feeling defeated; I'd hoped, against all good sense, that I might see Hunter there.

"We'll go to the fight," Juniper says.

As we spill out the side door, Loveless winks at me. "All the men who come to Love Inc. will have their eyes on you, wondering who you are. You'll have cocks across the stadium standing on end."

"I'm not sure how much I like that," I say as we walk across the parking lot.

"You should like it, honey. It means more money for you."

"Do you guys feel safe, out and about? I mean...after what happened?" I've taken her light moment and turned it deadly serious, but Loveless doesn't take the bait. She tosses her hair, which tonight she's wearing straight down her back, and gives me a funny look out of the corner of her eye—one I think says 'I'm not talking about that.' In a normal, cheery voice, she says, "I feel real safe." She opens her handbag and holds up a Taser, and I gape. For the remainder of our brief walk to a stretch limo, she shows me how to work it.

We pile into the limo, driven by Rod, a Peruvian man who's also an escort, who declares, once everyone is in, "I'm tired of my female clients. I need a man tonight."

So we set off to find Rod a man and watch a fight. I lean my forehead against the window and I hope more than I should that I will find one, too. I'm tired of Hunter's memory—and the mystery of what happened to the missing escort—following me around here like a ghost.

CHAPTER SIXTEEN

Hunter

BY THE TIME I get to the Joseph Club at ten o'clock on Monday night, I'm going on forty-eight hours without sleep, and I know I don't need to be here.

The last two days have been...intense. In addition to my adventures with Priscilla, Marchant and I are going after Lockwood with everything we have. We've expanded the team —Julie, Roberto, and Dave have been joined by a retired CIA guy named Ted Burts, as well as Julie's friend Lay1a, a forensic IT specialist who once worked for the Las Vegas mayor's office—and our surveillance is 24/7.

If wishes were fishes I'd have a fucking sea, because I've spent the last two days wishing I'd had the sense to use my phone's recorder the other night at Heat Mansion. When I'm not wishing that, I'm making absolutely sure I heard what I think I heard. Can I trust myself?

I know I can, because there is one thing I remember clearly. It's that gut-shot feeling I got when I heard Priscilla say "He doesn't want to hurt a lady." Before that, I'd let myself believe that if Priscilla actually had anything to do with Sarabelle, she was as much a pawn as myself.

But I know now she's not, and it feels like someone stuck their steel-toed boot through my abdomen. I've only felt that way one time before. It was when I was nine and Rita turned on me for the first time.

I'd had chicken pox, and I was itchy and whiny. I overheard Dad worrying about my fever, which was high enough that I'd been delirious—although I was lucid at that moment, wrapped up in my Power Rangers sheet and spying on them from behind the couch. Rita sighed and said, "Maybe he'll sleep for a few days." She did this funny laugh that was deeper and said, in hushed voice, "Or more than a few."

Dad just laughed, and he told her to drink another glass of wine, but I had known by the tone of her voice that there was *more*. And there was.

I don't like thinking about that, so I try to stop. I'm in the basement underneath the arena, in a small, tiled locker room that reminds me of another basement. I need my mind clear tonight, so I try hard to think of something else as I shower and wrap my back.

I've been given some small black shorts to wear, but I can't face thousands of people in something that looks like an overgrown Speedo. Those things are bad enough in the damn pool, but I'll be jumping around out there. I'm well-endowed, and half the town doesn't need to see it. I pull my black gym shorts out of my duffel bag and tug them on over boxer-briefs.

I take a long look in the mirror, running a critical eye over my sallow face and tense shoulders. If I went out shirtless with this gauze wrapped around my torso, I'd look like a hospital runaway, but I can't stand the thought of lifting my arms to put a shirt on. Tough shit. I pick a light blue shirt from a charity triathlon I did last year and I feel sick by the time I've got it on.

I think I have a fever, and I know why. It's because of my back. I should see about getting some antibiotics, but for some reason, I haven't. I tell myself it's because I can't go in for an exam; word would get around. Last time I went to the ER, with a fractured ankle from an impromptu game of soccer with one of the neighborhood kids in Napa, one of the local San Fran gossip rags ran some bullshit story about me coming from a 'certain' area of town where I used to get my coke.

That stroll down memory lane makes me pissed, which should be a good thing since I need a little energy boost for the fight. But pissed leads me only one direction, and that's Priscil-la's. All I want to do now is smash my own reflection in the mir-ror.

My fist curls, and I come so close to doing just that, I have to go sit on the bench beside the shower and start taping up my hands. A shrink once explained to me the concept of mindful-ness. It's been useful before, and I try it now—paying attention to the stickiness of the sports tape. To the shape of my fingers as I wrap each one. I even give some thought to the scalding pain on my back, telling myself it hurts like hell, but I'm not dead or anything. Just keep breathing.

And I do.

But with every breath, I want to punch that fucking mirror.

How could I be so stupid?

How could I let her get so close?

Even before I thought I was being set up to take the fall for—for whatever the fuck is going on, I knew she was trying to blackmail me for sex. Why did I ever go along with it?

You know why.

Rita's face follows me as I pace.

I check the clock on the counter: twenty minutes till show time. I inhale deeply, and I remember Marchant's reaction when I first told him Priscilla and Lockwood were trying to frame me, after the gala the other night. I remember the pity. He knows how much I loathe her, and he has to know there must be some-thing more to my fucking her. Something sick and twisted.

And he's right—he just has no idea about the details.

I start jumping jacks. It's mundane and makes me dizzy from the horrible pain in my back, but it takes the edge off for a minute. When I feel like I'm going to fall over, I return to the bench beside the shower. I close my eyes and try to be still.

I wonder for the dozenth time about motive. Why me? And how far back does this shit go? Did Priscilla find out about my mother and decide in advance that I would be the perfect man to take the fall for kidnapping an escort? Is that why she told Marchant she wanted me there that night while they were filming? Did Sarabelle get snatched simply because she was with me? Or was it just chance? Did Priscilla drug me out of spite, because I'd chosen Sarabelle over her, and Lockwood went for Sarabelle out of simple opportunism? Maybe that's why Priscilla fired him. He snatched Sarabelle, and when he did, he dragged Priscilla into it with him.

I think about the governor's mistress going missing a year and a half ago, right before he started fucking Priscilla. Right around the time Lockwood stopped working security for him and started doing cameras for Priscilla. I wonder how likely it is that Lockwood kidnapped her and disposed of her for the governor. Maybe that's how he got his taste for kidnapping.

I feel sick, because Sarabelle is alive somewhere, being forced into God knows what. I want to go get her right now. And tonight in this fight, I want to bathe in Michael Lockwood's blood.

I slide thin gloves over my taped knuckles and remind myself that I can't. First, because the sight of blood makes me sick. But more importantly, because he could be our only route to Sarabelle.

Ted Burts and Roberto are scouring San Luis at this very moment—starting with MIGHTY'S bar, the only lead we really have—and Julie and Dave are with Lay1a visiting Priscilla and Lockwood's homes while they're out. We think we're close.

I've decided we've got three days more. Three more days to find Sarabelle or I'm going to the FBI myself. Priscilla can say whatever she wants.

I stare at myself in the mirror again, hoping I won't have to take that risk. Just the thought of it has me vibrating with rage. I check the clock. Marchant will be here in two minutes. I inhale deeply, trying to find the chill zone before we have to walk upstairs.

There's not enough time. I swing at the mirror, shattering it—and maybe my knuckles—in one mighty punch that sends glass raining all around me. The pain in my fist is good, blazing like fire.

I let myself drink it up. Inhale it. I take it inside and turn it into fuel.

I don't have time to clean this mess, so I meet March outside in the hall. He's got an envelope containing the name of my match-up: **Lockwood.**

Elizabeth

THE JOSEPH CLUB is like nothing I've ever seen. As far as arenas go, it's fairly ordinary; the yellow circus-tent exterior, with its sparkling, blood-red sign and showgirl ticket-punchers remind me we're in Vegas, but it's the crowd inside that widens my eyes and makes my palms sweat.

"Got them packed in like sardines, no?" Juniper is pressed against me, a vision in a skin-tight white pant suit and red pumps, her dark hair pulled into an elegant pony tail. Swimming through a sea of shoulders and elbows on my other side is Loveless, wearing a flouncy peach-colored dress that whirls around her gorgeous legs.

"It's like this every year," Loveless tells me as we battle our way through the crowd. "Priscilla Heat knows how to throw a party."

I'm chewing fruity gum; I nearly choke. "Priscilla Heat?"

"The one and only." She says it casually, but when she glances at my face, I must have that swallowed-a-bug look—and that gives me away. "I sense a story here," she murmurs.

"There's no story."

"Sure there's not."

"Story?" Juniper pipes in.

"No." I shake my head, making my loosely curling pigtails tickle my bare shoulders. "There's no story, I swear there's not. I've just heard of her. Kind of surprised she's doing something for charity."

"Ooh, there is *so* a story here. One that perhaps will tell us more about who Scarlett really is." Juniper smiles slyly, like she's already dredged the rotten truth out of me.

"I'm not saying a thing." I mime zipping my lips and follow Loveless, who's flattened her body against a cement wall and is trying to make her way through the gate that leads to our seats. Finally we make it from the outer walkway and concessions area into the arena. Loveless stops, eliciting several irritated shouts from the stalled crowd behind Juniper and I, and holds up her ticket. "Looks like we're that way," she says, pointing at the bleachers below our walkway.

She takes one of my hands and Juniper grabs my other one, and behind Jupiter, Hannah, and on we go. I glance down at my bright red daisy dukes and loose, silk strapless top—it's white and sparkly—and I pray I don't stick out like a sore thumb. Already I've noticed that the biggest difference between these gorgeous women and myself is my lack of muscle tone. Yeah, I've lost weight, but you can see my flab and cellulite if you look closely; they, on the other hand, are built like gymnasts, plus big boobs.

When we finally make it to our seats, I'm stunned to find

how close we are to the fighting platform. It looks bigger than anything I've seen on TV: a bouncy-looking blue platform about a third the size of a basketball floor, surrounded by red ropes that are attached to four yellow square posts at each corner.

A sunken, moat-like space surrounds the platform. It's packed with men in tight pants and women in bikinis, milling around a few feet lower than the lowest row of spectator seats. I notice a lot of fake tans and faker boobs and even what I think is probably fake hair. I wonder how many of these people are porn stars, and feel kind of embarrassed that I have no idea. I've never watched a porno.

As I sink into my plastic bucket seat, I'm listening to Juniper and Loveless with only half an ear. So when I hear the name "Hunter" I actually whirl around toward Loveless. She's got her head craned toward Juniper, who's reading the program and speaking loudly to be heard over the crowd.

"He'll be fighting someone named Lockwood," Juniper is saying. "There are five fights. Theirs is fourth."

Loveless is nodding when I realize my mouth is hanging open. I shut it and turn back toward the ring, but it's too late. Juniper reaches around Loveless and grabs my elbow, shrieking, "You are holding out on me!"

I frown, trying my best to give her a 'what the hell' look, but Loveless turns to Juniper. "Do you think she knows him?"

"Oh, I'd bet on it."

"I don't know what you guys are talking about," I say loudly. A guy with taped fists and tiny black shorts is leaning up and waving to the crowd on the other side of the arena, so the noise level is at max.

Loveless gently grabs my chin and makes me meet her eyes. "Hunter West. You know him? Don't you lie to me, woman."

"I'm not," I say, but I can feel my stupid eye brows arching like they do sometimes when I lie. I look down at my knees, then Loveless shrieks and I put my head down in my hands.

"Holy shit, Scarlett! You sneaky little bitch!"

"I'm not sneaky," I wail. "There's not a story here!"

"Oh, I'm quite sure she's lying," Juniper confirms.

A blonde, gray-eyed girl leans around her, wiggling her eyebrows. "What are we talking about?" she asks in a Southern accent.

"Oh, nothing," Juniper says.

"Later," Loveless says in my ear. She gives me a pointed look, one that says I should be sorry for lying, and I shake my head a little guiltily.

A minute later, music I think I recognize from *Rocky* starts playing over the intercom, and everyone's attention is shifted to the platform, where two guys are now stretching. I try to feign interest, but all I can think about is Hunter. I wonder how much space stretches from my chair and the ring. Twenty yards? Fifteen? Could he see me from the fight? What if he gets hurt?

You can't care, I tell myself. *He's not your boyfriend.*

He's a guy who has sex with escorts and dates porn stars. A guy who has been nice to me a time or two. On a rational level, I know my feelings for him are about as realistic as a middle school girl's crush on a pop star—and the chances of it being realized are pretty much the same, too.

But I have a bad gut feeling when I try to feel okay with the idea of him dating Priscilla. It's her I should be worried about; I did see his hands around her neck. But when you look at Priscilla, you can see the bad in her. It's a woman thing, I think. Women convey so much without using words. Once you've seen one catty bitch, you've seen them all. And I know how to spot a catty bitch. Whatever Hunter is doing with her, she wants it, and what I really believe is that he does not. Maybe I'm kidding myself; I'll probably never find out.

The two men fighting first start to circle each other, and it's a good distraction. As I watch the fight, I'm buoyed slightly by the other girls' enthusiasm. It only takes a second before word reaches my ear that the fighter with long black hair, Dominique Domino, is one of Marie V.'s clients. His opponent, a muscled guy with buzzed hair, is a porn star.

Loveless cups her hands around my ear. "But *he* also pays for Marie V."

I gape. "Why?" I say near her ear. I try to lower my voice while still being audible. "Can't he get all the booty he wants, like...on the job?"

She nods. "But he likes it kinky," she hisses. "He wants to keep his image clean, so as not to limit his films. That's why he pays Marie V. for the weird stuff." I don't even want to imagine what kind of depraved acts could ruin a porn star's reputation.

"I think he kind of likes her more than just professional," Loveless adds, and I arch my brows. "Oh."

She rolls her eyes. "That's a nice way of saying it."

I spend the rest of the fight wondering what she means, eventually deciding Marie V. is probably not a fan of either of these men's affections.

The fight only lasts two more minutes before Domino clocks the porn star—hard—making his nose spray blood and gaining his title in a fit of screaming and applause, and Loveless leans in close to me. "Domino is the possessive kind. Marie V. will have to cut him soon."

I wonder how many of those types of situations working women find themselves in, and I think I'll ask later. I'm feeling more comfortable with Loveless and Juniper now—more like we're friends. For not the first time, I wonder if I'm just a job to them, just like the men are, but I shove the thought away. If they think of me that way, it's not a bad thing. I don't need to get too attached. Plus, it wouldn't be fair to pretend to be friends when they don't even know who I am.

Juniper passes me a huge tub of popcorn, smiling, and it's like a confirmation that I'm right. We are becoming friends. I don't want to enjoy the feeling, but I let myself off the hook. It's easier to face everything with friends, even ones that don't know your real name. I feel truly at ease for the first time since I arrived at the ranch.

That feeling lasts through two more fights. Then Hunter walks into the ring.

Hunter

LOCKWOOD IS IN the corner opposite mine, looking surly but not threatening in red shorts and black sneaks. He's shorter than I am—maybe five-foot-ten—and without clothes to give him bulk, I can see his upper body is well-defined but lean. His biceps and pecs are oiled and his black hair is slicked back, so his sunken cheeks and sharply square jaw stand out like a caricature. His wary brown eyes haven't left my body since I came into the ring, but I've noticed he doesn't like to look me in the eye. The crowd around us cheers and he widens his legs, trying to adopt a more intimidating posture.

Right.

I've got maybe forty pounds on this guy, four inches or so, and I hate him down to his fucking cells. I think I'd kill him with my bare hands here and now if I didn't need him alive. I flex my hands inside my gloves and try to ignore the pain radiating from my back.

We're announced, and then we step forward to tap gloves. I look into Lockwood's eyes, and for a second he looks into mine, and there's plenty of hate there. I keep my expression cool, because I can't let him know that I know what he's up to.

Lockwood swipes at the air as he bounces back to his corner, and the crowd cheers with excitement. In addition to doing camera stuff for Priscilla, Michael Lockwood also fights semi-professionally—meaning he has fans.

The fight begins with the loud honk of a bullhorn and the crowd roars. He steps out of his corner first, but he's waiting for me to come at him.

I circle, looking for an opening. Of course, he doesn't give me one, so I lower my guard. He takes a swing. I jump back. He gets me in the shoulder, a hard sting that sends pain across my back in waves, but I keep moving, arms up, ready when the moment comes.

He peeks up for a second, and I smack the bridge of his nose. It feels good. He swings, and I think it's wild but he's aiming for my back. He connects, and as the pain erupts I curse myself for not expecting that.

The crowd cheers when my fist hits his jaw, but he was already turning out of it. I get a kidney shot, and then he's on me. He hits me on the shoulder, and, choking back a scream, I catch him in the temple with my elbow.

He dances back, and I follow hard, thinking I've got him. I go for a knock-out punch, and he side-steps to evade. A hard jab to my stomach, then a blow to my jaw. Everything whirls. He gets me in the hip, he gets me in the ear. I think I see Libby in the audience, and that moment of hesitation earns me a glancing blow across my cheek.

I get him in the teeth, and he spits blood at me. I slam him again in the nose and he goes down on one knee. I kick him in the shoulder. I punch him in the neck.

He falls back, and when his eyes flicker, he smiles a bloody smile.

"You're an evil bastard," he hisses. "Making that escort disappear."

And I change my mind. I'm going to kill this rotten bastard here and now.

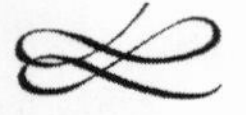

Elizabeth

SOMETHING'S WRONG WITH Hunter. I can tell the moment he steps into the ring. I've been watching him from afar for years, and I'm an old pro at his body language. Hunter West is a guy who's used to setting the agenda. His limbs are usually loose and relaxed, carried with the kind of self-assurance that comes from knowing you've got it all handled. So when he steps into the ring looking uncomfortable, those wide shoulders slightly hunched under a tight blue t-shirt, with eyes that look tired and heavy even from my vantage point, I feel worried.

Then the fight starts, and it's dirtier than the others. From Hunter's end and Lockwood's. A few times I catch his eye and I think he looks desperate. I cringe each time he gets hit, and I cringe each time he hits Lockwood, too. Eventually he knocks Lockwood down, and I sigh with relief. I watch Hunter lean over. Words must have been exchanged, because Hunter settles on one knee and starts punching Lockwood's face.

"Holy shit." Loveless, beside me, is leaning forward, both hands over her mouth.

My mouth is open, too, because Hunter is really going at it.

A whistle blows, but he won't stop. People in the crowd gasp. Men come and grab him, throw him down. Meanwhile, a nurse and a doctor are stepping in to check on Lockwood. Marchant steps in the ring behind them and helps Hunter to his feet. Someone throws a metal winner's chain sash over Hunter's head and I see him wince when it comes to rest on his back. He stalks away with Marchant, and I wonder where Priscilla is.

"Where's Priscilla?" I ask Juniper a minute later.

"She's out of town somewhere, in Canada I think. They're filming something huge there."

The crowd claps as Lockwood is helped to his feet. His face is a bloody mess, but he waves, drawing more applause.

The last fight is tamer, but the vibe inside this place is still a little...off. A little dark. I think about what Hunter did, and I begin to see holes in the story I created to make myself feel better about the whole Hunter-has-rough-sex-with-porn-stars thing. Because he certainly seemed to like violence in the fight.

"Want to go downstairs?" Loveless asks over the din of chatter. "See if we can get a view of the guys after they exit their prep rooms, post-shower?"

I do, but obviously I shouldn't. "I don't think so."

"Then let's get a drink. You can spill your Hunter story."

"Yes. You can," Juniper says.

I insist there is no story as I follow them to the bar that hangs out over the arena. We have to go up countless flights of stairs to get there, and when we finally arrive—in a dark den lit by flashing, multicolored strobe lights—I realize we've clomped to the very top of the arena.

Juniper goes to order our drinks, while Loveless and I take a seat at a yellow booth. She leans across the table, and I smile blandly, pretending I don't know what she's about to ask.

"What's your story, Scarlett? We trust you, now you trust us. What's your Hunter West story?"

I swallow hard, aware that I'm going to have to tell her something. It's only fair. Finally, after looking twice at the bar, hoping Juniper will be on her way back and I can postpone my sad tale until she arrives, I jump in head-first.

"I have a crush on him. But he doesn't know that I'm alive. I promise."

Loveless nods, like she's thinking this over carefully. She has a pretty good poker face, I realize as she purses her lips. "You know him from back home?"

I nod.

"So you are from Napa Valley?"

"Please don't tell anyone else. My family would be upset if—"

She reaches across the table, grabbing my hand, which is curled into a nervous fist. "Your secret's safe with me."

"Pinky swear?" I smile a little, and we latch pinkies.

"Pinky swear." Loveless stands abruptly and leans down. "Will you be okay for a minute by yourself?"

I nod. "Sure."

Without giving me an explanation, she slips into the crowd. I'm following her as she drifts over to the right, back toward the stairwell, when my eyes latch onto Hunter.

He's leaning against a corner of a smooth, mahogany bar, drinking something out of a glass. Probably West Bourbon. He looks really, really tired, and he's holding his left shoulder like it hurts. He's swaying gently back and forth, and I get the impression he's looking for someone.

I consider not going over to him, because I don't know for sure that Priscilla isn't here. But I can't stop myself.

I stop right in front of him, and it takes his eyes a second to lock onto my face.

"Libby?" The word is low and almost strangled, and I immediately wonder if he doesn't want to talk to me.

"It's Elizabeth," I say smiling a little ruefully, "but I answer to Libby as long as it's coming from you." I look into his eyes, waiting for him to smile, and when he doesn't—the left corner of his mouth twitches a little, but he can't seem to summon a smile—I feel that worried sting again.

I look him over: his damp blond hair, the handsome face that's bruised along the jaw and around his right eye, the green eyes he's barely holding open. He's wearing a faded blue button-up that's rolled up to his elbows, over black slacks and casual loafers. My eyes make it to his hands and I can't suppress a gasp.

They're wrapped in white gauze, but the brilliant stain of blood is already showing through the knuckles.

"Holy crabcakes."

"Lost my gloves," he murmurs, looking weary and distracted. I remember; he didn't lose them—he pulled them off, to go at Lockwood with his bare fists.

I step a little closer to him, enticed by the warm, earthy smell of his cologne. "What happened out there?" Immediately, I wish I hadn't asked that. It's so nosy. Prying. So I rephrase. "Are you okay? You just look...really tired and I noticed you were bleeding on your back."

He blinks, and whatever daze was over him, it's lifted. His eyes narrow, and he's back to shrewd Hunter. He brushes a hand down one of my pig-tails, fingering my brown hair gently. I can see his tired face soften as his eyes search mine. "What are you doing here, Libby? I saw you sitting with Geneese Loveless."

I shrug, scrambling for a way to play it off. "We're old friends."

"So you're friends, are you?" His tone sounds weird. Almost…too interested. *As if.* He chews his lip, and I think I just might die of Sexy. "It's...anthropology or sociology. Ethics?"

I grin, irrationally pleased. "How'd you know?"

He shakes his head, bringing the glass of amber liquid to his lips. When he lowers it, he's smirking. "Lucky guess."

My heart is probably about three beats away from bursting through my blouse.

But Hunter's expression quickly darkens. Worry creases his brows, and his full lips meld into a pensive line. "You should be careful with Loveless. She's...a hard-hitter. So are some of her friends."

I wonder what on earth he means by this, and then I realize and it takes every ounce of willpower I possess to swallow back a laugh. *That's* how he describes prostitutes? *Hard-hitters?* I lick my lips, somehow managing to restrain myself. It's probably best to play it off. I don't even crack a smile as I casually say, "Her friends have been nice so far, but I'll remember that. Although," I can't help adding, in defense of my new friend, "Loveless seems pretty level-headed to me."

"She is." He leans closer, so I get a magnificent whiff of his cologne. With his other hand he's swirling the liquid in his glass like he's starting to get edgy. I notice he's scanning the crowd again.

I edge away from him, and his fingers loosely curl around my hair as his attention boomerangs back to me—his eyes growing soft again. "Just be careful, that's all I'm saying."

I'm hit with the full force of those green eyes, and there's no mistaking the concern there. He withdraws his hand from the loose curls of my pigtail and grabs onto the bar counter behind him.

"Why do you care?" I whisper. The question comes from some self-destructive place, because I expect him to say, "Well, I don't, really." Part of me hopes he will say it. I hope he'll tell me that he and Priscilla are forever, and she might be a porn star but I'm fat virgin garbage.

Okay, crazy, we'll deal with that later. I smile tightly, blushing furiously in the dim lights of the bar. "I'm sorry. I appreciate your kindness. I'll be sure to think on my feet."

The universe smiles on me for a moment, because as I speak, Hunter is tossing down the rest of his drink; this means I can't see his face. In the last glimpse I have of him as I turn to go, he's rubbing his forehead with a pained look on his face.

"Have a good night, Hunter. You be careful, too."

I point myself toward the booth where I last saw Loveless and I tell my heart to keep beating. Hunter West is still a mystery to me, and a mystery he'll stay. We're moving through this world at two very different speeds: his is light, and mine is so much slower.

CHAPTER SEVENTEEN

Hunter

I'VE SCARED OFF Libby, but I can't go after her because I'm going to be sick.

I look down at my drink and groan at what a stupid S.O.B. I am, but then I remember Marchant ordered this drink, before he left to meet Dave. The drink's not drugged. It's me. My back. My shoulder. Lockwood got a knuckle shot right on my shoulder blade, and it's been bleeding ever since. Fever is pulling on me like undertow. Marchant got me a prescription painkiller, and he tried to make me 'talk' like he used to do in college sometimes, but in the end he just talked at me. Not smart to beat the shit out of Lockwood. Not smart to break mirrors. Not smart to let Priscilla whip your back to shreds.

Thanks, bro.

We came up to the bar together, and for a long time I was watching Lockwood, over in the corner surrounded by a bunch of strippers. He looked bad, but not as bad as I'd hoped. Both his eyes were black, and his nose was swollen—probably broken. But he was enjoying himself.

Marchant ordered me two drinks, and I downed one before he left and the second right after that. Combined with this fucking fever and not a lot of sleep...

Fuck me.

My eyes are almost closing on their own as I stumble down the dim hall to the men's room. I lost track of Lockwood when I saw Libby, but it's okay; one of our people is here somewhere and they've got their eyes on him, too. Christ, I can't even remember who it is. Was Julie gonna stop by here? I rub my burning eyes. Whatever.

My mind pulls me back to Libby and the look on her face when she asked me why I cared if she was safe. It bothers me that I couldn't think of anything to articulate that was...more significant than nothing.

I should be glad. She takes up way too much space in my thoughts anyway. I don't know what she's doing here, but I need to stay clear. I definitely don't need to be drawing the wrong kind of attention to her, and the thing with her and Priscilla…I still don't know what's going on there, but I don't need to aggravate the situation.

Speaking of…Lockwood deliberately goaded me—so now the whole damn town thinks I'm a hot-head. I should probably care about what's coming next. Should probably care about myself. What will happen if I'm drawn further into this cluster fuck?

The worst thing is, I just don't care.

Everything at the end of the hall has been moved around in the club's redesign last year, so I have a hard time finding the men's. I'm starting to feel like I might tip the fuck over when I get a text from Marchant. *Might have lead in SanL on SarB. Stay there, Balboa. You need an alibi in case it goes down.*

After tonight's show of rage, that's especially true, and I realize that's how Priscilla planned it—putting me with Lockwood. So I would look like a reckless, violent asshole in public. Fuck.

By the time I get to the bathroom, aqua blue and gold and tidy, I don't feel sick anymore—just dizzy—so I lean over the sink, painfully aware that my back is exposed. Someone could jump me.

The floor is tilting. I think about the way Sarabelle smiled when she came into my room that night. I see Rita's hand flying through the air, straight for my face, and I can feel that fucking whip bite my back.

"You're a whore's son, Hunter. Being an asshole is in your blood."

I splash my face, but I forget about my bandaged fists and one of them gets wet. I sit down on a glittery gold bench in front of a mirror. In a minute, I'll get up. I'll go home. I'm not making things any better by being here.

I decide to test my shoulder blade before I get to my feet again. It feels broken, but that might just be infection. I shudder just thinking of the pain I'll feel when the liquor wears off.

Priscilla has turned me into a masochist. Except I know it isn't her. I raise my left hand toward the ceiling, drifting under sparks of pain that point to a broken bone somewhere back there. I stand up and take a few deep breaths that only emphasize the pain's point. I step slowly into a bathroom stall and work my shirt off. Maybe if I re-work the bandages Marchant applied. He's not very handy with gauze and some of them are pulling...

Elizabeth

I CAN'T FIND Loveless. It seems strange that she would leave our booth and not return, but then again I wasn't there; maybe she did. Since I don't have anyone's number in my cell, I've started looking for Loveless or Juniper—or anyone. I've checked three dance floors, and now I've moved on to bathrooms and saunas. If I don't find someone in the next few minutes, I guess I'll go leave a message at the valet station asking our group to page me when they leave. Maybe I'll just wait there. It seems stupid, but I'm not sure what else to do. I could call Richard, but I'm too embarrassed.

When I get inside the ladies' room, dimly lit with a strobe light in the ceiling, the stall door swings open, revealing a man leaning against the inside of the stall. On another day his toned back and thick shoulders would have turned up my temperature, but the dude's exquisite body has been through the ringer. His back is marred by long, straight welts, covering him vertically and horizontally and every way in between. The streaks look painfully swollen, and up by his shoulder, there's an open gash that's oozing.

I try to catch my breath, but the twisty feeling in my stomach just won't leave. Slowly the man turns his head slightly, and I gasp. *Hunter*.

All of a sudden I'm overwhelmed by heat, a strong sensation that's at war with the concern I feel over the sad state of his back.

I hesitate a second, wondering if Priscilla put those marks on him. What must be wrong with him if he's in that kind of relationship? I remember the distracted look in his eyes back at the bar, the awkward way he looked behind his glass when I asked him why he cared, and wonder what is wrong with me for even caring.

Then I remember touching his face inside my mother's house, and I tell myself that *this is something*. This spark I feel when I'm around him—it's worth something. Then I picture him leaning over Priscilla, and I'm right back where I started.

When am I going to learn to stop spinning fantasies around this man? He's a rich-as-sin poker player who lives half his life in Vegas and is in a very weird relationship. What am I thinking? He hits a double, shows me a few moments of kindness, and now

I'm hanging on every word and reading into every glance.

Am I really that pathetic?

I reach for the handle on the big wooden door that leads from the bathroom into the hallway, and I hear the clatter of footsteps on the marble floor behind me. My mind spins madly, projecting its wicked wishes into reality. As I pull the door open, I can practically feel the rush of air from Hunter's body, moving after mine. His strong hand grips my bicep and his low, rough voice says, "Libby."

He turns me to face him, then pushes the door shut behind me. I stare at his face with suspended disbelief. The wide green eyes. The sweat-slick skin. His hair is wild, like someone's fingers have been in it, and his mouth is drawn.

I tug my arm away from him, or try to. His grip tightens as his gaze holds onto mine. "Were you leaving?" His voice sounds ragged, like he's out of breath.

"Yes. I...need to go."

"Because of me?"

I can't seem to find my voice, so I pull out of his grasp, grabbing the door handle and wrapping my fingers tightly around it. I don't pull it open. I don't even turn my face away from his.

Being this close to him is like stepping onto the surface of a star. I feel like I'm melting. My mind speeds up in time with my racing pulse, and all of a sudden I have to know. "What happened to your back?"

His eyes are still on mine, and I can't breathe as they flicker to my lips.

"I hurt it." The words are warm and gruff, like he's telling me a secret but he's not sure that he wants to. The simple answer surprises me. So does the bare look in his eyes.

"It looks awful," I say bluntly.

He shrugs, but his nonchalance is completely ruined by a wince. I look at his back through the reflection in the mirror.

There are a lot of welts, and they all seem to be about the same size. "Did Priscilla do that?"

"You think I'd let a woman do this to me?" He looks so stern and masculine, I feel stupid for asking. Not my business.

But there's something in his eyes. Something hard, almost a challenge, and I can't help feeling like I'm being warned away.

I suck in a breath, struggling to speak as I try to pull the answer from his eyes. "Did you?"

He's quiet again, giving me a chance to examine his face. There's a nasty bruise on his jaw. "This was a choice," he finally says.

A choice? My stomach rolls. "Are you saying that you did that to yourself?"

He reaches for me, grabs my hand, and as he pulls me closer, I know I'm in trouble.

"I'm not saying anything." His free hand comes behind my head, his fingers in my hair as I look into his handsome, bruised face. "You're the one talking."

"About you," I whisper.

"About me."

"I think you need to be more careful," I say, throwing what he said at the bar back at him. "I don't want to see you hurt."

His eyes flare, and for a second I think he's going to walk out, but then he groans and pulls me even closer. "You know what hurts?" he grits, his hand splaying over my ass, squeezing as he pushes me against his chest. "This hurts," he says, and I can feel him through my shorts.

He's hard and ready, totally jacked up. *For me*, I realize. I shock myself by reaching down—I want to touch him—but I stop and hover over his hard, smooth abs. His eyes widen and I feel his hand close over mine. That's all it takes. The world folds in on me, and the small, dim room becomes a fantasy. I'm rubbing my fingers up and down his bulge, amazed by the hard, stiff length of it.

Hunter moans, and I press a little harder. The way he flinches makes me worry I'm hurting him, but he's rocking into my hand like he wants me to press harder. I roll my palm around the round head of him, and he pushes his face into my shoulder. "Christ."

I stroke him up and down, eager to feel all of him.

"Maybe…you should unzip your pants," I say. It sounds unsteady, because I'm trembling.

He looks down at me, his face bent into a question, and I nod, nuzzling his throat as I pant. I'm still aware that this is a terrible idea—I'm going to get hurt; of that I'm sure—but right now, I want to keep his eyes wide and his mouth open, his body curled over mine, his hands clutching my shoulders.

He unzips his slacks and I reach for him, pushing past the elastic of his underpants so I can feel him skin-to-skin. Oh my God, he's hard as steel. So soft—and burning hot. The second that my fingers touch his velvet skin, he gasps and jerks inside my hand. I smooth my fingers down him, feather-light until I reach the base, and then I stroke a little, like I learned today.

He starts to pant, and I stroke up and down again before I tentatively cup my hand and reach lower. I've never fondled anyone's balls before, and I'm loving the shock on Hunter's face as he pulls away to look into my eyes. His are dazed, almost glowing.

"Libby," he groans. "Jesus."

Then he's pulling me against him, pushing my blouse up, shoving my strapless bra away and closing his lips over my breast.

I moan, and he cups my ass and pulls me closer, so I can feel him, big and hard, through what I can now see are boxer briefs. My hand comes out of his pants and I rock against him just a little; he groans and grips my hand in his. He thumbs me through my shorts and I whimper as his fingers push inside my shorts and past my underwear to stroke over my lips.

"Hunter," I pant, and his finger glides inside.

I could die happy right here, but then we would be Hunter 2, Elizabeth 0, and I can't let that score stand.

Using every bit of willpower I have, I reach around his arms, pushing past the elastic of his boxer-briefs to cup his head. My fingers glide down on each side of his cock and he moans, pressing his forehead against mine, kissing my mouth. His is open, panting. "Elizabeth."

The way he says my given name, all breathless and lustful, is intoxicating. I wrap my fingers around him, pumping him near the top. With my other hand I cup his balls. I'm surprised by how heavy they feel.

The hand that's stroking his cock moves over his head, finding it slick. *I made Hunter wet.* That thought makes me wet. His cock is pulsing and when I glide up and down again, he lays his cheek against my shoulder, holding onto my back with one hand while his other teases my clit.

"Libby..."

The nickname brings me back to the here and now, and I loosen my grip on him. His hand, holding onto my shoulder, trails down to cup my ass; his fingers in my panties shove deeper inside and I feel pressure building there. I shift my hips, desperate to relieve it.

"Hunter," I groan. I feel shaky, almost scared.

He tugs me to him, lifting me up and carrying me across the room. We go through a big, glass door and into somewhere hot —a sauna, where he gently lays me out on one of the benches. I watch through lust-heavy eyes as he grabs a red towel and lays it on the wood plank floor; then he lifts me in his arms again and spreads me out. My shorts are unzipped and folded down. His hand is moving and I'm gasping.

Hunter West.

Oh, yes.

No. I shouldn't be doing this.

"You're with Priscilla," I whimper.

He laughs, a hard, dry sound. "I'm not."

"I don't even...know you well," I pant. It doesn't matter to me, but it should.

He thumbs my clit and I arch against his hand. "What's to know?"

He's kissing my breasts, with one finger inside me. I've got one hand inside his boxer-briefs, and he is groaning in my ear.

This is wrong, this is so wrong. I know it is, but I can't stop.

"We're in a bathroom. I must be crazy."

"Sauna," he pants.

Then his finger glides out of me and skates over my clit. I clench my knees around his arm, barely able to keep my hand on his cock as I tremble.

"I can't do this," I whimper, although I obviously am doing it.

He rests his hand atop my mound, but I still have him by the shaft. My hand trembles, and it must feel good, because he shuts his eyes. As he does, his hips rock into me, and heat blooms all over my hand. His eyes flip open and I'm shocked to find that this is...wow.

I blink up at him, fuzzily aware that Hunter is coming and I should stroke him. He groans so loudly it hurts my ears, and his hands come down on my shoulders.

He pants, and drops his head against my shoulder in a way I love. I cup his cheek. My mind is racing, and as my pulse calms, I ask, only loud enough to rise above the sound of our deep breathing, "Why do you call me Libby?"

He lifts his head, his eyes on mine. His softens, like he's remembering something nice. "I used to know someone named Libby. She was kind...and when I met you, you reminded me of her."

I flush with shame. So the name is not for me. Of course not. He's dating a porn star, for crying out loud. Is he like this with everyone, I wonder? Sex on a stick, making women everywhere drop what they're doing and give him a hand-job in club bathrooms? I think about his back, unable to reconcile the grisly wounds with the look of kindness burning in his eyes right now. He must be some kind of fiend.

I draw my hands back to my sides, scooting away so I dislodge the hand that's still in my panties. I'm staring at his handsome face while telling myself that this is it. This insanity with Hunter West is over now.

"Libby, what's—" wrong?

How could I ever begin to explain?

I stagger to my feet and throw open the sauna door, and I'm rushing through the bathroom before Hunter is even on his feet. I'm crying before I get into the hall. By the time I sprint into the parking lot, I know I have a lot to learn about more than sex—starting with how to shield my fragile heart.

Hunter

I CAN'T GO after her. I can't even move. I'm shaking everywhere. I can't believe I told her that—the name Libby. I haven't thought of the original Libby in years, just like I haven't thought of what I talked about with her. But I had no problem telling Elizabeth Deville.

I told her something secret, something as personal to me as flesh and blood—and she looked at me like I'd just slapped her. Why did it make her so upset? Does she think Libby is a girlfriend?

'Libby' came into my mind the moment I saw Elizabeth trying to pop the hood of her mother's old Porsche in the middle of the road in the middle of the night. She'd begun as a neon blip on my infrared security camera, but even then I could see her temper, her determination. As she watched me in my garage later that night, her perceptive eyes brought the first Libby back to mind. I have a thing for names, so the few times I saw her again over the years, I would remember how she reminded me of the other Libby.

I don't bother asking myself why I always end up doing crazy things with Libby DeVille. I already know I don't have the answer. She just does it to me. Gets under my skin like a rash.

As I leave the sauna and stroll back into the stall where I left my shirt, everything on my body aches, but nothing more than the regret inside my chest.

CHAPTER EIGHTEEN

Elizabeth

"SCARLETT!"

"SCARLETT!"

"There she is!"

I'm standing in the parking lot by the side of the Joseph building, having just declined a ride from—of all people—Michael Lockwood, the guy who Hunter bashed to pieces, when my posse catches up to me. I turn around, and before I can get a good view of anything, Juniper smashes into me, surprising me with a ferocious hug. "We were dreadfully worried!"

"I'm sorry, girl." Loveless thumps one of my pigtails, and Bella says, "We've been looking for you for half an hour."

Juniper releases me, and I look down the row of concerned faces. "I'm really sorry. It's my fault. I went to the bar and..."

"That's when I saw Juan," Loveless says. "He was my client a few years ago and I hadn't seen him since then, so I guess I got distracted."

I feel relieved. None of them saw me with Hunter—at the bar or in the bathroom.

"I'm so sorry," Loveless says. She grabs my hand, and I'm being tugged behind the rest of them. I assume we're going to our ride, and a few seconds later, there is Rod in the Escalade. The other girls shuffle me inside first—"So you don't get lost,"

Bella teases—so I end up in the back, sandwiched between Loveless and a wall.

As we crawl onto the crowded Strip, I listen to the girls talk about the reason we're leaving 'early'. Apparently Domino, Marie V.'s overzealous client, started talking crap about the guy whose nose he broke in the fight, and Loveless thought it was a good idea for the Love Inc. crew to leave.

"So I held you guys up? I'm sorry."

"It was Loveless's fault for leaving you," Juniper says. "Don't worry. We're a family here. We forgive each other."

"How was Juan?" Bella asks Loveless. "Still looking fine as mama's apple pie?"

"Finer than a key lime pie," Loveless confirms.

She glances over at me, giving me an exaggerated wink. I don't really understand it, and it's not long before I find myself drifting off into my own little bubble of Lizzy angst. How is it possible that I'm selling my virginity as a fund-raising measure, but I'm so addicted to my crush that I'm all tied up in knots *not* over the auction but over who said crush is screwing and why.

By the time we make it off the strip, I've decided that I can console myself with something: Hunter is obviously in to me in the same way I am to him. I remember the way his green eyes burned when he grabbed my arm in the ladies' room. When I add everything together, I'm very tempted to say Hunter doesn't want to have a thing with me, but he can't help himself.

I smirk. *Maybe it's pheromones.*

The road darkens as we head southeast, toward the ranch, and in the privacy of the dark, I allow myself to remember Hunter's beautiful body. I'm pretty sure this will be the last time I ever see it—I'm not doing that to myself again—so I want to remember everything. But the thing that stands out most in my mind, other than the beautiful, blissful expression on his relaxed face as I worked him toward an orgasm, is his back.

And I know Priscilla did that. And I hate her for it.

And I wonder for the hundred-thousandth time, why? Why is he with her? Assuming for a second that her personality and her job don't matter at all (and I'm aware the job gripe is kind of hypocritical considering the company I'm presently keeping), she's not even that striking. She's attractive in a prefabricated kind of way, but there are lots of other fish in the sea—other pretty women with Crest-white smiles, fake tits, and mile-long legs.

I swallow, feeling weird. *I'm* one of them, aren't I? Okay, my boobs are real, but now that I've gotten into shape, I'm leggy, and I've always had a nice, white smile. It's strange to think of myself as pretty when I'm so accustomed to ignoring my appearance—but I'm not so bad. I'm striking. A few weeks under Brenda's care and I'll be just as cut as the next working girl. If he could have a normal woman like me, why is he with her?

I'm going to figure that out.

I've finally relax a little as the girls take turns describing features of their best-ever client, leaving the others to guess names. And then we turn onto the little asphalt road that's lined with billboards, and Loveless leans in close and whispers, "I didn't talk to Juan tonight. I saw him, but he went downstairs before I could get to him."

Her eyes widen purposefully, and I know what she's saying. She saw me disappear with Hunter. I expect her to ask me for details, but instead she pats my knee. "It's your story, Cinderella. Just tell me, did you lose a shoe?"

She has a habit of saying things that I don't understand, but I have a miserable sense that the answer is *yes*. Tears fill my eyes, and she whispers, "Oh, honey."

I nod, and I feel a little better.

I TRY TO tell myself that I'm not obsessed, but it's a lie. Suri calls Friday morning before I go down for breakfast, and I spill all—starting with the rendezvous at Hunter's house party and going all the way through the tryst in the women's sauna at the Joseph Club two nights ago.

I'm eagerly awaiting her response when I hear violent sobbing on the other end of the line.

"Oh my God." My stomach does a back-flip. "Is it something with Cross?"

"Adam," she wails. "We had a falling out and—" She sobs some more. "We're not getting married anymore!"

I sit down on my bed, clutching my stomach and feeling shell-shocked. "Suri, oh my God, what happened?"

"And Cross has his eyes open!"

"Whoa. Holy shit! Like, *for real* open?"

"For real!" She's still sobbing; I'm up and pacing the pale pink carpet.

"Suri, do you want to come here? Can you come here for like a day? An hour?" All I want is to be with her, but I know that I can't leave this close to auction time.

"*No.*" I hear her cry some more, and then she pulls it together, although she's still speaking in her sobbing voice. "Cross is doing...really good. Nanette is stunned. The doctors are surprised. He's had his eyes open for a day or so now, but he's not really saying much." She sniffs. "I just wish he would talk."

And then she's crying again—and so am I.

"They pulled him off some of the medicine yesterday. They think that might be why he's a little more alert. I think he's coming off some more today." Suri still sounds sniffly, and even though we're talking about Cross, I haven't forgotten what she told me about Adam.

"Holy cow, that's incredible. I want to see him so much. I just want to talk to him." My voice cracks a little and she says, "Why don't we call you? He and I? I'll give him my cell this afternoon and you can talk to him."

"Would you really? I would love that. I'll quit whatever I'm doing—promise."

"Don't worry, Lizzy. I'll take care of him."

"But what about you?"

She sniffs again. "I'll tell you all about it, but not right now. You're missing breakfast, aren't you?"

"Don't hold back on me because of this. I want to hear the whole story."

"I'm not," she pauses, still sounding teary, "I'm just not sure I want to go into it quite yet."

I hesitate before asking my next question, because I don't want to press her if she doesn't want to talk—but I want to know: "Do you think it's something that will last?"

Her voice breaks. "I think so. Yeah."

"Oh, Suri, I'm so sorry."

"I know." She's crying softly again, and I would give anything to zap myself to where she is. "I wish I was there," I say.

"I know." She takes a deep breath and I can practically see her steadying herself. Wiping her eyes. "How are you, Lizzy? Are you doing okay? Cold feet, warm feet?"

"Same as the day before yesterday." Suri and I talk almost every day, so she knows what this means. "I'm nervous, but I can do this. It's for Cross."

"Lizzy, he's going to flip if he ever finds out. You do know that."

"Let him," I say. "He can hunt me down. I hope he does."

"He might. Remember if you back out, I'll come get you."

"I won't, but thank you for the offer." I thumb the tiny framed snapshot of Suri and I that's sitting on my night stand. "I'm going to be thinking of you all day, okay?"

"Okay."

"I want you to promise me you'll call if you want or need to. Pinkie promise?"

"Pinkie promise. Love you, Liz-Liz."

"You too, Sur-Sur."

I spend the next few minutes thinking about everything that Suri told me. Then I call and talk to Nanette about Cross. He's got his eyes open when I call, but still hasn't really responded to anyone, which is disappointing, but I'm not complaining. In fact, I'm dancing as I get into my clothes: soft black slacks that make my butt look good, open-toe black heels, and a sea green blouse with wood buttons. I pull my reddish brown hair into barrettes and let it hang down to my shoulders.

By the time I go downstairs, the kitchen is closed; a quick glance at my cell phone reveals that it's time for my exam. I slowly make my way to the medical clinic, where for the next two hours, my virginity is verified through an uncomfortable series of pokes and palpitations. By the time I get out of the stirrups I'm red in the face and feeling distinctly undignified.

The moment I push through the door back out into the main hall, I'm greeted by the sound of kids' party bazookas and a single spray of silly-string, project across my face from a can in Loveless's left hand.

Juniper catches my arm, and Marie V. grins. "It's time for your sex class!"

"Sex class?" I put a hand on my stomach, which feels flip-floppy at the prospect. "Does that mean I—"

"You watch," Loveless says, winking at me. "Now, follow us."

So I do. I follow them around to the right side of the main manor house, into a spacious suite that's outfitted with more cameras than the rest of Love Incorporated.

A hot guy with silky blond-brown hair and pale blue eyes is waiting. When he sees Juniper, he grabs her hand, and I watch with a notch between my brows while the two of them step into another room, and a few of the girls I don't know well move in to give me hugs.

"We're leaving," Bella says. "Don't want to be a looky loo."

"Have a great day," a girl named Luri tells me.

"Juniper's the best," assures a slightly younger girl.

When the room clears out, it's only Loveless, Marie V., and I. On the other side of the window, Juniper and the guy—who I quickly find is named Aspen—are making out. We sit down on a plush couch, and I ask if the window is one-sided.

"Oh, yes. They can't see us," Marie V. tells me.

But I can definitely see Juniper. She's unzipping Aspen's pants, and I'm feeling a little awkward.

"Clients pay to watch this?" I ask them as Aspen pulls off her blouse.

"Some," Loveless says.

"Wow, that's weird."

"But not for you," Marie V. says. "It's good. They're going to show you the ropes. Feel free to walk up to the window. That's why they're doing it. So you can see what it's going to be like."

"Wow." I do end up at the window, only because Loveless prods me to. I'm still reeling an hour later as we eat a picnic lunch on the lawn behind the main manor house. When Juniper finally shows up, drinking a smoothie and wearing a long, pink robe, she grins. "Well, what did you think?"

"You were amazing."

She bats her lashes, and I realize they look longer—and her face looks more made up. "That's what I'm told."

"Well it's true." I gesture to her robe. "Are you working right now?"

"I am. I just came out between clients. I don't have one for another forty-five minutes, and it's you."

I nearly choke on my diet soda, and she laughs. "I'm going to be your model. It's the web cam preview, remember? I'll model the moves they'll want you to make, and then you'll make them. It won't be so bad."

"You can do it," Loveless assures me.

"Thank you. I'm nervous." Very. I've been here for days, but I still don't feel ready to pose for a camera. How could I?

"You're ready for this," Marie V. told me.

We shoot the shit a while longer, and then Juniper and I go film my web cam preview. It's easier than I think it will be; all the film people are nice. I'm wearing panties and a bra, but my face is shadowed, so on the screen, which I can see out of the corner of my eye, you can see the general shape of my head but not much else.

Afterward, Juniper and I practice some moves, which is funny and not at all sexual. I do dinner in the dining room, where I'm regaled with stories of everyone's day. Loveless is working all night, and so is Juniper. I have the night off, so I head back to my room, where I get a call from Suri and I get a chance to say a few things to Cross.

He murmurs something I think might be an answer to one of my questions, and that's enough for me.

When Suri gets the phone back in her hand, she says she's leaving rehab, so she'll call me back from her car. When she does, I get the story on her and Adam.

"For a really long time, it hasn't seemed logical to break things off because we have a lot of history and we care about each other, but it's not enough. I could talk for hours and give details, but it boils down to this: Neither one of us wants to make the sacrifices you should be making if you're going to get married." Her voice cracks a little, and she says, "So many things have changed these last few years. I've changed and so has he. We're just not...compatible anymore I guess. Does that make sense?"

"Of course it does."

"Really?"

"Yeah. Maybe that's why you've been fighting so much.

Feeling like you belong with someone is what makes the mundane stuff doable, right? Isn't that supposed to be what gets you through hard times? The fact that you believe you're with the right person, and you really love them and feel passion for them?"

"I think so," she sighs. "But I'm starting to think I don't know anything."

"You do, Suri. And you'll find someone else. Someone you do feel passionate and right about."

"I know. So will you, girl."

A few minutes later, we get off the phone, and I spend the rest of the night thinking about that. About whether I really want to find someone. So I can have a marriage like my mom and dad's? In my mind, marriage sucks, but what if both partners are normal? Okay, not normal, but less crazy than my mom. Less avoidant than my dad.

I curl up in my bed and just so happen to find *The Notebook* on TV. When Juniper calls my landline about thirty minutes in, asking me if I want to go to a poker tournament tonight, I decline. Until there's a real reason for me to think that there is hope for Hunter and I—hope that can be taken out into the light, rather than hidden away in a shadowy bedroom or a dark club sauna—I've got to keep my mind off him.

CHAPTER NINETEEN

Elizabeth

FOUR DAYS PASS without anything that registers on my Hunter -o-meter, and I fall into a soothing—if not comfortable—routine. Mornings I wake up and work my booty off with Brenda or one of her trainers. I take a quick shower in the gym and put on something comfy, then go up for lunch with all the girls, plus Rod, David, Slash, and a few other guys I don't know. After lunch, someone is usually assigned to teach me something. Yesterday it was Bella, showing me how to move in lingerie. How even the smallest crack between your legs can flash someone your va-jay-jay, and if you walk like a runway model, your teddy will look a lot better on you. Today I'm booked with Sonny for my morning work-out. I'm warmed to hear he thinks I look like "one of us."

I take a long time in the shower, because Loveless has a lunch session today and Juniper won't be in the café due to a scheduled phone call with her English boyfriend. I like the other girls, but there are still moments with them when I feel a little like an outsider.

I haven't seen Marchant yet, thank God, I realize as I slide into a muted aquamarine sundress. It hugs my bust, shows off my waist, and makes my legs look long; the fabric gets more sheer as it nears the floor. I take my time drying and straightening my hair and pull the top layers up into a barrette. I stick diamond earrings into my ears—they're loaners, and real—before spritzing myself with one of the house-approved perfumes and sliding my leather bag onto my shoulder.

Apparently I was going slower than I thought, because by the time I reach the café, it's mostly empty. I grab a muffin and a slice of turkey bacon and check my phone for a text to let me know where I'll be spending the afternoon.

My stomach roils when I see: Dr. Bernard—Love Inc. Psychologist

Immediately I dread it. I run back to my room, call and check on Suri and Cross—both about the same, Suri says—and grab a diet ginger ale for the trek down to the manor house where all the official business gets done.

I put on a calm face but my mind is racing. What does Dr. Bernard want with me? How can I talk to him or her if they don't even know my real name? What's the point, anyway?

I'm in knots by the time I reach the small office on the third floor of the building. The doctor's nameplate is mounted on the door, so I figure she must be the official Love Inc. shrink.

Elizabeth Bernard.

How much do I dread thee? Let me count the ways.

The door is closed and my phone tells me I'm a little early, so I drop down onto the plush mini recliner in the hallway and try not to bite my long, pretty, red nails. I'm obsessing over whether she will recognize me as the daughter of an addict—as if every shrink this side of the Mississippi has heard about my mom—when the door opens and a nice-looking woman about the age of my estranged grandmother steps out. A quick once-over reveals shoulder-length, gray-brown hair, a loose, floor-length brown skirt, and a surprisingly stylish, flowing beige blouse.

Her thin lips curl into a smile that looks more welcoming than anything, and she extends her hand; the nails, I notice, are as bare as her face. "Scarlett. Please, come in."

I don't take her hand, something I'm sure she notices, but I don't really care. I've seen enough therapists to last a life time, and now that I'm here, I don't plan to go out of my way to assure this woman of my sanity. I played those games my whole childhood. *I make good grades and have nice friends. So what if my mother slit her wrists last week?* If I want to flap my arms and cluck like a chicken, what will she do to me? Tell Richard that the ranch shouldn't host my auction? Um, I think not.

She waves to a cozy, suede-looking blue couch with gray pillows sporting cut-out felt daisies. I take a seat on the end nearest the door, because there's no reason not to. I don't want to be here and I'm not going to be anything but honest.

She sits down in a small, orange leather recliner and pulls a pillow under her elbow. "Shoulder surgery," she says with a wince. "I'm still recovering."

I nod. It's not like I care.

"What can I do for you, Dr. Bernard? What's the reason I'm here?"

She shrugs. "I'm not sure there is one. I speak to most people who come through the Love Inc. ranch as a matter of policy. You aren't an employee, of course, but you've been here for..."

"Over a week," I supply. "And in three days, I'll be gone."

She gives me a gentle, knowing smile. "You don't want to talk to me."

"Guilty." I feel a little awkward, but there's nothing I can do to stem the flow of animosity I feel for anyone sitting in an armchair with their PhD on the wall behind them.

"You've seen a therapist before."

"Dozens." I cross my legs. "One of the things I dislike the most is the questions, so let me answer them for you. My mom's crazy with a capital 'C'. She's been a drug addict or an alcoholic, in and out of rehab, since I was a young child. She married into money and my dad was in love with her at first, I think. Over the years that faded, and at some point he started traveling a lot for business. One of the...plants—" that would be bottling factories — "he visited regularly was in Salt Lake City, and about thirteen years ago, or maybe before then, he started seeing Linzie. He has two daughters with her—at least I'm pretty sure he does because one of them looks like him and the other one looks a lot like me. When I went to college he left Mom, sold the controlling share in his family's company, which had been in decline for some time, and moved to Utah to be with his new family. Yes, I'm bitter about it. And it doesn't help that Linzie is a bitch.

"My mom is in rehab as we speak—only it's not really rehab, it's more like a spa, and it's costing us more money than we have. My oldest friend, Cross, got into a motorcycle accident after a party where he and I had a fight, and he needed help paying for his care. I knew—well, knew of—Marchant Radcliffe, and I got the idea to sell my virginity."

I think that's a pretty tidy summation of what's the what. The first half, about my family, I've given several times before.

Dr. Bernard arches her delicate brows. "That's quite a story. Frankly I don't know which part is the most dramatic."

I wrinkle my nose. "I wouldn't call it dramatic as much as just...screwed up. Seriously screwed up. At least the part about my family. The part with my friend—" whose very distinctive name I should *not* have mentioned— "was just an accident, and the part where I sell my V-card is obviously an attempt to get money." I purse my lips, looking for some levity. "At least it's not a kidney."

"Did you consider that?"

I nod. "It's less profitable, crazy though that is."

"That is crazy." She looks down at her lap and makes a note on a pad. "Before we continue I want to make sure you are aware that I know your real name."

I gulp. "You do?"

She nods. "I'm sorry, but it's necessary. However, in my

notes I'm referring to you as Scarlett."

I frown. "Do you know who I am? Like, my identity?"

"Do you mean who your family is? Yes," she says. "For most of my career I ran a center that specialized in the dynamics of financially privileged families. You're the DeVille heiress."

"Not much left to inherit."

"You've been through a lot, with your mother. And your father."

"I guess so."

"I think the answer is a resounding 'yes.'"

I nod. "Yes."

"You know it's not uncommon for the children of addicts to harbor some resentment toward the therapists who treat their parents."

If I was a cartoon I'd be whistling a casual tune. "Oh?"

The good doctor shrugs. "You've watched therapists fail your entire life."

That's true.

"Hope can turn ugly when it's dashed over and over."

Her words strike so true that I have to bite my lip to keep from tearing up. Feeling desperate, I change the subject. "Are you from the New Orleans area, by any chance?"

She smiles. "How did you know?"

"Accent. How did you end up here?"

"I'm a child of privilege myself. I married a privileged man, a lawyer and later a politician. His last name isn't Bernard," she tells me, winking. "By the time I divorced, I knew Marchant and his adopted New Orleans social circle well. He's been a client of mine since his college years. In fact, it's thanks to him that I relocated. When he decided to bring a psychologist on board at Love Inc., he wanted it to be his own."

"Really." That surprises me. Marchant doesn't seem like the type of guy to see a shrink.

But Dr. Bernard nods. "He came to me after he lost his parents. In fact, we still talk. Maintenance therapy. I'm not sharing anything with you that he would mind. He's very open about it."

I nod, because I'm not sure what to say.

"I've got a question for you, Scarlett."

My stomach flips. "Okay."

"Why are you still a virgin?" She smiles a little. "Let me rephrase. There's no reason not to be a virgin, if that's what you want to be, but judging by your plans, you seem to have no religious or ethical qualms about experiencing intercourse."

I swallow hard, wanting to die. Does she actually expect me to answer this?

"I was curious, that's all. If you don't want to discuss it, you don't have to."

Well, dangit. Now I feel like I should discuss it. I play with my fingernail, then realize I'm doing it and force myself to look into her eyes.

"The question makes you uncomfortable?" she asks.

"Well, yeah."

"Does sex make you uncomfortable?"

I sigh. "That's not why. I guess it's just a little further than I like to go."

"With therapists."

"With anyone," I say. But, hey, I'm here. Why not? I chew my lip and then just jump in head-first. "I used to be kind of fat," I tell her. "And I have trust issues."

"What kind?"

"The because of my mom kind. The kind you get when you grow up in an unstable home. You know the story."

"I don't know your story. How does that go?"

I shrug. "I know my parents didn't have much sex. I overheard them talking about it a few times. Well, it was mostly my dad complaining. But that's just…I don't know, indicative of their whole relationship, which is to say there wasn't one. Everything was pretend with them. Like, our whole family was pretend. Probably because, with an addict, it's impossible to get any deeper than that. So we were all...I don't know...like roommates. I made friends with Suri and Cross, my two best friends, when I was young, so I grew to trust them without meaning to. But everybody else..." I bite my lip as the truth finally dawns on me with crystal clarity. I spit it out in a froggy voice. "I guess I just never considered that it was possible to have a good relationship with a man."

Her face is sympathetic. The kind of sympathy that almost hurts. I raise my hand to my chest. It kind of does hurt. "Geez, that's new to me. I didn't even know I felt that way."

She nods. "That's one of the reasons people—non-addict people—come to therapy. To learn more about themselves. How much time have you spent learning about Scarlett? Not Mom, not Dad, but Scarlett? Her issues? Her fears?"

I press my lips together. The answer is none, of course. "I never had time."

"That's very common for a young person with your history. And it's not your fault," she says with a reassuring smile. "The great thing about getting older is, you change yourself. And what's healthy and appropriate, you nourish."

I nod, relieved. *I'm not a freak who doesn't want a relationship. I just never really thought that one was possible. It makes sense!*

She looks up at the clock behind me, and I'm surprised to find an hour has passed since I walked through her door.

"Do you find yourself in Vegas very often?" she asks.

"Sometimes," I hedge. I sigh. "Not really." I feel my cheeks flush, and I tentatively say, "I wish I did. It was kind of nice talking to you."

She smiles. "Well I asked because I have an office in Los Angeles. I know it's not a speedy drive, but it is in driving range from the Napa area."

I nod, and she asks, "Would you like to talk again sometime?"

"It depends on how much money I get," I say, smirking. She hands me her card, and I put it in my purse. "I'll call some time."

"I'd like that. And Scarlett?" I turn with my hand on the door-knob. "Don't hesitate to come back if you'd like to talk again before you go."

CHAPTER TWENTY

Hunter

EVEN AS I'M playing, I know Lady Luck is with someone else tonight. I imagine the headlines, stupid puns arranged in that kind of cadence that journalists and bloggers like.

West doesn't know which way is up in tourney

Bourbon heir floats in first-day tourney

What-the-fuck-ever.

I screwed up last hand, and I'm screwing up again this time. A Zen master couldn't play with all the shit I've got bouncing around in my head. I want to tell that to the annoying blonde holding the camera. She looks a little too much like Priscilla for my liking, and I'm having trouble not snapping as she pushes her mic into my face.

Today has sucked. Scratch that. Everything has sucked since the other night at the Joseph.

For starters, Priscilla didn't really go to Canada. Today she rode down to San Luis and Julie tailed her, but she didn't seem to do anything except have dinner with a client at a swanky hotel.

I'm obsessed with her now. Priscilla. Obsessed with bringing her down. I go over every detail of her conversation with Lockwood at the gala again and again, and the worst thing is, without a recording, we've got no proof. Zip.

Doesn't help that Lisa from the FBI stopped by this morning to ask if I've ever been to Sarabelle's house. I don't say a word. I've got nothing to hide, but I'm not dumb enough to cooperate when I'm clearly emerging as suspect número uno. There are a million ways your words can be used against you once they leave your mouth.

Then there's Libby. *Libby, Libby, Libby*. I know she's been in Vegas, but Dave hasn't been able to find her. I finally broke down and texted Loveless an hour before play began.

'Elizabeth DeVille still with you?'

She texts me back near the end of the second hand, and I read her messages between the second and third hands.

'Who?'

'Elizabeth.'

'I don't know who that is. R u ok, Hunter?'

'Elizabeth,' I punch furiously. 'You were with her the other night at the Jo.'

When Loveless doesn't text me back, I take a few minutes during a commercial break and call Marchant.

I was right about my luck tonight. I lose the game.

I'm so furious I don't even give a shit.

Elizabeth

THE BIG DAY is a busy one. So busy, in fact, that I have almost no time to think of what's coming. I'm grateful for that as I'm waxed, worked out, fitted, and eventually sent to my room with a red lingerie set I will wear for bidding.

I review the contract, which is a lot longer than I anticipated but appears to contain everything that Richard and I worked out. The winning bidder is paying for six hours of my time, either at Love. Inc. or at another location. I can bring guards. I will provide vaginal intercourse. OH MY GOD, it sounds so technical this way! But luckily, I am only required to do this once to fulfill the contract.

If I provide only oral stimulation, the bidder will be refunded ninety percent of their bid. If my hymen is broken but I stop intercourse before the bidder reaches climax, the bidder receives a forty percent refund. Love Inc. takes a cut of my final total, regardless.

There's also a list of nos. No photography or video or audio recording. No hair pulling. No name-calling. No spanking. And no contacting me in any way after—although, oddly, there is a provision for me to contact the bidder. As if. This isn't *Pretty Woman*.

After eating a light lunch, I return to my room and have a last-minute freakout. I look in the mirror, at the stubborn bit of cellulite on the back of my thighs—it just won't go away, no matter how many lunges I do. I look at my not-quite-six-pack stomach and wonder if the winning bidder will want more. What about my breasts? They are nice, but they're not Ds. My fingernails are bare, but my toe-nails are painted red. I have weird toenails. The one on the big toe looks like a space helmet. And my voice... In third grade, Holcomb McVey said I had a stupid voice. I don't think I do, but—

My cell rings, and I whirl around naked to face my bed. Suri.

"Thank God," I answer.

"What is it?"

"I'm freaking out here."

"Do you need a getaway car?"

"No!" I laugh. "I need to remind myself that this was my choice and that I don't need a getaway car. Or anyone's approval."

So Suri talks me down, and she tells me about Cross—he told her he was tired, today—and when I get off the phone with her, there's a knock at my door and it's Marie V. She's wearing a pink robe and holding a small bag of lotions and perfumes.

"Are you nervous?" she asks.

"Um, hell yeah."

"Let me tell you something: They won't be expecting much. Every man knows virgins are kind of clueless. As long as your hymen is still intact, the guy will have a great time."

I scrunch my face up. "Um, thanks?"

She laughs, and surprises me by leaning in for a hug. "I enjoyed hanging out with you, Scarlett. I hope you have a great night."

"Thank you. I'm glad I met you, too."

"Any chance we might see you again?"

"I don't think so. I think if I do end up leaving the ranch to do the deed—"

"You probably will."

"You think?" I ask, wide-eyed.

"Just a guess."

My belly bats do a simultaneous dive. "Well if I do, I'll be picked up by a driver in my car, and I'll go home I guess."

"We're going to miss you."

"I'm going to miss this place, too."

I put the things that Marie V. gave me in my toiletries bag and answer the door again when a man named Max comes to do my hair. While he's using some super-powered hair dryer on me, Brenda comes in. She tells me how good I look and offers me a small, black box of condoms.

"He should have his own, but just in case."

"Thank you." I say goodbye to her, thanking her for my better-than-ever calves and biceps, and when the room is empty, I start zipping my bags. If I stay here to do the deed, I'll have to get my things out of them, but if I go, someone else will collect them for me, so I'll be glad they're packed. As I'm zipping my largest suitcase, there's another knock on my door.

I open it hesitantly, trying not to mess up my pretty hair, but it's all for naught: Juniper and Loveless throw their arms around me, and the last thing I care about is my hair.

"We came to help you dress!" Juniper says.

I don't think I've ever laughed so much in such a short period of time. Over the next half hour, my nerves nearly disappear, and I know I'll be forever grateful to them.

At nine-thirty, the girls walk with me to the showroom, where a huge king-sized bed is set up, all the bedding red to match my bra and panties. I lie out and they help pose me, spraying yummy scents in the air and lighting candles.

"You're beautiful," they tell me.

I thank them for their help, and they leave one at a time, each with a final word of encouragement. Juniper is last. "I remember my first time. Believe it or not," she laughs. "It's scary, and then it's over. You'll be fine."

I have about two seconds to myself, just enough time for my heartbeat to blast off, when the door opens and Marchant strides in. "Hi there, Scarlett DeVille."

My heart stops. I stare at his smiling face, and the only thing I can say is, "Uh…you know my name?"

He nods. "Don't worry, though. Our secret."

I say nothing, mortified beyond belief. I want to ask him if he'll be watching—I want to ask him to not watch. But of course he's going to watch. I almost drop dead when another thought occurs to me. If Marchant knows, does that mean—

"Bidding might get intense, but you'll only see the numbers. These things usually don't last but ten minutes or so."

I nod, still feeling totally panicked that Marchant Radcliffe —Marchant Radcliffe, Hunter's best friend, who knows my family—is here, and he knows what I'm doing. I tell myself it was probably inevitable, but I still feel nauseated.

He must misinterpret my anxious look, because he steps a little closer, sticking one hand in the pocket of his pinstriped coat. "You'll be okay. Everyone I know who's bidding is good people. I wouldn't put you in bad hands."

I don't know what to say, so I nod. "You look great, you'll do great," he says as he pats the bed. "No more than ten minutes, Scarlett." He winks, and then he's gone.

My muscles tremble as I try to keep my pose. I'm lying on my side, with my legs slightly scissored and my hand propping my head up. My fingers are threaded through my hair so it falls around my right shoulder.

I'm staring at the digital ticker near the ceiling, feeling like I might have a panic attack or pee myself, when the door bursts open and I gasp.

It's everyone. Not just a few, but all the escorts. Loveless is out in front, and she presents me with a little velvet box. She pops it open, and two beautiful, glittery diamond earrings wink at me.

"Surprise!" everyone shouts.

Loveless leans down. "I'll put them in your ears. Just hold your pose, girl."

As she puts the earrings on me, I feel a sense of total peace. And okay, it evaporates as soon as they leave the room and a little speaker on the bed tells me I'd be live in two minutes. But before that moment, I feel valued and loved. Here in a brothel.

The ticker clock—a two-foot-by-two-foot digital clock mounted by the crown molding—has big, red numbers, and as they inch closer to zero, I can feel my throat constricting like I might be sick. I focus on taking deep breaths and think about Dr. Bernard and how many good things have happened to me here. I feel older. Wiser. More capable. I can handle this.

Then the ticker reaches zero, and the windows surrounding my bed change subtly in hue—getting a little paler. This means people sitting outside the room can see me. I forget to breathe for a second, but then I smooth my mouth into a small, coy smile.

When the first bid flashes across the ticker, I nearly die.

$50,000, just like Marchant said. *That's a lot of money.*

The numbers quickly jump.

$80,000.

$100,000. *Oh my freaking God.*

$140,000.

$150,000.

$200,000.

$300,000. I feel dizzy, and it's hard to keep the shock off my face. With focus, I manage to keep my mouth twisted into that neutral/coy look, and keep my diaphragm in action. *You can do it, Lizzy. Just a little longer*. There is absolutely no way the bidding will go higher than three-hundred grand.

$400,000.

I want to barf, but I try to stay in pose as the light shines on my body. I tell myself again it's almost over. Then the ticker moves again.

$3,000,000. I'm shaking.

$3,200,000. This has got to be a joke.

$3,400,000.

Holy Moses.

$5,200,000.

$5,500,000. The hand inside my hair has clenched into a fist.

$5,900,000.

$6,000,000. The room spins around me.

$10,000,000.

This cannot be real.

I'm gasping for air as the windows grow darker, darker, darker still until I know I'm alone again. I bolt up, swinging my legs off the side of the bed and gasping at my chest. Oh my God, I can't believe what I've done. I've sold my virginity. I can't believe anyone paid $10 million for my hymen.

I'm not sure I can do this.

I can't do this!

I'm not worth that much. Maybe after a few rolls in the hay, but not now. I don't know how to do this.

I'm almost in tears as I pull the covers over myself, and Richard strides in. His eyes are wide. "I can't believe it. No offense, I thought you'd do well, but…" He shakes his head and laughs. "You're set for life."

I smile weakly, because if I don't smile, I'm going to start sobbing. "Is it...someone decent?"

I mean who bought me, and Richard gets it. He hands me a small, white card with the winning bidder's name printed in gold script. My heart really does stop this time.

Hunter West

CHAPTER TWENTY-ONE

Elizabeth

"I CAN'T DO this."

I'm sitting in a black velvet armchair, and Marchant Radcliffe is again standing in front of me. We've moved into a private room, one with no windows of any kind. I'm wearing a black silk robe, and I'm gritting my teeth as I try to come to terms with what just happened.

Marchant shakes his head, looking annoyed. "I've already taken the bid."

"I didn't say I wanted to back out." I don't want to back out. What I want is to disappear, right down to my ten million dollar atoms.

"Woman, you're giving me whiplash," he drawls. "You just said you couldn't do this."

"I didn't mean to say that," I say quietly. "I was thinking out loud."

"This is good for you," he tells me. "Really good. You got a price I wouldn't dream of and the bidder is a good guy. That's a Disney ending."

"It is?"

He narrows his eyes a little. "Yes."

I look down at my black robe. So this is what a princess looks like. I rub my eyes. Oh my God. How did this happen?

Marchant is tapping his foot, and I'm reminded that despite his easy charm and good looks, he's a business man—a business man in the people-selling business. He leans forward, putting a gentle hand on my head. "Are we good? C'mon...I want to hear you tell me that you're okay. You feel prepared?"

I nod, although it couldn't be further from the truth. I'm not ready to have ten million dollar sex with anybody, much less Hunter. The mere thought of seeing him in this position makes my eyes well up with tears again. I blink them back. I'm not going to be a prima donna or a baby about this. At least not when anyone can see.

"Does Hunter come here often?" I ask in a hoarse voice. I don't mean to ask it. The words just fall out of my mouth.

"He comes here to see me. He's an old friend. One of my best." Marchant's eyes are digging into mine, and I get the feeling he's trying to figure something out. A second passes, and his mouth draws up. He curses angrily and digs a hand through his hair.

"Goddamnit." He looks back over his shoulder. "I'm sorry for the French, but shit. You and him...you've got some sort of history." He says it like 'history' is a curse word.

I shake my head, wondering what it means that Hunter hasn't told his best friend about me. "I was just curious."

At that, he throws his head back and laughs. "Just curious. I'll put that down in your file." He takes a step closer, kneeling so we're at eye level. His brown ones look earnest. "You want the money?"

I nod.

"You sold your virginity to Hunter West for ten million dollars. Are you ready to fulfill your contract?"

"Well, yeah. I mean, if that's what he wants me for." I'm having a really hard time believing he paid that much money to get what he could get in a club bathroom—heck, just about *anywhere*—for free.

"If that's what he wants you for." Marchant snorts. "He just paid millions for you, honey. I'd say he fucking wants you." He gives me a pointed look, like he's expecting some explanation as to why his friend would do this. When I just blink at him, he rolls his eyes. "Well here's the deets. He wants to host you at his place. Tonight." He examines my face, which is bug-eyed, and shakes his head like he can't believe what he's about to say. "He's willing to pay an extra two million if you have any objecttions to moving to his ranch."

An extra two million to get me to his house *tonight*? I rub my lips together, freaking the F out and trying not to hyperventilate. "Okay," I whisper. I can do this. Oh God, can I?

"You gonna charge him the extra, or you want to amend the contract and settle with what he paid already?"

"Ten million dollars." It just can't be real.

But Marchant nods, those brown eyes holding mine, like he's looking for something. I sit up straighter, hell-bent on keeping him from finding it.

I take a deep breath, so I can speak without my voice shaking. "I'll do it without charging two million, unless there's something else to this. I mean, he doesn't want me for a threesome or something, right?"

"A threesome?" He laughs. "That's more my speed."

I remember the story about Priscilla Heat filming an orgy scene with Marchant. The thought disgusts me. I wrap the robe more tightly around my body and nod. "Well okay then. I'll go…tonight."

"I'll have Jeff ride with you if West wants to take his own wheels."

I smooth the robe over my knee. "I don't think I need him. Thank you, though."

He arches his brows—same color as his dark blond hair—and sticks his hands into the pockets of his suit. "I'm sorry you're unhappy with the outcome of the bidding."

I try to smirk, but my mouth just ends up quivering, so I press my lips together. “I don’t really believe you. You’re his best friend. Everybody knows that.”

“Guilty as charged. Hunter’s a good guy, Scarlett. He won’t hurt you. He...” Marchant looks like he’s going to confide in me about something, but then he shakes his head. “Hunter’s a good guy,” he says again.

He glances down at his iPhone, then back up into my eyes. “Are you okay to talk with him? He’d like to see you now.”

Right now? I look down at myself. I can’t talk to Hunter in *this*. Then it hits me, for the first time fully, that Hunter is the winner. He’s going to see me in a whole lot less than this.

I feel tears of panic pooling in my eyes. Hunter West. Not some stranger I can forget. My Hunter. Except he isn’t mine—and now he knows I sold my V-card. *I didn’t want anyone to know!*

I bite my lip so the tears dry and I straighten my posture, determined to master my emotions. Marchant’s mouth is puckered into a curious expression, but before he can throw any more of his questions at me, I nod briskly, in a way I hope looks professional. “I’ll talk to him.”

He turns to go, but he turns back around to me before he reaches the door. “Scarlett?”

“Yeah.”

“I don’t know what’s going on with you two, but I want you to know: Hunter’s my boy. He’s a good dude, and he’s got a lot on his plate. I mean a three-course meal of bullshit. So just make sure whatever happens tonight doesn’t turn into something else for him to deal with, okay?”

I’m so stunned, I can’t even nod. I just sit there with my mouth hanging halfway open, and after giving me a smile that looks almost *sad*, Marchant turns and leaves.

Holy cow.

I fold my arms around myself, trembling slightly. What is

Hunter playing at? I don't understand. I can't believe he paid so much money for me. Why did he do it? And 'three-course meal of bullshit'? Does Marchant mean the Sarabelle thing? Hunter's not a suspect, is he? I tell myself that obviously Marchant's a drama king. Look at his job. Showmanship. Drama. I'm sure it's nothing.

Still, I ball my hands into fists and bite my lip until I taste the tang of blood.

Pull it together, Elizabeth.

I can do this. I can keep my heart intact. Have no-strings, first-time-ever sex with Hunter, and go back home to Suri and Cross. I take a few deep breaths and start to feel a little better. Even a little angry. Marchant doesn't know what he's talking about. There's nothing vulnerable about Hunter. *I'm* the one who doesn't need any extra bullshit. Hunter is invincible. Capable of eating me for breakfast in one big CHOMP.

I drop my head into my hands, feeling like I'm being tugged in ten different directions. A few more deep breaths, and I remember that I just can't care. This is a one-night thing. Nothing more.

I'll be glad to get rid of my V-card. And holy belly bats, am I grateful for the money.

As for everything else...I don't know why Hunter bid on me, and I don't care. I don't have to. All I have to do is screw him.

I stand up, my black robe whirling around my ankles. I run my fingers through my long, loose hair and slide a tube of lipstick from the robe's pocket. I can do this.

And I believe that—right until the moment the door swings open and Hunter strides into the room.

He looks rough, his smooth skin pale, his mouth pinched tight. And God—that body. His massive shoulders draw my eyes, and my gaze falls down his flawless abs, visible through the tight, black t-shirt that is the top part of his trademark poker outfit. Poker outfit? I look down at his pants, and yep. They're the black jeans he always wears, along with big, black boots. He's Stetson-less, though, and his pretty golden hair is messy. His eyes, now fixed on me, are slightly red. I wonder if he's doing cocaine. I've heard he used to. My stomach twists. He looks me over, same as I did him, and I realize with a jolt that he looks genuinely angry.

His mouth pinches a little more, and he nods briskly at the door. "I've got my ride at the side entrance. Marchant says you're ready to go."

I lick my lips, looking into his face and searching for any hint of what he's thinking. But he's got a hell of a poker face. "That's it?"

"What do you mean, that's it? Are you expecting something more? A corsage?" he asks dryly.

I flinch. "No, of course not. I just mean...you look upset."

He stuffs his hands into his pockets. "Not so much upset as pissed."

"At me?"

"Just pissed," he says, folding his arms like he's daring me to challenge him. I couldn't if I wanted to. I have no idea what he's talking about. But I have a strong gut feeling that it's directed at me.

"I don't want to go off with someone who's angry at me."

His gorgeous green eyes are hard as nails. "Then reject my offer."

"No way," I say. "I mean...I can't. It's done already."

"Then go get into my car. You don't have to like it." His lips press flat. "I'm paying you, remember?"

I feel my face heat up. "I'd be a lot happier if you weren't. Seems we both have a better time when we hook up in bathrooms."

"I was thinking the same thing," he says. He sounds like he's being dry again, and I'm confused. He rubs his hand roughly over his forehead and turns toward the door. "Never mind about getting into my car. Wait here for me. I'll be right back."

I'm standing, frozen in place. I didn't know what I expected, but this isn't it.

He's back so fast I jump, but he doesn't notice. I bite the inside of my cheek as I eye the suede, fur-lined coat that will probably cover everything but my feet. He holds it out, and I just stare at him. He's got this haunted look to him, like he's seen something he doesn't want to see, or heard something he doesn't want to hear. He looks...worried. Worried and desperately unhappy.

He steps over to me, holding out the coat, and my traitorous heart aches for him.

"Your arms," he says, a little gruff.

I hold them out, and he helps me into the coat.

"Let's go."

His voice is still rough, and I think about saying something sarcastic. I would, if we were doing this at a party, or dare I dream it a date, or any other social function that didn't involve him paying me ten million dollars to have sex with him. As it is, I'm not sure how to act.

Eventually, I decide to salute him. I'm reaching all the way back to middle school for this one. "Yessir," I say smartly, snapping my feet together.

"Damn right," he mutters as he opens the door for me.

I step into the hall to find my posse waiting with hugs for both Hunter and me. The only Hunter hug I see, as I'm pulled into embrace after embrace, is the one between him and Loveless. She pulls him close, cradling his nape with her long fingers, and my heart bursts into jealous flames. The flames are quickly extinguished as I see her hug him tightly around the back. Hunter flinches. It's a barely there motion, subtle enough that I'm probably the only one who notices it.

She hugs him once more, and I see him push his face into

her shoulder. Then I'm swept up by Juniper, who gives me a crushing hug. Loveless joins after a minute.

"Take good care of him, and yourself, too."

I hug her hard, and then Hunter is there beside me, offering his arm. As we move toward the side door, crowded by the laughing, hooting girls, and Hunter wraps an arm around my waist, I can't help feeling just a little like we're bride and groom. Which is ridiculous. So, so silly. And feels more so as we burst through the door into a ring of guards. Hunter's arms are around me, guiding my steps, and then he's picking me up. I've got my eyes squeezed shut, but I can feel him stepping up, can feel his body under mine as we sit down; I'm in his lap.

He tucks me close, under his rock-hard arm, and leans up. "Drive," he tells someone.

I feel the car lurch forward and hear the familiar whirring sound of the thick, plastic partition going up between the front of an Escalade limousine and the back. Seconds later, I'm staring into Hunter's green cat eyes.

Hunter

I'VE GONE AND done it now. Lost my fucking mind. When Marchant started acting sketchy on the phone last night, I didn't know what the hell was going on, but then I remembered those billboards on the way to the ranch, and how I always get a giant hard-on when I see that woman's curves. I got a sick idea and when I really lit into March, he gave the old tired "I'm not going to say yes or no," and for Marchant that's always a "Yeah!"

Libby DeVille: virgin for sale.

I had half a mind to punch Marchant out until I realized what a hypocrite I was being. Well, until he pointed it out—that I myself pay for escorts, and what's different about Libby and those girls?

The answer: a thousand fucking things, and nothing at all. Is it wrong for me to make a distinction? Maybe, but I don't care. I stayed angry, and tonight, when I saw her wearing red, all that long dark hair splayed across the bed, it was like a holy vision. Except we weren't in heaven. We were in a fancy brothel, and there were a dozen other men with the same view I had—and they didn't deserve to be there. I know I didn't either, but this world's imperfect, and I couldn't stand to see her with somebody else.

So I bid on her.

I piled cash all the way to the ceiling for her, but now that I've won I'm wondering what the hell I'm gonna do with her. I don't plan to make her fulfill her contract, obviously… *I know, I know*, I've had a lot of sex with escorts, but Libby isn't an escort. If she fucks me, it'll be because she wants to.

Hal pulls away from the curb, and there's obvious confusion in Libby's ocean-colored eyes, like she has no idea why I'm so riled up. Scoots away from me and folds her arms over her middle, looking gorgeous with her hair rolling in waves over her shoulders. "I wish I understood what's going on with you."

I grit my teeth. The feeling is mutual. "Why did you do this?"

"Do what?" She crosses her legs, and I can see every line of her under the snug jacket I borrowed from Loveless.

I scowl, because I'm not in a game-playing mood. "Pursue your PhD," I say with as much sarcasm as I can muster. "What do you think?"

She's looking down at her hands, but her spine is stiff. She's got her hackles up. Her eyes rise to mine and I find her face blank. "I did it because I needed the money. Are *you* going to get all judgy?"

Me, who just paid for her. Me, who I assume she knows visited Love Inc. almost daily for several years. Of course I don't judge her for the idea, but the execution…it was dangerous and stupid.

I shudder to think of who she could have ended up with. I also don't understand why she's so hard up. "I know the value of your mother's home. Why not just sell it?" I rub my dry eyes.

"It's in my dad's name."

I frown. "You must have some other means. Some kind of trust fund—"

"Hunter," she cuts me off, quiet but firm, "you're not my keeper."

I inhale deeply, rubbing a hand across my face. I like the way my name sounds coming from her mouth. I think about the way she looked lying on that bed, and I'm hard again in an instant, even as she gives me a wide-eyed, serious look.

"I hope you didn't bid on me out of some misplaced feeling of responsibility." Her eyes drop, then raise to meet mine, and I can sense a rallying as she squares her shoulders slightly. "Why did you bid on me?"

My answer won't do, so I ignore her question. "Do you realize anyone could have won?"

"Anyone without a criminal record," she corrects. "And yes."

"Do you know who the runner-up was?" The runner up was Alexander Halford, a weasel corporate attorney who's fifty-five and only fucks women in their '20s.

She lifts her shoulders, staring straight ahead at the limousine's divider wall. "I don't care."

"Such trust in the world." Even to my own ears, I sound like a caricature of some cynical old man.

She arches a brow. "It's just sex, and it's just one time. I wanted what could be done with the money badly enough that it didn't matter who the winning bidder was."

My dick twitches, and I scoot a little farther away from her. "You're helping your friend, Cross Carlson." Remembering that day in court, I grit my molars. I'm probably about to stick my foot in my damn mouth again, so it's a good thing she cuts me a fed-up look and sighs.

"Why I want the money is no one's business but mine."

I snort. "I was in the courthouse that day. Unless you've got something else in the works..."

Her mouth tucks up, the little minx. "Maybe I do."

I turn toward her, wanting her to understand this. I pin her with my eyes and turn my gaze on high. "You can't trust just anyone. Definitely not a man that's going to pay millions to have sex with you."

"I have guards," she points out.

"Yeah, and you dismissed them to come with me. How well do you think you know me, Libby?"

"Well enough to know you're tired and grumpy, and your back's still sore." She sighs. "I know I don't know you very well, but am I really supposed to worry you're some kind of villain?"

"I'm a recovering addict who visits brothels and has a penthouse at a casino. You've seen me fucking a porn star—not too easy, either. You're riding an awful fucking lot on intuition."

"And you're not telling me anything I don't know," she murmurs. She looks away from me, and guilt grabs me by the throat. I sigh into my hands. Lift my head. Meet her eyes. "The other night at the Joseph—"

"Doesn't need to be rehashed. Seriously, Hunter, there was nothing complicated about that, so why make it complicated now?"

Now I do snort. I'd hate to see her version of complicated. I wonder if the mess I'm in up to my ears would qualify. Probably so.

She sits back against the heated seat, and I wonder how anything with us could ever be anything but complicated. I can't help being hard as a rock, sitting this near to her. All that long brown-red hair, that gorgeous face, the way she smells, like cinnamon and vanilla—delicious.

I'm silent as we roll toward Batshit Ranch. Not counting Priscilla, who comes by uninvited, I've never brought a woman here before.

CHAPTER TWENTY-TWO

Elizabeth

I FEEL LIKE I've fallen through the rabbit hole.

I'm sitting by Hunter on a plush, heated bench seat inside his stretch Escalade. We're rolling past fortress-like houses and sprawling, landscaped lawns, on our way to his ranch. He's been quizzing me about my choices, like a...well, I'm tempted to say a jealous boyfriend, except I know there's no way Hunter West is jealous over me.

I pull the coat closer around myself and wish I was wearing something different underneath. I think of what I just told him, about how our last encounter was no big deal. I wonder what it means that he wanted to talk about it.

Now that I've had some time to digest things, I'm incredibly glad it's Hunter I wound up with. I can't account for what he does with other women—especially Priscilla Heat—but he's never been anything but gentle with me, and I can't picture him being different tonight.

I slide a glance his way, admiring his body in those tight, black clothes. *I'm going to have sex with him!* I shiver a little, and Hunter puts his hand on my knee. "Cold?"

"I'm okay."

He pushes a button on his door, and I feel more heat coming from the vents.

"Thank you."

He doesn't speak, but he seems to notice that his hand is still on my knee. He lifts his palm up, looking like he's not sure how it got there. We endure a few more minutes of weird silence before the limo passes through massive, iron gates and starts rolling down a long driveway. A few hundred yards later I see a huge stone house surrounded by big, lush oak trees. We turn into a circle drive and park between a fountain and the bib-shaped stairs.

Hunter is out before I am, coming around to my side and opening the door before the driver can reach me.

His hand in mine feels warm and calloused. He tugs me gently toward the stairs before he stops, cupping my cheek with his other hand, looking contrite. "Libby, I know I've been a dick tonight, but...I don't want you to worry. I'll make sure you're comfortable."

"Thanks." It sounds awkward, but then I am awkward. What does he mean, make sure I'm comfortable? It's sex, not a bikini waxing. Is he talking about how much it hurts the woman when—

My stomach clenches when he tucks an arm around my shoulders, and then we're going up the stairs. He pushes through the double doors and leads me into a massive foyer with gorgeous, hardwood ribbon stairs curling up to a second-floor, a massive wood-carved chandelier with dancing gas flames, and a marble tabletop with a curved, scroll mirror that rises toward a vaulted ceiling.

"Wow—your place is beautiful."

I feel a little embarrassed as I say it—a little bourgeoisie—but why be embarrassed now? He's seen my mom's 1990s kitchen, and I know he knows about my family's financial woes. Heck, he's paying me ten million dollars to be here right now.

His hand around mine tightens. "Decorator." In the dancing light of the chandelier, his face looks beautiful and hard. "Are you hungry?"

"No, not right now." I'm too nervous for that.

He nods. "Then follow me."

I'm all eyes as he leads me down a wide hallway with a marble, checkerboard floor and gorgeous wood walls. It's very masculine, elegantly understated, with few frou-frou decorations.

We pass a huge, lit painting of a bird dog prancing and another of a Gothic, shotgun home, and I say, "You're from New Orleans, right?"

He nods, but doesn't speak, and I feel kind of foolish for acting like we just met.

Really, our relationship—if you can call it that—has been pretty much the same since that night at his party. Nothing personal, just physical. Which, again, makes me wonder why he paid so much for this. I wonder if it's possible he really likes the idea of being the first man in between my legs. It's a little crude, so I hope not.

I follow him into a comfortable men's parlor with two plush soft couches, a recliner, and a fireplace, plus an emerald marble bar and shelves filled with old, hardback books. His laptop, a sleek, black Mac, sits on an end table, half cracked. I'm filled with the low-level buzz that comes from being in his personal space.

"Have a seat," he tells me, motioning to the couches.

He strides over to the bar and pours two drinks. Bourbon, of course. Mine is shallow, his is not. He sits across from me in a wing-backed chair, one ankle propped on his knee, and I feel the belly bats again. He looks so serious, even more imposing than usual here in his own home.

"I have a proposition for you, Scarlett."

I swallow. "Okay."

"You stay for a week, and sex is optional. Initiated by you. If, by week's end, you haven't done so, you can return home to Napa."

My mouth falls open. That's how shocked I am. I can feel my face redden as I falter, "I-I don't understand."

"Take it at face value," he advises.

I shake my head, feeling shocked and...kind of stung. "I just don't get...why did you do this? Why pay so much tonight if you don't want to... If you don't want this. Does this have to do with Priscilla Heat?" It doesn't seem logical, but then again, nothing about him does. Maybe bidding on me was just a means to an end. A bet or something. Maybe he wants me to be in a film.

"Priscilla and I are not an item," he says wearily. "Trust me."

I have no reason to trust him, as he's already pointed out, but even if I did, it still doesn't explain why he just paid millions of dollars to take my virginity, only to now offer me this bizarre…I don't even know what to call it.

Then I have a terrible thought. What if he's decided he doesn't want me anymore, and this is the best way he can think of to let me down gently? I swallow back my humiliation.

"Have some of your drink, Libby. Hal will have your luggage in soon and I'll show you to your room." He rubs a hand through his blond hair and once again, I find myself fighting to control my emotions.

I run my gaze over him, focusing on how he looks, on the way the dim light shadows him.

"You look tired."

One eyebrow arches, a similar expression to the one that Marchant Radcliffe makes. When it's clear he's not answering, and the ensuing silence has stolen all my bolder questions, I decide to ask about that. "You and Marchant have been friends since college, right?"

He nods.

"Tulane?"

"Right." He takes a swallow of his bourbon. "I'm surprised you know."

I know I have to be red as an apple, but I try to cover. "You're kind of famous."

"It's the television," he says. "People watch you play poker, they feel like they know you."

That hits a little close to home, and I smirk to cover my nervousness. "Do you consider yourself easy to get to know?"

He regards me over the rim of his glass, looking like a grumpy bear. "What do you think?"

I lift an eyebrow. "I think our relationship is...weird. Our interactions, rather. I'm not sure I'm in a position to say."

He stares at me—almost through me—for a second before bringing his glass back to his mouth. I get the feeling he wants to say something, but he doesn't. He just sits there, looking tense and tired, and I'm blabbing again out of nervousness.

"Did you play tonight? You're wearing black."

"I did."

"Did you win?"

"No."

"You didn't win?"

He looks grave—but maybe he's just giving me his poker face. "Shocking, isn't it?"

I press my lips together. "I thought you hadn't lost in almost a year."

"I hadn't."

"Oh. Well I'm sorry to hear that."

He snorts. "I don't give a shit."

He looks behind my head, in the direction of a clock I hear ticking, and stands, leaving his glass on one of the shelves. "Come with me. I'll show you to your room."

I watch him out of the corner of my eye as he leads me back down the elegant hallway, toward the foyer and its staircase.

"What will it be?" He asks gruffly, after a moment of silence, in which all I hear is the swishing of our clothes and the soft pad of our shoes. "Would you rather stay the week or get the deed done now?"

We round a corner to the entry hall, and I ball my hands into fists. Why did I ever think I could handle this? My heart is pounding and my knees feel weak. I'm so confused; I want to run, but I take a deep breath instead.

I manage to flash Hunter a nonchalant look. "You're the winning bidder. It's your choice," I say as we reach the stairs.

"Then we'll wait."

It takes a few seconds for the shock of that to sink in. Hunter doesn't want to have sex with me? *Or maybe he wants me around longer.* "If you're doing this for my benefit, please don't. You get what you want. You paid enough."

"I'll keep that in mind."

I'm going to ask him more about his week-long plan—as well as how that will affect the terms of our agreement with Love Inc.—when I notice how carefully he's moving up the stairs. I think about his back again, which reminds me of Priscilla and how wrong it is that I'm here, in his house, but still, I feel a swell of sympathy for him.

"How is your back? Are you feeling any better?"

"Are you always so solicitous, or is it my charm that brings that side of you out?"

I think he's teasing, but I don't realize that until after I've spoken honestly. "I'm not sure." Then I add this little gem: "I've never had a boyfriend."

It was relevant in my head; whatever this is with Hunter is the closest I've ever come to Romantic Relationship Land. But he didn't need to know that.

He sounds strangled when he asks, "Never?"

I want to die. My hand actually comes to cover my mouth. I jerk it down, so frazzled I actually stop my ascent. I look into his surprised face, feeling like an idiot.

"I don't mean I've never done...anything ever. Never dated, I mean. I just mean…it was nothing serious." I clench and unclench my fists as we step onto the second floor, done in vibrant navy blue, pale green, and gold.

I run a hand back through my hair, now sweaty, and Hunter looks at me like I've grown horns. "Are you a lesbian?"

"Do I seem like one?" I ask him pointedly.

He smirks, and I tell myself to get back on my game. *You're okay. You can do this.*

We go about twenty feet down the hallway on the left, and Hunter opens the door to a room that's done in green—just like another room, in another of his homes. "This will be yours."

"It's lovely."

He nods once. "It should have everything you need."

"Thank you." But I'm still confused. I wish I had the nerve to ask him why he wants me hanging around here for a week, and why he seems fine with the possibility that he might not get what he paid for. We do have chemistry. I know that much. So what gives?

He looks me over, head to toe, and I feel a blush cover my cheeks. "You can dress however you want." I look at him like he's crazy, and he adds, "I mean, I don't want you to feel like you have to walk around the house half-naked."

Really? "Are you sure you don't want me to just go home? Because I can. If this isn't...you know, working out."

He puts his hand on the small of my back and pushes me gently into the room. "I'm sure, Libby." He leans on the doorway. "Call for me if you need something. Press one on the phone, and it will ring my cell."

And that's it. He's gone, and I'm alone in my lingerie and silky robe, feeling more confused than ever.

CHAPTER TWENTY-THREE

Hunter

THIS IS A fucking mess.

I am a fucking mess.

I gave her the room adjoining mine? *Really?* I drop my head into my hand and use my fingertips to rub my throbbing temples. I haven't slept in days and having Libby next door isn't going to help. Shit is hitting the fan with this Sarabelle situation, which means having Libby here is an even worse idea.

So why did I do it?

It's not all that hard to figure out. I didn't want anybody else fucking her. And it's not a caveman thing. I don't want to possess her—I don't want to possess any woman.

And yet…I just can't stand the idea of another man...

Jesus H.

Libby DeVille, a fucking virgin. I thought she felt tight when I had my fingers inside her, but I thought she was just inexperienced. Not a goddamned virgin.

I'm leaning against the hallway wall, hard as a baseball bat and straining against my fly, when I get a call from Dave.

"What's up, man?"

"Bad news." My stomach sinks, and I hustle down the hall. "In addition to claiming all Sarabelle's client logs earlier today, the FBI is out at Love Inc. right now. Went in the back way, across that desert and that patch of grass behind the left manor. One of my people says they're hot for you. They're even interested in tonight's bidding."

"Fuck."

"I'd feel the same way if I were in your position."

I grit my teeth. "Keep me posted, okay?"

"Sure thing."

The line goes dead, and I suck a big breath down. Fucking Priscilla.

I practically run to my office, where I page my head of Batshit Ranch security, Julian, and give him instructions on how I want this place protected. Then I pull out my .38, stick it in the holster I wear against my abs, and pull my tight black t-shirt off. I stride to one of the guest rooms, grabbing a white undershirt out of a package I keep in the top drawer for visitors. Then I pull on my ragged bomber jacket and go back into my office.

I pull out my phone and call Priscilla. It rings four times before I'm sent to voice mail.

Shit.

It was a stupid move, maybe, but I don't care. I'm tired of being a sitting duck. I want to move on this.

I slump down in my desk chair and pour myself another glass of bourbon. West Bourbon. Truth is, I find the shit a little bitter. How's that for a secret?

I'm comforted by the familiar warm glow in my belly, and I call Priscilla again. This time I'm sent to voice mail after one ring.

Shit!

I'm up and pacing, and Rita is on my mind. I've known for a while now that if Priscilla leaks the story of who my real mother was, it could lead to scrutiny of the West family. It could lead to what happened between Rita and me.

At least one person other than the coroner knows the truth: Libby Bernard, Marchant's favorite shrink. That's one way it could come out. There could be other people who know; people my father has trusted over the years. I've never asked him for a list.

I prop my cheek against my palm and try my best to think about something else. But all I can think about is handcuffs. I don't think I could be prosecuted for what happened, but it could sure as hell make me look guiltier in the Sarabelle disappearance.

But I didn't do that.

So what?

Innocent people go to prison all the time.

I've been cuffed one time before, after a bar fight at the Wynn a few years ago. I still remember how much it reminded me of my wrists, years ago, pinched together by long fingernails.

"Piece of shit! You little bastard!"

And fuck it: that calls for another glass.

I'm halfway on the road to plastered when my cell rings again. Marchant.

"Yello."

His voice is tight. "How you doing, man?"

I rub my eyes. "I'm doing. Sleeping beauty's upstairs."

There's a long pause, during which I expect Marchant to ask about my semi-drunkenness. Instead, he says, "You haven't heard from Dave yet?"

"Just a little while ago."

"So you know?"

"Know what?"

"So you don't know."

"What the fuck are you talking about?!" Through the haze of liquor, I feel something prickly and cold. There's silence on the other end, and I want to come through the phone and throttle him. "Know what, dickhead?"

"Sarabelle is dead." His voice cracks. "They found her in San Luis. Dave says they found her with one of your cuff links in her hand."

Elizabeth

MY PHONE RINGS a few minutes after Hunter leaves, and it's Suri—sobbing. I know it's about Cross, and my heart is in my throat when she says, "HE'S AWAKE! TALKING A LOT!"

"Holy crabcakes! Are you kidding me?!"

She isn't.

Cross woke up two—really woke up—two and a half hours ago, with Suri in his room. She was holding his hand just before the end of visiting hours and reading him a magazine about vintage motorcycles.

The news makes me so excited, I actually shriek, then promptly sit down on the bed, because my knees are shaking.

"Suri, I want every freakin' detail."

"The last day or so, he was different," she says. "I didn't tell you because it wasn't something I could explain, but he was looking around the room some and sometimes he seemed... uncomfortable or something. I would look down at a book and then back up and it seemed like he had shifted. I don't know, it's hard to explain.

"Then tonight he made this choking noise, and I thought something was wrong so I pushed the nurse button, and as soon as I did he said my name! I was worried it was a fluke, but he's still awake now and they're checking him over. They're even going to give him orange soda." Her voice breaks on the word, and I sink down in a chair. "Nanette said he might be asleep by the time I get back, but they were doing some man stuff so I didn't need to be in there and I just had to tell you. Am I interrupting anything?"

I tell her an abbreviated version of the Hunter saga, and then I steer things back to Cross. He's so much more important than my romantic angst.

"Suri, did he seem okay? I mean...did he seem the same?"

I can hear her voice break as she says, "He really does."

"I can't believe it," I breathe. "I mean, after the stroke, I was worried he would..."

"I know," Suri says, "me, too. But he seems okay. At first glance, anyway." She laughs a little. "I asked him all the silly TV questions, like did he remember the year and who's president, and he did. He even asked about his bike."

I wipe my eyes. "That's just amazing." And it really makes the anxiety and drama of tonight seem about a million times more worthwhile.

"You should feel really proud of yourself for having the guts to do what you did," Suri tells me. "It wouldn't be a course I would have taken, but you got what you needed, and for Hunter to be the winning bidder...call me crazy, Liz, but I think it's the universe repaying you."

I snort. "I'm not so sure about that, but I'm over the moon about Cross. Suri, I want to hear from you soon. I mean very soon. Within hours."

"We'll call you, Lizzy! As soon as we can, I promise."

'We'...

That sounds strange.

By the time I hang up the phone, my mind is reeling in three different directions. I take my time in the luxurious, over-sized shower attached to my room, then change into a big, old University of San Francisco t-shirt and my favorite pair of comfy, bikini-cut panties—deep red, with a white pattern of Xs and Os. The huge, canopy bed is cold, and the pillow smells strange, like vanilla and lavender, and I can hear the air whooshing through the ducts somewhere nearby.

It takes me a long time to go to sleep, and I remember the last thought I have before I shut my eyes is 'I hope I sleep through some of the awkwardness of tomorrow', followed by 'I don't want to miss a thing with Cross'.

So when I find myself staring at a pitch-black bedroom sometime in the wee hours, I feel confused and ill at ease. The curtains are deep green with gold accents. They're thick, so they stand out as black against the creamy wall. I can still hear the air whooshing through the noisy vent somewhere near my head, and I wonder if anyone's ever had the balls to tell Hunter it's annoying.

Hunter...

I'm at Hunter's house. And I'm still a virgin.

I feel so disarmed, I push myself up on my elbow, reaching for the bottle of DeVille bottled water on my night stand. I take a deep chug, and then I sit, still as a portrait, listening to the sounds of the house and wondering what woke me. Is it something with Cross? Maybe I got a text.

I'm reaching for my phone when I hear it: a moan. I can tell it comes from inside his chest, and it reminds me of the way he sounded with Priscilla.

It isn't long before shame, anger, and hurt are pounding through me. I feel sick. Disgusted—with myself or him? As I slide from the bed, I wonder why he's doing this. Is he really so awful that he would bring me to his house and then screw Priscilla Heat in the room next door?

I clutch my chest as I step closer to the door where I can hear another moan. I'm devastated, certain she really is in there with him, when I hear another moan. Only this time it's more groan than moan. There's no mistaking: this is pain, not pleasure.

I pause at the door, but only for a moment. I'm here, and I have nothing left to lose. I lean against the cool, wood door, listening for Priscilla's breathing or her voice, but all I hear is Hunter.

I try the handle. I'm shocked when it turns. I hesitate again, but then my legs are moving, carrying me into a den of darkness—so dark, I can't even make out shadows. I'm tense, listening, and just as my eyes start to adjust I hear another low moan.

My eyes fly to a chair on the other side of the room, and there's a person. Hunter...alone. He's hunched over, clutching his head, breathing like someone on the verge of hyperventilating. He's naked except for a pair of boxer-briefs, and sweet Jesus he is beautiful. My eyes can't help appraising him. My body warms. I glide closer, arms stretched out, and when I get within leaping distance of him I can smell liquor.

Oh no.

I remember how rough he looked earlier today, and at the bar the other night, and fear twists my gut. Is he an alcoholic?

"Hunter?" His massive shoulders rise and fall and I can hear his labored breathing, but otherwise he doesn't stir. I glide my palm along his beautiful, thick shoulder, stroking lightly near his nape. "Hunter?" I try again. "Are you okay?"

He curls over more tightly, clutching his golden hair—too hard. On instinct, I grab his fingers to loosen their grip. He puts a hand over his face and moans again, his body twisting.

"Hunter?"

I feel lost. What do I do for him? Did he drink himself into this state? I can't believe he'd do that. And besides, I know a head-screwed drunk when I see one. This seems like something else.

"Hunter? Are you sick?" He continues breathing hard, almost like he's struggling, and I wonder about the drugs he's said he doesn't do. For some reason, the thought of Hunter doing drugs makes me feel devastated.

He shifts so he's lying back against the chair, so when I step in front of him, I have full view of his glorious, ripped chest. The way his abs and hips taper down to... *Oh, no, Liz. Don't look there.*

With all my self-control, I pull my gaze back to his face. He's got it covered with his hand, but I can see his nose and mouth between his fingers. His lips are twisted. Like he's having a nightmare. His body still seems...asleep.

Moving hesitantly, I reach for the arm that's lying on his leg to see if I can rouse him, but when I touch his forearm, he jerks back. He moans, and it's an awful sound.

"It's okay," I whisper. The only thing I can think of is to take his hand in mine. I do it quickly, grasping and then squeezing. I sandwich his hand between both of mine, and he leans forward a little. His shoulders relax some, but he's still covering his face with his free hand.

"Hunter. It's okay." I trace his bruised and scraped knuckles. My mind is racing. Maybe he's feverish, but his hand feels cool.

"Come to bed," I murmur. I stand, tugging on his hand, and I'm surprised when he rises. The way he walks over to his bed—the dazed look in his eyes and the stiff movements of his body—lets me know he's somewhere else. Not here. He stops beside the bedside and I touch the small of his back, where he doesn't have any fresh cuts. He collapses onto the bed, face-up. His eyes are shut, his body slack.

I rub his shoulder. "Turn onto your side."

He shifts his hips, and I get full view of his back. It still looks bad, striped with pinkish marks and painful for sure, but not infected. A shudder rolls through him and I put my hand on the firm skin of his side.

"It's okay, Hunter. Go to sleep."

I step up, near his head, and find his eyes are open. I'm shocked when they roll over my face. "Libby?" He sounds strangled.

I nod and whisper, "Go to sleep." His eyes drift shut, and I am brave enough to stroke his golden hair. It's soft, so soft and pretty, like his creamy tanned neck and his cute little ear.

"Go to sleep, Hunter. Everything's okay."

Finally he's breathing evenly, his body relaxed.

I bring him the bottle of water from my bedside, and fish some crackers and Advil from my purse. I leave them on the table beside his bed and stroke his hair once more before I go.

CHAPTER TWENTY-FOUR

Elizabeth

I OPEN MY eyes to streams of golden light. They push their way past the edges of the thick green curtains that cover the massive, wall-long windows. The first thing I think is *something important happened*, but for that first minute, I can't remember what. All I know is that I feel rested, and my huge oak bed, with its sheer, flowing canopy and satin duvet, makes me feel like a princess.

Holy crap. I'm at Hunter's house. And...what the fudge was that last night? There's no reason my memory of the previous night should make me nervous, but suddenly that's what I am. I can't move from the bed. I can hardly even breathe as I think about the man who slept next door to me. Is he okay? Still sleeping?

What the hell am I doing here, in this bedroom that connects to his? I feel almost crushed by a wave of surreality. I sold my V-card. For ten million dollars. To Hunter West.

How am I ever going to pull this off? Have sex with Hunter? I imagine a fully awake and fully erect Hunter, naked and lying over me...

Dear God.

I hop off the bed and fly through my morning preparations. Since I showered last night, I consider skipping, but considering what might be on today's agenda, I give myself another quick rinse. I dress in a pair of brown leggings and a long, sexy red sweater that dips down just a little low in front. I pull on some ankle-length boots I borrowed from Suri and put on just a dash of makeup. If Hunter might be seeing me up close, I don't want to look fake, but I don't want him to see the sprinkling of freckles on my nose, either.

But will he be seeing me up close?

I feel silly for over-thinking things when I've messed around with Hunter before, but those times were different. Spontaneous. This…well, isn't.

I send a quick text to Suri, demanding updates about Cross. I want so badly to tell her what happened in Hunter's room last night, but I don't. I do enjoy a moment of glee, where I want to fall down on my knees and thank the heavens that Cross is *awake*. Then I tuck my purse and phone under the bed, give myself one more glance in the mirror, and step out into the hall.

The first thing I'll do after reassuring myself that Hunter is okay is let him know I'm not cool with our plan. I don't want to initiate sex. I've never done it before and he is, after all, the winning bidder. He should chose the moment. If he doesn't, our contract might fall through. I might not get paid at all.

Slowly—so slowly that I'm almost not moving at all—I step to the door beside mine and raise my fist to knock. My knuckles connect with the cold cherry wood, and I hold my breath as I listen for his footsteps. Nothing. I knock twice more, trying not to worry when he doesn't answer. Then I tuck my hair behind my ears and head for the stairs. Maybe I'll find him in his study.

My pulse is pounding by the time I reach the bottom of the curling staircase. With sunlight streaming through the windows, I can fully appreciate the beauty of the foyer, with its glossy marble floors and sleek wood walls. The chandelier hanging from the high ceiling is made of what looks like an old-school wagon wheel and some kind of copper. It's just the right blend of eclectic and classic.

I'm thinking of going left, toward the study, but then I catch a whiff of something delicious. It's pretty unlikely that Hunter's wearing an apron, but I'm so hungry, I don't care who's cooking. I come down off the bottom stair and follow my nose, toward the right, past a grand dining room with a fireplace and a long table topped with what looks like a pewter sculpture of a sailboat. I'm walking past that room, toward another room that looks like a formal living area, when I see, through a half-cracked doorway in the dining room, a posh black and white kitchen.

I'm stepping past the table when Hunter's beautiful body fills the doorway. I'm shocked to see his lips spread in a cat-like grin as he looks me over from head to boot.

He tilts his blond head at the room behind him. "I've got breakfast."

As he turns back into the kitchen, I realize he's holding a wooden spoon. Holy belly bats, that's sexy. Hunter in house clothes, cooking breakfast. Dark jeans hang off his hips, with a worn-out spot over the left back pocket. A scruffy green button-up shirt is rolled up to his elbows. Rugged boots with real live mud clomp on the tile floor as he heads for the stove.

As I step into the kitchen, which smells like butter and sugar and bacon, he turns around from the stove and flashes me a cautious smile.

"How are ya?"

I surprise myself by sliding a look up and down his delectable body. I just can't resist. I notice that despite his sunnier attitude, his eyes are still tired and, underneath a day's worth of stubble, his normally tanned face looks slightly pale.

"How are *you*?" I ask, praying he'll mistake the ogle I just gave him for friendly concern.

"Up and kicking," he says, turning back to what he's doing so I get a view of his broad back and tight ass. The double oven and industrial-sized sink face a massive window overlooking rolling acres of flat farmland. Framing the sink are rows of counter space, complete with black stools, place mats, and silverware.

I take a seat at the bar stool nearest me, choosing the spot closest to the oven, so Hunter is standing right in front of me. I prop my elbow on the counter—black granite with coppery swirls—and try to pretend that this is normal for us. Hunter and I, regular breakfast buddies.

He's pushing some bacon around a skillet, not looking my way, when I begin to wonder if this will be a repeat of last night. I'm not sure if I can stand the awkwardness again. Then he lifts his head and pins me with a warm gaze I can feel between my legs.

"You cook?" he asks, and I notice for the first time that there are two big platters on the counter on Hunter's other side, already piled high with biscuits and cinnamon rolls. Wowzers.

"I don't," I say, hanging my head. "Suri, my roommate, cooks like a champ, so I'm kind of spoiled. I'm surprised you do," I add. "I would have thought you had somebody."

"All honesty?" He arches a brow. "I gave my chef the day off." He picks up a gooey-looking cinnamon roll and hands it to me. Then he gives a slight shake of his head and grabs a plate from one of the cabinets. "Try that," he says, pushing the plate my way, "and tell me if you're still skeptical."

I do, and oh my God. I shut my eyes, and when I open them, he's grinning. "That's just sinful."

"Our cook in New Orleans taught me to make these things from scratch," he tells me, biting into one. His eyes widen, like he's realized he can't speak around the cinnamon roll, so he quickly tries to chew, which makes me laugh.

Our gazes hold like magnets as we both finish our rolls, and then Hunter turns back to the stove, where the bacon is popping and crackling.

His eyes flick over me as he works on the pan. "I have to

say, I miss the getup from last night."

I smile at him. "Do you now?"

"I do."

He quickly moves the bacon from the skillet to another plate, then pushes it toward me. He grabs a basket of eggs out of the fridge, and watching his shoulders move as he cracks them into a giant bowl is one of the sexiest things I've ever seen.

He seems so...different in his own space. Not at all like the Hunter from my sex fantasies, or the anguished man from the last few nights.

I wish there was some way to ask about last night in particular, but I can't think of one.

"How do you like your scrambled eggs?" he asks over his shoulder.

"Hard, I guess," I say, and yeah, I blush a second after I say it.

He doesn't notice though, and I munch on my bacon. He's quiet, again, so I have time to work up my nerve. A few minutes into his egg scrambling, I bring up the subject of our deal.

"I'm not sure I like it."

His green eyes flicker over mine, then return to the eggs. I can see his shoulders tense.

"I'm glad you mentioned that," he says, sliding a glance at me as he stirs the eggs. "I've thought about it more, and I'm thinking it might be best if you head home a little earlier."

He pauses, looking pensive, and I rest my hand on my stomach. I'm not sure what to say. I just don't understand.

"You can go whenever you want," he says, meeting my eyes. "You'll still get your money."

His words hit me like a drop-kick to the chest, and I blurt, "You don't want me?"

"I didn't say that." His words are hot—and so sincere that it's impossible not to believe him. "If you really want to do this, I do too. But it needs to happen today."

"Why?"

His jaw tightens, and again, he won't look at me. "I've got some business that just came up. You'd be more comfortable back at your own place."

Oh, so that's how it's going to be. My temper flares. "You're bullshitting me. Not that it matters. You did pay for this, so you can do whatever you want."

"It's not Priscilla," he says, pressing his lips together. "It's not like that."

He moves the eggs off the stove and checks the oven before walking around the counter to stand in front of me.

His hands tunnel into my hair. "I want you," he says in a husky voice, and I can feel how much as he leans against my hip. "I'm disappointed about the change of plans. Believe me. But this is how it's got to be."

"Why did you do it? Why did you say...to stay the week? Why did you even bid on me?"

"I want this to be yours. On your terms. That's how it should be, Libby. You should be comfortable. I thought you'd like a few days here to get your footing." His fingers, in my hair, trail up my cheeks; his thumb strokes my brow and I shiver. "I didn't buy you for sex, although I'd love to take you to my bed. I bought you because I can't stand the thought of some other bastard pawing at you. Not you."

"But it's okay for other girls?"

He strokes my hair off my forehead. "At Marchant's, all the girls choose their clients. It's invitation only out there, I'm sure you know. They set their own prices. Get paid well. And most of them aren't doing it for altruistic reasons."

He strokes his calloused thumb over my lower lip, and I tremble. My insides have gone liquid. "You used to go out there," I whisper.

"I did."

"How come?" He cups my cheek, still gentle, but I can

sense him closing off.

"I've got my reasons."

"But you could sleep with any woman."

Loosening his grip on me, he laughs, and I look up at him. "I'm glad you find me so appealing, Miss DeVille."

I blush. "Almost any woman."

His jaw drops open in a funny way, and I grin so hard I can feel the dimples in my cheeks.

"Is it because you like to keep your distance?" I ask.

"Wow." He sort of chuckles a little bit. "Sneak attack."

I shrug, because I didn't really mean to sneak attack. It's just, pretense has never been stripped away like it is now between the two of us, so I figure I should take advantage of it.

Hunter seems to feel the same way. "Keep my distance?" He strokes up and down my cheek bone, and I feel hypnotized as I reach out and touch his hip. "What do you mean, keep my distance?"

My knees part a little as he steps closer, coming in between them.

"Do I strike you as a man who keeps my distance?"

"I don't mean that," I say, breathless. "I mean, no relationships."

"I have a better question: How is it a pretty girl like you still has a V-card to sell?"

"I'm not a girl," I whisper.

"No, you're not."

He leans down and covers my mouth with his, and I pull him close, feeling his hardness with a heady rush as he rocks his body into mine.

"You're a woman," he says, between hard kisses. "Goddamned gorgeous one at that."

My hands drift into the pockets of his jeans, and oh my God, that ass. It's tight and firm and everything a man's ass should be. I want to pull his jeans off. Squeeze it. Kiss it.

I'm panting, elated by his compliments, as he trails gently down my throat and kisses my collar bone.

"I'm like you," I whisper into his hair. "Want to keep my distance."

"Not doing a very good job of it," he pants.

He comes up for air, pushing his forehead against mine, so close that I can count the yellow flecks in his irises. "You know what I mean," I murmur. "I don't want a relationship. I never do. I mean I never have."

His eyes change, from aroused to something more shrouded as runs his fingers down my arm. "Probably your mother."

I lean back, stunned that he said that to me. "Probably so." I guess I come off as the screwed-up daughter of a drug addict. Lovely.

"I'm only saying because I've had my share of therapy," he says, squeezing my hand before he walks back around the counter, to the oven. He opens it, and a heavenly sweet smell wafts out.

"You have?"

"Yes ma'am. Mostly when I was a kid."

"After your mother passed away?" It's a forward question, but then he's been forward with me.

Something passes over his face—something ugly. He covers it quickly and nods. "That was part of it."

"Well you're probably right." I lean against the counter, propping my head in one of my palms. "Relationships, other than with Suri and a few other friends—they just don't seem worth it to me."

"That's because you don't want to get hurt."

"You're quite the Ann Landers, Hunter West. I'm shocked."

He looks at me without any trace of a smile. "I do write an advice column. Vegas High-Rolling. For the *Las Vegas Sun News*."

I gape, and he laughs. "Kidding, of course."

"You're a funny guy."

I'm feeling a little more relaxed now, and happy to flirt with him, and willing to broach sensitive subjects—like: "So what's up with you and Priscilla?"

"Nothing but the sky," he says, pouring two tall glasses of orange juice.

"You don't care about her, but there's chemistry?"

"I don't care about her," he says flatly.

His eyes meet mine, and they're so cold, and all of a sudden it's painfully obvious to me that we're not really friends, or breakfast buddies, or anything at all. We don't know each other, and I've struck a bad cord with my prying question.

Hunter turns back to the stove and begins to pile two plates with food. When he speaks again, his tone is lighter. "I've got a question for you: Weren't you even a little worried about who would win your bid?"

"Uh, yeah. My friend Suri kept joking that it would be some–one old and slimy."

He smirks, piling scrambled eggs on two big, square plates. "Are you saying I'm over the hill?"

"I didn't know you'd swoop in to rescue me."

"That wasn't a rescue. Believe me." He checks the oven again, then shuts it. "Do your parents know?" He sticks his hands into his pockets and leans against the sink. "I assume not."

"They don't."

"I'm surprised your friends let you go through with it."

"I needed the money," I say. "And it was one friend. I didn't really let her argue."

"Well, I'm good for it." He rubs the bridge of his nose, like he has a headache.

"Do you win a lot at poker?"

"I do. I win more at Wall Street." He peeks into the oven one more time, and I think how sexy he looks in chef mode. "What kind of jam do you like?"

"Strawberry."

"I'm a strawberry man myself."

He sets a jar of homemade jam on the counter, then puts the oven mitt back on and opens the oven, pulling out a tray of...

"Beignets! Holy crap, I love beignets!" He puts two on a plate and slides it across the counter, then piles three on his own plate. He does not come around to sit beside me.

I pick one up and turn the hot pastry around in my burning fingertips. "You're incredible."

"You think so?" He regards me silently over the counter as he polishes off a piece of bacon, then says, "I know you're doing this for Cross Carlson. I'm not sure if I think you're stupid or amazing."

I scrunch my face up. "That's not the only reason. I'm also doing it because I'm tired of being a virgin."

That draws a chuckle from him. "What's so tiring about it?"

"I guess I'm tired of all the anticipation."

He grins wickedly. "I'd say anticipation is one of the best parts."

"I wouldn't know," I murmur, biting into my beignet.

"Are you saying that you want to know?"

"Oh yeahh." I squeeze my eyes shut, blissed out over the warm, doughy goodness. When I open them Hunter is smirking at me. I blush. "I meant oh yeah, that stuff is really good. But yeah, I do I guess. Otherwise I would have hung onto it."

Slowly, languidly, tiger-like, Hunter walks around the counter. He wraps his hands around my biceps, turning me gently to face him, and pulls me close. Then he bends down slowly, bringing his face close enough so I have an amazing view of his lips. As I sit there, brainless and overheated, he leans closer and licks the corner of my mouth.

"Powdered sugar," he purrs.

I'm panting, halfway to a heart attack, when he stands back up, looking down on me with a suddenly serious expression.

"You think about this, Libby. Really think about if you want to be with me. It'll be a one-time thing. You said it—I don't do relationships, and I don't make exceptions, even when I'm tempted."

"I don't either." Although I haven't ever had the chance, and with him, I'm sure I totally would.

"Well I'm in if you are." He strokes his palm over my hair. "You give me half an hour and I'll come find you. Sound good?"

I nod, clutching the bar stool so I don't fall off.

"Okay." He trails his hand down my arm and squeezes my fingers, so gentle it almost takes my breath away. Then he kisses my cheek and starts to back out of the kitchen. "One V-card," he says, making a check mark with his finger, "claimed."

CHAPTER TWENTY-FIVE

Hunter

I FEEL LIKE I'm living in a dream: part nightmare, part fantasy. The fantasy is easy enough to dwell on. I've got Libby in my house, and soon I'll have her in my bed, underneath me, with those long legs spread and her hot pussy just waiting for my cock. It's a good feeling. One I could enjoy for hours. But I don't have hours, because of the nightmare part.

I walk into my study, shutting the doors behind me, and go immediately to the bar beside the shelves. If I'm going to call Marchant, I'll need this.

As I toss some back, I try to remember what I did after I heard about her death the night before. I know I drank. I had a dream about Libby, but it almost feels like a memory. I awoke this morning with an awful headache, and even now, after a shower and breakfast, I feel like absolute shit.

I feel worse when I think about telling Libby. About Sarabella. It has nothing to do with her, but if I am declared a suspect, I don't want her to feel duped—like she gave herself to me under false pretenses.

I don't think I'd be found guilty were I to be charged, being that I didn't actually do anything, but I'm not naïve. I know my father has his enemies, and so do I. I also know Governor Carlson is involved in this. Powerful players produce powerful results.

I feel queasy thinking of that, so instead I think of Libby's breasts. How I'll get to kiss them soon. We'll have a good fuck, and I'll make it one to remember.

I pull my cell phone out. I need to hurry, get upstairs to Libby before she turns on the news. I don't think my name would be on it, but I can't be sure, and I don't want to lose my chance to touch her one more time.

I lock the doors of the study and dial Marchant. He answers on the second ring.

"Hey, dude. You free?" he asks.

I frown. Wasn't I the one who called him? "What do you mean, am I free?"

"I'm surprised no one's knocking at your door. I've had someone in a dark suit poking around my penthouse, trying to get past security."

I frown. "You're not at the ranch?"

"We've closed for a few days for Sarabelle."

"How you holding up?" Sarabelle was one of the women I visited from time to time, but she was Marchant's employee and friend. He feels the responsibility of this even harder than I do.

I can see him clenching that square jaw of his when he says, "If Priscilla Heat did this, I swear I will kill her with my own two hands."

I shut my eyes and rub them. "You and me both. Tell me what you know."

"Dave heard it on the police scanners about ten minutes before I called you last night. He's also got a guy inside the FBI. Says the cufflink has your initials in capital letters. He called me asking if I thought you did it."

Fucking great—our own guy turning on me. "What'd you say?"

"What do you think I said?"

I rub my eyes. "What's going on with Priscilla and Lockwood now?"

"Lockwood's been MIA since yesterday. All our people are looking for him."

That's news. "And Priscilla?"

"She's at her house. Hasn't moved."

I take a swallow of my drink and force myself to ask: "Sarabelle was...found in San Luis?"

"Yes," Marchant says tightly.

He doesn't tell me where, and I don't ask. It'd be best if I don't know, in case I'm questioned.

I hesitate before asking my next question, because I'm pretty sure I don't want to know. "What color was the cuff link?"

"Color. Uh…I think Dave said that it was black."

"Goddamnit." I jump up, curling my hands around the phone although I want to smash it. "That one came from my dresser drawer."

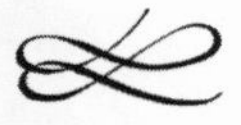

Elizabeth

AS SOON AS I get back to my room, I see a message on my phone from Loveless. 'Call me ASAP.'

That seems random. I hope nothing is wrong. I pick a soft-looking wing-backed chair to sit in, prop my feet on the foot stool, and count the rings. She answers on the third, and I can hear in her voice that she's been crying. "Scarlett. How are you?"

"I'm fine, but what's wrong?"

She sniffs, and there's a long pause before she whispers, "It's Sarabelle. They...found her body."

I press my hand over my mouth. "Oh my God. Loveless, I'm so sorry."

"We're all in a state of shock. But that's not all." She speaks even more softly, so I can barely hear her. "FBI agents came by today." I hear a shuffling sound, and when she speaks again her voice is muffled. "Scarlett...you can't tell anybody but...they think Hunter did it."

My stomach bottoms out. "Holy shit."

"But he didn't, Scarlett. I've known him for years. He would never do this."

I lean my head against the chair back, feeling dizzy. "If he didn't do it, why do they think he did?"

"That's what I don't know. But I thought that you would want to know that something's going down."

I nod, feeling...stunned. "That's so crazy." And then I remember myself, and what this call is really about. "I'm so sorry about your friend, Loveless."

"It could have been me. It could have been any of us." Her voice breaks. "But Sarabelle was so sweet. It shouldn't have been her."

"It shouldn't have been anyone," I say.

Loveless sniffs, then says, "Just be careful. Not from Hunter —well, you should be if you get a bad feeling, but I don't think you will. Be careful because something's going on, and now that you've been here at Love Inc., you're one of us."

For some reason, her words make my eyes water. "Thank you, Loveless. Thank you so much. I'll be thinking about you. About all you guys. Take care of yourself, okay?"

I hang up the phone with a heavy feeling in my stomach and read two texts from Sur.

'Did u know one of escorts frm brothel found dead??!!'

And from almost thirty minutes after the first. *'U ok? Msg me back. Paranoid here!'*

I take a deep breath and tell myself that I can handle this. I don't need to message Suri for backup, and I don't need to go running home like a chicken.

All of a sudden it hits me that this must be why Hunter was so weird last night. He must have found out about Sarabelle then. Wow. I can't even imagine what it would be like to be falsely accused of something like that.

Unless he did it.

He *didn't* kidnap her, did he?

Of course not. I shake my head and send a reply to Suri: *'I'm fine. Cross??'*

'Doing gr8. I'm here now.'

'Gr8. Can I call him l8r, even if u not there?'

While I wait for her reply, I change into my sexy clothes—a fresh red teddy and crotchless panties, followed by my black, silky robe—but I don't feel sexy. I feel sad. Sad for Sarabelle, sad for my friends at Love Inc., sad for Hunter. Last night he was clearly grieving.

I'm walking to my en suite bathroom, ready to lather myself with lotion in anticipation of the big event, when I hear a deep boom from somewhere in the house. I stop mid-step, all the hair on my arms standing on end as I realize the sound is shouting. Hunter's shouting. It grows louder in time with wall-rattling stomps.

For half a second, I want to shut myself inside the bathroom and barricade the door. I've seen way too many freak outs in my life. But my feet seem glued to the Oriental rug as I listen to Hunter coming down the hall. The rhythm of his footsteps is unsteady, but there's no more shouting. He stops, and I hear a loud bang that reminds me, eerily, of Cross's fist against the wall that night at Hunter's vineyard party. I hear a muttered curse, followed by the sound of a door swishing open, then slamming shut.

I stand doe-still, barely even breathing as shuffling sounds start to come from the room next door. A creaking sound that reminds me of a drawer being opened. A slamming sound. A few heavy footsteps. The unmistakable sound of something shattering.

I'm shaking now. Sometimes Mom got drunk or wasted and broke things. Sometimes in proximity to me. It's not that she meant to hurt me; she simply never noticed I was there. Once, when I was nine, I had to have stitches in my left eyebrow because a piece of a glass bowl caught me as I came into the kitchen to check on her.

I don't want to go into Hunter's room this time, but just like last night, I can't seem to stop myself. I'm sweating, my fingers trembling as I wrap my hand around the doorknob. I know better than to knock. Angry people almost universally want to be left alone—only when they're breaking things, they probably shouldn't be.

As I turn the doorknob, I remind myself that he isn't doing drugs. He isn't drinking. At least not like my mom does. He's upset because someone he knew died.

Or maybe he killed them.

"Shut up," I murmur to myself. He didn't kill Sarabelle. He was playing televised poker for the last two nights, and last night he was here with me.

I take a fortifying breath and throw the door open. At first I'm not sure I'm in the right room. What last night stood out to me as a large space with elegant, imposing furniture is now a clothes tornado. I immediately notice his huge dresser is missing two of its drawers, and atop the dresser, I can see a picture frame lying face-down, surrounded by shards of broken glass.

A quick glance around the room reveals Hunter standing by his hulking, four-post bed, pawing through a sea of undershirts and boxer briefs. Mixed in with the crimson pillows and blankets of his bed are two hefty dresser drawers. He's bent over one, arms moving in a frenzy as he throws clothes every which way.

He doesn't even glance up as I step closer. He doesn't seem

to know I'm here. His face twists in fury, and he grabs one of the drawers with both hands and hurls it at his headboard, where it bounces off and lands on a pile of pillows.

"Hunter?"

He's breathing hard, his face white, his mouth and green eyes standing out vibrantly against his skin.

He straightens, shoulders heaving as he sucks back air. He looks so furious, it's like he's in a daze. He's not looking at me, but rather at something behind me.

Without moving a muscle or glancing my way, he whispers, "Go away."

I follow his vacant gaze to the wall behind me and find that he is staring at a mirror. Staring blankly at himself. No, not blankly. Desolately.

As I watch, he leans down against his bed, elbows on the mattress, face going into his palms as his shoulders hunch and one of his hands tunnels back through his messy hair.

"I heard about Sarabelle."

He whirls toward me. His mouth is twisted into a bitter pinch, and his eyes are harder than I think I've ever seen.

"I'm so sorry. I know you knew her."

"You don't know the half of it," he murmurs hoarsely.

"I'm sure that's true." I hold his gaze. "But I know throwing things won't help," I say softly.

"Nothing will." I watch the edge in his eyes fade back into dazed desolation, and I take two steps closer. When he doesn't react, I close the distance between us and gently touch his elbow.

He jumps a little. "Jesus, Libby." He lifts up his hand, like he's going to touch me, but instead he takes an unsteady step back. "You need to get your shit and go. Just *go*."

"I don't want to go yet." I want to wrap my arms around him, but he grabs my hand. His fingers grip mine and his pretty eyes grow tortured. "I can't make any promises...unless you go. Sometimes when I'm angry, I..."

"Throw things?"

He swallows, and my eyes rake over his body. I can't miss the erection straining against his jeans.

"Sometimes when you're upset, you want to have sex?" I whisper.

He nods, just barely.

"That night at your house, you were upset, weren't you? I saw your room. There was a broken wine glass and the pillows were all over the floor." That was just after I'd heard him having sex with Priscilla. "Hunter...what's going on with you? I'm worried."

His eyes slide over me, and I think it's the most honest I've ever seen him look. I'm reminded, oddly, of an angry, despondent child before he reaches out and grips my shoulder. "You should leave." His voice is hoarse and low. "Libby, please. Turn around and *leave*."

I bite my lip, and I consider doing just that. But I can't. This is Hunter. And maybe I'm a crazy idiot for feeling how I do, but when I'm with him, I feel better. More *me* than I am without him, and that's not something I can just let go of, even if it is insane.

"Do you think that you could talk to me?"

Hunter looks into my eyes and I feel like he's seeing everything inside my past and future. Then, suddenly—*roughly* —he tugs me to his chest and wraps himself around me. I feel his head come down on top of mine and my gut clenches.

"Libby." It sounds like he's pleading with me. I look up at him, wishing I knew what he needed, and his hands come up frame my face. "Libby...why don't you just do what I say?"

"I don't want to leave yet." I clutch his biceps and press my cheek against his chest. "I really wish that you would talk to me."

He nuzzles my face with his, his cheek stroking mine as our mouths join in a kiss. I expect that it will quickly turn hard and fierce, but instead his lips are feather gentle, so soft it doesn't feel quite real.

I pull him close and hungrily deepen our kiss. His tongue glides past mine and he's tugging in deep breaths while never moving off of me. I'm feeling dizzy when he whispers, "Keep your eyes closed."

I think about the strangeness of his request, the way I saw him with his hand on Priscilla's throat, and I can hear him in the limo: *"You're riding an awful fucking lot on intuition."* I try to feel some of the recommended skepticism as his fingers stroke my cheeks, his lips moving over my temples, teasing my ear. And, right there, he groans and presses his heavy body into mine.

"No, open them. Open them, Libby. I want to see your beautiful blue eyes."

His eyes are wide, and when I look into them, I feel like my insides have gone molten. I nod, then arch up and press my lips to his. We kiss for what seems like hours. Hunter's body is warm and weighty, and as things between us heat up, I grab his hips and he rocks into me with increased frenzy, panting, "Oh God, Lib. Oh God."

He's got my robe unfastened and it lies in heaps around me. His lips are sucking my breast, his hand holding my teddy up, and I can feel him trembling.

"Hunter, can I...?" I fumble with the button of his jeans, and he groans.

"Oh no." He pants. "You first."

He ducks and pulls my panties down, and before I know it his mouth is covering me right where I'm throbbing. I'm coming off the mattress, tugging on his hair, and he is moaning like he loves it.

I find my release with a strangled scream, clamping my legs around his head. He grins when he disentangles himself, and I can feel his stiff length pressing against my leg through the denim of his jeans. I try to reach for it, but he lifts his weight off me.

"Why not?" I murmur.

His eyes are wide. "Do you want to?"

"Yes. Of course."

I grab his shoulders and push him down beside me. This time it's me between his legs, unzipping his pants and freeing that huge, hard length. I pull his blue jeans down, his boxers down, and there is all of Hunter—cock and balls and hair-strewn thighs. I can feel a spurt of warmth between my own legs as I lean down and ease him into my mouth.

He nearly comes off the bed. I suck his head against the soft inside of my mouth and stroke his shaft while my other hand cups his balls. I take him deeper, licking his rod-stiff length just like an ice cream cone—the way I practiced. I lap around the edges of his head and he tugs my hair. I suck some more and pump him just a little harder. I can feel his balls stiffen in my hand. His cock throbs, and I taste a tinge of salt before he jerks away from me, coming over both our hands.

He's pushed himself up onto his elbows and I think he will lie back. Instead he wraps his arms around me and brings me down beside him, curling his body around mine.

"Hunter." I reach behind me and feel the delicious hardness of his abs.

"You're a fucking angel," he rasps.

"No," I whisper, grinning. "Just a girl."

"My favorite girl." He gathers me into his arms and pulls me to the top of the bed, then urges me underneath the covers as he sets the drawers down on the floor. I realize I never figured out what he was doing when I came into the room, but he's not doing it anymore, so it doesn't matter quite as much.

Especially now that we're under the covers, our warm, sated bodies pressed together. Our arms and legs are tangled and I stroke his face, because he's just so handsome.

Soon his breathing is even and his body slack. I stroke his hair and face until my arm muscles are aching from the strain of hovering up over him. I tuck my arm back by my side and kiss his cheek. "Get some rest," I whisper.

Then I snuggle down beside him. I might have drifted off. I can't be sure, but when I open my eyes, I know it's afternoon by the amber and pink tone of the light streaming through the curtains. I blink up at the ceiling, realizing with a pleasant burst of warmth inside my chest that Hunter is wrapped around me, his face hidden in my hair.

I grin. Then I look across the room and see Priscilla.

CHAPTER TWENTY-SIX

Elizabeth

HOLY SHIT. THIS is not good. I'm lying here with Hunter, and there is Priscilla, leaning against the door to his room. Her eyes and mine collide, and I drag my gaze down her lithe body. She's wearing a black pantsuit and tall red heels. Her blonde hair flows over her shoulders like she's just come from a beauty parlor.

Her red lips curve into a twisted smile, and she purrs, "Scarlett."

I sit up and glance wide-eyed at Hunter. He's still sleeping. On his stomach. So I can see all the half-healed welts on his back. It's all I need to get angry—for what she's done him, and that she's even here at all, ruining our moment. I have no idea why Hunter's tied up with her, but I know he shouldn't be.

I pull the sheet around myself as I hop off the bed, moving with borrowed bravado. Hunter, still sleeping peacefully behind me, is my inspiration. He's got enough on his plate with this Sarabelle stuff. He doesn't need a drop by from Priscilla.

Normally my insecurity might cause me to question that—maybe he's in love with her; blah blah blah—but after today, I know he's not. I'm not even sure he likes her, and if nothing else, I know she won't be as gentle with him as I will.

Holding the sheet tightly around myself with one hand, I use the other one to point at the door. "I have no idea what you're doing here, but it's creepy and you need to leave. He's asleep, as you can see. He isn't feeling well."

Priscilla laughs. "His little hooker. What a spitfire you are." She rakes her mean gaze up and down my figure. "I'd like to know what you did to lose all that weight. That night I saw you at Hunter's party you were quite the fat ass."

Her comment bounces off me. I stalk closer to her and jerk my finger at the door. "Get out of here. I'll tell Hunter you came by, and he can decide if he wants to see you." If she doesn't leave in just a second, I might claw her.

She laughs, a throaty, knowing sound. "I see what this is. You actually have a thing for him."

"I think it's clearly mutual."

She shakes her head and makes a tsk-ing sound. "Believe me sweetheart, you don't want to get involved with him. He's poison."

I frown at her. This makes no sense. Hasn't she spent the last few months—or even longer—having sex with him? Good sex, from what I saw through the powder room keyhole.

Intuition tells me she's full of crap, so I roll my eyes as I wave at her again. "I know what I want, and I don't trust a word out of your mouth."

She shrugs. "Your choice Triple X. But if you think he's yours, keep dreaming."

It takes me a second to realize she's not calling me X-rated; she's calling me plus-sized. I snort. "You're ridiculous, and believe me, you really need to leave before I call security." It's a bluff—a stupid one, since I have no idea how much she knows about his house—but she takes a small step backward, the backs of her heels bumping the door.

"Get out of here and don't come back. You sadist."

I march forward, and to my shock, Priscilla turns, opens the door, and steps into the hall. "I'm going," she says in an airy tone, "but it's not because of you, Elizabeth DeVille. I'll be back when Hunter has time to *enjoy* himself."

I open my mouth, but a gray-haired man dressed in butler's uniform beats me to it. Ms. Heat?" He asks as he strides down the hall. I'm surprised when he snatches her arm.

"Hal, I—"

"Mr. West has placed you on the do-not-admit list," he says, as he hauls her off. "I don't know how you got in, but it's time for you to go."

Priscilla shrieks, and I watch as he tosses her over his shoulders and marches toward the stairs.

As they disappear from sight, and I sink down in front of Hunter's door, shaking. What have I gotten myself into?

WHEN I RETURN to Hunter's room, he's still sleeping. I hesitate only a minute before unraveling the sheet from around my body and lying it gently over his. I slip back into my teddy and robe and go next door to call Suri.

"Hi." I smile, feeling oddly content after my little run-in with Priscilla.

"Hi! Lizzy, how is everything? I want to hear about it all. I'm sorry I haven't been a good friend this last little while. Has he put the moves on you?"

"Sort of." I blush. "But I want to hear about Cross first."

She says Cross is awake, but he's quiet and moody. I smile, because that sounds about right.

"I'm sure he'd love to talk to you, but there's a social worker in there with him now. Do you want to call back later?"

I agree to do that, and after a few more minutes of filling her in on the days' events, I hang up and go back into the room with Hunter. I slip into the bed and snuggle up to him. Within seconds, his eyes are open and he's blinking at me.

He reaches out and thumps my nose as a gentle smile

spreads over his lips. "How are you?"

"Good. How are you?"

He sits up, revealing his amazing chest, and I worry I may combust. I think he notices, because he smirks and runs his finger up my throat, the way you might stroke a cat. It makes me shiver, and I find myself giggling like a teenager.

As he slides off the bed, totally, gloriously nude, and begins to look for his clothes, he peeks over his shoulder. "I'm sorry about earlier. Damned embarrassing." It takes me a second to realize he's talking about the mess he made of his room—not about Priscilla.

"It's okay. Don't be embarrassed."

He grabs some boxer-briefs off the floor, and my eyes linger on his perfect package as he steps into them. *Holy moly.*

"I've thrown things around since I was a kid. It's how I used to deal with anger I guess."

I nod, toying with the silky sheets. "You lost your mom. It makes sense that you would have had anger issues."

He gives me a charming little sideways smile. "You're wise for your age."

I arch a brow. "My mom has been hard in other ways."

"I can believe that." I watch in bliss as he throws a few handfuls of clothes into one of the drawers, his chest rippling. As he steps toward my side of the bed, I know I must be flushed. I watch as he swallows, his Adam's apple bobbing. "I know we haven't had the main event yet. I just wanted you to know that it's not because I don't want to."

Holy cow. My blush gets blushier. "Thank you," I say awkwardly. "That's nice to know."

He leans against the bed and pulls me up against his chest. "If I'd known what I was missing out on, I'd have looked you up a while ago. Actually," he adds, smiling a little, "I sort of did."

"You did?"

He nods. "One day I just got curious about little Libby

DeVille, and I looked you up in the campus registry. Kind of a pervy thing to do when you're in your mid-20s."

I laugh. "You liar. You're thirty."

"Indeed I am, but I wasn't then."

Holy crap. Hunter looked me up when I was an undergrad? The belly bats turn into butterflies, and they soar around my stomach.

He squeezes my shoulder as he steps away, grabbing another handful of clothes and hauling them over to his dresser, and I work hard at not overheating as I watch his taut ass. Ah, and those long, muscled legs.

His back still makes me sad. The welts make me feel a little sick. I open my mouth to tell him about Priscilla. At that moment, though, he stuffs the clothes into his drawer and comes back over to me. He leans against the bed, and I notice how radiant his face looks as he gazes at me. I have to struggle not to grin, because it feels so good.

"I'm sorry that you saw me act the fool, but I'm glad you're here. It's been...a break. A nice break, Libby DeVille." He twirls the end of a strand of my hair, the way he likes to do sometimes.

I wink. "Maybe you need to take breaks more often."

His fingers rumple my hair, and he brings his mouth down over mine. I'm lost in the warmth and softness of his lips and tongue, the nibbling teases of his teeth. He climbs into bed, resting his delicious weight on top of me, and he's hard and I'm wet and I'm grabbing that golden hair and staring into those cat eyes. When I pull away to gasp for air between our kisses, I really think this might be it. Maybe I'm finally going to lose my V-card.

I go for his boxer-briefs, but his hand clamps over mine. His gaze on mine is hard, which I don't understand. His chest is pumping, and I can feel how hard he is against my knee.

"Libby—no."

I frown. Did I do something wrong?

"It's not you," he pants. "You're perfect. It's just...I don't want your first time to be like this. With me like this." He looks down at himself, and when he looks back up, he leans his head against my neck and speaks his warm words on my collar bone: "You could do better."

I sit up a little, jarring him, and then I lie back down and cradle his shoulder. "Better how?"

"Better place, better circumstances...probably a better guy."

"What's wrong with this guy?"

He swallows. "You deserve someone who's got his shit together."

"You seem pretty together."

He chuckles, but it's a dry, humorless sound. "That's just because you don't know me." He runs a gentle finger down from my throat, between my breasts. "You deserve the whole package, Libby."

"I'm not sure anyone has that." I haven't called to check on Mom since I left California—because I just don't care. I'm still angry enough to spit nails at my dad. The more I think about seeing Dr. Bernard again, the more afraid I feel. "No one's perfect, Hunter. You need to give yourself a break."

He swallows, and his eyes look so clear, like a river. "Don't try to know me. Don't try to get close to me. It's not a good idea, Lib."

"I don't care if it's a good idea. I don't think I can stay away from you. Now that I know you..."

He shakes his head. "You're wrong." He pushes himself up and lithely shifts his body off the bed. "You don't know me. And what you do know should not make you want to learn anything more. You need to trust me, Libby. Stay in your own world, and leave me in mine. We can have a little fun together before you go home, but that's it."

I'm surprised and humiliated when my eyes well with tears. "That's all you want from me?" I can't believe this. That he's giving me no chance to go beyond just sex. And after what I told Dr. Bernard. Since I've been here and we've spent some time together, I'd actually started thinking…I don't know. That we click. That there is something here worth exploring.

He rubs his face roughly, like he's frustrated or his shadow is itching. "It doesn't matter what I want. I've got...a lot going on, and I don't want to get your hopes up falsely. *If* you're crazy enough to have those kinds of hopes," he adds, pulling his mouth into an ominous frown. "Maybe you're not."

I push myself off the bed. "All I said was 'You don't give yourself a break much'. It's not like I got down on one knee."

He just looks at me, his jaw locked. For the longest time, I think I'm being stonewalled. Then his mouth softens, and he sighs. "Then maybe it's me," he says, very, very softly. "Maybe it's me who's wanting more."

He grabs my arm, gentle even as he steers me to the door that joins our rooms. I drag my feet, mostly because I'm shocked —and thrilled—and totally confused. Hunter wants more! But he doesn't want to let himself have it?

I frown up at him, but he's shaking his head again. "Libby, I'm so sorry I didn't think it through. You should leave. Tonight or tomorrow—as soon as you can get away. Tap your red slippers and go home to Napa."

My chest aches, and I'm shocked to find I can't speak over the lump in my throat. I swallow hard and try my best to look dignified, instead of like a beggar. "Hunter...I don't understand."

"This is how it's got to be."

He opens the door that joins our rooms, but I don't move. He puts his hand on the small of my back. "C'mon, Libby…I don't have room for wherever this might be headed, so why not end it while we're both ahead?"

"We're not," I whisper.

He tugs me through the door to my room and sweeps his palm over my hair, giving me a look of what can only be longing before he holds up his hand in a goodbye pose. "Take care of yourself, Libby."

I can't even form an answer as he steps back through the door.

Hunter

I WOKE UP sometime after Priscilla arrived. At first I thought it was a nightmare. Then I heard Libby, telling her to go away. I'm so ashamed that I just lay there, eyes closed, listening to that bitch talk shit about me—and listening to Libby, my guardian angel. I soaked it up. It soothed something inside me. Made me feel like I'm alive instead of dying.

That's what it's been like with Priscilla. Like suffocation. A slow snuffing out of everything I want and everything I need.

Just like it was with Rita.

I don't understand how Libby is so different.

After I peeked into the hallway and realized Priscilla was being dealt with, I feigned sleep, listening as Libby came back into my room and then slipped into hers to make a phone call. I was about to get up when she came back and got in bed with me. I stayed completely still while she wrapped her arm gently around the lower part of my back and nuzzled her face into the crook between my shoulder and my neck. Why did it feel so good? I've been touched before, but it never felt like that. What's so different about her?

I stand for a long time in front of the door I sent her through. I shut my eyes and try to feel the shadow of her presence in my room. There's a part of me—a raging, senseless part—that wants to burst the door open, rip her clothes off and fuck her until she can't walk anymore. She'll be stuck in my bed, the smell of vanilla and cinnamon surrounding me forever.

However, the part of me that actually cares about her wins the day. I wasn't lying when I told her she deserved the whole package. She is selfless, kind, beautiful, smart, good, and in so many other ways out of my league.

I don't know what she sees in me, but I shut my eyes and try to drown in the peaceful feeling I get whenever she's around. It's like the amplification of that feeling I had the very first night I saw her, with the broken Porsche. Peaceful. Pleasant. Beautiful. Good.

As I listen to the room around me, I think that I can hear her voice. She sounds upset, and it kills me that I'm the reason why.

My body's sore, so I sink down to the rug, leaning over my knees with my head propped in my hands.

"I fucked up... I fucked it all up... I fucked up..."

Sometimes when I close my eyes, I can hear myself sobbing and my dad yelling and I see all that blood.

I inhale deeply.

Libby. Think of Libby.

I've got her face pinned to the forefront of my mind like a motherfucking screensaver when the phone rings. Not my cell phone, but my land line. Shit.

CHAPTER TWENTY-SEVEN

Elizabeth

I DON'T WANT to leave, but I'm not sure what else to do. Hunter doesn't want me here, and I can't force him to, regardless of how much I want to stay. This is the second time he's said I should leave, and Priscilla *was* just here. He has a whole life outside me, and if he means what he says about not wanting to take things any further with me, I don't see the point of trying to force myself on him.

I'm packing my bags, feeling numb and desolate, when Suri calls.

"Lizzy—hi." She pauses for a second. "How are things?"

"They're good. I'm headed home."

"Really? Wow. So I guess things must have progressed?"

"Kind of," I hedge. I don't even try to go into it, because I can tell by her voice that something's wrong. My stomach's tied in knots, because I'm worried that it's Cross.

"Is something going on? You sound weird."

She sighs. "Girl, you always know, don't you?"

"I'm your bestie. That's my job. So spit it out."

"It's Cross. He's saying... He told me that what happened that night wasn't an accident. That someone *did* it. He's upset, like he pulled out all his IVs and cursed at Nanette, and then he told me to leave because he needs some time to think." Her voice breaks on the word 'leave' and I know something is going on with the two of them.

"Wow." I clutch the phone a little tighter. Cross has had some serious issues with his father, but I don't think he has any real enemies. Does he? I lean against the bedpost, feeling sick—over this, over Hunter. Over everything. "Is he doing better now? I mean, when you left was he..."

"I didn't leave. I'm outside, in a waiting area. I think they sedated him. He was really upset." She drags in a teary breath and I can hear a sniffle, followed by the rustle I'm sure must be a tissue. "I'm sorry to burden you with this while you're at Hunter's, but I didn't know who else to call. He said that when he left to go...after the fight the two of you had, there was this guy messing with his bike. Like, touching it and stuff. The guy told him he liked the bike. It doesn't sound like much, but Cross says when he got onto the road he had trouble controlling it. He said the steering had been messed up, and the breaks seemed messed up too, but not completely. So he didn't flip like he might have, he just lost control of the steering...because of how much he had to drink, but mostly because the bike was ruined."

"Holy shitballs. Did he know this guy?"

"Cross said he looked like someone he used to know. I asked if it was an enemy or something, and he acted kind of weird. I don't know if we can trust him, though, Liz. He thinks you two had a fight because he was jealous over you messing around with Hunter."

"He *was* jealous," I whisper.

Suri huffs her breath out, and I can feel her censure. Her irritation that I kept it from her. "I guess I don't know all the details." The next second, I'm left there standing with the dead line in my hand, and no way home. How nice.

A few seconds later, a phone rings, and for a moment I think it's Suri. It's actually the landline on the table in the corner. It rings once, twice, three times before I reluctantly lift the earpiece.

"Hello," I hear Hunter say, just as I'm opening my mouth. His voice is extra low and slightly raspy, and if I'm not mistaken, I can hear the echo of it through the door that joins our rooms.

Almost immediately, there is another voice.

"Hunter." It sends a shiver down my spine, because I know that voice from TV. Hunter's father. Shit. "Are you alone?" Conrad West's voice has always been a little creepy: a cross between Darth Vader and a used car salesperson.

"I'm at my house and yeah, I'm by myself. What can I do for you, Sir?" Hunter sounds weary. Under that, I hear a ring of irritation.

"It's been a long time since I've heard from you," Conrad says.

"Yep."

"You feel no obligation to keep in touch with your father? Your sister says she never hears from you either."

"What do you want, Dad?"

"What do you think?"

"I don't know." His voice tightens. "To wish me a good day?"

"You know damn well why I called!" Conrad snaps. "You're in water hot enough to boil a pound of crawfish. Is there anything you care to tell me?"

"I don't care to tell you shit. That's why I never call."

I can practically feel Conrad's anger through the phone line. My palm around the phone starts sweating as Hunter's dad growls, "You don't want to talk? Then allow me. You are being investigated for the murder of a Las Vegas escort. Does that ring a bell?" Conrad's voice has gotten more Southern; he's practically drawling. "Sometime between the night you engaged her services and the next morning, she disappeared. Right out of your bed. She was found dead last night in a ditch in Arizona, with your cuff link in her cold fingers."

"I didn't—"

"That is immaterial, Hunter. You can't *be* investigated. Do you understand how badly you've fucked up?"

The line is quiet.

"Okay, then let me spell it out. Rita died because of *you*. Because you couldn't learn to quit pushing that woman's buttons. Are you intentionally trying to ruin your life? Because you're doing exceedingly well." Hunter says nothing, and his dad continues. "You tend to do that. Ruin things. Well let me tell you, this sort of scandal is below our family.

"You know, for years after you moved to Vegas I had patience with you. I, too, had some oats to sow, but unlike you, I moved forward."

Hunter's voice warbles on the line, then comes through loud and strong; condemning. "You fell in love with a hooker. And she died in childbirth, because you wanted her to labor at your house. *That's* how you 'moved forward.' Because my mother died. Rita weaseled her way back into your life and you took her, and you pretended she was my mom, too. This scandal's not below our family. This scandal is our family."

"No it's not! The only scandal comes from you!" Conrad snaps in a rush of anger.

"I'm not the one who hit a little fucking kid!"

There's a pause, and then Conrad's voice lowers, soft and deadly. "Neither am I, but sometimes I wish I had. Clean this mess up, Hunter. Pay off the cops. Do whatever you need to do to bury this. But let me warn you, you may have to go farther than I did for you. Priscilla Heat is close enough to Carlson to suck his fat, red cock, and she is covering for him. From what I've been able to gather, this somehow goes back to one of Carlson's mistresses. This is hearsay now and I'm working to find evidence, but I am not going public with it. It will hurt my career. You need to find someone who can. Check your e-mail.

Check it daily. Check it hourly. Right this course or so help me. Goodbye."

Hunter

I'VE BEEN POUNDING the bag so long that things have started getting blurry. When I hear Libby's voice say my name, it's like a salve, but I can't stop what I'm doing. My knuckles are bleeding, the scabs from the charity fight split open, and for once, I want to see blood.

I was playing cards online in the basement that afternoon. For months, it had been the only place I knew she couldn't reach me. The cancer had advanced so much, she couldn't make it down the stairs without risking a fall. It's ironic—I think it's ironic—because that used to be her favorite place to find me. The walls always muffled the sounds of her slaps and screams. They bounced off the tile, magnifying in my ears. But my father could pretend he didn't hear.

These were different days, though. Rita was spending most of her waking time in the bedroom she shared with my father. When I got hungry or wanted to go outside, I typically only had to avoid the bedroom or the sitting room.

That afternoon, when I heard her creeping down the stairs, hanging onto the banister, I half wondered if she'd died and come to haunt me on her way to hell.

She was thinner than I was used to seeing her, with thinning patches in her black hair, but I remember feeling anxious when I saw her reflection in the computer monitor. She might have been sick, but she still hated my guts.

She raised her arm and I whipped around, my arms already up in front of my face. But she wasn't trying to hit me. She was clutching a hot pink t-shirt. As she shook it out, I noticed spots of bleach.

"Did…you do this?" Her voice was reedy, weaker than it used to be, but still, I knew to keep my answer short and to the point.

"No."

She held the shirt out, her manicured hand shaking slightly. "You're a liar."

"No I'm not." Her eyes were bugging out, the way they sometimes did before she hit me. My heart was racing, and I remember the way I fumbled for what to do next; the way I tried to curb my fear. "You should go back upstairs," I told her flatly.

No emotion. Sometimes if I kept my voice very neutral, she would just leave me alone.

Faster than I thought possible for her, she wrapped her frigid hand around my wrist and dug her brittle nails into my skin. I remember looking into her dull, brown eyes. Her mouth—her trembling lips—were pulled into a sneer. She sank her nails in deep enough that I could feel the blood well and she hissed, "You're a…selfish little bastard."

She slapped me on the cheek then—and it wasn't even hard. I remember thinking that it didn't echo like it sometimes did.

I remember I looked into her face again, and I noticed for the first time how thin she really was. How different she looked since being diagnosed three months ago and doing chemo. How skeletal. How frail.

Maybe that's why I did it. Because for the first time ever, I felt like I was strong enough to take her on.

Maybe it's because she cupped my cheek then, just after she'd hit me.

I've had years to think about it, and I'll never know for sure.

All I know is that I hit her. *Hard*.

I knew as soon as I punched her that I'd made a horrible mistake. I even tried to grab her, but her knees just crumpled. She hit the floor, and blood was everywhere in a heartbeat. I tried to find the source, but it was everywhere: not just her nose, but her mouth, her eyes, even her ears.

I still can't get away from all that blood. I wake up covered in it. It's there when I have a good hand. When someone orders their steak rare. When I'm tagging cattle here at the ranch.

Rita is always bleeding out on me.

Right now, I want the blood. I punch the bag again.

"Hunter..."

Shit. I whirl around, panting. I had almost forgotten she was here. "Scarlett" DeVille. She reaches for me, but I step away, holding my bleeding hands near my sides. "Libby—go away."

"I can't." She sounds like she's crying. When I blink the sweat out of my eyes, I find that hers are wet. Without thinking, I pull her into my arms, pressing my lips against her hair as I speak quietly near her ear. "Do you see why you need to leave now? I'm a fucking mess."

"I know you are." Her voice breaks as she wraps her arm around my waist. "That's why I can't leave." I inhale vanilla and cinnamon, allow my eyes to close. "Hunter, I know what happened with Sarabelle."

I freeze. "What are you talking about?"

Her eyes are huge, but she doesn't back away. "I wasn't being nosy, but I heard it at the ranch. You slept with Sarabelle, and then she disappeared. And now...they found her. That's why you were upset last night, wasn't it?"

I rub my hair, noting the stinging of my knuckles. "You don't need to worry about any of this."

"Did you hurt her?"

"What?" I suck in a breath. I can feel the blood rush out of my head, the way it used to when I heard Rita coming down the stairs. "Fucking hell, Libby, do you really think that I would hurt a woman?"

"Did you?"

"Jesus—*no.* I would never hurt her." My throat goes tight and I have to work my jaw. I look away, and Libby takes a step closer.

"The police think you did it?"

"She had one of my cufflinks in her hand when they found her."

She looks into my eyes, and I see only sadness. "Oh, Hunter. How did you get into this?"

"I don't know. And I wouldn't tell you even if I did. You've got no business anywhere near this."

"I already am. I'm a Junior Ranger Prostitute now, and more importantly I care about you. And I'm sorry this happened, but…" She pauses, obviously working herself up to something. I definitely don't expect her to say, "I didn't mean too, but I overheard some of your conversation with your dad."

I can feel the air leave the room. My knees go weak. I start to sway.

"I'm so sorry. I answered when it rang and—"

"You shouldn't have," I rasp.

"I know." A tear falls down her cheek. "He was really horrible to you."

I turn my back to her as blood roars in my head. I've got a hand covering my face, but I can sense her movement as she comes to stand in front of me. "I heard him say something about Priscilla. Is that why you and her are...I mean, is that why you have sex with her? Because of the—"

"There is no why!" I snap. "There is no why! Where you're concerned, there is no *why*! Quit asking questions and just GO! Fuck it, Libby! Can't you see I'm trying to protect you!"

"From what?" Her blue eyes blink. "What's going on? Is she trying to frame you, Hunter?"

"I don't know," I answer finally.

She touches my shoulder. "Your back..."

I raise my head to look her in the eye. The pity on her face cracks something in me open. I shift my weight, trying to draw a breath. I can't take the pity, so I dip into my reservoir of anger, instead. It makes my tone sharper when I ask, "Did you ever think maybe I like that shit?"

"Do you?"

"What do you think?" I grab her shoulder without thinking about my bloody hands. As soon as I see my stained fingers on her, I feel dizzy. "Do you think I like it?" I rasp.

"I don't know." Her eyes, holding onto mine, are huge. Her face looks pale and worried. Out of nowhere, guilt slams through me like a train. I should never have brought her to my home. And if she heard any of that conversation with my dad…

Damnit!

I do the only thing I can to say I'm sorry.

Elizabeth

BEFORE HUNTER KISSES me, I really think he's going to throw me out of his house. He's bleeding, upset, radiating anger and frustration, and I'm just...here. Useless. Totally unable to help him. Unwanted, even, if what he said earlier was true.

Then he cups his palm around my head and pulls me close and plants his mouth on mine, and my knees turn to jelly. He holds me against him and kisses me like he's drowning and I'm air.

I kiss him back, returning fire for fire, because he's Hunter, and my body just responds. But my mind is spinning. Someone hit him when he was a kid? His stepmother, Rita, the one his father accused him of killing? Is that why he lets Priscilla hurt him? And Priscilla is having sex with Cross's father!? Is that why Cross hates her so much? And Holy Jesus! Cross's dad had another mistress killed?!

It dawns on me that Hunter is right. This is some really big shit. Some huge shit, and I don't know what's going on. But soon Hunter's tongue sweeps through my mouth, and just like that, I forget my worries.

I tug his hair and run my free hand up his hard shoulder. He's shirtless now, here in his gym, and I can feel the line of every muscle. My hand settles over his strong nape as he kisses roughly down my neck and I moan, "Hunter."

"You're a stubborn...woman...Libby," he pants as he kisses down my chest and rips my button-up blouse open. His hands tickle behind my back and my bra is off in seconds. My breath is in his mouth as his fingers make quick work of my slacks. He lays me on the bright blue work-out mat and sticks one big forearm inside my slacks, moaning in pleasure when his fingers find their mark. I'm not wearing panties. I didn't want a panty line.

"Jesus, Libby. This is so damn hot."

He slides a finger in and I'm clinging to his shoulders as he rocks his hips into my thigh. I can feel his swollen length, and I want it inside me.

"Hunter," I pant. I want to tell him what I need but I can't find my voice.

Hunter

I SHOULDN'T TAKE this any further, but her mouth on mine is so soft, it's like a vindication. Her hands, reaching for my cock and stroking through my jeans, are so tender. I can't resist her. I crawl down her legs and position myself over her, then dip down and taste her salty sweetness, showing her just how hungry I am.

When she finds her release, she screams, then pushes herself up on one arm, leaning her forehead against my shoulder. I'm astonished when I realize she's not leaning on me; she's trying to reach past my torso.

"Why are you doing this?" I grate out as she works my zipper.

"I don't know." She laughs. "I'm crazy, I think. Every time I see you, I..."

"You what." I grab her chin, because I want to hear this, and I want to see her eyes when she says it.

"Every time I see you I want you," she whispers. "Ever since I was sixteen."

"The Porsche?"

She nods, and I kiss her mouth. She kisses me back with all her might. She ends up on top of me, pulling my jeans off like a sexy-crazed nymph. The denim rubs my cock and I'm at full-mast, pushed painfully into my boxer-briefs. She yanks them off, pops me into her mouth, and I groan. I want to ask her if she's sure, but my ass is rising off the floor and I can't keep from pumping my hips. Her hands are...God. "Yes, there!" She's gliding over my balls and pumping my cock and licking my head and—

I come fast and hard, pulling out of her mouth only just in time.

She grins, and I push my tired self up to kiss her lips.

CHAPTER TWENTY-EIGHT

Elizabeth

I DON'T THINK I've ever seen anything hotter than Hunter's face as he comes. But in the seconds after he finishes, I'm worried again. He grabs a towel off a bench and cleans us up, and then he pulls me to my feet and hands me my clothes—and he's gentle, with his eyes on me as we both dress, clearly concerned about whether I enjoyed myself.

I look into his eyes and tell him, "That was wonderful."

"Good," he says. But the little smile he gives me doesn't reach his eyes at all. He looks distracted. Worried, even. Like maybe he regrets what happened. *And why wouldn't he*, says a little voice inside my head. *He told you to leave, Lizzy—and you didn't.*

I'm staring at the floor, trying to decide what to do next without making all this ten times more awkward, when he reaches out and tucks a strand of hair behind my ear. "Want to go upstairs?"

"Of course."

There's no smile from him, no sign at first that he's relived or happy that I'm still around. But after we step off the elevator onto the main floor, he wraps his arm around my shoulder as we walk toward the staircase. Every time our sides and hips bump, I feel a jolt.

He loosens his grip on me a little as we take the stairs, but we're still close. His eyes glide over me. He looks pensive. "I want you to get a shower."

Oh, no. He's sending me away now.

I swallow, because I don't trust myself not to make embarrassing noises. If he wants me to leave, I need to go.

"Okay," I say quietly.

He holds out his hand, and for a second, I'm confused. "I didn't think about this when I touched you, but my hands are bloody."

Panic flashes through me. "Are you positive for something?"

"No. I'm not. Just…I thought you might like to clean it off."

He says nothing more as we make our way through his room into and his massive bathroom, done in sleek whites and grays, with Kandinsky abstracts on the wall.

There's a shower, which I figure he will turn on, but instead he reaches over the sunken, square gardener's tub and turns the knobs. He pulls some bottles from a cabinet, squirting something from one of them into the tub as it fills.

"Take as long as you want," he tells me. He sits a towel and a wash cloth on the tub's edge, and then he disappears, closing the door behind him.

What the heck? I strip out of my clothes and hop into the bath only as a courtesy to Hunter. I don't feel dirty, and I don't want to sit in here by myself, curious about what's going on inside his head, but maybe he has a thing about cleanliness.

I take the world's shortest bath, and as I reach for my towel, I notice the mess of fluffy, black terrycloth isn't all towel. There's a robe there, too.

I bring it to my nose and a quick sniff reveals it's Hunter's. It smells like shaving cream, deodorant, and him. As I slide it on my damp body, I actually shiver.

Holy wow.

After only a moment's deliberation, I use a comb on the counter to brush my hair and then I gather my dirty clothes into a bundle and walk into Hunter's bedroom. It's been entirely put to rights—by Hunter while I bathed, or by a housekeeper, I'm not sure; I was so focused on Hunter I didn't pay attention to the room when we passed through it before.

I guess I'm still not paying attention, because suddenly there's a tap on my ankle, and I realize I just walked right past him. He's sitting on the plush rug with his back against the wall, just outside the bathroom.

"Hi." Despite the weirdness of our circumstances, I can't help but smile.

"Hi." He returns the smile, but his is weary. I jerk my thumb toward the still-steaming bathroom. "You should shower, too." He's sweaty and his hands are still bloody. "I bet you'd feel better."

When he makes no move to get up, I lean down, grab his forearm, and tug lightly. "Come into the bathroom with me. I want to help you wash your hands."

"I can do it," he says softly, getting up.

I run my fingers over his. "You need to put some gauze on them."

I catch a flicker of something on his face that I think might be embarrassment, but it's gone just as fast, and for a long moment as he gets a first aid kit from a bathroom cabinet, he's Hunter West, the enigma/fantasy.

When he's back in range, I put my hands on his smooth shoulders and urge him onto the side of the tub. "Sit." I grab a chair from behind me and pop open the kit.

Cleaning his fists is surprisingly intimate. It makes my belly clench, not because he's beautiful—and he is, especially with his torso bare—but because I feel so much for him.

I run a damp towel over his right hand, and I'm hit with the memory of what I heard his father say—about him killing Rita. And what I heard Hunter say, too: *"I'm not the one who hit a little fucking kid!"*

My stomach clenches. I have so many questions, especially about this, but I know now's not the time. I want to keep it light right now. I briefly meet his gaze. "When's your next tournament?"

"Supposed to be in two weeks."

"Do you split your time pretty evenly between here and your vineyard?"

He shakes his head. "I prefer the vineyard. When I can be there."

Which I hope is a lot. I'm practically gleeful when I think of him being so close.

I glance up at him as I switch hands, and I find him looking down at me through long, dark eye-lashes. His face is so handsome, it's hard to think about anything else. I take a deep breath as I tie off the gauze around his left wrist. "I was wondering ...how do you think Sarabelle ended up with your cuff-link?"

He locks his jaw. "Do you really want to hear this?"

Now holding onto his right wrist, I nod. "Not only do I think you would never do something like this, but you didn't sound guilty on the phone, and no one at Love Inc. thinks you are. Those three things are good enough for me."

He rubs a hand back through his hair. "I don't want to drag you into this."

"Is it because you don't trust me?"

"No. It's because I'm worried for you." He doesn't meet my eyes, but he does take my right hand with his bandaged left one and leads me next door. On the way, he grabs an undershirt from a bathroom closet and slides it on.

When we get into my room, he says, "Let me help you pack. There's too much going on; I don't know who might show up here." He presses a tender kiss on my cheek. "Libby, I can't stand to worry about you."

"I'll go tomorrow if you still think I should. But for tonight let's just talk, or...I don't know. Watch movies or something."

He gives me a skeptical look. "Watch movies?"

"I bet you have a hell of a home studio somewhere in here."

"And if the FBI shows up and takes me off in handcuffs?"

"I'll post your bail." I smirk a little. "I have the money."

I start to fold and organize my clothes, which are laid out by outfit all over the room, and Hunter leans against the bed. It's a little awkward, but also kind of companionable. "I'm surprised you went to a brothel for sex," I say after a few minutes.

"Are you?" he smiles a little ruefully.

"You could get it on your own."

"True. But I'm emotionally detached. Women don't like that."

"Do you really think so?" I don't see him that way at all.

He shrugs. "I'm not saying it's not attractive to some. But eventually most people want more."

"That's not what I meant. Why do you think you're detached?"

He shrugs. "Nurture shaping nature." One eyebrow lifts when he sees my face. "You look surprised."

"I am," I say, sticking the last of my stray outfits into my suitcase. "I don't see you that way at all."

He presses his lips together, then says, "I don't act that way with you."

And he doesn't—which is the only thing that gives me hope when I think about how this thing between us might work out.

I link my arm through his, and we take the elevator up to the third floor. We follow a long, beige rug past closed doors Hunter doesn't bother to explain. One of them is cracked, and I can see some hunting gear. I'm wondering what's in the rest of them, still wondering at what his dad said—about Rita, who was apparently his stepmother—when Hunter stops walking, and I realize we've reached the end of the hall.

"The movie room," he tells me simply.

He opens the heavy door and leads me into a vast space brightly lit with in-ceiling globe lights. Arranged on two sides of a long, red-carpeted aisle are dozens of rows of comfortable-looking leather recliners, facing a screen that rivals that at any theater I've visited.

Hunter drops my arm and points to a row of dark wood cabinets lining the right wall. "You pick something. I need to call Marchant, okay?"

I nod. "I need to make a call, too."

We go into separate corners. Suri tells me Cross is calmer now, wants to see me, and is now saying he might be wrong about someone trying to kill him at Hunter's party. Maybe it was the drugs, he's told her. Suri is both worried and confused. I tell her I'll be back tomorrow and am glad when someone beeps in and she has to go before I can give her my own update. I'm not sure where I would even start.

After I slide my phone into my pocket, I turn my attention to the cabinets, and have five minutes to pick my way through what must literally be more than a thousand movies before Hunter is back. "Something...um, happened. Having to do with the situation you heard my father mention. If they don't get it straightened out, I might have to go help."

I raise my eyebrows. "Who's they?"

"Marchant and I have a team of private investigators looking into Sarabelle's disappearance."

I nod slowly. "I see." I guess I shouldn't be surprised.

He arches his brows and asks, "What did you pick?"

"*The Notebook*."

The horrified look on his face is priceless.

I laugh, pulling the DVD out from behind my back. "What about *The Princess Bride*?"

"Now that'll work."

"I want to watch this and have fun. But tell me one thing first. Was it all fake? You and Priscilla?"

He nods, and I can't help myself. "So she's framing you. Blackmailing you or something." I wonder if it has anything to do with what Hunter's father mentioned—with that bit about his stepmother—but I can feel that it's the wrong time to ask.

I can be patient.

Hunter puts the BluRay into the player, then falls into one of the leather chairs. He holds out his hand as he reclines it, and when I step between his legs, he pulls me into his lap. I'm surprised, but I adore the closeness.

"Don't worry about me," he says as I settle against his chest. He tucks his chin atop my head and wraps both arms around me from behind. "You know...I still remember the first night I ever saw you."

"You had a woman over."

"An escort."

I frown, wondering about his biological mother. She was an escort, or so his father said. "Do you only like escorts? Is that why you're not having sex with me?"

"I have sex with escorts because they don't want anything. Remember? I'm a no strings attached kind of guy."

"You seem like you would make a good boyfriend," I say, stroking his arm. Not that I can really say, having even less experience in relationship matters than he does. "I mean, if you found the right person."

He's silent for a second, and I kick myself for being so obvious.

Eventually, he says, "I think ultimately I just can't take that risk."

He kisses my temple. I snuggle up to him as the movie starts to play, and want to cry.

Hunter

LIBBY FALLS ASLEEP against my chest sometime before the credits roll, and I carry her to my bed. Then I discuss the Priscilla incident with Hal. It seems at some point Priscilla—or one of her friends—hacked my system wirelessly, rewriting its security protocols to admit her 24/7. Hal has reset the system, put a better firewall on it, and he's called in his brothers, Jake and Gilly. I have him post them both outside my door.

As I dress, I think about everything that's transpired between Libby and I. Everything that's been said. And I wish, for the first time, that I was a free man. Really free. I wish that I could have her. Not just for a night. She's not that kind of woman. And when I'm with her, I'm not that kind of man.

I think about all the food I cooked for her breakfast. I never cook. I never want to. But I want to feed Libby. I think about how I let her touch me with her eyes open. I let her look at me, and I didn't feel anxious the way I used to when I slept with escorts. In fact, it's the opposite; I like looking into her blue eyes. I think about her up there in my bed, and I'd give anything to be there with her. Kiss her. Fuck her. Fly around the world with her. I'd like to take her to New Zealand. The Alps. Lake Como. Some place that's as beautiful as she is.

Instead, I get my gun and call Marchant to see if any of our people have a lead on Priscilla's location. He tells me no one has—she's still M.I.A.—so I head out to try to find her. I check out with Hal and open the doors to my front porch, already thinking about how I'll get the little recorder stashed in my glove box and put it in my pocket, just in case I actually find Priscilla and can get her talking.

I lock the door, turn around, and jump as a slender arm encircles my waist.

"Hunter."

Priscilla! Now that's a surprise. She's standing in the nook where a huge potted palm blooms, right beside my doors. The porch light is on, and in the amber glow, her hair looks white, her eyes almost black.

"Priscilla," I growl. I want to throttle her right here and now, but I need the recorder to make any of this worthwhile. I push her against the side of the house, pressing my palm against her ribcage, and look into her coy face. "You and I need to talk. Somewhere not here."

I guess she sees the rage twisting my face, because her eyes widen, and she arches up against the stone wall. "I didn't pick you, Hunter," she says quickly. I try not to let my surprise show as she leaps right into a confession. "Not for anything but sex. I wanted you beside me on screen. We look great together. That's really all I cared about."

"So it was all Lockwood?" I murmur.

She leans up to kiss me, but I move my hand from her chest to her throat. "Don't try that shit," I hiss.

She sticks her hands up like I'm holding her at gunpoint. She's worried, and I've never seen her worried. Is this a game? Why is she here? Why is she talking?

"He knew I had drugged you that night—just for fun," she insists, "and he wanted to fuck Sarabelle. She never took him as a client. He didn't like that."

"So he—what? What did he do to her?" I need to know, but I'm afraid to know, and that just stokes my anger. I wrap my fist around Priscilla's blouse and tug her down the stairs, toward my truck. She slips and falls, but I'm not thinking clearly. I don't care if she gets scraped up. I jerk her forward.

"Hunter, stop!" She shrieks, and it's loud enough to wake the fucking dead. "Listen to me! Listen to me!" She wraps her arms around a large rock that's in the flower bed by the bottom stair and looks up at me with her mouth hanging half open. "I can't control what he does, Hunter!"

"What did he do?" I growl.

"He slipped into the room. She was asleep and you were out. I think he gave her some of what I gave you and then he—" She swallows. "It's disgusting—I know it is, but I had nothing to do with it!"

"And then what?"

"You can't expect me to tell you anything extra," she says, suddenly haughty again. "You've made your bed, and now you'll have to lie in it. *You* took her out to the car and put her in! I asked you to, and you did it without question!"

"No I didn't!" I'm completely stunned. "You're a god-damned liar."

"You did it," she snaps.

"I was fucking drugged!" I grab her by the wrists and drag her toward my truck. "You're a sick bitch, Priscilla," I say, wanting to get her riled up before we get into my truck. "Do you think I believe Lockwood did this alone?" I want to throw out what I know about the governor's missing mistress, but I'm not sure it's the time to play that card.

I shove Priscilla the rest of the way to my truck and pin her against the side of it as I fumble for my keys.

"I don't care what you think, Hunter! Sarabelle had your cuff link! Did you know that? And your real mother? Roxanne the escort? *The Los Angeles Times* knows all about her. In fact, about now they should be learning a lot about you, Hunter West. I came upon a whole stockpile of your history."

I'm so shocked my hands stop working, and I let her go.

She dances out of reach, blonde hair flying around her face. "It was so easy," she laughs. "What I told you was true—we didn't plan this. But Lockwood has a cousin on the police force. Someone really powerful." Lead Detective Josh Smith. "Once he heard that they were really going to make a case out of this, he let Michael know, and we had to come up with a solution. At that point I was pissed off." She gestures at her body, laughing shrilly. "If you think you're too good to be in one of my films, I've got no care for you, so I helped him set you up."

I lunge forward, grabbing her wrist, and she shrieks again as I jingle my keys. "Let me go!"

I fumble with the "unlock" button on my key as I try to keep her talking. As I try to keep myself calm enough to keep from smacking her. I suck back a deep breath as I unlock the doors. "I still don't understand why you're helping him at all."

"Who?"

"Lockwood. Are you in love with him?" I know she's not before she snorts, and I'm correct that the question will elicit an elaboration.

"In love with that disgusting boar? Of course not!"

I swing the door open, tightening my grip around Priscilla's forearm. I'm going to get this shit recorded if it kills me.

"So it's the governor," I murmur as I shove her toward the cab.

I guess it is, because she shrieks and goes nuts, kicking at my crotch and biting at my arm. "LET ME GO! LET ME GO! LET ME GO!"

"No," I growl. I throw her skinny ass into the front seat and Priscilla starts to claw at me. As I try to climb in behind her, planning to hold onto her arm until we take off driving, she pulls a can of Mace and sticks it in my face. I move so fast I'm out of the car before she can press the button on it; she tumbles out into the dirt.

As she gets to her feet, I try to grab her again, but she slaps me in the face, and I reel.

"You can't win this, you stupid motherfucker. It's got roots you can't imagine, and you're the FBI's suspect number one. That's what I came to tell you!" She takes off into the lawn, her hair trailing behind her as she dashes to her Camaro. She stops mid-way, turning around to face me with a deviant little smile and dancing eyes. "You know, I am a little sorry, Hunter. Good men don't belong in prison." She shrugs. "Guess that's what happens when you fuck hookers. Even virgin ones."

"If you touch her, I will kill you slowly," I warn.

She laughs, throwing back her head. "Fits your MO so perfectly." She waves, and she's walking around her car—gone, and my opportunity is lost.

CHAPTER TWENTY-NINE

Elizabeth

I WAKE UP the next morning feeling like something is missing. I roll over in my cozy bed, and that's when I notice where I am. *Holy crap, I'm in Hunter's room!* That makes me grin into the pillows. My smile slips a little when I realize I'm in his bed alone, and it goes away completely when I remember that today's the day I promised I would leave.

And I'm leaving a virgin.

I don't want to leave, and not just because I still have my V-card. I don't want to leave Hunter. He needs me right now—I feel certain he does. I roll over in the sheets, inhaling his scent, and I have to swallow back a sob. If I leave now, we might never spend this kind of time together again. And what about the trouble Hunter's in? Who's going to help him?

I go into my room, check to see if there's a text from Suri—there's not—and then I slide into a red wrap-around dress and pin my hair back with red barrettes. I check my phone again, not quite ready to leave the room and set this day in motion. The clothes I slept in still smell like Hunter, so I bring them to my nose.

How am I ever going to get over him? How will I move beyond any of this? Not just the experience with Hunter, but the dark story weaving itself around him. Sarabelle, Priscilla,

Cross's dad? I want to know more—for Cross's sake, and for Hunter's—but I know he won't tell me more.

I leave the room without zipping my bags. I inhale deeply when I reach the stairs, hoping I'll smell breakfast—but there is nothing in the air except the smell of cleaner and hardwood. Where is Hunter? Is he even here?

I'm headed to his study, not sure exactly what I'll find. As soon as I reach the first floor, the doorbell rings. Doorbells at surprising times remind me of the accidents my mom has had—accidents or incidents in which the cops showed up at our house. So hearing it now stops me in my tracks.

I look around.

It rings again.

I step over to the hallway that leads to Hunter's study. "Hunter?" I call. Surely a house like this has speakers in most rooms; in fact, I think I've seen them. He'd be able to hear the doorbell, wouldn't he?

The doorbell rings again, and I step slowly to the glass panes surrounding the doors. Against my better judgment, I peek out. I'm shocked to find the person on the porch is Dr. Bernard. My stomach clenches. She can only be here for me. Did something happen to my mother?

Without a second thought, I unlock the door and pull it open.

I'm holding my breath, bracing myself for her news, when she reaches her hand out to me like she wants to shake mine. Her face is curious, not grave.

"I'm surprised to find you here, Elizabeth. How are you?"

"I'm surprised to find you here," I manage. I suck a deep breath in. "Are you here to see me?"

"Actually I'm not." She smiles, a little awkward, but friendly. "Would you mind letting Hunter know I'm here?"

"Uh…one second." I shut the door in her face without even thinking of asking her in. As soon as I turn around, Hunter is there. He's wearing black jeans and a brown shirt, and he looks pissed. Behind him are three men, all beefy, with guns on their belts.

"Is that Elizabeth Bernard?" he asks, frowning.

"Yes. She says she wants to see you."

He nods, looking kind of dazed. "I was in a meeting. I thought you were asleep."

One of the men—they are all still standing in a row beside the stairs—tips a baseball cap at me, and I say, "That's okay. I only answered because I thought she was here for me."

Hunter looks over his shoulder. "Dave, Jake, Gilly, why don't you wait for me in the kitchen. My chef, Bernita, is there. She can feed you."

One of them says, "Sure," and the group takes off. I know I should do the same, but I'm too curious to get myself moving quite yet.

I watch Hunter smile as he squeezes Dr. Bernard's hand. "How can I help you, Libby?"

My jaw drops. That—Dr. Bernard—is the other Libby? Someone kind from Hunter's past. Someone I remind him of. How weird is that?

I don't get the chance to find out exactly how weird it is, because Hunter steers the psychologist toward his office.

I should probably go upstairs and figure out how I'm going to get back to California, but I decide to wait for him outside his office. I won't get too close while they talk, just close enough so I can see him when he comes out. If I don't, I'm afraid I won't even get to say goodbye.

I sit on the stairs for a moment, giving them a chance to get into the office and close the door. Then I follow the hall in that direction. I'm not surprised to find the big, wooden doors shut, but I am surprised that I can hear Dr. Bernard's voice clearly through them. It's not loud, but it's crisp and clear. The woman has excellent enunciation. I take a step back, wanting to respect

Hunter's privacy but then I hear "girl who disappeared" and my curiosity keeps my feet planted.

I inch closer, and I can faintly hear Dr. Bernard say: "...looking back through some of my files. Quite a few women at the ranch were friends with Missy King. I trust you know with what happened to her."

"I do."

"I spoke with several of our girls after she went missing. One of those women is still employed at the ranch, and she spoke with me yesterday about Sarabelle's disappearance."

"Do you have something?" Hunter asks. I'm shocked, because he sounds…*desperate*.

"I think so," the doctor says. "One of the things that bothered this particular Love Inc. employee most was a connection she saw between Sarabelle's disappearance and Missy King's. She said that Missy was rumored to've entered into a relationship with a man from San Luis in the weeks before she disappeared."

"Do you have a name?"

"Jim Gunn. She's sure."

"How sure?"

There's a brief pause. "She seemed certain."

Hunter is silent. So is Dr. Bernard. Eventually, Hunter asks, "Did she say anything else helpful?"

"Nothing that stood out, but if I think of anything else, I'll let you know."

For a long second, no sound comes from the room.

Then I hear Hunter's voice. He sounds choked up as he says, "Thank you."

"I know Marchant and you are looking into this on your own. He doesn't mind me telling you, he mentioned it during one of his sessions. I know you don't like that I moved to Nevada, and I know you don't like me knowing so much about your past. But I'm on your side, Hunter. I always was."

I hear what sounds like a squeak from Dr. Bernard, and through the crack between the doors I can see Hunter's arms around her shoulders.

"Thank you, Libby." His voice is low and sounds like it's coming from the back of his throat, and suddenly I understand the subtext here: Back in New Orleans, Dr. Bernard was Hunter's shrink, too. Which is why she wants to help him now.

With questions spinning in my mind and an ache in my chest, I hurry toward the stairs.

I'M IN THE bedroom Hunter gave me, sipping a chilled latte I got from the refrigerator, when I hear footsteps coming down the hall. I've spent the last thirty or so minutes thinking over what Dr. Bernard said. Thinking about what Dr. Bernard knows. Thinking about how it all applies to Hunter. The truth is, I know so little I really can't even speculate. All I know for sure is that Hunter's in a mess.

I sigh and allow my mind to chew on other, more personal details. Like how his real mother was an escort. Rita, the woman I thought was his mother, is thought to have died of cancer when Hunter was fourteen, but based on the conversation he had with his father, it sounds like there was more to it than that. I can't bring myself to believe that Hunter would have deliberately killed the woman; he looked appalled when I asked him if he'd killed Sarabelle, but maybe, if she was in the habit of hitting him, he hit her back and…I don't know…an accident happened.

There are so many things I want to know—I want to know *everything* about Hunter—but he's up to his eyeballs in this awful situation, and if he wants me to leave so he can focus on getting all this figured out, I will.

I hear him turn the doorknob and my stomach twists. I don't want to go. I don't want to leave him here in this big house by himself. I think that we might never share any time together again, and I feel terribly depressed. Before, Hunter was an unavailable male for me to idealize but never get to know. I *do* know Hunter now. And I like what I know.

He strides into the room with his usual commanding energy, and as usual, I can't breathe for half a second. He's such a handsome man. It's not just his high cheekbones or his beautiful, lash-framed cat eyes, or his soft, firm lips, or his messy, tug-able golden hair. It's the way he moves. The sound of his voice. Which, right now, is low and rough.

"How you doing up here?"

I shrug. "Fine. How are you?"

He lifts a shoulder. "Just got a visit from an old friend."

I smile. "I talked to her at the ranch. She's really nice."

I'm surprised when his lips tuck up into a lazy grin. "I thought you might say that. You know, when we first met, you reminded me of her."

I can barely contain my own grin. I love that I remind him of someone who cares about him. "Oh yeah?"

"Yep. You're both...just really nice."

"I think you're the nice one, Mr. Southern Gentleman." I take his hand and pull him close. His other hand curls around a piece of my hair.

"You think I'm a gentleman?" he smirks, then kisses me soft and slow. His eyes burn when he pulls away.

"I want a rain check," I murmur.

"Isn't that my line?"

I stroke my finger down his chest. "You deserve to get what you paid for."

I'm shocked when he pulls me close. His arms close hard and firm around my back, and his face is buried in my hair. "I already got it. And more."

He holds me for the longest time, and I hold him. My eyes are hot with tears.

"I wish things weren't like this," I choke.

After I say this, my heart pounds. I've never been so open with anyone, and if Hunter sees me as nothing but a bed buddy, I think my heart will break in two. I'm holding my breath when he says, "So do I."

My voice cracks. "Will you call me sometime soon?"

"As soon as I can."

I look up at him, and I'm surprised to see the sadness in his green eyes. He's still got one arm around my back; the other hand is smoothing my hair off my forehead.

"I could stay here with you," I say. "I don't mind if you're busy getting everything sorted out."

He slowly shakes his head. Before I can argue, he brings a finger to my lips. Then his mouth meets mine for a kiss so gentle it makes me shiver. "I'm going to miss you."

I nod. "I'm going to miss you, too."

Half an hour later, I'm gone.

CHAPTER THIRTY

Elizabeth

"SERIOUSLY, LIZZY. YOU just can't make this stuff up." Suri looks at me from behind the wheel of her lavender Land Rover. We're driving on the lonely, two-lane roads between Crestwood Place and Napa Valley Involved Rehab, and I've just finished my story—or at least, the censored version. Suri doesn't know all the heavy details, and she probably never will, which kind of sucks, because I don't think she has any clue how ripped up I am over leaving Hunter.

This is confirmed when she shakes her head in wonder. "Do the girls from the ranch know yet? That it didn't happen?"

"Yet?" I snort. "You think I'm just going to call and tell them? No way." Sarabelle's funeral is today. I'm sure they're all too busy to care about how my sex life isn't going.

"Are you going to tell the truth if one of them asks you?"

"I don't know." I look out the window, at the bleak gray day. "I can't see myself lying, but it is kind of embarrassing."

"I don't think so. I think it sounds like he really likes you, Liz."

"Maybe. Maybe not." It's been three days, and I haven't heard a word from Hunter. I worry that he was too gentlemanly to take my V-card, but the amount of affection he felt for me never quite reached the next level.

He's got his own life and I've got mine. Yeah, he has a vineyard home, but that doesn't mean he has time for or interest in having a California girlfriend. "There's no question, we have chemistry, but chemistry isn't everything." In fact, he outright told me in the movie room that night that he didn't think he'd take the risk of getting into a relationship. The sudden memory makes me feel even worse.

"Isn't it?" Suri murmurs.

And I know she's referencing Adam and her. She hasn't talked about it much, but her sadness is obvious.

I check my phone's screen—I'm pathetic, and have put Hunter's name into a search engine's alert system, so I'll know if anything about him is published online. Nothing new has popped up.

I slide my phone between my thighs and try to think of something non-Hunter-related. "I want to hear more about you and Cross."

It's an intentional turn of phrase, because I think there's something going on, even though Suri won't spill.

She shrugs. "We've been hanging."

I haven't had a chance to visit Cross yet, unbelievably. My first day back, Mom's rehab called and wanted me to do a discharge visit. It actually went better than they usually do. Mom looked more fit and happy than I've seen her in a long time. They've got her on a new antidepressant, and I'm trying to be positive about her recovery. I even stayed the night in one of the guest rooms at the 'spa'—where I lay awake on my little cot until the sun rose, combing Google for news about Hunter or the investigation into Sarabelle's death. The next day, yesterday, Cross got a visit from his father, so I couldn't visit then, either.

"I can't wait to hear how the visit with his dad went," Suri says. "I hope he wasn't an asshole to Cross."

"I hope so too." I try to squash the awful curiosity about what Hunter's father said—about the governor and his bygone mistress—but I can't. So I look out the window and focus on the grass and trees.

A few minutes later, we pull into the parking lot of NVIR and I start getting butterflies. "Are you sure he doesn't mind if I come?"

It seems ridiculous asking. Cross has always been slightly closer to me than to Suri. But I'm struggling with the feeling that in just two weeks, Suri has taken my place.

"Of course, you silly goose. He's dying to see you and hear how your 'class trip' went."

"Ugh. I hate having to lie to him."

"Are you actually going to write about it for school?" she asks as we get out of the car.

"I don't know. Maybe. Probably not." I had to un-enroll for the semester to make the trip, and when I get back to it next semester, I doubt I'll feel like rehashing an old situation.

We're quiet as we walk through the door, and there's Nanette. She's got her long brown hair pulled up into a pretty bun, and she's wearing purple scrubs. She reaches out her arms for me, and I'm kind of surprised and kind of thrilled.

"Nanette. Long time!"

"Too long. How are you?"

"I'm good."

"That's great."

I smile—genuine, because I really like her. "How is Cross?"

"He's up and moving. He shaved today and he's been playing games on my cell phone. He's still having some trouble with his left hand and leg, as well as some occasional pain in his neck, but we're seeing improvement in the leg."

"Not his hand?" Suri asks.

"Not much," Nanette says. "But we think the pain he's having in his neck might have something to do with his hand. Besides, we're not anywhere near the end of his rehab."

I tear up, because it's so amazing to hear that. Cross is

awake, and he's doing rehab. Suri and I hold hands as we walk back to his room.

"Ready?" she whispers.

I nod.

She pushes the door open, and I feel like a kid at Christmas.

Cross is leaning against his bed, wearing gray scrubs and a dark blue t-shirt, which is enough to knock me off my feet. Then I see his face, and I feel like I've been sucker punched. As soon as his eyes land on me, he looks...infuriated.

I open my mouth to say his name, but he beats me to the punch. "Suri," he says, his eyes never leaving mine. "Give us a minute. In fact, come back sometime later."

Suri looks confused. She shakes her head, and there's no mistaking the worry on her face. Cross notices it, too, and sighs. "Everything is fine. I'm doing fine," he tells her. "I just want a minute to talk to Liz—alone."

After shooting me a clueless look, she steps into the hall, and I'm alone with Cross.

"What's wrong?" I walk slowly to him, crumbling under the weight of his horrible, accusing gaze.

"Why did you do it?" he asks hoarsely.

"Do what?"

He swallows, and for the first time he looks upset instead of mad. "Why did you think that I would be okay with that?"

Obviously he knows I went to Love Inc. I feel like a kid getting scolded by my dad, and I play like I don't know what he's talking about. "Okay with what?"

"So you're going to deny it?"

"Deny what?"

"You sold your virginity! For me!" His voice cracks, and I'm filled with dread. Cross steps toward me, and for the first time I notice his limp. His face still looks the same. Except colder. "My father told me. You know how he feels about Vegas. He's got spies there. Lizzy, tell me what would make you do a thing like that."

"Why do you think?" I croak. "I couldn't stand to see you in that awful place! And," I add quickly, "I didn't need to be a virgin. What's the point? At twenty-three, it's almost a joke."

He opens his mouth, looking anguished, and I hold up my hand. "It went just fine, Cross. I'm okay. Right here, in one piece."

"You went home with Hunter West." His voice is soft fury —and it makes me mad.

"What do you have against Hunter?"

"He fucks Priscilla Heat. Don't you know that, Lizzy? Don't you care?"

I can't say anything to that. It's not my secret to tell, so instead I say, "Do you believe everything you hear?"

"I saw them that night. They were having sex before the party. Did he tell you that?"

"I didn't ask."

"So you *don't* care." His mad face crumples into hurt. Frus–tration. "What is it about him?"

I still don't have the answer to that question, and I definitely don't want to talk about it with Cross. "I've got a better idea: Why don't you finally tell me why you hate Priscilla Heat."

"She fucked my father," Cross says bluntly. I blink, and he rubs his eyes with his right hand. "I told you that he had affairs."

"With *her*?" He chose Priscilla Heat over Cross's beautiful mother? My mouth hangs open.

"Yeah, tell me about it." Cross rolls his eyes. "He likes hookers."

What pops out of my mouth next is unplanned. It's only meant to be a thought, but I guess it's so powerful it escapes. "One of them was Missy King."

Cross's eyes pop. "What do you know about Missy King?"

I bite my lip, not sure what to say now that I've divulged that I know something. *That was stupid.* I don't want to point anything back toward Hunter, so I shrug. "What do you know?" I ask him.

"What do *you* know?" he snaps.

I hug myself, feeling stupid, but I've already put my foot in my mouth. Might as well keep going now. "Is that why you and your dad don't talk? Is that the secret you found out last year? That he was seeing an escort, and she disappeared?"

Cross's eyes squeeze shut, and my heart pounds—hard.

"It is, isn't it?" Holy shit, this is big news. I fumble for the other name I heard in Hunter's conversation with his father. "Cross, have you ever heard of someone named Lockwood?"

He frowns and shakes his head. "Who is that?"

"What about Jim Gunn?"

He blinks slowly, his face losing all its color. "How do you know that name?" he asks hoarsely.

"I heard he dated Missy King."

Cross swallows, wrapping one arm around his stomach. "You don't need to say that, Lizzy."

"Why not?"

He gives me a sharp look that makes me feel like I'm being warned. "Just don't say it. Don't ask me about it. Sometimes there's stuff you just don't need to know. Do you get that?"

His face is deadly serious, and I almost feel like I'm in some kind of crime drama. I bite my lip, and for a long second, I consider letting it lie. But then the stern look on his face starts looking kind of...fearful.

"Cross—what's going on? Do you know something bad?" He shakes his head, and groans instead of answer. "How do you know Jim Gunn? Did he have something to do with Missy King disappearing?"

My question seems to hit Cross like a punch. He bends at the waist, clutching his head and moaning. "How do you know this shit, Elizabeth?"

"So he *did*?" My eyes are a centimeter away from popping

clean out of my head.

Cross looks at me through his hands, and when he speaks, his voice is ragged. "Suri told you, didn't she? She told you what I said about the guy I saw who was messing with my bike. I was out of it—all fucked up on Dilaudid for my neck."

I shake my head. "But if Jim Gunn really *did* something bad to Missy King and you know about it, and if you think the guy beside your bike that night was him... That's bad, Cross. That's scary bad."

Cross is leaning heavily on the side of the bed, breathing hard, and I notice there are wires running out of the bottom of his t-shirt. One of the machines starts to hum. I step close enough to touch his shoulder. "Oh my God, are you okay?"

He sucks his breath in, and just as I get really worried, his right hand clutches mine. I lace my fingers through his, and there's a knock at the door. "You okay in there?" Nanette calls.

"Fine," Cross says, but it sounds like he's gasping.

"Oh my God, Cross." I wrap my arms around him and he pulls me close.

I breathe deeply as we hold on to each other, and finally the monitor stops beeping. I run my palm over his soft, short hair and look into the handsome face I've known almost my whole life. I can't imagine someone hurting Cross. "I'm sorry that I mentioned that stuff. I didn't mean to upset you."

I'm expecting him to brush his freakout off, the way Cross would. I'm expecting anything but what he does, which is push my hair back and kiss me, his lips touching mine for half a second before he jerks away.

I touch my mouth, horrified. "Cross—"

"I know, okay?" He holds his hands up. "I know I'm not the one you want. Jesus, Lizzy, just give me a second." He turns away, and out of nowhere, tears are spilling down my cheeks. I feel like I can't do anything—for Cross or Hunter.

I'm standing there with my arms around myself, wishing I

had never come here today, when Cross turns back to face me. There's space between us this time. "I'm sorry, Lizzy. Please forgive me."

"I do. Of course I do." I look into his blue eyes. "But I'm worried about you. If you know details of a...I don't know, some kind of crime—"

"Shhh." He reaches for me, but he doesn't touch me. He brings his right hand back to his side. "Don't talk about that, please. And don't think about it either, okay? I'm fine now. I'm good."

I wipe my eyes, smirking. "Are you trying to make *me* feel better?"

"Would that be so bad?"

"Yes." It would be terrible for Cross to go through this alone. Just like it's terrible for Hunter. "It was him, wasn't it?" I whisper. "Jim Gunn did something to make Missy King disappear, and you know he did."

He shuts his eyes.

"Did your father...ask him to?" It's such a horrible question, I can barely get the words out. It seems impossible, but if Missy King turned into trouble...did something that might put Drake Carlson in jeopardy… God, he really might have done something horrible. I drop my voice an octave lower. "Do you have, like, evidence or something?"

Cross hesitates, his lips pressed into a firm line. And I know Cross. That's a confirmation.

I feel cold all over. Icy. For a long second, I can't even find my voice. When I do, it's high and squeaky. *Scared.* "What are you going to do about it?"

He holds his arms out, then lets them fall against his scrubs. "What is there to do?"

"There's gotta be something. Especially if the guy found out you know. Cross, that's terrifying."

"My dad's a terrifying guy."

I don't plan to tell him, especially after what happened a few minutes ago with that monitor when he got freaked out, but his face is so defeated, I can't help myself. Cross is in danger and I *have* to tell him what I know and find out what he knows.

It takes me almost an hour with the two of us sitting hip to hip on his bed. I whisper near his ear as we play music on my iPhone in the background. He whispers back. When we're finished, we get approval for Cross to leave the grounds tomorrow.

CHAPTER THIRTY-ONE

Hunter

I'M IN MY library at the vineyard playing cards with myself when Marchant calls. I ignore him. My head is aching and I didn't get a damn bit of sleep last night. I don't want to talk to his hen-pecking ass. I'm sleeping worse since Libby left than I did before she got here. I guess I know now what I'm missing. I finish the game and re-deal my cards. I'm looking at them as I play, but I'm seeing Libby's face.

And I'm thinking about the other Libby—Dr. Libby—who called today, to "talk." I know March put her up to it, but I can't find the energy to be angry. It's kind of nice to have my old shrink tell me I'm a good guy. Even nicer since it looks like that might hold.

Priscilla's threats are seeming more and more empty. For the first few days after our struggle in my truck, I waited for the other shoe to fall, but it just hasn't. The FBI has stopped coming around, and Josh Smith from the LVPD has closed his case without enough evidence to make an arrest. For the past few days, Lockwood has been at his house doing nothing but watching satellite TV. Priscilla has been fucking a cop buddy of Smith's. If her phone conversations—recorded by Dave—are to be trusted, she's thinking of putting him in one of her films.

Sarabelle is dead, and that can't be changed. Her funeral

was this morning. And while the FBI seems to be kicking up their heels, I'm working on my own play for Lockwood and Priscilla. Mainly Lockwood. But Priscilla will get hers, too.

Marchant calls again.

I hit ignore.

Again five minutes later. "What is it, dude?"

"Hunter—*fuck*. Have you read the *L.A. Times* today?"

"No." My whole body tenses. "Why?"

"There's allusions to you left and right in that story. House in California, one in Vegas. Heir who visits brothels. They're quoting an anonymous source who says that the FBI has you as their prime suspect. I'm surprised you haven't had them show up at your fucking house. The *Times* even put a bit in there about Roxanne. Damn, man, I'm glad I knew that or I'd be shocked."

"How'd you know?" I whisper.

"Dave found out. Man, are you okay?"

I swallow. "Yeah."

"You want me to catch a plane out for some bro time? I've got Dave all over this; he's checking with his contacts at the FBI. But he's started acting suspicious, dude. Says he found some shit in your family's closet that he wants to talk to me about. What do you think—"

I kill the call and walk slowly to the liquor cabinet. I've downed two shots when three men in gray suits ring my doorbell.

Elizabeth

"ARE YOU SURE this is a solid plan?"

Cross is sitting beside me in the Camry, wearing a ball cap and looking grumpy.

"Oh, yeah. Hunter will tell me everything he's found about Jim Gunn. I'm willing to bet there's something that can help you." I look back at Cross. "Hunter trusts me enough to share info, I think, and I trust him. It might turn out to be lucky for you both."

Cross gazes out the window, the way he's done most of our drive, and I feel so sad for him. I take his hand before I think about which hand it is: his left one, the one whose fingers don't work. I only have it for a second before he draws it back into his lap.

"It'll get stronger," I murmur.

He looks down at the hand. "Can't draw up any new design plans." He means for the motorcycles he designs. "Can't steer, either."

I want to cry for him. To scream about how unfair it is, that Cross was almost killed for knowing something he hadn't even meant to find out. Instead, I try to keep the pity off my face and say, "I know."

He uses his right hand to give my hand a squeeze, and then he's looking out the window again as we roll through the valley. It's a sunny morning, with a crisp blue sky stretching over miles of vineyards. Even the grass beside the road looks especially vibrant. But the pretty day doesn't do much to calm my nerves.

"So in and out?" Cross asks, tapping his right hand on his knee. "Wham bam?"

"Maybe. Maybe not." I shrug. "You said you didn't mind—

remember? And it's worth it. I promise."

He shrugs. I can tell he's down, and I wish so much that I could help more. We're almost there when he says, "Change of subject."

"Okay." I wait a beat and he blows his breath out of puffed cheeks.

"Suri's been acting…a little off since I woke up. You know anything about that?"

His question throws me off so much, I actually cough. It's everything I can do to keep my eyes from widening. "You think so?" I ask neutrally.

"C'mon, Liz. Shoot straight with me."

She's been acting 'off' because she's developed feelings for him. I'm ninety-nine percent sure.

"Fine. Then yes. I do know something, but it's just a guess. I'm guessing that she maybe…maybe she has feelings for you." I'm breaking the girl code by telling him, but Cross is as good a friend to me as Suri is, and he's got enough drama in his life at the moment without having to wonder about that.

Cross sighs. He looks out the window, at the vines, and I can tell he's not going to say anymore right now.

We're on the last stretch of the dusty little road to Hunter's octagonal home, and I'm getting nervous. Nervous about taking Cross back here to the site of his accident, and nervous about coming here myself.

I'm quiet as we pass the spot to the right of the road where the grass is black and frayed. Cross lets out a deep breath, and I press my right arm into his left.

"You remember it, don't you?" he asks after a moment.

I nod, and he does something funny with his mouth—a thing he does when he's trying to push something down instead of show his feelings.

For the next fourth of a mile, I try to think of something soothing to say. When I can't, I wrap my right hand around his left one, not threading our fingers together but enveloping his hand with mine. He leans his head a little my way on his head rest and closes his eyes.

I'm worried he's asleep as we pull into the driveway, but when I park and touch him lightly on the knee, he looks right at me.

"Wish me luck." I force a smile.

"Good luck. And, Lizzy—thank you."

"You're welcome." I hug his neck, and out I go.

The belly bats are swarming as I walk to the front door. I've tried to get in touch with Hunter six times in the last twenty-four hours, and each time he's hit the 'ignore' button on his phone. I don't even know for sure he's here, although I did read in this morning's *Los Angeles Times* online that he was questioned at his Napa home by the FBI yesterday.

I knock once, then twice, then three times before I try the handle. As my fist closes around it, it's jerked open from the inside, and I'm yanked off-balance. I bump into Hunter's beautiful bare chest.

The second we make contact, he shoves me off him. His eyes widen as he sees my face. "Libby."

I nod, and my eyes widen, too. He's shirtless in black gym shorts, and his bare chest is every bit as delicious as I remember. I pull my eyes up to his face, steamrolled by another wave of emotion as I think of all he's been through in the last day.

"Hunter, hi." I swallow, because suddenly my throat is dry and tight. "I tried to call you."

"I know." He looks put out, but now that we're face to face, I find that I'm so glad to be here, I don't care.

"How are you? I read that you were questioned by the FBI yesterday."

I search his eyes for some sign of how he's doing, but they're carefully blank. "That's kind of you, but I'm still standing."

I can tell he's trying to sound strong, but for just a second as he speaks, his eyes look lost.

"I miss you," I say softly, which is what I feel the strongest. His brows draw together, just a little, and for a second I think he's going to hold out his arms and say he misses me, too. Instead he rearranges his mouth and folds his arms across his chest. "What can I do for you, Libby?"

I'm silent for too long—stung that this is the reception that I get. His lips tighten. "I said I would call you if I could. I haven't had the time."

"I don't get it." I lower my voice, stepping closer, and Hunter retreats, taking a step back into his foyer. "You didn't hurt Sarabelle, so I don't get why you haven't told the FBI what's really going on."

"What's really going on?" he asks flatly.

I shake my head. "I thought you had people investigating. Your father, too." All of a sudden, my eyes are swimming with tears. I try my best to blink them back.

I look at the floor, because there's nothing emotional about the floor, and that's when I see Hunter's ankle. There's a metal band around it.

I cover my mouth. "Oh my God! You have one of the—the things." I point.

He scowls, shuffling his foot a little bit behind him, and hot tears start to trickle down my cheeks.

He reaches to catch them, then drops his arm, like touching me would violate some rule. "Libby, please don't cry for me."

I throw my arms around him. "Hunter—how?"

He folds his arms around my back and whispers into my hair. "She had my cufflink. I'm the only lead they have."

I squeeze him harder, like the strength of my hug can fix this mess. "Tell them about Priscilla and Michael Lockwood, and their connection to Governor Carlson. Tell them what you know. I don't know the whole story, but I know there is one. I know your father doesn't have bad information."

I feel him shake his head as my cheek is mashed against his chest. "You don't understand."

I pull away and look into his sad eyes. "So explain it. I'm tired of not understanding."

Now he drops his arms off me and steps back, away from the light that streams through the windows of the door and into the darkness of the foyer. His eyes search my face as he brings his lower lip between his teeth. "Libby...there's more to this than you think."

"What do you mean?"

"It wasn't Sarabelle," he says. "It's something else. You don't need to know the story, Libby." But I do. My mind is racing. I remember what his father said. *"Let me warn you, you may have to go farther than I did for you."*

"Did you do something bad when you were younger? Something with…with Rita?"

His face hardens, and he looks out over my shoulder. I pull the door shut behind me and step forward to grab his hand. I pull him into the hall where Cross punched the wall that night, what feels like two lifetimes ago. Looking up into his eyes, I can't believe the guilt I see.

"Hunter, talk to me. Please."

His head snaps up, those green eyes flashing. "Libby, I *can't*. Don't you think I would if I could? You're the only person I *want* to talk to."

"So do it."

He shakes his head. His jaw is locked, his shoulders set. "I can't," he says. "I *won't*."

"But it's not a secret? Whatever it is, the FBI knows it happened and they're using it against you somehow?"

He grits his teeth, looking stoic. I take the answer as a 'yes'.

"Are you ashamed?" I ask. "Embarrassed? Please don't tell me that you think I'll judge you."

He grabs my shoulders. "Libby, please. You need to go."

"No." I'm tired of being sent away, dismissed, denied access to people I want, people that I need. "I—I've never liked anyone the way I like you, Hunter. And I don't want to have what's going on with us cut off before it even has a chance to start, all because of someone like Priscilla or that Lockwood guy. I can't let you get dragged further into this because you won't accept some freakin' help. I heard Dr. Bernard that day, and I heard her say that she was on your side. She knows about this secret of yours, doesn't she?"

His mouth quirks into a little frown, and as he looks into my eyes, I swear I can feel how much he wants me. Not my body—me. But then he stalks to the front door and pushes it open.

"I'm sorry, Libby. You think you get things, about me and everything that's going on, but you're just wrong." His gaze rolls over me, and I'm left with the poker face. "Did you get the check?"

"I don't know if I got the check!" I snap, suddenly furious. "I haven't checked the mail because I've been so damn worried about you I forgot there was mail!" I whip out my phone and text Cross: 'It might b a while. U prob have time to take that walk u mentioned.'

I hold it up. "My ride is gone. You're stuck with me." I sink down to the floor, cross my legs, and glare up at him. "While I'm here let me tell you something that I need from you. Something I think might help you, too. Because I've found out something that could possibly be important.

"My friend Cross says a man with black hair and prominent cheekbones was messing with his bike that night at your house, and that's one of the reasons he lost control of the bike. The guy's name, he thinks, is Jim Gunn, a man who used to be an acquaintance of Missy King. Cross knows about Missy. He knows his father made her disappear and he says Jim Gunn is the one who did it. I need to know what you know about Jim Gunn."

If Hunter was wearing his poker face before, now his features go completely slack. He turns a wobbly half circle before he crouches, jerking a hand back through his messy golden hair. "Is this a fucking joke?"

"No. Of course it's not. Hunter, just bear with me for a second. I want to show you a picture of him." I pull the image up on my cell phone but am hesitant to hand it over to Hunter. The snapshot came from Governor Carlson's computer, and Cross found it—and a whole bunch of other crazy shit—by accident one day almost a year ago. I meet Hunter's eyes and hold his gaze as I pass him my phone.

I can tell the moment he sees what I saw: a face that looks an awful lot like the face of the guy who offered me a ride that night outside the Joseph. Like the face Hunter bashed in during his fight: Michael Lockwood's face. Jim Gunn has different hair in this photo, but his face is unmistakable: the sunken cheekbones, thin lip, super square jaw. His hair is blond instead of dark, like it is now, but he even wears it the same: greasy and brushed back.

Hunter's eyes widen. "Holy shit." His gaze bores into mine. "How does Cross know this? How does he have a photo?"

"His computer died, and he was living at his parents' at the time so he got on his dad's computer. I don't really remember how he found it, but he found a bunch of e-mails, too."

"Does he still have them?"

"Yes, I think. He had the picture in his inbox. He logged in on my phone and there it was. He's got it on some USBs, too, though, I think."

"Holy shit." He's on his feet again, pacing. "Holy shit, Libby."

"What do you know about him? Do you have any kind of evidence? Jim Gunn is Michael Lockwood, am I right? They look the same."

He nods, then shakes his head. "They look the same, but I

don't have any proof. Jim Gunn is just a name. A name Dr. Libby knows, and one Cross knows and associates with this picture. Unless Cross has info that's very damning, and that also happen to deal with the Sarabelle situation specifically…I don't know how much it will help me."

He looks into my eyes, and his are so bleak, my heart sinks before he even continues. "I'm a good suspect, Libby. They'll charge me before they pin it to the governor."

"But...why? What makes you such a good suspect?" I let go of his hands and raise mine in the air, ready to launch into a passionate attempt try to get his deep, dark secret out of him again. But before I can start talking, he bows his head.

"Because. I killed my stepmother."

I frown at him. "Explain how. I thought she had cancer." Everybody knows this. When his father ran for U.S. Senate, his wife Rita's untimely death was a major part of his sympathetic story. "Hunter...?"

He slumps down against the wall and pulls his knees up to his chest. He props his forearms there and rests his head on top of them. All I can see is the top of his hair. But I can hear his voice.

I slide down beside him, and he tells me.

CHAPTER THIRTY-TWO

Hunter

I TELL HER everything. I don't see why not. I don't worry about how it will make her feel, either. This secret, with me for so long, can't wait to leap out.

To understand how the FBI knows what they know, she has to understand that Priscilla—or Lockwood, AKA Jim Gunn—found out I spent a year or so talking to Libby back in New Orleans when I was a teenager, and sometime in the last week, the digital file cabinet in Dr. Libby's inbox got hacked. The information was turned over to the FBI, presumably by Priscilla.

"So if I were to try to pin this all on her, they'd immediately suspect I was just playing tit for tat with the person who turned in the files from Dr. Bernard. But even if they didn't think that, I'm going to have a real tough time proving that I'm innocent ...when I'm not."

I tell her about that day in the basement with Rita. I'm hesitant at first, but then I don't spare her any details. I tell it to her like I told the doctor. And, just like Dr. Libby, my Libby can't believe it.

"You wouldn't do that. Not without a reason." And I can see it in her eyes that she knows I had a reason. I know she must, because she listened to my phone call with my dad, and it's not hard to deduce.

"She treated you badly, didn't she?"

"She wasn't good to me," I hedge.

"She was abusive," Libby whispers.

I shrug. "If you ask my father, he'll tell you I antagonized her all the time."

"Well that's bullshit."

"How can you be so sure?" Even I don't know half of the time. Not after hearing for so long that it was my fault.

"Because you didn't mean to kill her, for one!"

I open my mouth, but I'm not sure what to say.

A shadow crosses Libby's face. "You didn't, did you?"

The other Libby asked me the same thing, and the answer to that question is what's tormented me all these years. Did I intend to kill her? Did I think to myself, "Time to kill Rita!"? No. But the relief that I felt… Sometimes it's easy to forget it was an accident. That I just snapped and lost my temper—finally.

Libby clears her throat, and she has my attention again. I can tell from her face I've been silent for too long. "Hunter?"

I shake my head. "No." Even with my fucked up point of view, I know that's the appropriate answer. I didn't set out to kill her. Didn't even pre-meditate punching her. It just…happened.

"You couldn't be charged for something like that. All you did was punch her. It's not your fault she died from it."

I shake my head. "There was no chance to charge me anyway. My father kept that shit quiet. Covered it up, even. Bought off the coroner. He was in the middle of a tough race, and the truth wasn't even an option." I chuckle sourly as I consider what I'm going to say next. "In the end, Rita's 'cancer' death and our family's story of loss is probably what won him the election."

"So he never called it what it was? He acted like it was your fault—that she treated you that way and then one day you finally had enough?"

"He thought it was my fault," I tell her bitterly.

"Hunter, that's just not true. You don't have her blood on

your hands." Her voice drops. "She has yours."

I shrug. I've told myself that before, but to little effect.

"Here's something I don't get," Libby says. "Those files from your talks with Dr. Bernard should be inadmissible. Right? They were stolen."

This is also true, although the files could certainly point the FBI in the direction of the coroner my father bought. Probably did, if what Dave told Marchant can be believed. The information, which will surely be leaked, will cause a big stink for my family—my father in particular. But, "Even if I don't face any legal consequences from that incident, and from my father's cover-up of it, in the court of public opinion about Sarabelle, I'm pretty fucked."

"But there must be some way—"

I sit up straighter and lean my head back against the foyer wall. "There's too much we don't know. All March and I have pertaining to Sarabelle is a bunch of phone recordings of our villains talking in code. Lockwood—Gunn—if he has a place down in San Luis, none of our guys have ever seen it. Sarabelle was found in a damn ditch.

"I know." Her eyes glisten with tears. "But Hunter, we have to try to find the truth."

"And wait and see how long it takes them to drag out more of my story? The part about how Rita liked to hit me? The world already knows my mother was an escort. The media is having a fucking field day with all my so-called mommy issues. You know what it will be like when it comes out that I killed my goddamned child-abusing stepmother?"

"You didn't mean to kill her!"

I shrug. "It makes no difference to them."

"What do Dr. Bernard's notes even say? I've been to enough shrinks with my mom to know she probably didn't write HUNTER IS A MURDERER in red caps."

That's true. I have no idea what's in those files. Libby Bernard hadn't looked at them in seven or eight years, she said. But it doesn't matter. "I don't know, but that's not the point. There's a good chance the FBI already knows about the cover up, which would sure as shit makes me *look* guilty."

"So we have to set the record straight," she says. "We have to try. Please try. Please." She kisses my mouth, and I can't help groaning. "Libby. You're so good."

"You are."

She's tugging at my gym shorts, and all of a sudden I'm hard as fucking rock and aching for her. I sweep her hair out of her face and press my palms against her warm cheeks. "Libby, are you sure?"

She knows what I'm asking, and she leans in closer for a kiss. As I lap into her sweet, warm mouth, I realize I just told her. I just told her everything. My eyes flip open and I squeeze her shoulder. "You don't care? What I told you—it doesn't... change anything?"

"Hell yeah, it changes things. It makes me want to kill your father, but that's about it."

I let out a long breath, and she shakes her head. "I'm so mad for you, that you had to go through that. That you still are." She leans her head against my cheek. "But does it change my feelings for you? No."

That's all I need to hear. I swoop her up, throw her over my shoulder, and stomp to the bedroom doing my cave man impression. She's trying to grab my ass and giggling as I spank hers. I carry her to the green room—it's clean, this time—and toss her on the pillow-stacked bed. I climb up after her and tug her shirt over her head.

"I think it's time to cash that check."

"Yes, please," she gasps.

My cock twitches as my gaze rakes her shirtless body, and I bend over and start to work her bra. "Is this okay?" I murmur between our kisses.

"Oh yes." She leans up, kissing my throat as her warm hands pull my shorts down, and when my dick springs out, I swear to God she actually shivers.

"Oh...Hunter. I want you so badly."

"You can have me. But I want to taste you first."

Elizabeth

HIS EYES ARE molten as he crawls over my limp body and pinches my nipple in between his teeth. "Oh," I moan. "Hunter!"

He sucks me for another second before he lifts up and kisses both my eyelids, then my cheeks, my nose, my mouth. He's breathing hard, and his dick is rubbing against my thigh.

I lean up and kiss his mouth. "I want you inside me."

He nods, his shoulders rising and falling with his need. "No promises, remember? You know I can't yet."

I stroke his jaw, feeling warm inside because he said *yet*. "I only need you, Hunter. I just need to know you feel this, too—right now."

"Yes. I feel you." He cups his hand between my legs and glides a finger inside. I'm wet and ready for him. I reach down between his legs and gently stroke his head. He pushes himself into my hand. His breath is coming in harsh tugs, and I can tell by the way he kisses my mouth that he's getting hungry.

"Christ," he pants, "you're so beautiful."

"You are." I kiss his shoulder and his pec and his mouth and his knuckles. He's got his fingers inside me and I'm trembling and needy.

"Please, Hunter."

I roll over the edge with a shuddering gasp, and Hunter reaches for the drawer beside the bed. He pulls out a rubber and I sit up a little. "Can I help?"

I work it over his weeping, plum-sized head, and he gasps as I curl it down his shaft.

He dips down and licks me one more time, and slides another finger in. "You're so wet."

"Ready for you," I say, breathless. I want to scream it at him.

He crouches his body over me, leaning down to nibble at my throat. "It's going to hurt. I wish it didn't."

I nod.

He strokes me some more, bringing me close to climax again. I'm aching. "Hunter..."

And then he's taking himself in hand, pressing his head against my heat and gliding gently over my entrance. He rocks against me, sliding his head against my wetness until I'm desperate. Then his hands find mine, our fingers intertwine, and his wide, green eyes cling to mine.

"Baby." I feel him, hard and hot against me. Then with a press of his lips on mine and a thrust of his hips, he pushes in. It stings—badly. I gasp. He's wincing, still pressing my hands against the mattress. His eyes close as he pushes once more, deep, and I'm impaled.

"Oh God."

"Are you okay?"

He leans down for a trembling, open-mouthed kiss, and I can feel the vibration from the movement deep inside me. It makes me...want to move. "Oh...Hunter."

It still hurts, but as I rock against him, just a little, it also feels really, really good. Like I might burst. I open my legs a little. Gently lift my hips to take in more of him. I'm rewarded by a strangled groan, and Hunter's forehead falls against my cheek.

"Jesus Christ, you're so fucking tight."

He kisses my lips; our tongues stroke, and then he's pumping in and out. I'm moaning—loud, deep mews that spring from my mouth unbidden. As we find a rhythm, I begin to lose myself. This is not like other things we've done. This is... hypnotizing. We're rocking together, and I'm clinging to his shoulders and he's bowed over my chest. He drops a quick kiss on my mouth, gasping as he rocks in such a way that his shaft glides down my clit. It feels so good, I grab his ass. I want him all.

"Hunter," I pant. I'm flying high, my eyes squeezed shut, raising my hips, gripping his shoulders. *"Hunter!"*

"Libby."

"Hunter!"

His thrusts come harder. My legs are boneless as I push against him. Heat blooms inside me, sweeping through my body like a tidal wave, and my eyes flip open. I can see his nipples tighten as I feel him stiffen. He groans. "Libby." I think he shudders, but I don't know. I'm shivering, half sobbing and he's panting so hard. And then I'm aware of him pulling out, leaving me stinging and empty, but it's okay because he's pulling the covers over me, pressing his body against mine.

"Thank you," he breathes.

"Oh my God." I laugh. He grins, and I can see his hair is damp and sticking up. His eyes glow with deep warmth as they look into mine. "That was amazing," I say.

He smooths the covers over me. "I hope it didn't hurt too much."

"It was perfect." He kisses my lips and then my hair, and then he's getting up.

"Hunter?"

"Just grabbing some food." I watch him walk, in all his naked glory, to a small refrigerator that looks like a wooden chest. He returns with a big bottle of DeVille bottled water and a bowl of strawberries. He lies on his side and offers me the bottle.

I grin as I take a long swig. "This stuff's handy."

"Never even have to leave my room." He winks.

"Oh, I bet you keep this stuff in here for just you," I tease.

"I do." He feeds me a strawberry, and I shut my eyes as I chew. I want to lie here forever.

"Will you shower with me?" he asks.

I lean my head against his chest. "I actually just remembered...Cross drove me, and he's probably waiting. He'll notice and I'd be embarrassed." I flush. "I think I'm already going to be embarrassed."

He toys with a strand of my hair. "Well you look beautiful. Can you stay here for a minute? Let me get a warm towel for you?"

I nod. "Thank you."

I watch him disappear into the bathroom, and I think how different I feel from last time I was in this room. Abruptly, I wonder about Cross. There's a window to my right, and I can see out of it if I lean off the bed and peek between the wooden blinds. I sit up, feeling kind of woozy, but very sated.

As I turn to face the window, I see movement on the other side of it. I freeze. Then the thing swings on its hinges, and I find myself staring at one Michael Lockwood.

CHAPTER THIRTY-THREE

Hunter

I DID IT. I had sex with Libby—and it was incredible.

I clean up in the bathroom, then find a glass bowl, rinse it out, and fill it with warm water. I go search my cabinet for the softest towel I can find. As I sift through washcloths, I'm surprised to find my hands are unsteady. I'm excited. I can't wait to get back in bed with Libby.

My thoughts naturally return to our conversation about Rita. I might always blame myself, but knowing Libby doesn't—knowing she can look past it—is an unexpected gift. I'm surprised I feel better, getting it off my chest. And the Cross thing—that might be a lucky break. I felt pessimistic about it at first, but at this moment it's hard to feel anything but hopeful.

I wrap myself in a robe and grab one for her. I'm already smiling like a moron as I push the door open. My eyes fly to the bed, eager to see Libby's face. But she's not there. I stride into my room and turn a full circle. Empty. The blinds to the right of the bed are cracked, and the window is open. Libby's clothes are on the floor where I tossed them, and as I look that way, I see the bedroom door is still locked—the way I left it when I carried her in here.

I go look out the window. "Libby?"

I look out at the lawn, but it's quiet and seems normal. I

push the window open and get half my torso out before I notice the blood spots on the grass.

Elizabeth

WHEN I COME to, the first thing I notice is the roar of a plane. I wince, because it makes my head throb. Why am I flying when I have such a bad headache?

My eyes snap open and I bite back a scream. I pull in a few shallow breaths through the cloth that's tied around my mouth. I listen, but hear only the plane. I see...a ceiling. It's round, of course, and not too wide. I shut my eyes again, hoping for some clarity, but there's nothing. I remember making love to Hunter ...and then Lockwood was at the window.

Holy cow. I can't believe this really happened.

I open my eyes a little wider and look down at my body. I'm lying on a narrow cot, with my arms bound in front of me, and holy crap, I'm almost naked. I'm wearing an oversized, dirty green t-shirt, but it barely reaches my upper thighs. I register some soreness between my legs before my eyes are bouncing around the space again. I slide them to my right, and there's Cross! He's slumped over a small chair beside me. Seeing him so limp makes me panic. I gasp, and when I do, I smell the bitter scent again. Some kind of chemical. That must be what put me out.

I turn my head, ignoring the ache that threatens to split my skull, and try to get a better look at Cross. But there's nothing to see. He looks...unconscious. Slowly, and with great effort, I turn my head to the left, hoping—no praying—I see Hunter on the bed beside me. When I don't, I feel crestfallen, but this is a good thing. If Hunter was with us, who would rescue us?

And someone has to rescue us...don't they?

That's the last thing I think before the door to our room opens, and Priscilla steps in, a smile splitting her face.

"You're on your way to Mexico," she says.

She steps a little closer to me, and I lean away. "Don't worry, *I'm* not going to hurt you." She walks behind me chuckling. A moment later I feel a pinch in my upper arm, and her face, above me, starts to blur.

I don't know how much time has passed when I wake up and find myself lying on my back in a dingy motel room. Long enough to land a plane, and long enough for my stomach to cramp with hunger, despite a brain-killing headache and the stench of garbage.

I glance down at my aching body. Wrists still tied; ankles now tied. My gaze drifts up to the cracked ceiling, and then back to my body, which feels weak and strange, like I haven't moved in years. I'm lying on a twin bed, on the most disgusting pale yellow bedspread I've ever seen in all my life. Right in front of me, pushed against a cracked yellow wall, is a rickety-looking wooden table with a chipped ceramic flower vase on top. I assume, based on the heat, that we've arrived in Mexico.

God, are we really in Mexico? Part of me can still see Hunter moving over me. Taste the strawberries. How did this happen—and why?

I summon the energy to lift my head and glance over to my right, where I find Cross lying face-down on the other bed. He looks so...still. My pulse starts pounding.

"C-cross?" As soon as I say it, I wish I hadn't spoken aloud. I lie there for a minute, tense, worried that Priscilla or Lockwood will burst through the warped wood door. When no one does, I try to sit up. Maybe if I kick and strain enough, I can get myself untied. Unfortunately, I find that with my arms tied in front of me and my legs bound, plus the effects of whatever drug I've been given, I have no balance. I can barely even get my shoulders off the mattress.

I press my hands together and try to get some slack in the dirty rope that's squeezing my wrists. No luck.

Oh, shit. Now I start to panic. What's going to happen to us? Is Cross okay? Where is Hunter? Even thinking about him makes tears spring into my eyes. I need him so much right now. What if he can't find us?

If he can't find us, I tell myself sternly, *you will save the day.* Hunter may have no idea how to reach us; I can't wait for him. If I can just get Cross awake, he and I can try to come up with a plan. In the meantime, I shut my eyes and try to figure out Priscilla and Lockwood's game. Is Cross's dad in on it? Surely not. He and Cross don't get along, but I can't imagine him wanting to hurt his own son. So it's just Priscilla and Lockwood.

I take a deep breath and cast my eyes on Cross, looking desperately for the rise and fall of his shoulders. He's breathing, thank God, but his face seems to be pressed into a pillow. I think about the monitors Nanette had to take off of him for our field trip today. One was for his pulse, the other for his blood oxygen saturation. I forgot what the third monitored. Nanette said he really didn't need them anymore. He's doing extraordinarily well, but that was before this. What if the drugs he got today make him go back into his coma?

I inhale deeply. *Positive thoughts, Elizabeth. You'll find a way out of this*. I can't really vanish into Mexico—can I?

I hear a creaking sound, and before I can think to play dead, Lockwood strolls through the door. He's wearing dirty-looking brown workman's pants and a gray button-up shirt. He's got on some kind of big, floppy cowboy hat, which shields most of his sunken-cheeked face. I also notice he's wearing a gun on his belt.

Of course.

Belatedly, I want to shut my eyes, but his gaze is already on me. "What do you think?" He spreads his arms out. "You like your comfy little Mexican hideaway?"

I swallow back a string of curse words. I need to appear calm or he might put me back to sleep. "My wrists hurt," I answer.

"I didn't ask about your wrists. I asked about your room." He looks up at the cracked ceiling. "Believe it or not, this is big shit in Mexico."

"Where are we?" I ask him.

He grins, looking genuinely amused. "You think I'm telling you? All you need to know is this is where we sell 'em. You'll fetch a good price. He may, too," he says, nodding at Cross's broad back. "He's got nice blue eyes."

Hearing this news, I feel nothing. Maybe I'm in shock. The only thought I have is that I want to get more information from him. Not want to, have to. I have to stay in control if I want to get away. I try a simple statement. "You killed Sarabelle."

"Only because I had to," Lockwood says, hooking his thumbs through his belt-loops. "I was gonna take her here to market but she got too frisky." He chuckles as he shakes his head. "Silly bitch acted like she was going to give me head and bit my cock." He grimaces, fondling himself, and I grit my teeth. "Sarabelle, she wasn't like the other chicka, little Miss Lucky."

When he says her name, I remember it. She was the escort who went missing a little while before Sarabelle. I raise my eyebrows and paste on a surprised, slightly impressed look. "You took Ginnifer Lucky, too?"

Lockwood nods, standing up a little taller. "She fetched a good price. But you…well, they're paying better these days. All that drug money." He grins, revealing stained teeth.

I try my best to keep my disgust off my face. I want to sound curious, keep him talking but not make him mad. "You're the one behind Missy King, too, aren't you?"

At the mention of her name, his eyes dance. "Missy? Yeah, I sold her. She's still in the country, actually. Somewhere," he says, grinning. "She was a good fuck, that little Missy. Spirited. Gave the governor trouble, that's what happened to that little lady. Bet she's keeping some Mexican drug lord real happy."

That thought makes my stomach churn. "What's the point of selling Cross and I? People will notice we're gone. If you need the money that badly, I recently came into some—"

He interrupts me with a coarse laugh. "I was disappointed to see the deal was already done." I really might be sick this time. I clench my legs together and ignore the humiliation I feel. So far, the shirt's still covering my goods, but if I move, it won't be. This is a man who raped Sarabelle. "You would have fetched a much higher price yesterday."

"I have money!" I say desperately.

He snickers. "We're moving you two downstream because you're all up in our business. And I do mean business. Tail like yours goes for high dollar." He grins, and I squeeze my legs even closer together.

Lockwood is definitely leering at me. He walks a little closer to my bed, so when Priscilla strolls through the door, I actually feel almost glad.

"How's our prince and princess?" she asks.

Lockwood's dark eyes rove over her body, clad in a skin-tight black dress, before he glances back at me. "This one's a Curious Cassie."

I scowl at Priscilla. "I can't believe you help him sell women into sex slavery."

She laughs. "You over-estimate my moral code, darlin'. Besides, sex with strangers isn't as bad as you think."

"It is when you're forced to do it!"

She gives me a patronizing grin. "I guess you'll find out."

"I just don't understand," I say evenly. "What's in this for you?"

"You should know I'm not in it for the money," she chides. "In fact, I'm usually not involved in Michael's extracurriculars at all. But this situation needed some tidying up."

"I used to work for that kid's dad," Lockwood says, pointing at Cross. "Missy was his mistress before she started getting in the way. I had worked for him in security, and then I started talking to Priscilla. She wanted the governor and after a night of drinkin' she and I got the idea. It was really more my idea," he says with a little nod. "That little slut needed to be taken care of, and the governor asked me to take care of it, and, like that—" he snaps "—a new enterprise was born."

"I never liked her," Priscilla says. She rolls her eyes, like Missy was *such a twat*, and I realize she's psycho. They both are.

"But you dated!" I exclaim to Lockwood.

He shrugs. "Didn't really, but I'll take the rumor. She was not an ugly woman. I think she had her eye on me. That made it even easier to get her across the border."

"And after that, Governor Carlson got to be with me," Priscilla says.

"He didn't stay with you," I point out.

"Yes he did." She grins. "He just got better at sneaking around."

I don't know what to do with this information. I glance at Cross, glad he's still asleep. "His father doesn't know about this, does he?"

Priscilla shakes her head. "Definitely not, but if he did, I'm not sure he'd try to stop me. I've got enough dirt on him to fill the Grand Canyon."

I need time to process all of this, but time I do not have.

"Why is Hunter involved?"

She shrugs. "He was in the wrong place at the wrong time, really." She knocks Lockwood with her hip, and I want to vomit. "Besides, it's Michael's fault, not mine. I have restraint. He doesn't. When he heard what I did to your cocky little poker player, he made a rash decision, and then I had to cover for him. If we get charged with something, it could lead back to Carlson."

As Priscilla explains things to me, Lockwood pulls her dress aside and kisses her breasts. I stare, dumbfounded, as he starts to hump her. She steps back and swats him away, leaving him panting like a horny dog. "Do you know what time it is?" she asks him.

"We've still got an hour," he says.

"Until what?" I nearly shriek.

Priscilla smiles. "Don't you like surprises?"

Lockwood laces his fingers through hers, and together they leave the room. Cross is still asleep. My mind is racing. I can't believe what Cross's father did. I can't believe Priscilla is such a monster. I can't believe we're trapped here. Everything about this situation is horrible.

Hunter. Where are you?

I try to wake Cross. I call his name, I try to talk to him; I even sing Katy Perry songs. He hates Katy Perry. I'm thrilled when, after only a few minutes, he rolls onto his back, giving me a full view of his unbound hands. Why didn't they tie him? His eyes flutter at the ceiling, and he grimaces like he's in pain.

"Cross?"

He moans, then rolls back on his stomach. Crap!

I hear Priscilla's voice nearby and she comes back through the door, holding a bottle opener. She opens a cooler on the other side of Cross's bed and pulls out a bottle of beer.

"What did you give him?" I ask as she opens it.

She shrugs. "A couple of tranquilizers. Not everyone has a good reaction to them."

"What do you mean, not everyone has a good reaction?!" I've managed to sit halfway up now. I jerk against the binds around my wrists. I want to slap her.

With another shrug and not a glance my way, Priscilla saunters out of the room. "Cross," I call.

He moans.

"Cross, wake up! Please!"

But he doesn't move or say another word. Why did I take him with me to Hunter's house? He said he wanted to see the outside world. I try not to feel too guilty, though. That was my first chance to have sex. So what if I took it? It's not my fault a crazy guy kidnapped us.

I push my breath out. Suck in another one.

It's okay. At least I won't die a virgin.

I laugh out loud. Only for a second, but it's enough to draw Lockwood's attention. He saunters back inside, sans hat, giving me a full view of his rotten, shit-eating grin.

I glare at him. "What's happening in an hour?"

"The buyers are coming."

"To get me and Cross?"

He shrugs. "Maybe just you. Depends on if they want a dude."

"And if they don't?"

"Maybe I'll cook him and eat him." I can feel the blood drain from my face. Lockwood bursts out laughing. It's jerky and gaspy, and makes him sound kind of like a choking bird. "Naw. Naw. That's not the plan."

"You tried to kill him, didn't you? That's why you didn't tie his hands." Horror washes through me as I realize this makes sense.

He nods. "Nothing personal. But he knows a bunch of things he shouldn't."

"How do you know he knows?" I challenge.

"His father told Priscilla. She don't keep secrets for anybody."

Of course. Freakin' Priscilla. Oh my God, I want to slap that bitch.

From somewhere behind me, I notice a clock ticking. I

guess it's mounted on the wall. "How much longer?" I ask Lockwood. It's kind of ridiculous to ask, but I figure why not.

His gaze drifts over my head. "Looks like about thirty-seven minutes, seniorita."

I shut my eyes, and a minute later, I hear a rustling in the cooler, followed by his footsteps and the closing of the door.

Holy cow. This is really about to happen. I'm really getting sold! Not my V-card; *me*. I strain my abs and get myself half-sitting. I pull against the binds so hard my wrists sport blood-red lines. I've got to do something!

As I work my wrists against the rope, the ticking of the clock threatens to drive me crazy.

Try as I might, I just can't undo the freakin' knot! It's complicated and tight.

I wiggle my ankles. Nothing.

I'm lying there, praying and trying to regulate my breathing, when I hear a moan. My eyes flip open. "Cross!"

He sits up, looking dazed, and I think I might pass out from glee.

"Cross," I hiss, trying harder to be quiet. "Come untie me!"

He blinks at me, and my heart sinks as I realize he's not really seeing me.

"Cross," I whisper. "It's me—Lizzy! I need your help!"

He blinks, the slack look on his face never changing as he rolls his shoulder. Squinting, he looks slowly around the room. "I feel...stiff." His voice is croaky. His eyes wander over the ceiling and the walls, and then finally to me. They widen. "Lizzy?" He flinches as he notices my binds, and I can see some of the stupor fading. "What the hell is going on?"

"You don't remember?"

He frowns. "I fell asleep, waiting for you." He looks around the room again, but I hiss. "Cross! Come and untie me! I'll explain later, but you have to untie your feet and then help me!"

He swallows as he blinks down at his feet. He leans over,

placing one palm on his ankle, and I urge him, "C'mon! You've gotta move fast!"

"Okay." He gives me a concerned look while his fingers grapple with the rope. "Damn," he mutters, "I'm thirsty."

"I'm so sorry, Cross. But Priscilla Heat and Jim Gunn have kidnapped us!"

His eyes bug out. "Holy fuck." He grits his teeth and goes harder at the ropes on his ankles. "Where are we?" he asks while he works.

"Mexico."

"Are we getting sold or something, like Missy King? Because that would be unbelievable."

I nod. "I really think we are. Except you..." I'm about to speculate on why they didn't feel a need to tie Cross's hands when the door opens again, and a tall Mexican man walks in.

CHAPTER THIRTY-FOUR

Elizabeth

HE'S WEARING ALL black, from his boots to the fedora-like hat on his head. He has light brown skin and Spanish features. Once I see the dead look in his eyes, all I know is that he's not here to help us. In fact, he's probably here to buy us. *Crap*.

His assessing gaze flicks over me, then over Cross, who I quickly realize has managed to slump over on his side. Did he do that in time to fool the buyer? I'm not sure, because I wasn't watching him. I watch the buyer's face; he's looking down his thin nose at Cross. I don't think he's spared a look for me yet.

He steps closer to Cross, poking his bicep with his long fingers.

Then he turns toward the door, flicks his hand in a come hither motion, and two other men walk in. Neither is as tall as the buyer, and it's clear they're working for him, rather than the other way around. They're wearing black like he is, but they don't look as clean or well-groomed, and where he points, they scurry.

I tense, terrified because I expect them to skip right over Cross and come to me, but instead they each grab one of Cross's shoulders, and they roll him over. He's so limp I wonder if he actually passed out. One of them starts to unbutton his blue jeans, and I shriek.

The buyer's gaze snaps to me. "You can't do that!"

"You be quiet," he hisses. His accent makes his voice sound like a snake.

"He's not for sale."

"What about you?" He steps closer to me, taking my face in his hand and running his finger over my cheek. "Are you for sale?" he asks me. "We get many requests for feisty American girls." His gaze flicks between my legs. "They told me you are barely used."

I blink up at him, too terrified to say anything.

He releases my face and chuckles. "She is just a baby."

Abruptly he's leaving my bed and walking toward the door. I glance over at Cross, and I'm relieved to find his jeans still zipped.

The buyer pulls something out of his back pocket, and as he reaches the doorway, his two sidekicks lean in to hear what he has to say. I gasp as I notice they're both holding machine guns.

The shock of it is so horrible, I forget to translate what he's telling them. The two sidekicks move to stand behind the buyer, and all of a sudden they're all talking at once. Then the three of them step back, and Priscilla and Lockwood come in.

This time, I can hear their conversation clearly.

The buyer speaks in Spanish: "We'll take them both. The man, especially, will fetch a good price in a larger market. Dark hair and blue eyes is a good look. For the woman, I am thinking Asia."

I keep my eyes trained on the ceiling as my heart races. I dare a quick glance over at Cross. He seems asleep, but is he really?

Lockwood says, "How much?"

The buyer makes a tsking noise and continues speaking in Spanish. "I want to see more of them. A fresh woman is a fresh woman, but how big is the man?"

"He is large," Lockwood says in Spanish.

Oh my God. Does he actually know that? My cheeks and head feel too hot, like any moment now, steam might start flowing from my ears. *Please, no.*

"I want to inspect the girl."

"Please," Lockwood says, also in Spanish. "Her legs still have blood on them."

He waves at me, and Priscilla holds her arm out like a game show display girl.

I'm swallowing convulsively. The man nears me, and I wonder if I throw my legs up, if I can kick him with my knees despite my tied up ankles. He scrutinizes my face and then he reaches for my chest.

As his hand comes down to grope me, I experience my first real moment of hopelessness. What if this is really my new life? His fingers are inches from my breast when I close my eyes, but his hand never makes it. He crashes to the floor, knocking me off the bed, and his two sidekicks start yelling. The buyer jumps up as I fumble onto my elbows, leaning on the bed's frame. I'm shocked to see Cross standing over me, clutching a handgun.

It must belong to the buyer, because the buyer's face is a mask of shock as he reaches to the now empty holster on his right side.

For the longest moment in the history of moments, Cross and the buyer stare each other down. Then, out of nowhere, Lockwood fires a shot at Cross. Cross ducks, and the sidekicks at the door come in screaming. One of them has Lockwood on the ground in seconds, aiming what looks like an AK-47 at his face. Priscilla is screaming, sticking her arms in the air, her huge boobs bouncing as she jumps in place. "I give blow jobs! Don't hurt me! I'll give you a blow job!"

At first I think she must have lost her mind, but one of the gunmen actually lowers his rifle and makes a grab at her crotch.

She thrusts toward him, leaving Lockwood, Cross, the buyer, and me in our standoff. I shift my attention to translating

Cross's Spanish, and I'm stunned to realize he's negotiating some kind of deal.

I catch something about, "Giant stockpile of guns" and "American airplane, not far from here" before my eyes and my attention drift to the buyer.

A small part of me will forever regret that I'll never know if Cross would have been able to lie us to a happy ending. Priscilla is on her knees, Lockwood is on his back, and Cross, only days out of a coma, has elicited a respectful—if skeptical—expression from the buyer, who is obviously more interested in getting an airplane loaded with weapons than he is in whatever money he could make from us.

The buyer is wearing his skeptical-but-coming-around expression, and Cross is owning it, and I'm just sitting there, not like a badass heroine at all, wondering if they're just going to kill us when they realize there's no plane, when a third sidekick with a big machine gun runs into the room and cries, "Chota!"

"Chota?" the buyer snaps.

"Chota!"

"CHOTA!"

And, just like that, the buyer and his sidekicks run like hell.

I'm freaking out now, too, so I struggle to stand up, and Cross grabs me and pushes me under the bed. Right before my face mashes into the dirty, tile floor, I notice Cross's ankles are still bound, and he's balancing on the outside of his soles.

Then there's a gunshot...but it's not Cross firing. He's in the process of crouching down behind me; I can feel something sharp between my skin and the rope, first on my hands and then my ankles. I turn to find Cross freeing his feet. Then he stands and whirls toward the door, where the sound of footsteps echoes.

He mutters a confused-sounding curse. "Hunter West?"

I jump up and get a glimpse of Hunter, leaning in the doorway. I know the exact moment he sees me, because his eyes widen and his mouth falls open in relief. His gaze flies over me, and he rushes toward me. I'm already anticipating his arms around me. I can practically feel them. But before he reaches me, a loud boom wrenches the air, and Hunter flies into the wall.

"OH MY GOD!"

I watch in horror as he slumps down to the floor, his face twisting in agony as his right hand fumbles toward his bright red, left shoulder. He lifts his head, and his wild eyes comb the room until they settle on my face.

"Hunter!" I rush him, noting dimly as I fly across the room that Cross is on top of Lockwood, pummeling his face.

"Hunter! HUNTER! NO, no, no, *no, please!*" I grab his body, shocked and terrified by how limp he is already.

"Libby." His hands grab at me as he starts panting, which quickly turns to horrible choking. "Libby..." he gasps, "you ...okay?"

That's the last thing he says before his eyes roll back into his head.

I start to scream, and somewhere far away, I hear one of my would-be kidnappers cry: "Chota!"

CHAPTER THIRTY-FIVE

Hunter

I MUST HAVE died and gone to hell, because I'm burning. The fire spreads through my upper body, quickly overwhelming all my senses. Then I'm dragged down into darkness. How many layers of hell are there supposed to be? I can't remember, but I must be going deep.

The burning is more intense now. I hear a man moaning and wonder if it's me. I hear a woman moan, too, and I'm worried the woman is Libby. I scream her name over and over, but I don't get an answer. Libby's not here. Michael Lockwood took her.

I relive the moments after she disappeared from my vineyard. I'm outside screaming her name, and Dave is there almost immediately. By chance he'd picked up Lockwood's trail late the night before and eventually followed him to my home.

Dave was at the side of the house when he heard two cars pull up, and he got to the front just in time to see a silver Audi he didn't recognize spirit Cross and Libby away.

We jump on Dave's bike and give chase, but we haven't caught them by the time we leave the neighborhood. Dave has an idea. A terrible one. Lockwood spent two hours at a tiny airstrip before coming to my house.

We arrive just as a Lear Jet goes airborne. I call the FBI,

and it takes them almost an hour to give the local cops the clearance to examine the flight records. They arrive in time to spend another hour figuring out the records have been falsified. The plane claimed to be headed north, toward Redding, California, but tracking software shows it actually went south.

The FBI has to wait for orders, but I don't. Hal and I get on my plane. It's several hellish hours before the plane we're chasing lands—in a rural area outside San Luis Rio Colorado, Mexico. My pilot, Victor, lands in a field, and Hal and I start trying to trace a path from the empty plane to Libby. Fifty bucks gets us a hotel name, and two hundred gets us a dinged up dirt bike. We pull out just as another plane—the FBI, Hal says—flies low overhead.

I'm moaning again, and just like before, the woman is crying. There's something clutching my hand. Someone, and I feel sure it's Libby. She's the woman crying.

I squeeze her hand as hard as I can, and the crying stops. "It's okay, Libby."

I have the strange suspicion that I'm only managing a whisper. She's crying again. I mean, she is really going at it. I squeeze her hand, and the crying turns to breathless sobbing.

Damnit, Libby.

Her sobs make the burn worse. Darkness starts to fade, and I can see white flames. I feel like I'm choking and I start to struggle against the invisible hands that hold me.

Fuck—oh fuck. I don't like this. Not at all. There are so many voices rising up around me. Someone slaps my face, and I don't think it's hard, but I'm already on edge.

And then there is light. Fluorescent light.

Holy shit. I turn my head left and right, squeezing my eyes shut against the searing pain, and there is Libby, bent over me and crying. And I really must be confused about what's going on, because she's wearing scrubs. Libby looks beautiful in scrubs.

Elizabeth

HUNTER IS IN and out of consciousness for almost two days. They say it's not that long considering the bullet's trajectory—through his left lung—and where it lodged, by one of the branches of his axillary artery. He almost bled to death in the hour-long helicopter ride to the UC San Diego Hospital, and when we got here, they wheeled him straight into surgery, which lasted four excruciating hours.

The nurses let me stay by him in the ICU when he came out. I think because Marchant Radcliffe told everyone that I'm his fiancé.

The first forty-eight hours in the ICU, Hunter's mostly sleeping. The incision, on his back, around his shoulder blade, is called a thoracotomy and is supposed to be one of the most painful sites for surgery. So they have to keep him sedated. I hate it, and spend probably too much time sitting by his bed, crying. Cross stays with me for most of the first day, but he has to go back to rehab the next. Suri gives me some company, too, and of course Marchant is in and out.

The weirdest thing that happens in the first forty-eight hours is that my mom visits. She's wearing a pant suit—my designer-loving mother's definition of drab—and her hair, which she normally pulls into a dramatic up-do, is flowing down her shoulders, much like mine. I meet her in the ICU waiting room, and when she hugs me, I start sobbing. I have to say, it's one of the weirdest experiences I've had in years. It's even weirder when she says she's staying.

So that's what happens. While I'm asked every imaginable

question by the FBI, my mother keeps me fed and brings me clean clothes and tries to make me get some sleep.

On the second night after we arrive—the night Dave tells me that Michael Lockwood, AKA Jim Gunn, AKA a few other names, is being charged with the abduction of Missy King, Ginnifer Lucky, Cross, and I, plus the murder of Sarabelle—I'm a teary mess. I cry a lot, and Marchant charms his way in so the two of us sit side by side in plastic chairs and talk about the mess Hunter's been in. We also speculate about Priscilla, who hasn't been seen since Mexico.

I go into the waiting room and eat some fast food with my mother. This is when I find out that she knows what I did at the ranch. I guess she overheard one of the investigators talking about it. When she first brings it up, I sort of freak out, but it turns out all she wants to say is sorry.

"I'm so sorry for what I've done to our family with my addiction, Elizabeth. I can't stand to think of how much money I've wasted. It makes me sad that you were so desperate."

I try to explain to her that I wasn't just desperate—I was also tired of being a virgin—and to my surprise, she says she understands, at least a little.

That actually feels good.

Later in the night, I talk a lot to Hunter. His vitals are looking stronger now, and they want to see some improvement in his breathing, so they've started weaning him off some of his sedatives. I'm sitting by his bed, staring at his monitors, when all of a sudden he moans, and I get a peek of his green eyes. He's been squeezing my hand since yesterday, but seeing his eyes...it's amazing.

"Hunter," I whisper.

He grimaces and turns his head toward me. His eyelids are heavy, his eyes barely open, but I can see him trying to focus on my face. His hand, in mine, squeezes. He gives me the smallest little smile, and in his hoarse voice, he says, "I missed you."

Tears fill my eyes. "I missed you, too."

The third day, sometime in mid-morning, Hunter opens his eyes again. He looks dazed, then panicked.

I rub his fingers. "Hi. Are you okay?"

He frowns, then looks around the little room. His eyes return to mine and his hand squeezes me a little harder. "Libby... I don't know where we are."

"That's okay." I stroke his palm. "You don't remember because you got hurt."

He looks me over. His brows are drawn together and his lips look dry. "I saw you. You were wearing scrubs."

I nod. That was before I had my own clothes, shortly after we got here. "I just borrowed them to wear for a little while."

I can see it dawn on him. His face loses some of his color, and his heart rate rises just a little. "Lockwood got you."

I nod. "Yeah, but then you came."

He makes a sour face. "That bastard shot me."

I blink through tears. "Yes, he did."

Hunter frowns, looking down at our hands before meeting my eyes again. "Did I shoot him first?"

"I think you did. Cross says you leaned into the room and got a perfect gut shot."

Hunter's eyes are slightly wide. He's nodding, but I can tell he's not completely following, or more likely, he just doesn't remember.

I hesitate before asking my next question. "Do you remember anything from the helicopter?"

After a second squeezing my hand, he shakes his head. I'm not surprised. In fact, I'm glad. The times he was conscious were horrible. I wish I could forget them, too.

"Did you go with me?" he whispers.

I nod. I have to bite the sides of my tongue to keep from crying, because as I sat there in the helicopter, watching those FBI people—or "chota," as the Mexicans were screaming—work on him, I really, really thought he was going to die.

"I was with you," I finally manage.

His eyes close as his fingers squeeze my hand. "Stay."

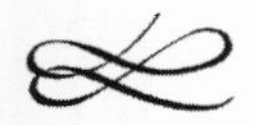

Hunter

GENTLE HANDS ARE playing in my hair. It feels so good, I want to keep my eyes closed, but I miss Libby and I need to know it's her.

Damn the effort it takes to get my eyes open. And when I do, I have to struggle to focus on her face.

"Libby..."

She looks up. She's so pretty. I'm so glad she's here.

She smiles her sweet smile, the one I've only ever seen her smile for me. "Hi, you."

My throat's dry, and I start to cough. Libby holds out a cup with a straw, and I gulp down a few sips of water. I feel really... stiff, so I try to shift my body weight. Pain like a hot poker lances through my shoulder and I have to bite my lip to keep from whimpering.

Now I'm in a cold sweat.

"Do you want some more pain meds?" Libby looks concerned.

I nod once, then shake my head. I already feel dizzy. If I take a pain pill, I might fall asleep.

"Are you sure? You look a little rough around the edges." She strokes my hair off my forehead, and I shut my eyes. All I can think about is Lockwood taking her. I have another awful thought: What if I'm arrested for skipping the country? Who will watch out for Libby then?

I swallow and crack my eyes open. "Am I being arrested?"

She shakes her head. "But Lockwood has been."

"For what?"

"For Sarabelle," she says quietly. "And all the abductions."

"No shit?"

She nods. "Actually, I think your dad had a hand in getting it done quickly. Lockwood was taken as soon as they got him back into the states. And, for the record, you just missed your father."

I blink my gritty eyes. "He was here?"

Libby nods. "Yep. And he had news. He's resigning."

My shock makes my back hurt. "What the fuck?"

"Apparently he's fallen in love with one of his aides. She looked a little younger than him, maybe in her thirties."

I snort. "Oh."

"But I don't think that was all. He told me he had some personal things to settle. He's coming back to talk to you tomorrow."

I nod, because I don't expect much from that bullshit. I shift my weight again, testing the pain around my left arm. It streaks through me, and I find myself panting.

"You need pain meds." Libby's frowning.

"I want to know...about Priscilla."

Her frown deepens as she leans a little closer, resting her chin on my bed rail. "She's missing, Hunter. We didn't get her out of Mexico. Cross says she might have gone with some of the cartel guys."

I shut my eyes. That's fucking weird.

"Dr. Libby has been here. So has Marchant. And Loveless."

I'm surprised. Not about Marchant, but about the others. "How is Loveless?"

"She left you those," Libby says, pointing to a bouquet of yellow flowers, "and the others will all be back to see you tomorrow."

Libby's fingers stroke my face, and I reach out and grab her arm. I tug her closer, and she leans over the rail and presses her face into my side. She eases an arm over my waist. With my right hand, I reach out and touch her pretty red-brown hair.

"What about you?" I whisper. "How long have you been here?"

"A while," she murmurs.

"The whole time?"

"Maybe."

I smile a little, tightening my grip on her. "I can't get rid of you."

She sits up, so I can see her face. "You can't," she whispers, smiling. But her eyes look serious.

"I didn't really want to," I confess.

EPILOGUE

Elizabeth

IT'S ONE OF the first warm days in March, and Hunter has a poker tournament this afternoon. This one's at the Wynn, which is convenient since that's where we've been staying. After he was discharged from the hospital, we sort of took a two-month vacation here.

He offered to take me home to Crestwood Place and recuperate in Vegas on his own, but there was no way. After everything that's happened, I just can't stand to be away from him.

Suri understands.

Cross is here tonight, wedged between Marchant and I. Marchant invited him. It's pretty weird how they've gotten to be friends. Maybe it's motorcycles. I didn't know it until recently, but Marchant has six.

It's taken Hunter the last two months to return to play. For the first few weeks, he had trouble raising his left arm. Once he was completely healed, he went through a brief phase where he didn't want to be seen on TV.

"Everyone thinks they know my whole life-story now," he complained. "How can I have a poker face?"

And it's true—the part about everyone thinking they know Hunter. Everywhere we go, I feel the stares. People outside Vegas and California and D.C. and New Orleans might not know what happened, but around those parts, we're notorious. When I came downstairs tonight with Cross and Marchant, about thirty minutes after Hunter and the other players began filming, we were ushered to front-row seats marked for family only, and I saw the camera get a shot of us.

There are more poster-board signs in the small audience tonight for Hunter than for all the other players combined, and I get my drinks for free.

Priscilla Heat finally surfaced a few weeks ago, trying to cross the border with a Mexican drug dealer. She was arrested and is now awaiting her trial, along with Lockwood. Priscilla's production company has been shut down, and I've heard her nasty films are selling for twice their old price. Further proof that the world doesn't make a bit of sense sometimes.

In the last two months, so much has happened between Hunter and me, sometimes it's hard to remember that's what really brought us together.

Sometimes I wonder what would have happened if he'd simply won my bid, we'd had sex, and I'd left his house a few hours later. I like to think we would have found our way back to each other no matter what. When I asked Hunter what he thought, snuggled up in his hospital bed a few days before he finally got discharged, he smiled and winked and said he would have thrown another house party.

"You're mine, Libby DeVille. That's how it's supposed to be."

Ever since he woke up after his surgery, Hunter hasn't been shy about saying things like that. Neither have I. Some mornings I wake up beside him in his penthouse here and I'm amazed at what we have together. It isn't always easy, but I can honestly say it's always fun.

His wounds have healed up perfectly. Except for a small, round scar on his chest and the Captain Hook slash on his shoulder-blade, you'd never know he collapsed a lung or that a bullet barely missed a crucial artery. The FBI has completely closed its files on Hunter, and on one of those early days in the hospital, his dad even offered an apology of sorts for not doing more to protect Hunter from Rita. I'm not sure how much Hunter cares, but it's a first step, anyway.

Marchant has given Dr. Libby one day off each week, and on that day, she comes to Hunter's penthouse to talk to one or both of us. I think it's doing Hunter good to talk to her again, and I've even begun dealing with the resentment I've always carried toward my mom. It hasn't been two months yet, but she's still sober.

Tonight after the tournament, Hunter and I are flying back to Napa. I haven't seen Suri in weeks, and Hunter and I need to spend some time in the vineyard house together. I think we both need to make some new memories there, since the last one involved Lockwood.

Marchant and Cross get along like old friends as we watch the tournament, talking about cars and bikes and women as I train my eyes on Hunter's infamous poker face.

"Can you tell if he's got a winning hand?" Cross asks me.

I tell him, "no, of course not, silly," but the truth is—I kind of can. I'm getting to know all of Hunter's tells.

It's fun to watch him play. Even with that fixed expression on his face, I can tell he's in his element. Maybe it's because of his experience with Rita, but Hunter likes a certain element of control. Playing poker seems to give him just enough so he can handle the lack of it in other areas.

The tournament passes quickly as I sip my diet and bourbon and Cross and Marchant load up on the straight stuff.

This is Cross's first time out since leaving rehab. The good news is, he's doing great for the most part. The bad news is, he's still taking painkillers for his neck, and his hand's still not back to normal. Suri tells me he hasn't re-opened his bike business, and I don't think he's ridden yet, either. Every time I've seen him, he's put on a good act, like he's doing fine—no more of that sullenness he had in the weeks after he first woke up—but I'm not betting on it. As far as I know, neither of his parents have made a move to reconcile with him.

The FBI's investigation doesn't appear to have reached past Lockwood, to the governor, and since the day we had our talk in Hunter's room at rehab—right before the day we both got nabbed—Cross hasn't mentioned anything about going forward with whatever evidence he may have. I can't imagine that's good for him.

To make things worse, now that my mother is living in her house again, Cross has moved into his bike shop. I'm hoping when Hunter and I get back to Napa, I can try to get a better feel for what's going on. If Cross needs help, I'll be there.

Hunter wins the final hand and he, Cross, Marchant, and I have a few drinks in one of the lounges before Cross and Marchant head to—dear God— the ranch—and Hunter and I make our way toward his plane. As we drive his Aston Martin to the airport where he rents a parking spot and stores his plane, he holds my hand tightly and looks at me often. If I didn't know better, I'd say he was tense, but Hunter is always tired and relaxed after a good game.

His eyes flicker across my face once more before he turns onto Airport Lane. "Are you sure you're not too tired to go tonight?"

I nod. "I'm sure. I miss Napa."

We roll into the airport parking lot, and his face grows serious. "Are you sure it's not Crestwood you miss?"

I frown. "Yeah, I'm sure. Suri is a great roommate, but it's nothing compared to living with you." As soon as I say it, I wonder if the question was more about Hunter than me. "Why? Do you think I should go back to Crestwood?"

Things have been going so well the last few weeks, I haven't really thought about them changing. But maybe I should have. Maybe Hunter's decided it's too soon for us to be spending all our time together.

I force a smile. "Are you getting Libby overload?"

His eyes widen. "Oh, no. Hell no. You're not getting sick of my ass, are you?"

I giggle at his wording. "Your ass—yes. Totally sick of it. The rest of you I'll take, but not that ass." I stick my hand into his seat, grabbing at it, and Hunter's hand captures mine and guides it to the bulge in front.

He hits a button on his steering wheel, and the door to the car garage lifts as he drops his head back against the seat and murmurs, "Mmmm."

He guides the car into his spot—three walls of cement and a drop-door, a lot like a unit in a storage shed—and darkness closes over us. I laugh and unbuckle as he shifts us into park. I throw myself onto his lap and go straight for his belt.

"Get this off so I can show you what a real win looks like," I say, grinning.

"Yes ma'am."

I had my mind on something oral, but Hunter opens his door and pulls me out onto the cement floor. There's a window and door here in our little garage, but with the lights out, I don't think anyone could see us. Which is a good thing, because Hunter pushes my skirt up and lays me spread-eagle on the hood.

The warmth of the motor burns a little bit against my ass, and Hunter's mouth burns somewhere else. It's not long before I'm gasping for release. He doesn't give it to me, so I sit up and grab at him until I get my hands on his pants. I tug them down, lie back, and beg him: "Please..."

"What the lady wants..."

"The lady gets," I finish, panting.

I gasp as Hunter pushes inside me, and when we start to rock, I gasp some more. The sex tonight is hard and fast, a little rough. I like it this way. It's not long before I'm screeching

Hunter's name, and he's shuddering over me.

When we leave the garage and walk back out into the parking lot, I'm feeling sleepy, but totally satisfied. I squeeze Hunter's hand as we come into view of his plane.

He squeezes back. "It'll be nice to get back to the vineyard."

I look him over, studying his face, but it's one of those moments where I just can't read him—so I ask. "Do you think you're ready?"

He shrugs. "It's my house."

"We'll have to christen it." We did the same thing at the penthouse, making love in all the spots where he was with Priscilla. At first it was hard for me to know details like that, but any doubts I might have been carrying are all gone now.

We follow the row of runway lights and Hunter helps me up the stairs and into the cabin, then goes out and talks to some of the techs. A few minutes later, he comes back in, with his hands in the pockets of his black pants. I'm surprised to find he looks tense.

I walk over to him and wrap my arms around his neck, rocking my hips into his. "You okay?"

He nods. "Yeah." He leans down for a hungry-seeming kiss, and we're still going at it in one of the chairs when the pilot turns the 'buckle seat belt' light on and we have to take our seats. I slide the arm rest up, so our two seats are more like one, and lean my head against his shoulder. Hunter's arm goes around my back.

"Thank you for coming with me," he murmurs as he kisses my hair.

"To Napa?"

He nods.

"Of course. You know I would go anywhere with you." I lace my hand through his.

"Would you?" he asks. I search his face for hints of teasing, but he's not.

"Hunter, what's wrong?"

He shuts his eyes and leans his head against the seat.

"Are you feeling bad?"

He shakes his head.

"What is it?"

He takes a deep breath and unbuckles his seat belt. At first I think he's going to be sick, but when he gets down on one knee, my heart starts pounding.

"Libby, I was going to wait for some time memorable and romantic, but I don't think I can keep this to myself anymore." He reaches into the pocket of his pants and I stop breathing. "Libby—I love you more than anything in this world. Will you marry me?"

He takes my hand and squeezes my fingers, while his other hand brings out a small, red box. I expect him to open it, but instead he closes his fist around it and looks into my eyes. "I know you're young and you've still got some school to finish. You might want to do things you haven't done, but we can travel. We can do anything you want. Anything it takes to make you happy. If you want to sell the place in Vegas, we can. If you want to—"

"YES!" I throw my arms around his neck. "Hunter, we don't have to do any of that. Yes, I'll marry you!" I smash my lips against his, and I'm laughing. "I love you!" I can feel his smile under my mouth. He deepens the kiss, and I can feel him shudder as I wrap myself around him.

"We don't have to do anything different," I murmur. "I don't want to." I lean down to kiss his temple and he locks his arms around me. His forehead presses against my throat, and I kiss his cheek.

"How long have you been thinking of this?" I ask, giggling maniacally.

His eyes flick up to mine, and a grin spreads across his face. "You really want to know?"

"Um...yes."

"I designed the ring when you would take naps at the hospital. It shipped to Dr. Libby and I got it from her weeks ago." He arches one eyebrow. "I would have dropped it on you earlier, but I was worried you weren't ready."

"I'm ready! Hunter, let me freakin' see it!"

With one arm locked around me, he opens the box, revealing a beautiful, oval ruby ringed with diamonds.

His green eyes hold mine as he fumbles with the box and slides the ring on my finger. I giggle and wave my hand around, buoyant enough to float through the roof and into the sky. "Thank you." I throw myself into his lap and straddle him, and Hunter's face burrows into my shoulder.

We sit there wrapped up in each other as the plane soars through the clouds, swooping lower as we near Napa—our home.

After a few minutes of blissful silence and lots of little kisses, Hunter looks down at me, smiling a little slyly. "I kind of already made some preparations."

"That confident, were we?" I smirk, and he grins. I poke his ribs. "C'mon now. Out with it!"

"I had our room re-done...and I got you a new car. I hope you're not upset."

"Upset?"

"I know how loyal you are to your Camry. This can just be a weekend car if you want."

"What kind of car is it?"

"A Porsche." His eyes are dancing as he thumbs my cheek. "One time I fell in love with a woman in a Porsche."

"I didn't think that happened until a good bit later."

He smiles, looking lazy and comfortable and handsome. My fiancé. He looks into my eyes. "I don't know when it happened, but I'm damn sure glad it did."

"Me too." I snuggle up against his hard, warm body as we

soar through midnight clouds. “Me, too.”

ABOUT ELLA

ELLA JAMES IS A Colorado author who writes teen and adult romance. She is happily married to a man who knows how to wield a red pen, and together they are raising two children under three who will probably grow up believing everyone's parents go to war over the placement of a comma.

Ella's books have been listed on numerous Amazon bestseller lists; two were listed among Amazon's Top 100 Young Adult Ebooks of 2012.

To find out more about Ella's projects and get dates on upcoming releases, find her on Facebook at *facebook.com/ellajamesauthorpage* and follow her blog, *www.ellajamesbooks.com*. Questions or comments? Tweet her at *author_ellaj* or e-mail her at *ella_f_james@ymail.com*

OTHER TITLES BY ELLA JAMES

STAINED SERIES
Stained
Stolen
Chosen
Exalted

HERE TRILOGY
Here
Trapped

LOVE, INC. SERIES
Selling Scarlett
Taming Cross
Unmaking Marchant

Made in the USA
San Bernardino, CA
18 June 2014